Reviews for *The Last Day*

'A tender, beautifully written book about marriage, love, grief and fear: how all can be lost in a moment, and how hope survives.' **Julie Cohen,** author of *Together*

'Exquisitely written and completely immersive, *The Last Day* caught me up from the very first page. With taut, page-turning plotting, intense emotion, and characters who live and breathe – so real, I now feel I know them – this book was a complete joy, one I didn't want to finish, but which I know will stay with me for a very long time' **Jenny Ashcroft,** author of *Beneath a Burning Sky*

'*The Last Day* is an exquisitely written story of love and loss. With a poet's hand, calm clarity and true wisdom, Claire Dyer paints a picture of real people dealing with very real emotions. Turn your phone off, put a Do Not Disturb sign on the door, and curl up with this gem of a book' **Amanda Jennings,** author of *In Her Wake*

'Exquisitely written and utterly compelling. Claire Dyer is a master of perfectly-pitched emotion, and *The Last Day* is an unforgettable book' **Iona Grey**, author of *Letters to the Lost*

'Impossible not to read on. Highly recommended' **Jane Cable**, author of *Another You*

'A beautifully observed story of love, loss and longing. Claire Dyer writes with a poet's precision and a compassionate heart' **Stephanie Butland,** auth

'I just read *Th*   rending situation, beautiful writ   cters' **Tracy Rees,** author of *Amy*

C016447573

THE LAST DAY

Claire Dyer

THE
DOME
PRESS

Published by The Dome Press, 2018
Copyright © 2018 Claire Dyer
The moral right of Claire Dyer to be recognised as the author
of this work has been asserted in accordance with the
Copyright, Designs and Patents Act 1988.

This is a work of fiction. All characters, organisations and events portrayed in
this novel are either products of the author's imagination or are used
fictitiously.

A CIP catalogue record for this book is available from the British Library

ISBN 9780995751064

The Dome Press
23 Cecil Court
London WC2N 4EZ

www.thedomepress.com

Printed and bound in Great Britain by Clays., St. Ives PLC

Typeset in Garamond by Elaine Sharples

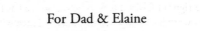

For Dad & Elaine

Though we covered it, over
and over with the snow
of the years, one day,

another life later, it surprises us

Robert Seatter, 'Afterwards', *The Book of Snow*

Vita

It's late April. The light in the studio today has been flat and constant and perfect – the kind of light we'd hoped its north-facing windows and its clear view of the sky would give us.

I've been working for hours and I'm tired. A bit earlier I'd had some lunch in the house and gone for a walk around the block, down Albert Terrace, along the perimeter of the park to the footpath, then through the gate into the garden and back to the studio.

Classic FM's on the radio and the picture's going well, for a change. I'm normally in the throes of despair by now, but this one's behaving itself and for that I'm grateful.

I'm just starting to wash out my brushes when my phone rings.

It's Boyd.

I see his name flash across the screen and for a second I wonder where he is, why he's calling. We've haven't talked for a month or two, which is fine, of course: there's been nothing to say. I'm planning on sending him a birthday card on the 27th like I normally do, but we haven't actually spoken to one another since Christmas.

The ringtone burbles and his name is still on the screen, but for some reason I can't answer it and so I let the call go to voicemail,

1

telling myself I'm busy with my brushes, telling myself it's fine for me to wait, it doesn't matter – nothing matters, not now.

I finish with my brushes, cover the easel, switch off the heater and the radio and lock the studio door behind me. The light is fading and there is a slight chill in the air; I wrap my shawl around me. My phone is a weight in the pocket of my jeans.

Inside the house I put the kettle on and pick up today's crossword. Two across is 'Business Baron' and the second letter is Z; it's been puzzling me all day.

'Bloody thing,' I say out loud as I throw the paper down onto the sofa at the back of the kitchen extension.

My fingers are itching, the back of my throat is dry; I know I'll have to listen to Boyd's message but I can't bring myself to do it. Taking the phone out of my pocket, I stare at it for a long minute. There's a text saying 'Voicemail has 1 new message. Please dial 121.'

The kettle has finished boiling; the noise of it subsides into the quiet. The only other sounds are the distant growl of traffic and the drum of my pulse in my ears.

'Bloody stupid woman,' I say, out loud again.

But there is no one to hear me.

And so eventually I dial 121 and there's his voice once more, the low rumble of it.

'Vita?' he says. 'It's Boyd.'

Well that's bloody obvious, I think. Who else would it be?

'Um …' There's a pause and, in the background, I can hear people talking and distant music. 'Um …' he says again. 'Hope you're well. I'm fine and Mum's OK too. Not sure why I said that, but anyway she is.'

He clears his throat.

'Look,' he continues, 'I was wondering if we could meet up. There's a favour I'd like to ask you. It's a bit awkward so I don't really want to talk about it on the phone. So, could we meet do you think? I could come round to the house, or we could grab a coffee, or a drink, or something. Anyway, it would be nice to see you. It's been too long ...'

Another pause, and then, 'Let me know, Vita? As I say, it would be nice to see you.'

Nice? I let the phone drop onto the counter, snort, whip off my glasses and start cleaning them with the hem of my shawl.

I know I will have to reply and will need to do it quickly before I lose my nerve. Not that it matters; it doesn't matter whether I see him or if I don't, but I guess I am curious. It must be the puzzle solver in me. I decide not to call him but to send a text instead, so I type, 'Got your message. Am in this evening if that's convenient. Any time from 7.' I don't say, 'Love, Vita' because I don't love him and he doesn't love me and that's all perfectly fine.

I pick up the paper again and stare at the crossword. Second letter Z? What the fuck can the answer be?

He texts straight back. The message says, 'Thanks. Will be with you around 7.30 if that's OK. Shall I bring some supper?'

I send a reply: 'OK.' It's up to him to decide whether I'm saying OK to the time or the supper, or both. I really can't be bothered.

By six-thirty I've had a shower and put on my black linen trousers and a sweater which Boyd once said was the colour of an aubergine and, standing in front of the mirror in our bedroom the first time I'd worn it, I'd said to him, 'I'm not sure where you buy your aubergines, Boyd, but to me it's taupe.'

'Taupe?' He'd laughed then, and added, 'That's a real Farrow & Ball word! I'd expected better of you.'

'Sod off,' I'd replied and as I turned around he'd cupped my chin with his right hand and kissed me lightly on the nose.

'Love you too,' he'd said and had gone downstairs where he'd turned on the radio and started to empty the dishwasher.

It had been a normal day.

Just before seven-thirty I hear his car pull up outside and busy myself plumping up the cushions on the chairs in the lounge. I gaze about me, at my furniture, at the spaces and the calm I live among and in. It has taken a long time for me to learn to live alone, not to miss the hum of being part of something bigger than myself, but I've done it and I wouldn't change it for anything.

* * *

He knocks on the door. I let him in.

'Vita,' he says.

'Hello.'

'How are you?'

'Fine, thank you. How are you?'

'I'm well, thank you.' He hands me a carrier bag. 'I bought us some supper.'

I want to scream.

We move through to the kitchen and I start unpacking the bag. He's bought soup, pâté, a farmhouse loaf, a bottle of Merlot. He's also brought a bunch of late daffodils; I will have to put them in a vase when he's gone.

'What are you working on at the moment?' he asks as he rummages in a drawer for the corkscrew.

'I've moved it.'

'What?' he asks.

'The corkscrew. It's in that jug.' I point along the counter.

'Oh, OK.'

He walks behind me and plucks the corkscrew out; I can smell his aftershave. If I closed my eyes I could pretend he'd never left. I stare at the soup: minted pea and ham hock. The bloody man has only gone and bought one of my favourites. And flowers? Why on earth would he bring me flowers? I take the lid off the soup, tip it into a saucepan and stir it vigorously, impatient for it to come to the boil.

'Here,' he puts a glass of wine down next to me. 'I'll join you but better not have more than one glass as I'm driving.'

'OK,' I say.

As I heat the soup he wanders around, picking things up, putting them down again. He moves over to the sofa, studies the newspaper, and the crossword. 'It's Czar,' he says. 'Two across. It's Czar.'

'Of course it is,' I reply, getting two bowls out of the cupboard.

Bloody man. I would have got it in time.

We sit at the dining table and he cuts the bread and pours me another glass of wine. The soup is hot and delicious; I hadn't realised how hungry I was.

'So, what *are* you working on now?' he asks again.

'Oh, same old, same old,' I reply. 'But that's not why you're here. What's this favour you want my help with?'

Boyd is a big man: tall and broad with a shock of grey hair and big brown eyes. He used to fit this house, but recently it and I have got used to him not being here. I have filled the space he left with other people, other things.

'Um,' he says, moving a knife and then picking up the salt cellar

5

and twisting it around in his hands. 'Um, I've got myself into a bit of a pickle.'

'What sort of pickle?'

For some inexplicable reason my heart is thundering in my chest. Stop it, woman, I say to myself. Whatever it is won't matter, can't touch you, not now.

'There's someone else.' He blurts it out. 'Someone at work.'

'Trixie?' I ask, incredulous.

'No, not Trixie. Her name's Honey. We took her on a while ago, as a sort of a junior.'

'Junior? How old is she then?'

'Twenty-seven.'

'Oh, Boyd,' I say and I'm thinking, *Honey?* What sort of fucking stupid name is that?

'But that's not it. That's not the problem.'

Isn't it? What is then? I take another mouthful of wine. I notice he hasn't touched his.

'I've miscalculated the tax bill …'

'What about Anthony? Didn't he warn you?'

Boyd looks at his bowl. He's put down the salt cellar, the soup is still steaming. There are crumbs scattered over the table top.

'Yes, he did. But I didn't listen.'

'Oh, Boyd,' I say again. 'What does it mean? How much do you owe? What are you going to do about it?'

'It's a fair sum; I'm going to have to rent out the flat to help cover the costs and obviously tighten my belt.'

He looks down at his stomach and then lifts his head and gives me one of his lopsided grins, his left eyebrow raised just a little. Bloody man, I think. Bloody, bloody man.

'So where will you live?'

'Well, that's the thing.' He passes me the pâté, I shake my head. 'I was wondering if I could move back in here in the summer, just for a while. A few months, that's all.'

What can I say? The house is still half his. He has every right to ask.

'Um …' I say.

'Before you answer though,' he reaches out a hand and touches my arm, 'when I say "I", I mean "we", I mean Honey and me. Could Honey and I move in? We've …' he hesitates, swallows, '… been living together for a few months now. She gave up her lease for me, hasn't anywhere else to go. Would there be room?'

I look at him; I see him; I know him. It doesn't matter to me either way, does it?

'Of course,' I say brightly. 'Of course you can.'

* * *

And of course I'm watching.

They're not expecting me to be there but I am. I've hidden my bicycle behind the horse chestnut tree at the end of the cul-de-sac; each leaf on it is the size of a man's hand. It's sunny, it's hot; it's been a bitch of a day.

I'm standing in the shade and am at enough of a distance that they won't be able to see me unless they look carefully. I doubt very much that they will; they'll be too busy.

I take my glasses off and clean the lenses with the hem of my smock. Without them everything is satisfyingly blurry; if only life could always be like this, I think.

Boyd's car pulls up as I'm putting them back on. He turns to say something to the girl in the passenger seat but I avoid looking directly at her. He parks the car and they get out. He's wearing suit trousers, a blue and white striped shirt, no tie. She is graceful, willowy, blonde; her walk reminds me of a cheetah's. As they approach the house, he leans into her and says something, resting the palm of his hand on her lower back. I shiver involuntarily and this surprises me because enough water has passed under enough bridges by now for this not to matter. Boyd and I are friends, always have been. And I'm fine with this. I really am.

As they go through the gate, he takes her hand in one of his. He unlocks the door and they step inside. I can only imagine what she's thinking. Not Boyd, though, I know exactly how his mind works, just as I know my own. And I am fine, I know I am. This is all going to work out perfectly, because I'm over him – I've told myself enough times that I am. I am immune; nothing can touch me now.

Honey

Boyd takes her hand as the gate closes behind them with a squeak and a click. She imagines he's heard it do so a thousand times before. The house looks smaller than she thought it would be. When he's spoken about it, he's always made it out to be something other, something bigger.

The path they're on leads to a blue-painted door, the kind of navy worn by school girls and matrons in hospitals. Around the door a Virginia creeper has spread like a tapestry; it will look amazing come autumn. The front garden is a rainbow of summer flowers: stocks, mallows, delphiniums, poppies. To the left of the door is a sash window on the ground floor and another one above it on the first floor. The glass in the windows is, Honey notices, very clean.

To the left of the house are trees: youthful horse chestnuts, full-leafed and jaunty. They border a park. There is a brick wall and a pathway separating the trees and the park from the house. He's told her that Vita wheels her bicycle out of the gate at the bottom of the garden and up this path when she goes out.

Next door, on the right of Boyd's house, is another house, the mirror image of this one. Boyd's also told her that the terrace was

9

named after Prince Albert and Honey likes this sense of continuity, of history. For someone like her who has so little of it, it is pleasing.

Boyd squeezes her hand. 'She won't be here. You know that, don't you?'

Honey nods her head. Boyd gets a key out of his pocket.

'You've still got a key?' she asks. She wants her voice to sound normal, but it comes out as a croak.

In the horse chestnut trees pigeons are making the sounds pigeons make: *hoo* follows *hoo*, reminding her – bizarrely – of a ship's horn. Then they beat their wings in amongst the leaves, a sound like gunfire which blooms and settles into quiet once more.

'It's still my house,' Boyd says. 'Well, half of it is anyway.'

He's a large man and the house is small; he looks like a giant going into a dolls' house as he ducks before entering the front door. Boyd is big and solid and warm and wonderful and Honey loves him with all of her heart even when he's wrong. And he'd been wrong when he said Vita wouldn't be here because she is, everything about the house shouts her presence.

In Honey's bag is the end of an old loaf of bread and the salt cellar from the flat. They step into the front room; she turns and sprinkles some salt on the threshold. She truly believes both the bread and the salt will keep the evil spirits away.

The room is crowded with furniture: two chintz-covered chairs; a tall, dark, Victorian fireplace; and a small, squishy sofa under the window. The walls are bare apart from a huge, abstract oil painting above the fireplace. There is a vase of summer phlox on the mantelpiece and Vita's left a newspaper on the arm of one of the chairs, the crossword half done. It's mid-afternoon and the house is stuffy with captured heat.

'Shall I show you around first?' Boyd asks, his left eyebrow raised in its quirky way.

It's as though her feet are glued to the carpet. She wants to move but can't. 'Shouldn't we open some windows first?' she says. 'It's hot in here.'

She watches as Boyd undoes the catches on the front window and lifts it up. Then he strides into the back of the house and does the same with another window. Another key turns in a lock and there's a puff of fresher air. He must have opened the back door.

'Come on then, slowcoach,' he calls.

She peels her shoes from the floor and takes a step, then another and another until she's walking past the staircase which runs up to her left between the front and back rooms. She glances up; the upstairs of the house is silent and waiting.

In the dining room there's a battered oak table with a bowl of fruit on it and four mismatched chairs around it, another fireplace, and the window that Boyd has opened which looks out at a small passageway between the kitchen and the side wall. In the distance there is a long, narrow garden, the borders of which practically meet in the middle. He's told her that Vita's studio is at the bottom of the garden, behind the apple tree and that it's not visible from the house. It's where she works and keeps her bicycle. 'She's crazily independent,' he's said on a number of occasions.

Boyd's standing in the kitchen, one large hand resting on the counter top. The units are new, white and shiny; the floor is wooden. To the right of the back door is a small extension in which there's a battered, leather, two-seater sofa with a low table in front of it. There are more flowers in a vase on it, an open magazine and some junk mail. On the wall behind it is a mirror. Honey can see the back of Boyd's head in it.

The house is homely and lived-in. It appears that it barely has room for them and the stuff they've brought from the flat in the boxes and bags that are in Boyd's car on the road out front.

'What do you think?' he asks.

She knows he wants her to like it, it would make everything so much easier if she did; it is their only option after all.

'It's sweet,' she says, looking up at him.

As he says, 'Shall I show you our room?' his phone buzzes.

'I'll leave it; whatever it is can wait.'

'It might be about the sale of the house in Merlin Crescent,' Honey says.

'Mmmm, it may be, but I'm going to leave it anyway. This,' he takes a step towards her and gently cups her face with the fingers of his right hand, 'is more important. *You* are more important.'

Honey feels as though she's being watched, that Vita is watching her, that she's doing something wrong. She feels like she did in the early days when she and Boyd were just beginning, when she wasn't so sure of him, when she felt everything she did was brazen and dangerous. And now, it's still like she's the other woman and that they shouldn't be here, he shouldn't be touching her face in the kitchen of this house. He bends down and brushes his lips against hers. Instinctively her insides tighten and she leans in towards him; she can feel herself melding her body to his; she fits into it perfectly. It's corny, but it's true.

'Come on,' he says, turning her around so she's facing the front of the house again. 'Upstairs with you, wench!'

Boyd's voice is low and gravelly. She's never been brave enough to question why she fell for him in the first place. She guesses some therapist or do-gooder would say that, because they're both fatherless, she sees him as a father substitute and he sees himself as one too, and that with him at forty-six and her at twenty-seven, he's far too old and wise for her and she's far too young and inexperienced for him.

Well, perhaps not too old or wise, otherwise they wouldn't be here, with their possessions in the car, the flat they lived in up until this morning rented out to a stranger. Perhaps, if he was wiser, he would have power of attorney over his mother's affairs and have persuaded her to make a will, his estate agency wouldn't be in the parlous state it's in right now and he wouldn't be making this sacrifice for her and Trixie's sakes.

And, as for her? She may be young, but she's not inexperienced. No, sir. There's still a great deal about her that Boyd doesn't know, that he mustn't know.

He's following her; she can feel his breath on her neck. She wants him. Even here, even now, she wants his body on hers; his weight on her and in her. She wants to be on her back, lifting her hips to meet his.

They go up the stairs. At the top, the landing splits and, to their right, leading to the back of the house, is a corridor at the end of which is the bathroom. A doorway along the corridor opens on to what will be their room; it had been the spare room when Boyd lived here before, or so he'd told her.

She pauses in the doorway. Time is passing. He said Vita had agreed to wait for them to get settled in before she came back, but Honey hadn't thought to ask him what time this may be. Somewhere in the house there must be clocks ticking. Seconds are pulsing through the phones in their pockets. Outside the sun is ever so slowly slipping down the afternoon sky.

The room obviously faces west as it's flooded with light. The bed's covered with a white counterpane. There's a mahogany wardrobe in the far corner and a dressing table under the window. Yet again, there is a fireplace. This time it's been painted white. The grate is empty and everything in the room looks clean, clinical almost, like a stage that's been set and is waiting for the actors to arrive with their messy dramas, their clothes strewn about, clusters of jewellery, a pile of books to read.

'Will it be big enough?' Honey asks. 'For all our stuff, I mean. There's no TV downstairs, not that I could see. Is there room in here for one do you think?'

Boyd's still standing behind her so she's looking over her shoulder as she says this. He kisses her neck. Again, that thrill passes through her.

'We'll sort something out, I'm sure,' he says. 'Maybe I can persuade Vita to have one installed downstairs, you never know!' He laughs a small laugh, then adds, 'Come on, woman, let's start bringing our stuff in. It'll be best to do it before she gets back.'

'OK,' Honey says and they turn and go back out of the doorway. She's following him this time; his body sways from side to side. He doesn't pause at the top of the stairs to look into what used to be his and Vita's room but she can't stop herself from doing so. She glances in. Because it's facing the front, away from the sun, the light is less savage inside it, is gentler almost. She sees a vast, unmade bed, full-length green curtains made out of some silky material, a pair of trainers on the floor, the laces of which are white and luminous. A red chiffon scarf on the bed looks like a wound. On the fireplace there's a black and white photograph of a couple in a silver frame.

Honey thinks of the bread and the salt. She has to stay positive. If she doesn't, this isn't going to work.

Because the house is at the end of the row and because the road is a cul-de-sac, it's quiet out the front. When she steps out of the front door, she can hear Boyd huffing and puffing as he starts lifting stuff from the car. She should be helping him but instead she's watching him stack their belongings in neat piles.

She'd always promised herself to journey light; this is the most she's ever moved from one place to the next. And it's not just clothes and things like that this time. Now she has photographs, books with her name in them, a job, a phone and charger. She has a debit card. And she has Boyd. She is moving with him too.

She knows Boyd. She knows he'll hope that as she's not helping, she'll be inside the house, breathing it in, making herself feel at home. But instead she's watching him, transfixed, remembering.

* * *

It's later and Vita still hasn't arrived. Boyd and Honey have almost finished unpacking. A blackbird is shouting his evening news from the apple tree, the sun is getting larger and lower, the sky is striped with thin, silky clouds.

Honey's putting her and Boyd's toothbrushes in a glass on the shelf above the basin in the bathroom when she hears it: the unmistakable whirr of a bicycle being wheeled down the path next to the house. A latch lifts. A gate opens and closes. Slowly she moves back into their bedroom but stops by the bed; she can't look out of the window. She doesn't want to see her yet. She's not ready.

Next there are footsteps up the garden path, Boyd's wife is clearing her throat, then she coughs. Still Honey can't look; she doesn't move.

Downstairs, the back door opens. Boyd's voice is low and achingly familiar as he says, 'Oh, hi Vita. You're home.'

Vita

I've been rehearsing this moment all day. Well, if I'm honest, I've been rehearsing it for weeks, ever since Boyd asked if he could move back in. But why should I need to rehearse? It doesn't matter whether he's here or not.

But, I've had a bad day. I've been waiting in the park since they arrived, am hot and tired and the job I'm on isn't going well: bloody stupid dog, bloody stupid owner. And now, I'm walking in the back door of my house and Boyd is there, a massive presence again and there is something solid and permanent about him and he's saying, 'Oh, hi Vita. You're home.'

'So, you got a degree in the bleeding obvious or what?' I say, hurling my bag on to the sofa at the back of the kitchen. I choose not to look at him but can sense his shoulders tense. After all, I know him. We may have been separated for six years but we'd been married, and happily married, for fifteen years before that. Well, we'd been happy for most of them. The last one had been a bit shit.

There's a noise from upstairs: a bump and a shuffle. I'd momentarily forgotten about that bloody girl. Honey. Again, what sort of damn stupid name is that?

The noise is a timely reminder. Boyd must have heard it too.

'Thanks for making us welcome,' he says. 'The bedroom looks comfy.'

We've never admitted it, not even subconsciously, but it was in that room that our marriage had, to all intents and purposes, ended. After he'd gone, I'd washed down the paintwork with bleach and repainted the walls. Now it's bland and magnolia and the evening sun will be streaming through the window. I imagine Honey up there, her bare feet on the carpet.

I snort, tucking a stray strand of hair behind my ear and, in one deft move, take off my glasses and start cleaning the lenses with the hem of my smock again.

'It's OK,' I say, still not looking at Boyd. 'It's not like I had a choice. Not really.'

'I thought,' he says, 'I'd rustle us up some supper. For all of us. We can have it outside. It's a lovely evening. What do you think?'

I know he's asking for more than my agreement to a cold meat and salad supper. He wants this to work. For the three of us to get on. And why shouldn't we? I've spent six years convincing myself that us being friends is the ideal solution. The rest? Well, that's been parked as just something that was so fucking sad, such a fucking waste.

'Oh. OK,' I say, putting my glasses back on.

I'm known for them, my glasses, that is. They're big and red and like something from the eighties, but they're my trademark now. I'm wearing them in the headshots I've had done to publicise my stupid pet portrait business; I'm wearing them in the self-portrait on the homepage of my website; my logo is a pair of large red spectacles, the frames spelling out my name. 'All very Dame Edna Everage,' Boyd used to joke. Back in the day. Back then, before …

'I'll be down in a bit,' I say now. 'I'll just pop upstairs first.'

'Honey's up there.'

'I kind of guessed she would be.'

I take a deep breath and tell myself everything's fine. This is what I expected, what I agreed to. Yet, when I get to the top of the stairs I find I can't look to the right, can't propel my feet along the landing, can't nonchalantly pop my head around the bedroom door and say, 'Hi, settling in OK?' like I'd rehearsed.

Their stuff seems to fill the house; there are still some boxes in the lounge that Boyd hasn't unpacked. I imagine them both as giants, ten feet tall, with voices that boom and echo. I imagine their toothbrushes in the bathroom leering at mine, leering and laughing.

But it's quiet up here, so quiet I think I can hear the girl breathing. I turn left into my room, saying, Fuck it, to myself.

I thought I'd made my bed earlier but no, here it is resplendently unmade, a pair of trainers on the floor and a blood red scarf, the same shade as my glasses, snaking across the scrunched up duvet. The photograph of my parents stares at me from the mantelpiece.

The scarf was a present from Colin. I move forward, pick it up and wind it through my fingers. Colin. Bugger, I'd forgotten all about Colin. I think back to when Boyd told me about Honey and asked if they could move in. The words 'pot', 'kettle' and 'black' had ricocheted around my head, but no way was I going to tell Boyd about Colin. Not then, and, it seems, not now either.

But was I supposed to be seeing Colin tonight? I can't remember. I track back through the day. We'd spoken this morning as I was getting on my bike and he was walking down his path to the road. He'd said, 'Hope it goes OK,' and I'd wondered at the time whether he meant the job I'm on – the bloody dog, his bloody owner – or whether he'd meant this evening and me getting home to find that Boyd and that girl had moved in.

No. We weren't due to see one another tonight. We'd agreed it would be best to do things slowly. Let me get used to having Boyd back in the house and at least to be able to string a coherent sentence together to Honey (yet again, what sort of name is that?) before introducing them to Colin. It should be OK to introduce my husband to my lover, shouldn't it? After all isn't that what Boyd is doing now, introducing *his* wife to *his* lover? But I don't want to; I'm not ready to do it yet.

I sit on the bed, the scarf still threaded through my fingers. I should open the window. Let in some air.

It had been a Saturday morning in early May, a week after Boyd had asked his 'favour'. We were naked, Colin kneeling behind me on the bed. We'd just made love and he was brushing my hair and asking, 'Are you sure you're going be all right? All the other stuff notwithstanding …' (Colin uses words like 'notwithstanding' and it's one of the reasons I like him so much), '… you're kind of used to living on your own these days, aren't you? Won't it be crowded with the three of you in the house?'

'What choice do I have?'

Colin was still brushing my hair. I've always worn it in a long, thick plait down my back, it has hints of grey streaking it now but when I was younger it was glossy and a kind of bluey-black. Boyd used to call it my 'raven-wing hair' and Colin loves brushing it.

'After all,' I continued. 'It's still his house, or half of it is. We've never bothered to get all that bollocky stuff sorted, you know: a divorce, splitting the assets. The business was doing well enough then for him to buy his flat and let me stay here. There wasn't any need to do anything more formal. We only had ourselves to worry about in those days.'

'And now?' Colin's hands are smaller than Boyd's. Everything about Colin is compact, tidy and unsurprising.

Colin had moved in next door about a year after Boyd moved out. He'd hung two artificial lavender-coloured topiary balls outside his front door and, for a while, I'd presumed he was gay and so started an easy and uncomplicated friendship with him which, when I realised he wasn't gay but very much heterosexual and unattached, had developed into an uncomplicated relationship where we had uncomplicated sex now and again and went to see plays and out for the odd meal, and where he bought me a red silk scarf for my forty-fifth birthday.

'Well, I guess it is a little bit more complex now,' I said, leaning up against him. He'd carefully put the brush on the bed and cupped my breasts in his small, neat hands. It was a gesture of comfort, nothing more. Colin isn't the sort of lover who wants to make love more than once a session, he would consider it an extravagance. His small, neat fingers had made me come in a very satisfying way and he'd come too, quietly and efficiently and with the minimum of fuss.

I often have to stop myself comparing Colin's lovemaking to Boyd's which, when we'd been younger and life had been easier, had been big and boisterous and unpredictable.

'I mean,' I continued, 'now he's got this massive tax bill to pay which, in true Boyd fashion, he hasn't planned for properly and, instead of doing something sensible like making cutbacks – reducing Trixie's hours again for starters and getting rid of that pop-princess Honey – he'd rather get the money together by renting out his flat and moving in here for the duration. He's promised me it won't be for long …' I'd tailed off.

Trixie had been nothing but kind to both me and Boyd when we'd been together and had been especially thoughtful after it all went wrong, bringing round casseroles and quietly ironing Boyd's shirts when all I could do was lie in bed and stare at the wall.

As I talked, I could taste the soup I'd cooked and the wine I'd drunk the evening Boyd called round. It felt strange telling Colin, as if I was translating something from a foreign language into English, into words that could be better understood.

And, of course, Colin had been fine about Boyd and Honey moving in. He's the most unthreatening, and unthreatened, person I know. He's my polar opposite; I know I've always been prickly, difficult and intense. Maybe it's the artist in me. That's what Boyd used to say anyway.

There's another noise from the other bedroom: a kind of snuffle and a soft tread. I really should get cracking; I should brave the trip to the bathroom and wash my face, do my teeth. I still feel grubby from working in that bloody woman's house with her bloody dog's hairs everywhere. Anyone who knows me would think I like pets, seeing as I'm a pet portraitist but, truth be told, I prefer painting human faces and definitely prefer larger animals, such as horses, to small, yappy dogs with bad breath.

I unwind the scarf and stand up. It seems like hours have passed, but it's probably only been a few minutes. I can still hear small, woodland-creature-like noises from along the landing. I really must go and say hello to the girl Boyd has brought here to live with us.

I'm in the doorway to my room when Honey appears. Low sunlight is still pouring through the back of the house, through the bathroom window and dotting the walls and carpet with a kind of golden confetti. All I can see is her outline: small-shouldered, slim-hipped, the long legs I'd seen earlier. Already I feel a bubble of resentment; she's so bloody young. And then Honey steps out of the light and we are face to face.

In the gloom, I gasp. Or I think I do. I'm aware of some sort of sound coming out of my mouth. It seems stupid now that I didn't insist on meeting her beforehand, maybe I was too afraid of what I'd see and that it would either make me change my mind, or make it impossible to change it.

No, this way was, I'd thought, better. But, even the snatched view of her I'd had when they'd arrived hadn't prepared me for this. Now, I can see what Boyd sees, has seen every day since he's been involved with her: a huge pair of violet eyes, a perfect brow, a rosebud mouth, cheekbones you could cut paper on and hair so short you can see the shape of her head which is, of course, faultless. It is smooth and round and I have an irrepressible urge to lay my hands on it.

'Hi,' Honey says, shyly, dipping her head to one side so she looks like an inquisitive bird, one that's half-ready to hop into my hand and half-ready to fly away.

'Hello.'

There is a pause.

'Did you …' I say.

'Thank you …' Honey says at the same time.

We laugh, both of us, together.

There is another pause.

'Did you …' I try again. 'Did you find everything you need?'

'Yes. Thank you. The room's great. And thank you for having us to stay. Boyd calls you his god-send.'

The girl's laughter is, I think crossly, like a gentle waterfall with the sun beading through it. Fuck it, I say to myself. Fuck it. I don't want to like her. I don't need to like her. It's not in the plan.

'Humph.' The noise comes out like the noise dogs make when they're dreaming. 'It's not like I had a choice,' I say curtly.

'Even so,' and there's that laughter again, 'it's kind of you. No, not kind. It's actually really amazing. I don't think I could do it.' As she says this, Honey reaches out a hand and touches me on the arm. Instinctively I recoil.

'Oh, I'm sorry,' Honey says. 'I didn't mean to …'

'Boyd's making something to eat,' I say instead. 'Tell him I'll be down in a bit, will you?'

And with that I brush past Honey and stride along the landing to the bathroom. Once there I shut the door behind me and rest my head against it. The sun is still beating through the window.

'Fuck,' I say out loud. 'Fuck, fuck, fuck.'

And there they are, their toothbrushes in a glass on the shelf: one green, one pink. They are nestled up against one another. Mine is in its own glass on the window sill where it always is, where it had been when Boyd's toothbrush had been nestled up against it.

I hadn't minded Honey touching me. In actual fact, I'd quite liked it. It was the kind of touch I imagine a child giving a parent; possessive, careless, full of a nameless love. The kind of touch I'd once believed would be mine for always.

Boyd

'Well, that didn't go too badly, I thought,' Boyd says to Honey as he pulls back the duvet and gets into the bed.

He says it quietly, afraid that Vita will hear him, and he's lying of course. The evening had been terrible.

But then he whispers, 'What the fuck is that?'

Honey's wearing some sort of Victorian nightgown buttoned up to her chin. When they'd lived in the flat, she'd slept naked.

'I thought I ought to, you know,' she says. 'Just in case I bump into her in the corridor during the night.'

'But it's ridiculous! You look sixteen in it.'

'I quite like it,' she says, climbing in beside him.

Her eyes are enormous in the low light from the bedside lamp. Outside the night sky is navy. When he'd drawn the curtains to, the moon had been high and small, as small and bright as a pearl. 'Aw, take it off. It's hideous.' He laughs and, leaning over her, runs his hand up inside the thick material until he finds the top of her thigh.

'We can't,' she murmurs. 'We shouldn't.'

'Why not?' His fingers are pushing her legs apart. Her mouth is half open, he knows this look. She wants it too.

'She might hear us. It wouldn't be seemly.'

'Seemly? Ye gods woman, are you speaking like you're from the nineteenth century now too?'

'But I'm right, aren't I?'

She clamps her legs together trapping his hand. Next she pulls his face down to hers and kisses him softly on the lips.

'Boyd?'

He loves it when she says his name. 'OK. You win,' he says, reluctantly withdrawing his hand and smoothing her nightgown down again. He kisses her forehead. 'But promise me that we will, and soon? OK? And promise me you'll get rid of this thing?' Again, he tugs at the nightgown. 'Or I might be forced to rip it off you!'

He's joking of course.

'Perhaps you should get some britches and one of those flouncy Darcy shirts …'

'You're mixing your fashion eras!'

'OK, Mr Know-It-All. Anyway, you were saying, you thought it went OK tonight? Dinner and all that? Did I do all right?'

'You were fine. It's gonna be fine here. Trust me.'

'What time you setting the alarm for?'

She tucks her hands under her chin in her customary adorable way. She has absolutely no idea how gorgeous she is, Boyd thinks as Honey asks him this.

'Seven should do it. We've got that valuation in Morris Road to do first thing.'

'I think I drank a bit too much,' she says drowsily.

'It's never easy, the first night in a new place but I see you've already chosen which side you'll be sleeping on.'

'You know me. Always a door to my left and able to see a window. I'm kind of superstitious that way.'

'Are you? I hadn't noticed,' Boyd nudges her gently with his arm.

'And apparently there's a film star who always has to sleep with his head pointing north. Or maybe it's a poet, or a writer, or an explorer. I'm not sure.' She sighs sleepily.

Boyd smiles to himself. She'd told him exactly the same thing the first night she slept in his bed at the flat.

'Is there?' he says.

'But it's not new to you, is it?' she asks after a brief pause.

'What isn't?'

'Sleeping here. It's not your first night here. You've lived here before.'

'Never in this room though. In the front bedroom and on the sofa, yes, but not in here,' he says, leaning down and kissing her lightly on the lips. 'Night, Honey.'

'Night, Boyd.'

He turns off the light. There is a strip of yellow from the landing light at the bottom of the door. He can sense, but can't hear, Vita in her room on the other side of the staircase. He thought them being here wouldn't matter, but it's odd, it does feel odd. He hadn't expected it to.

He forces his mind to concentrate on what's outside the house, rather than what's inside it: he thinks about the park, the trees keeping guard, the grass silver in the spotlight moon. He imagines urban foxes following their night-time trails, or a badger walking across the playing field, rocking its body from side to side. Listening carefully, he waits for the nightlife to make its sounds: the purr of an owl calling, hedgehogs rustling through leaves. But there's nothing. Just the distant hum of traffic, Honey's gentle breathing.

Dinner had been bread, thick-cut ham, cheese, chutney, beefsteak tomatoes and too much wine. The three of them had sat around the small wooden table on the patio outside the back door and he'd tried very hard not to focus on what had changed since he'd left. The table itself was new, as were the chairs they were sitting on. Vita had obviously taken to growing herbs too, there were pots of them dotted around the patio's edge and she'd hung a basket crammed with red begonias on the back wall of the house. The garden had become much more overgrown. He could hardly see her studio now. He remembered building it and thought – maybe unfairly – how, whilst he'd moved on, she'd chosen not to.

He turns over in bed to face the door. Honey's back and shoulders are rising and falling in time with her breathing. She always seems so childlike when she sleeps and doesn't dream, he thinks, the wariness she carries with her seems to fade then.

Has he really moved on though? After all, he's back here now, isn't he? He studies Honey's neck, how it tapers, how her hair line tapers too. He cracks his knuckles and closes his eyes. It's only temporary, he tells himself and it's not as if he has anywhere else to go.

He sees the three of them as they were at dinner, as a tableau printed on the back of his eyelids. He'd tried to keep the conversation flowing. 'Apparently, Farnham Road Hospital in Guildford was opened in 1866 in memory of Prince Albert. Queen Victoria was a patron, donating one hundred guineas to the cost of building it. I've often wondered if there's a link somewhere between that and why this terrace is named after him. Do you think he visited Farnham at some point, or maybe passed through it on a royal progress or whatever it's called? We never bothered to find out, did we Vita?'

Vita was playing with the stem of her wineglass.

'No, Boyd. We never bothered,' she said. Then she turned to

Honey and, in a voice much sharper than Boyd reckoned she'd intended, asked, 'Are you a monarchist?'

'Never really thought about it,' Honey said, swallowing hard. She put down the piece of bread she was holding and dropped her hands on her lap so that they couldn't be seen. Boyd recognised this move. She did it when she was worried or nervous or felt herself under scrutiny because, when she is, her hands shake.

'No, I suppose someone your age wouldn't really need to worry about stuff like that,' Vita said pointedly.

And then bless her, Honey bit back. 'Well, are you a monarchist or a republican then, Vita? You've obviously had a lot more experience than me, so no doubt you have a point of view.'

She said it charmingly, her lips twitching with a half-smile, but she still had her hands in her lap.

Vita's shoulders relaxed a bit and she looked at Honey with a hint of respect. Fifteen all, Boyd said to himself, cutting a corner off the piece of cheddar and popping it into his mouth.

'I guess if I thought the way my parents claim they do, I'd have the Royals' heads on spikes,' Vita said, 'but, realistically, I think they do a good job. They're obviously a bit pompous and detached from the real world of mortgages and benefits and two-for-ones at Aldi, but they represent something that means well, that does the country good.'

Vita looked almost surprised at herself for having said so much. If Boyd had imagined how tonight would be, he'd have thought, knowing Vita as he does, that she'd keep her own counsel, play it cool, but here she was almost having a conversation with Honey.

'More wine?' Boyd asked.

'OK,' Vita said.

'Yes please,' Honey replied.

At that moment a man came out of the back door of the neighbouring house. He looked over the fence at them. Boyd realised then that Vita had never replaced the fence like they'd planned to do once upon a time; it was still low and tatty, threaded through with the clematis he'd planted the year before he left. The clematis obviously hadn't been cut back properly for a while.

The man raised a hand in greeting.

'Hi there,' he said jovially.

Vita shifted in her chair, picked up her glass and took a gulp of wine.

The man was, Boyd noticed, small and neat, wearing a faded denim shirt and pale chinos. His skin was the colour of cappuccino and he sported a tidy beard, the same dark brown as his short hair. He had kind eyes and a frank, open smile. He must, Boyd reckoned, be about forty.

'I'm Colin. Next-door neighbour, for my sins!'

He didn't seem surprised to find Boyd and Honey there which made Boyd wonder what Vita had told him about them. Boyd stood up and went to shake Colin's hand. It was compact, warm and dry and, not for the first time, Boyd had to remind himself not to squeeze too tight; it is easy to forget sometimes with hands the size of his.

'I'm Boyd and this is Honey,' Boyd said, pointing at Honey who smiled at Colin.

'Yes, Vita said you'd be coming to stay. It's nice to meet you.'

'Likewise.'

It was all so perfectly reasonable and grown-up and Boyd was on the cusp of asking how long ago he'd moved in when Colin said, 'Better leave you to it. Just giving my tomato plants a quick water and then I'm off out. No doubt we'll bump into one another again sometime.'

'No doubt,' Boyd said, moving back towards the table and sitting down again. Honey was still smiling at the new neighbour but, Boyd noticed, Vita hadn't said a word throughout the exchange. 'He seems nice,' he said, as Colin made his way down his garden, carrying a watering can.

'Mmmm,' Vita replied and then she added, 'Well, I'd better get this lot cleared away,' and she pushed back her chair and stood up, taking some of the empty plates with her into the house.

It was nicer when she'd gone inside. The atmosphere in the garden softened. Boyd could hear Colin whistling something tuneless as he pottered amongst his plants; the sky had turned a kind of translucent lilac. Birds were shouting from the trees.

'You OK?' he asked, reaching under the table for Honey's knee and giving it a squeeze.

She nodded. 'Not sure who won that round,' she said.

'It doesn't need to be like that,' he said. 'It shouldn't be like that. Vita is …'

But just at that moment Boyd didn't know how to describe the woman who had been and was still, technically, his wife. Vita was just Vita: sharp-edged, vivid, angry and disappointed and, although he didn't want to, Boyd had to admit that some of this was down to him. She hadn't always been this way. There'd been a time when …

Honey makes a small sound in her sleep which rouses Boyd from his musings. He inches closer to her, feels the heat from her body and he reaches out to rest his hand on her leg. All is still quiet in Vita's room. Outside the night is still turning and somewhere in the sky there will be a shooting star, he thinks. Eventually he sleeps.

* * *

When his alarm goes off in the morning, it takes Boyd a few seconds to remember where he is. Yesterday he'd woken up in his flat to its usual light and the shapes made by his furniture. It's different here. He tracks back in his memory to see if he recognises it from before, when he used to live here, but he can't. The house is the same; its fittings and decor may have changed a bit but the house is fundamentally the same, so maybe it's him who's changed. He is a different person now.

Next to him Honey stirs.

'Morning, sleepyhead,' he says.

'Piss off.' She burrows deeper in the duvet.

He kisses her shoulder through the inconvenient cotton of her nightgown.

'Piss off,' she says again. She's always a nightmare first thing.

'I'll go and get you a coffee, shall I? And use the bathroom. That way at least I'll be out of Vita's way.'

Honey snuffles in agreement, at least he takes it to be agreement.

He hadn't thought through how it would be: the three of them negotiating one another's morning routines. It had all been so simple in the past. Vita would rise at six-thirty, drink two mugs of tea sitting in the alcove at the back of the kitchen, a newspaper on her knee open at the crossword, a pen behind her ear. Then she'd shower and dress and eat one piece of thickly buttered toast thickly covered with Rose's Lime Marmalade before either going down the path to her studio or down the path to get her bicycle and go off to see a client, or a gallery owner, or a picture framer. And he'd get up, get dressed and go out the front door. He'd drive to the office where Trixie would make him his first coffee of the day.

Back then it had been as though he and Vita were at either end of a piece of elastic and, come the evening, they'd be pulled back toward one another again, back toward the house, to an evening by the fire or sitting in the garden. And it had all worked splendidly for a while.

He wanders downstairs and there she is, sitting on the sofa in the alcove, a newspaper on her lap, a pen behind her ear, a cup of tea on the table in front of her. She's wrapped in an orange pashmina under which she's wearing a pair of striped, men's pyjamas. Her hair is in its customary plait.

'Oh,' Vita says, looking up at him. 'I'd forgotten you were here.'

'Really? Who did you think it was coming down the stairs?'

'I mean, I'd forgotten you were both here. For a moment ...' She takes a gulp of her tea. 'Oh, it doesn't matter.'

Her voice is angry and she plucks the pen out from behind her ear and writes something in one of the boxes in the crossword. 'Nine down,' she says. 'Oblivion. The answer's Lethe, of course. It's been staring me in the face for the last ten minutes. Sodding thing.' She slaps the paper down and stands up. 'OK if I use the bathroom? It's time for my shower.'

'Sure', he answers. 'We'll fit in around you. That's the deal.'

She makes a kind of harrumphing noise as she puts her mug in the sink and gathers her pashmina around her shoulders more tightly. 'I shouldn't be long,' she says. 'And, by the way ...'

'Yes?' He's putting the kettle on. She's standing just behind him. He can feel an untamed energy buzzing through her.

'... put some clothes on before you come down tomorrow morning OK?'

Boyd looks down. 'Shit,' he says. 'Sorry.'

He's wearing nothing but his boxers. It may have been appropriate yesterday morning in his own flat. It may have been appropriate six years ago when he was still living here. But now, this morning? No, it wasn't appropriate at all.

The kettle is making a noise as it comes up to the boil, but he's convinced he can hear Vita talking to herself as she climbs the stairs.

Half an hour later, when Vita has had her toast and marmalade and has slammed the back door and gone down the path to her studio, Honey is sitting up in bed holding a cup of coffee and Boyd is putting on a tie in front of the dressing table mirror.

'Shall I drop you at the office on the way to Morris Road?' he asks her.

'Sure, but if you drop me at the front, then I'll have to leave by the front door this evening. You know that. I can't mix and match my doors.'

'I know,' he says, watching her reflection in the mirror, her eyes huge and dark in the room's half-light, her neck so slender it's amazing it can hold the weight of her head. 'You getting up soon or what?' he asks her. 'You have ten minutes and then I'm leaving without you.'

'You wouldn't.' She's laughing at him and she's right. He wouldn't.

'Let me just check my horoscope and then I'll get up, I promise,' she says, putting her coffee down and picking up her phone. 'I'll check yours and Vita's at the same time.'

'Mumbo jumbo if you ask me.'

'But I'm not asking you, am I?' She's smiling as she scrolls down on her phone. 'Mmmm,' she says, 'looks like someone is going to contact me from afar today. I sincerely hope not!' She says this almost crossly, defiantly but, he notices, she doesn't check his and Vita's. She puts the phone back down and gets out of bed.

And then it comes to him. He knows what gift he can get her for her birthday next month.

He concentrates hard, thinking only of Honey as he leaves the house and walks out on to the pavement. He doesn't think of the countless other times he's left for work from here, the sound the key makes turning in the lock, Vita's flowers providing a kind of guard of honour each side of the pathway. He doesn't think of Vita.

Colin, the guy from next door, is also leaving for work, or so Boyd presumes. He doesn't know what Colin does for a living. 'Good morning,' Boyd says.

Colin says good morning back.

'It's going to be another hot one.'

'Sure is.'

And that's it. Honey is getting in the car as Colin strides off up the road, a small, neat knapsack on his back.

It's the summer holidays so traffic is light.

'Did you see Vita this morning?' Honey asks as they turn into Castle Street.

'Yep. She seemed fine.'

'She working today?'

'Yep, in her studio I think.'

'We won't all have to eat together tonight will we? Shall we go out for dinner instead?'

'We can do, but we mustn't make a habit of it. We can't really afford to.'

'I know, but ...'

Boyd pulls up outside the office. Inside he can see Trixie at her desk. 'She's in early,' he says, then adds, 'But what?'

'It might send a message that we're our own bosses.'

'OK, I'm sure she knows we are, but I'll text her anyway and let her know.'

'Thanks,' she says and kisses him lightly on the cheek. 'See you in a bit,' she says. 'Good luck in Morris Road.'

'Thanks. Just going to pop the car through the car wash first.'

'Sure you don't want me to join you?' she asks, licking her lips and giving him a lewd wink.

He laughs. He knows what she's referring to. 'Get away with you, you minx, and let me go and do my job the way it should be done: maturely and with probity.'

She opens the door to the office and walks in. He hears her say, 'Hi there,' to Trixie, who raises a hand in greeting but doesn't look up from what she's doing.

Boyd indicates and pulls out into the flow of traffic.

He's a few minutes early for the valuation and so parks round the corner from Morris Road. He opens the car window and leans an elbow out. The morning around him is busy and already the air is warm.

If he can, he always parks away from the house in question. When houses are put on the market it can unsettle a neighbourhood, so he likes to check with the vendor first whether it's all right to be an obvious presence. He likes to know whether the move is prompted by something good such as a promotion, or an older couple moving closer to their daughter and her family maybe or, in some cases, a new start in a completely different part of the country. When it's due to death or divorce, it's never as pleasant and it's good to find out what the neighbours know before he parks his big blue car outside a house and walks his obvious estate-agent walk up the path.

As he's pondering, he watches a cat hop over a garden wall and swagger along the pavement, keeping close to the wall. The cat gives off an aura of not giving a fuck but his ears are pricked and his tail is twitching. For all his bravado, he is watchful and wary.

Droplets of water from the car wash are clinging on to the car's bodywork. Against the paint they are shaped like cabochon jewels. Boyd wonders where he knows that word from. It must be from Vita and her crosswords he thinks. There's a strange tightness in his chest at the thought of Vita and he feels a bit like the cat he's just seen. To all intents and purposes he's swaggering through this experience of taking Honey to live in the same house as his wife whereas, in reality, maybe he too should be more wary, more watchful.

He checks the time. Five minutes to go – and so he lets himself remember the valuation he did at 'Chimneys' last year, the valuation after the car wash when he'd been alone with Honey for the first time.

* * *

Boyd had been dubious when Trixie recruited Honey. He hadn't seen the need for an office junior, but thought maybe he was being blinkered and didn't realise just how much work Trixie was doing. Anyway, Honey had arrived: a cautious, shy, dowdily-dressed girl who was far too thin and nervous. She'd reminded him of a wild bird – a sparrow, or something like that.

But gradually, she'd relaxed. He'd come across her humming to herself as she washed up the cups, or filled the photocopier with more paper. She'd started to dress differently too. Gone were the plain woollens, the knee-length skirts. Instead she'd begun to wear brighter colours, her skin glowed, she'd had her hair cut and dyed and when she walked, she reminded him less of a bird and more of a wild cat: long-limbed, graceful, powerful.

He'd had no idea then what would happen. How could he, when it came out of the blue the way it did?

'What star sign are you?' she'd asked him.

It seemed all they'd said so far was 'I shouldn't ...' and 'I know ...'

'Um, I have no idea.' His hand was itching to touch her leg again. He felt magnetised.

'Well, when's your birthday?' She looked at him, the lilac of her eyes almost purple in the low light. The car was being rocked by the whirr and whizz of the mammoth brushes.

'April 27th,' he said.

'That's OK then.'

'Why?'

It was hot, the car airless and each sound seemed magnified. He could feel sweat prickling his neck under the collar of his shirt.

'We're compatible then.'

'Why, what's yours?'

'Virgo. Mine's the 7th September.'

There was a pause after this and Boyd could sense her thoughts veering away from the there and then of them in the car. He had no idea what she might be thinking.

'So it's my birthday first?' He tried to make a joke of it. 'I expect cakes in the office, you know. Trixie always remembers.'

'Does she?' Honey asked. Another pause. 'That's nice,' she added.

At 'Chimneys' it was as though the air between them was charged with static. Mrs Chambers bustled around them, making tea, offering them biscuits on a plate with a doily underneath them. She was a short, compact woman with impeccable hair and a sweet, round face. However, her eyes betrayed a sadness; they spoke of grief, of love lost too soon.

Boyd scanned the room for photographs; there weren't many but there was one, on the mantelpiece in the lounge, of a man leaning against a farm gate, a dog at his feet. Behind him, fields stretched away to the horizon. The sunshine, although in black and white, appeared fierce and the man was holding a hand to shield his eyes from the glare of it. To Boyd it could have been a gesture of welcome or farewell.

As the valuation progressed, Boyd was acutely aware of Honey. They were in Mrs Chambers' bedroom with its perfectly-made bed, its dark wood dressing table with a triptych of mirrors reflecting themselves back at one another. Honey's reflection moved in and out of view and every time she came back into view, his breath caught in his throat.

Eventually it was over. They agreed on an asking price and all the other practicalities.

'Thank you,' Mrs Chambers said, 'for coming, for being so gentle with the house.'

Even then, even after the innumerable houses Boyd had bought and sold, he tried never to lose sight of the fact that his job was predicated on people leaving the homes they were used to and going somewhere else. There is a huge difference between the word 'house' and the word 'home'. This was the kind of estate agent he wanted to be.

Honey had been quiet on the journey back to the office.

'You OK?' he asked as they drove into the car park at the back of their building and he pulled up by the Grundon bin.

'Sure,' she said. 'It's just been a bit of a morning. A lot to take in.'

'I hope not too much?'

'No. I'm a resilient soul,' she answered, smiling at him. But it was a tight, unsure smile.

'Look,' he said. He had no idea what to say but just that something definite needed to be said. They needed to agree on a plan. So far their time alone together that morning had been beautiful but insubstantial – achingly insubstantial. He needed something concrete to hold on to. He felt as though there was a butterfly cupped in his hands, beating its wings against his palms. 'Look, before we go in, there's something I need to know.'

'What's that?' she asked, her voice an almost-whisper.

'Can I woo you?'

'Can you what?'

'Woo you.'

She laughed then, a loud, carefree laugh. She threw back her head so he could see the smooth, pale skin of her neck.

'What's funny?' He switched off the engine and shifted in his seat. The silence was almost deafening. Shit, he thought. I've blown it. What the fuck made me say something so corny? It had been years since he'd last done anything like this, he was obviously very rusty.

But she turned to him and rested her hand against his face. 'Yes please,' she said, adding, 'I'm sorry I laughed. It's just that no one has ever asked me that before, not ever.'

'So, dinner? Tonight maybe?'

'Tomorrow night. Tonight, I'm washing my hair!'

She was teasing him.

'OK. I'll book somewhere.'

'Thank you.'

She let her hand fall. He wanted to reach across and kiss her mouth but forced himself to open his door and get out of the car.

'Best not say anything to Trixie, for the time being at least,' he said.

'OK,' she said. 'Business as usual then.'

'Absolutely.'

But when they got back to the office, everything had changed. All comfort and certainty was gone. He was a schoolboy again and every minute that ticked by seemed to carry something huge and portentous along with it.

The biggest change though was in Trixie. Normally she'd bring him a coffee and custard cream and say, 'So, how was it? Spill all.' And then she'd sort the paperwork in her quiet, efficient way, updating him on the calls he'd missed while he was out and maybe telling him that the searches on the property in Makepeace Avenue had come in. But not that day. That day she stayed at her desk, staring resolutely at her screen. Boyd had assumed she'd had bad news at home. He would ask her about it later.

He didn't. He forgot to.

And the dinner with Honey the following night had been torture. He was clumsy and, he believed, boorish. Out of his mouth came all the things he'd vowed not to talk about: their age difference, the fact they worked together, the fact he was still, technically, married.

But Honey had dismissed all of it. She'd listened to him, her chin resting on her upturned hand, the candlelight making shooting stars of her eyes. And she'd said, 'Bollocks to the lot of it, Boyd. Who cares? It's nobody's business but ours.' Then she'd leant across the table and whispered, 'And you're going to fuck me tonight, OK?'

Out of the car and away from the office, she seemed a different person. It was as though she were the adult and he the twenty-something-year-old.

'Come on,' she said when he'd paid the bill. 'Let's do this then. It'll be better after we do.'

And it was.

'Touch me here,' she said, her hand resting on her belly.

She was lying on his bed, naked and beautiful. Moonlight made her skin the colour of milk.

He pressed a fingertip on her belly button, she groaned. She lifted her hips a fraction and he watched her.

She was slender and long, her waist a shallow curve. He bent his head and kissed her breasts.

She opened her legs for him. She guided him towards her. He covered her body with his.

It was like nothing he'd ever experienced before: that jolt, her gasp, the way she held on to him, drawing him in.

'I won't break,' she said, smiling up at him, her breath hot on his chest.

He came fiercely, suddenly. She was the first since Vita. She was different from Vita and the violence of this difference shocked him.

'Now my turn?' she said.

'With pleasure, madam!'

And, still inside her, he moved his hand down.

After she came, she kissed him on the lips. She tasted of wine and sugar. She tasted of honey.

* * *

Boyd checks the clock again. It's time to go. He gets out of the car and starts walking down Morris Road. His heart is full of his rememberings and a bursting, nameless love for this girl who has brought this change to his life, this fresh start.

All they have to do is get through this next little while living in the house in Albert Terrace with Vita, pay the tax bill and, although he hates the thought of it, wait for his mother to die so he can give both

Honey and Vita the lives they deserve: proper homes, income, security. He owes it to Vita and to Honey. For all Honey's sweetness, there is still something fragile about her; something that tells him that one day he could wake and find her gone. He believes he must do everything he can to stop this from happening.

Boyd has promised himself he will make amends to his wife and love Honey the best way he can. This is the man he wants to be.

* * *

When he gets back to the office, Honey is out at lunch and Trixie is staring at her screen, her fingers poised over the keyboard. Boyd switches on his computer and while it's turning on, he texts Vita to say he and Honey will be eating out that evening. She doesn't reply.

Next, he puts his phone down on his desk and swivels his chair round so he's facing Trixie.

'Hey there,' he says, smiling at her. 'You going to say hello or what?'

The last day

On the last day Graham Silverton's alarm goes off as usual.

Shit, he thinks, rolling onto his back and staring at the crack in the ceiling.

Next to him, his wife stirs, her hair dark on the pillow case.

'Morning, sleepyhead,' he says, reaching over and kissing her lightly on the lips. Her breath is musty and tastes faintly of garlic. They'd had chicken Kiev for tea last night.

At the bottom of the bed, Henry the cat lifts his massive head and stares malevolently at Graham. The two of them have never really got on.

His wife grunts in reply but doesn't wake up fully, so he slips out of bed and pads along the landing to the bathroom. Around him the house is quiet; the kids are still asleep. He'd promised that he'd go to B&Q before his shift started and get the new bath panel she'd been on at him about for months.

In the shower, the water pricks his skin like a million hot needles and it feels good. Perhaps he should get some stuff to patch up the crack in the bedroom ceiling as well, while he's out, he thinks.

Honey

It's only their second night in Albert Terrace and yet, already, Honey feels as though she's lived here for ever. Waking up in Boyd's flat yesterday morning is like a distant dream, almost as though it happened to someone else.

They get back from dinner around nine. It's Friday night and the restaurant was busy; the men wore chinos, pale shirts and loafers and the women were tanned, dressed in tight white jeans and nautical tops. It seems this is the uniform here. Most of the men had expensive watches on their wrists, the women had huge diamonds on their wedding fingers. But she doesn't envy them. She has enough, sometimes she thinks she has too much.

Vita's not home. She can sense it as soon as they walk in the door. But she's not as worried now; not now she's seen the whites of her eyes.

Yet still Boyd calls out, 'Vita, you home?'

Silence.

He turns to Honey, his eyebrow does that strange lift and fall.

'While the cat's away!' she says, pressing her body against his.

She senses he's going to saying something, but he doesn't. Instead he bends his head and kisses her neck.

'You've changed your tune,' he says at last. 'It was a different matter last night!'

'That was then. This is now,' she says.

She wants him. Here. Now. She wants to do it with him in the house he used to live in with Vita. This, she believes, will help her establish her claim here. She rests her hand against his groin.

'Come on then,' he says. His voice comes out as a breathless rush and, for a second, she takes this as hesitation and has to work hard to banish the image of him and Vita from her mind, all the times they must have been together here in the past: the closeness, the whispered secrets, the laughter. She banishes other memories, the things she's done before too. They have no place here, not now.

She takes his hand and they run up the stairs.

'I wish we had a lock on our door,' she says as Boyd shuts it behind them and she pulls the curtains to.

'I'll put one on it as soon as I can,' he says, moving a chair and lodging the top of it under the door handle.

'I feel like a naughty schoolgirl,' she says, stripping off to her underwear. Her stomach is full of fine food and her limbs liquid from the wine they drank with dinner. Outside the evening is drawing in, it's amazing how quickly summer turns. One day it stays kind of light, that luminescent, pearly light, until ten, ten-thirty and then you blink and the sky is the colour of sapphires at a time when it shouldn't be and, when only a few days before, it wasn't.

Boyd knows her body now. He knows when she likes it fast and when she likes it slow. Tonight, they fuck quickly, expertly. She has her knees by her ears and is holding on to her thighs when he comes. She rocks in time with his thrusts and then stretches her legs out while he's still in her. She feels safe and treasured; perhaps too safe. It seems she is losing her ability to stay alert, ready to run.

'Hey,' he whispers. 'You OK?'

'Yes, sure.'

'You're not normally this quiet!' He kisses her mouth, pulling on her lips with his teeth.

'It's just it's the first time here, you know. We haven't made it ours yet.'

There's a mumble of voices from the bedroom in the next door house.

'Colin-next-door must have a guest,' Boyd says.

Honey nods, sleepy now.

'Do you want me to …?' Boyd is smiling. She can hear the duvet rustle as he gently withdraws and moves off her.

She nods again.

And he makes her come with his tongue. She is still sleepy but comes quickly and fiercely under him. Neither of them speaks. She's on autopilot, overtaken by instinct and, for a second as the ripples spread and fade, she relaxes; really relaxes. This is unusual. She keeps her eyes closed because she doesn't want to break the spell.

Also, she feels there is the presence of something else in this room, something delicate and fragile, something she's afraid of acknowledging.

'There,' he says. 'We're all done.'

'Mmmm.' She turns and curls into a ball and he wraps his body around her.

They stay like that for a while until he says, 'I need to pee.'

After he's used the bathroom, he moves the chair back to where he'd got it from and gets into bed and soon he's asleep, his breaths rumbling out of him like a bear's, but she can't drop off. Her brain is humming as though she's waiting for something. To distract herself, she lets herself think back to when she got the job working for Boyd.

She'd been lucky to get it. Lucky that the Job Centre sent her the details. Lucky that Ali, whose corner shop she'd worked in now and again, was happy to give her a reference. She really needed the money. It had taken her a long time to shake off the past: the well-meaning foster carers who didn't quite know what to make of her; the battles she'd fought at school; the unsavoury company she'd kept; the sex; the grubby money; the long, bitterly cold nights; the hunger; the night it all changed. She'd hoped this job was going to save her.

She guesses it must have taken a huge leap of faith on Trixie's part to take her on. She was as honest as she could be with her. 'My background hasn't been what you may call orthodox,' she said as they sat either side of a meeting table in a small, airless room at the back of the office. Trixie was drinking coffee. Honey had a glass of water in front of her and, in her lap, her hands were shaking.

'Give me someone's whose has been!' Trixie said. 'We're all made up of fault lines and scars.'

'Are you sure though?' Honey asked. She'd told her about her recent past, but not the rest. She still didn't know the words to describe the rest of it.

She'd dressed carefully. Dark skirt, tights, a thistle coloured jumper which she thought suited her complexion, sensible shoes, knickers inside out for good luck. Everything, apart from the underwear, had been purchased from the local charity shop, but then charity shops in Farnham aren't your common or garden ones, so the clothes were smart enough; smarter than she'd worn in a long time.

'You have GSCEs,' Trixie said. 'You have retail experience. You have an address and a bank account and what's more, I like your smile. It's honest and open. And I know Boyd will like you too.'

'Boyd?' Honey asked. It was the first time she'd heard his name.

'It's his agency. Boyd is Boyd Harrison, hence Harrison's Residential.'

'Oh, I thought you were the boss!'

'Well, I guess I am really.' Trixie grinned at her and winked.

Trixie's in her late forties. She has shoulder-length auburn hair, pale skin and green eyes. It was autumn then and she was wearing a simple, black dress with a cowl neck and long sleeves. She's short and petite and, Honey was to learn, married to Richard who had once done something with money in the City but who'd recently lost his job. They had two sons at university who, she said, seldom rang or came to visit.

Honey had lifted her hands from her lap and rested them on the table. Trixie touched them briefly and stood up. 'Well,' Trixie said. 'I think we're done here. Come back tomorrow and meet Boyd, just in a belt and braces exercise. I know he's going to love you too.'

And he did.

And he does.

Honey went back in the morning. Boyd was at his desk but stood up when she approached him.

'Honey,' she said. 'My name's Honey. Trixie said …' she tailed off nervously.

He smiled down at her from his great height, his left eyebrow raised a little.

'Ah, Miss Honey,' he said. 'Welcome to our happy family! Did Trixie show you around properly yesterday?'

She managed to stammer out, 'I had a short tour, but it would be good to know where everything lives, what I'm expected to do.'

'All in good time. Let's show you the essentials first. Kettle, loo, back yard in case you need to smoke, our stationery store – you have to be careful of the step down to it, it's a health and safety hazard that step, I've been saying so to Trixie for ages.'

'Oh,' Honey said, interrupting him, 'I don't smoke.'

'Good, you've passed that test then!'

Again, he looked at her and this time she noticed the brown of his eyes, brown as melted chocolate. His lips were full, his body on the bulky side; there was certainly no six pack under that brightly-striped shirt but he held his height and this weight well. Instinctively she checked for a wedding ring. There wasn't one.

She settled in. She settled down. She worked hard and each night she caught the bus back to her tiny bedsit and thought of Boyd and imagined a life for him: a life where he lived in a detached, mock-Tudor home, had a small, well-kept wife, some children, a dog.

Of course, his life was and is nothing like that.

Boyd was, she discovered, separated and lived alone in a two-bed apartment on the main drag through town. The flat was in a Georgian house which had been tastefully divided up and, looking at it from the outside, as she often did, she thought of him in its spacious rooms, she imagined his body spread out on a dark leather sofa; there would be a widescreen TV and a glass of full-bodied red wine on the table in front of him.

Neither Boyd nor Trixie ever spoke of Boyd's home life but she gathered he didn't have children, had never owned a dog.

Most of Boyd's non-work attention seemed to centre on his mother, who lived at great expense in a local care home. Boyd had persuaded her to sell her house to finance her stay there but she wouldn't sign over the money to him, wouldn't let him have power of attorney or even, she'd told him, make a will. He moaned about this a lot to Trixie.

Boyd had told Honey that his mother had said, 'When I'm gone, I'm gone, and you can clear up the mess. I'm not going to make it easy for you.' Boyd had also told her later that he believed that his mother was punishing him for something he'd done when he was younger. He seemed unwilling, however, to say what this might have been.

He and Trixie rarely spoke about Boyd's wife. She was just a presence in the shadows, someone Honey didn't pay much attention to. Not at the beginning. It didn't seem important then.

And then there was the day they put his car through the car wash.

Honey had been working at Harrison's for about four months. It was early spring. The weather was clement, business was OK, or so she thought, and she was happy; happier than she'd been in a long while. Life was simple and good. She was making good choices, staying on the right side of herself, showing her best self to the world. It was an effort and she was taking a huge risk, but she was doing it. She was holding on.

'Boyd suggested you go out with him on a valuation today, if that's all right,' Trixie said as Honey sat down at her desk, putting her bag underneath it and bending down to switch on her computer. 'Mrs Chambers is putting 'Chimneys' up for sale.'

'Oh,' Honey said. 'What a shame. It's a lovely house. I hope whoever buys it doesn't change it too much.'

'Yes it is. Original Arts and Crafts, I think. Anyway, Boyd thinks it would be good if you got an idea of what he does when he's drawing up details; all that guff about 'estate-agent-speak' is unfair when you do business like he does. He has integrity …'

'Who does?' Boyd asked, coming out of the meeting room and

surprising both women. With him was a small, beaky man with thinning hair, carrying two A4 lever arch files in his arms.

'Ooh,' Trixie blushed. 'Doesn't matter, we were only gossiping.'

'Ah, gossip. The lifeblood of any self-respecting business,' Boyd said, laughing. 'This, by the way, Honey, is Anthony, my accountant, for his sins.'

Anthony lifted the files in greeting and Honey waved back. It would have been impossible to shake his hand.

'I'll be off then,' Anthony dipped his head in Boyd's direction. 'Remember what we talked about. The time for caution and all that. You need to start making provisions ...'

'Yes, yes,' Boyd swept a large dismissive arm in the air. 'Point taken, point taken.'

As Anthony left, Honey noticed one of his trouser legs had got stuck in the top of his sock and wondered who he lived with who could have let him go out like that.

'So, Trixie's given you the order of the day then?' Boyd asked Honey. 'Ready to roll in about five?'

After wondering about Anthony, Honey wondered when Boyd was going to stop talking to her as if they were on the set of a forties' movie or in the pages of an Enid Blyton novel. But she played along nonetheless, saying, 'Sure thing boss,' and doing a mock curtsey.

A short time later they left the office. Trixie was on the phone and Boyd was humming as they stepped out into the street.

'We'll go out the front if that's OK? I'd like to see the window displays. We can use the alleyway three doors down through to the service yard.'

Honey knew this and also knew she'd have to come back through the same door later. It was one of her things.

Harrison's was on the corner next to the Swan's Head and opposite Costa. Honey had redone the window displays the day before and Boyd stopped for a moment to study them before he nodded and strode on. She had to take two steps for each one of his to keep up.

'We'll go in the car,' he said. 'Creates a better impression than arriving on foot.'

'Oh, OK,' she replied, panting slightly.

'But first, I want to take the car to the garage, give it a whoosh through the wash.'

'OK,' she said again.

Boyd's car was a large dark blue Lexus, he would have looked ridiculous in a smaller car – he would have looked pretentious in an even bigger one. This one fitted him perfectly.

He opened the car door for her and she could smell his aftershave; it was tropical, coconuty, at odds with the fresh, early spring day in Surrey. She sat in the front, sinking into the soft cream leather.

'It's nice,' she said. 'You have a nice car.'

'Mmmm,' he snorted, 'would be even nicer if it was actually mine. Still paying for the bloody thing to tell you the truth.'

The door shut with an expensive click and then he was getting in beside her and that was the moment she realised they'd never been so close to one another, or alone, before.

She could feel the warmth of his body; she could feel the size and shape of him beside her. As he did up his seat belt his arm brushed against hers. A memory from her past buzzed through her, like electricity almost.

This memory wasn't a good sort of memory though. It was uncomfortable, like bonfire smoke caught at the back of your throat. He was supposed to have looked after her, the man who'd been married to her first foster mother. But he hadn't, not really. He'd never done anything more than brush his hand over some part of her – her arm, the small of her back, her knee when they were sitting on the sofa watching TV – but there'd been something menacing about him, as though there was a switch somewhere which, if flicked, would create a shift in the balance of power that, as a child, she hadn't completely understood but which, she'd known, had posed a threat.

It hadn't made for an easy life. At school, she'd tried to keep her head down, do her homework on time, stay out of bother, but trouble always seemed to find her. There were the girls who waited for her round the back of the gym and who pelted her with soil, saying, 'Yo, bitch. You got no mum, yeah? You a bastard girl, that's what you are.' And Honey had hit back, had kicked, had spat in their faces.

And there'd been that cow of a science teacher who always seemed to have it in for her, picking on her in class, never letting an opportunity pass to undermine her. And, of course, eventually Honey had snapped, called the teacher a 'fucking whore' and had been excluded for a day.

Her foster parents at the time had grounded her, put her on short rations, taken away her TV privileges, but Honey had never wanted to be the sort of girl who lashes out. She spent years struggling to manage the two sides of herself: the girl who stays and fights and the girl who runs away.

Maybe it's because of all this that she believes so fervently in her superstitions. She has to have something to hold on to, to keep some kind of control.

And all she's ever really wanted is someone who loves her unconditionally. She'd never known it, not until she met Boyd. And now her greatest fear is that this unconditional love would, if he knew the real her, prove to be conditional: this is why she must keep her secret self a secret.

To Boyd she was – is – something new, untried, umblemished. He must never know she's damaged goods.

'Oops,' Boyd had said, as he bumped into her in the car. 'Sorry.'

'No problem,' she'd replied, adjusting her skirt and stretching out her legs in the footwell.

She could hear his bones click and stretch as he turned to look over his shoulder and reverse out of the space; his hands were spread over the steering wheel and, for the first time, she noticed the tiny, boyish hairs on his wrists.

'So,' he said, stopping at the junction into the main road, 'how are you getting on? Enjoying it?'

'Yes,' she managed to say, 'very much. Thank you.'

'Don't thank me. Trixie says you're doing a good job. It's nice to have you around.'

She thought he might glance at her when he said this, but he didn't. He kept looking at the road and then, when there was a gap in the traffic, he indicated and pulled out.

There was a silence she thought she ought to fill and so she said, 'I've never …'

He put his hand on her knee; his hand was huge and hot and she liked having it there. This time she didn't think there was anything remotely untoward about it. It's odd how instinct kicks in. In the past, a hand on her knee would have been a threat; now it was a comfort, a gesture that promised something good.

'Hang on,' Boyd said lifting his hand off, 'let me just get round this stupid parked car and then you can say what you've never …'

She realised then that his hand on her knee had been to stop her from talking, nothing more, and a weird kind of disappointment knotted itself into a ball inside her chest. Stupid car, stupid Honey, she thought.

'Well?' he said after a moment. They were waiting at a set of traffic lights. Ahead on the right was the garage. 'What have you never …?'

'I was going to say that I've never had a job like this before. It's great. Thank you.'

'I told you that you don't have to thank me!' He laughed and this time he did glance at her. His eyes were dark and shining. Then they were turning into the garage forecourt. Again the indicator made its soft tick-tock noise. 'Right, here we are. You wait here; I'll pop inside and get the token. Unless you want anything?'

Suddenly he seemed shy, unsure.

'No, I'm OK,' she said. 'I don't want anything.'

But she did. She wanted him. She hadn't realised until he'd put his hand on her leg, until he'd turned and looked at her. She'd had lovers, many lovers, many kinds of lovers: some she remembered almost fondly, some with shame, others with relief that she'd got away from them when she did, and one with terror that he may yet come to find her.

It seemed she'd spent a lifetime kissing frogs, but there seemed something good and different about Boyd. Of course it was inappropriate and a thousand shades of wrong, but by then her palms were sweating, the skin on the back of her neck prickling. She hadn't felt this kind of rush, this innocent type of desire for as long as she could remember, if ever. It flooded through her like words from the hymns she used to sing in assembly at school. It was a kind of comfort she craved, a sense of belonging.

But she mustn't, she thought. She shouldn't. She can't. She'd just got everything back on track and wanting something good, like this promised to be, was surely pushing her luck. She'd long believed that aiming for the stars was the occupation of fools.

Boyd got back into the car, flourishing a slip of paper. 'No token, just a code. I'd forgotten for a moment that we're now in the twenty-first century,' he said, smiling at her.

He drove forward, punched in the code on the control panel. He drove forward again until the green light turned red and his front tyres were on the buffers. The door behind them rolled shut. The door in front did the same. They were enclosed, cut off, completely alone.

The jets whooshed water at the car, the brushes whirred and spun. The noise was deafening. She watched, mesmerised, as the mechanism rolled slowly towards them. The car rocked slightly. There was a brief pause as the brushes slowed to a stop as they reached the end of the car and, in this pause, Boyd turned to her and said, 'I …'

The air inside the car was crackly; she could almost hear it sparking.

'I shouldn't but …' he said.

'Shouldn't what?' she asked. But she thought she already knew.

Then he thumped the steering wheel and bent his head so that it rested on it. 'I can't,' he said. He turned and looked at her, as if seeing her for the first time. 'Honey?' he said. 'I don't understand this. It's like a body blow. There's been no one, not since … I don't understand,' he said again. 'Why now, when I've seen you every day? Why has this happened now?'

She studied the collar of his shirt; the skin on his neck was rubbing up against the inside of it.

'I wasn't expecting this,' he continued. 'What can we do?'

He looked like he was on the verge of tears and as if he wanted to say much more than he had done.

She knew that love could happen in an instant, well a type of love anyway. She'd read of it in books and seen it at the movies and, if it wasn't love, then it was a connection, an understanding stretching from one person to another. It was something in the other person's eyes, how you felt seen by them, the way they tipped their head on one side, their smile, the set of their shoulders, the tiny movements they made that caused your heart to flip and your life to realign – whatever it was you were expecting to happen changed course and you had no control over where you were headed from there on in.

Maybe it was this type of love they'd felt that day in the car. Maybe it was something else altogether. What was for certain was that he raised his head and lifted a hand and rested it on her face and she covered it with one of hers as if by doing this they would find the answers to all the questions he'd just asked.

They sat there like that for what seemed like hours and then, peeling it away from her cheek he flipped his hand over and brought her palm to his lips. He kissed away the sweat. His lips moved up her wrist; he leant across, pushed up the sleeve of her jacket and kissed the inside of her elbow.

The brushes had started up again by now. The mechanism rolled again. The car rocked again. The noise was deafening and in her chest her heart was hammering, telling her that something amazing, wonderful and terrible had been done that couldn't be undone.

'We will need to talk about this. I've never, not ever, not before, with anyone from work. Not for years and not with anyone other than …' he said sombrely, uncertainly, as the doors started to lift and the light above them turned green and he pressed the car's ignition switch and the engine rumbled into life.

'I know,' she said. It seemed she had lost the power to say anything else and her heart was still thumping, her head reeling. This was wrong, this was not allowed. She didn't deserve any goodness and Boyd was a good man and he must never know what she was. She wanted to carry on being this version of herself.

But she had let Boyd kiss her palm, her wrist, her elbow and she hadn't been loved for as long as she could remember, not properly, and she wanted to, oh, how she wanted to, and so now months have gone by and Boyd is in bed beside her in his and Vita's house and in her head she can still hear the pulse of the car's indicator, the beat of the car wash's brushes against the windows of his Lexus.

* * *

Towards dawn she hears Vita come home and realises it was her she was waiting for. Vita goes into the kitchen and runs the tap for a bit and then she comes upstairs. Honey hears a floorboard creak and the soft click of the bedroom door as Vita closes it behind her. She doesn't use the bathroom and Honey's curious as to why, but this curiosity doesn't last and soon she tumbles into a deep and dreamless sleep.

Or, she thinks it's dreamless until she realises that the darkness is water and she's swimming, or trying to. She's lifting her arms and her hands are slicing through the water but she's not moving. She kicks her legs but, again, she's not moving. Then she remembers.

She remembers the boat, and the man on the boat. He is dark-skinned and wiry and smells of cinnamon and one of his arms is pinned across her chest. He's holding on to her free arm, her other arm is wedged under her. He's pulling at her clothes and she's saying 'No' and his mouth is opening and closing but no words are coming out of it.

58

The space they're in is small and there is a distant smack of waves against the hull and he's hurting her, she needs to tell him he's scaring her.

She doesn't know what time it is, but it's dark outside.

His mouth moves again, his eyes are black buttons, like a toy's eyes.

She feels his weight shift a fraction and slips out from under him. It's like she has scales, like a fish does, and that she'll die if she doesn't get into the water. Her lungs are gills. She has openings in her chest that flap with her breaths.

She shakes her head and her vision blurs. She is inching away from the man who has his back turned to her now and has lifted his head as if he is an animal scenting danger in the air.

Then there is an explosion somewhere behind her and she wants to think it came before she started running but time is concertinaing and she hears a crackle, like someone is screwing up a sheet of tinfoil.

There is a huge white moon in the sky and behind the boat is a strip of lights which must be the shore. She jumps off the deck but there is roaring in her ears and she doesn't hear herself hit the water. All she can feel is the cold judder her bones and that the clothes she's wearing are weighing her down. She is a flag or a jelly fish and she's lost all the bones that had juddered a second ago; they are floating somewhere just out of reach.

But she starts to swim and she swims until her chest is burning with the effort. Then there are arms around her: strong, muscled arms that are dry and warm but she is still swimming and the arms are holding her tighter and tighter until she has to stop. She tries to tread water. Water laps at her mouth; there is still roaring in her ears. She raises her head and howls and she hears a voice saying, 'Honey! Wake up. My god. You were dreaming again.'

And the door to the bedroom bursts open, the light from the landing is the colour of custard and Vita is standing in the doorway in a pair of men's pyjamas, her hair like a curtain over her shoulders.

'Boyd?' she's saying. 'Is everything OK? I heard crying. I heard crying and I thought for a moment ...'

'It's OK, Vita. It's Honey. She was dreaming. I'm sorry we woke you.'

'Oh.'

Vita's disappointment is a solid thing. It stands next to her. Honey can sense it even though she can't see it. Her breathing is steadying. She knows now she was dreaming and that it must almost be morning.

'I'm sorry,' she says both to Boyd and Vita. Boyd is still holding her but he's looking at his former wife. Honey follows the trajectory of the look as it leaves the bed and travels across the room. It falls with a thump at Vita's feet as if it is exhausted, as if it has been travelling between them for years.

'As long as you're OK,' Vita says, turning swiftly and marching away. She doesn't shut the door behind her so Boyd lets go of Honey, gets out of bed and gently closes it.

'You haven't had a dream like that for a while, have you?' he asks. 'Do you want to talk about it?'

'No. It's all right. Must be something about being in a new place. Perhaps it'll just take time for me to get used to being here.'

But, as Boyd checks the clock and says, 'Five-thirty. We could get another hour or so's sleep,' and settles himself under the covers, she knows what she dreamt didn't have anything to do with being unsettled here and it wasn't a dream. It was a memory; it was her unconscious telling her that she'd never really be free. One day he will find her.

She lies next to Boyd and listens to the birds and the occasional car gun its engine down the main road which intersects with Albert Terrace. She thinks of the nurses coming off night duty, and milkmen picking up crates and loading them onto the backs of their floats. She thinks of postal workers sorting letters and farmers walking their cows to the sheds. And she thinks of the heat of the sun on her face and of flowers opening their petals and refuses to let herself think of the boat, and the man with the dark skin and the black-button eyes, and the fire, and how the water weighed down her arms and legs, how she swam, how she staggered onto the beach and how cold the sand was under her feet.

* * *

It's Saturday morning and they don't have to be in the office until ten. At eight-thirty Boyd goes downstairs to make them a cup of coffee and Honey hears him and Vita talking, their voices making a soft humming sound. She imagines they are discussing her and the dream. She wishes they wouldn't. She's still thinking about the look that passed between them, how Vita seemed to reject it. She doesn't want Boyd to be treated that way. Also, she wants to know what her crying out reminded Vita of.

Then, Boyd's back. He's wearing joggers and a t-shirt. Yesterday morning he went down in his boxers. She remarks silently on this but doesn't think anything more about it. She drinks her drink but her head is sore from the wine and sex and lack of sleep and the intensity of the dream. It is almost as though she imagines there to be saltwater stains and small heaps of sand in the bed. She sips, but struggles to distance the dream from reality. She must pull herself together. Dwelling on the past won't do her any good at all.

'What's Vita doing today?' she asks Boyd as he picks out a shirt from the wardrobe.

'Working in her studio I think. That's what she said just now, anyway.'

He peels off the t-shirt and drops it onto the bed.

'Do you think,' she says, 'I should pop down and say thank you to her, you know for being concerned in the night? I'd quite like to take a look in her studio anyway and I'd rather do it when she was there.'

'Sure, I guess she wouldn't mind. She doesn't normally. One good thing about Vita is …' he pauses as if trying to choose one good thing from many good things, or so she imagines, '… is,' he continues, 'her lack of pretension. She's a no-nonsense kind of girl.'

Honey lets the definition of Vita as a 'girl' pass, after all she guesses she must have been one once.

And so, just before they set out for work, Honey makes her way down the garden and knocks on the door of Vita's studio.

'Mmmm,' Vita says.

The studio is flooded with light; its windows seem out of proportion to the size of the walls and there are canvasses stacked everywhere, six or seven deep at times. Vita's bike is propped up in one corner, Classic FM is playing on the radio and Vita is sitting on a stool in front of her easel. She looks at one with where she is, as if the studio has grown around her. She wears it like a coat.

There is a faint sketch of a dog's head on the easel. From this distance Honey can't make out the breed.

'Um,' she says. 'I just wanted to pop down to say thank you. You know for checking in on us earlier and,' she pauses. Vita picks up a brush and studies its bristles. She doesn't look at her. 'And …' Honey continues, 'I'm sorry, for disturbing you and everything.'

Vita glances up, her expression unreadable. 'As long as everything's OK,' she says. 'It's never easy in a new place.'

There's a moment of silence. Honey waits for Vita to say something more but she doesn't. Honey doesn't know what to say. It seems she has run out of words.

'Best I let you get on then.' The words splutter out at last.

'OK.'

Vita's looking at her brush again.

And then she sees it. Tucked in a corner, half-covered by another painting but unmistakably him, is a portrait of Boyd. 'Oh!' she says, 'you've painted Boyd.'

'Well, of course,' Vita replies.

It is a remarkable likeness; it's as though he's about to break into a smile. The picture of him is everything he is, from his eyebrow, to the curve of his cheek. Honey feels as though he is going to say something that matters.

'It's extraordinary,' she says.

'I'll take that as a compliment.'

'Oh, yes. I meant it as one. I really did.'

Again, there is silence and she is aware she should go. She needs to go to work. The day must go on.

And this is what Honey's learnt in the life she's living now. There can be no remission, now she's here with all that she has; even being here in Vita's studio with the picture of Boyd she'd painted once when they were really married to one another, Honey must take that next step, one foot in front of the other. She needs to go on so she doesn't stop.

If she stops the cracks may appear and if they do, Boyd may see them and Honey must never let this happen.

The last day

On the last day, Graham Silverton is carrying the bath panel back to the car. In his jacket pocket is a tube of Polyfilla for the ceiling crack and the Twix he'd treated himself to from the vending machine behind the tills.

It's nine-thirty. He's not due at work until eleven and so decides to go home first.

When he gets there, everyone is out; the kids are at school, his wife at work, even Henry the cat is on manoeuvres. Graham puts some food in a bowl for him anyway, should he decide to come back before the others get home.

He leaves the bath panel leaning up against the banisters and the Polyfilla on the kitchen counter. Opening the fridge, he takes out a carton of milk and takes a swig from it. This, obviously, is a banned activity: he should use a glass, or so his wife has always stipulated. He looks over his shoulder to check she's really not there. She isn't. He puts the milk back in the fridge and closes the door.

He gets to the yard just before eleven and asks his boss, 'What've you got for me today, Darren?'

Vita

I'm standing outside their bedroom door. I know I mustn't go in, but they're both at work and I'm bored with the painting I'm doing: bloody stupid dog, its bloody stupid owner.

Boyd and Honey have been here for two nights now, but it seems longer. The first night I was worried I would hear them, but I couldn't, and then last night I was with Colin, coming home in the early hours only to be woken by Honey crying out the way she did.

It had been instinct that got me out of bed; I don't remember doing it, but there I was, standing at the door looking at them in the bed, a clamour of sounds in my head. Without my glasses on I couldn't see all that well, they were more shape than substance in the glow from the lamp on the landing.

But even so, I had refused to acknowledge the look Boyd gave me and had hurried back to bed, burying myself deep in the duvet. It had reminded me of other times, other nights, the taste of the despair in my mouth was the same.

And now I'm turning the door handle and stepping inside the room. The bed is unmade; the dents in the pillows where their heads have been are still there, the covers thrown back, Honey's things are strewn about: some jewellery, a book by her bedside, a pair of jeans that look like they'd fit a child, inside out on the floor. The sun is streaming through the window and dust motes are spinning in the air. The silence is overwhelming.

And I can smell Boyd: his aftershave, the lingering scent of his skin, his Boydness.

I put my hand on my chest and tell myself that my heart is still in one piece. This will not break it. This will not break me. If you don't love, then you can't be hurt. If you no longer miss something, you can't grieve for it, can you?

I turn around and slam the door behind me. The sound is like thunder.

Boyd

Boyd has a few significant regrets. He regrets not getting into lettings when he first started up his business. Back then he'd believed there was a certain cachet about having the word 'Residential' after his name, but now he knows better. After all, now the business is just him. It has no inherent value so if he were ever to sell it, the return on the investment of his time and energy would be disproportionately small.

Maybe he'd believed that one day he'd have a child to pass the business on to. The fact that he hasn't is another of his regrets.

He does well enough, given how small a fish he is in the pool of agents in the town, including the mighty creatures that have swum out of London to set up base here. Despite the size and pulling power of these giants of the deep, and that of the new breed of internet agents offering their one-click service, there are still people here who favour the more personal touch, people to whom Boyd can say, 'I sold this house to your parents. I know how much it meant to them.'

If only he'd managed his money a bit better they wouldn't be in the fix they're in now. If he's honest with himself, he did take his eye off the ball in the early days with Honey. But, who could blame him? He'd been like a rabbit in headlights. However, ignoring his accountant's warning was, he's come to learn, a foolhardy thing to have done.

He also regrets not having been a better husband to Vita. He'd started out with all the best intentions, of course he had. But now she doesn't love him and he doesn't love her – not in the way they did before. And if, as they say, grief is the price you pay for love, then because there is so little love left, he shouldn't still be grieving. And yet he is, it overwhelms him on occasions, like a punch to the stomach, and he finds himself bent double, with his hands on his knees trying to breathe through the pain, but he can't tell either of them, not Honey and especially not Vita. It wouldn't do any good for him to do so.

And so these are the thoughts Boyd has as he stops off to buy a lock for the bedroom door on his way to work. Honey had wanted to walk to work today, she'd said.

If only life were as simple as having a bolt on a door, he thinks as he waits at the counter to pay. If it were, we could choose when to lock ourselves in and the world out.

'Thank you,' he says to the assistant. He's young, a schoolboy still. He's obviously been made to work here by parents keen for him to have something on his CV other than 'IT Skills' which actually means all he's good at is playing video games.

The boy nods at him, but hasn't yet learnt the art of saying anything back.

For all she did wrong, his mother did at least instil a work ethic in Boyd. He too had worked behind shop counters, done deliveries and washed the neighbours' cars. But, unlike this boy perhaps, Boyd's choices had been predicated by the need to earn. If he hadn't, then they'd have had no money, at least at the start, before his mother started on her campaign of finding men with money. She'd been remarkably successful at that, in the end.

When he gets to the office, Trixie is on the phone, the bangles on her wrist knocking against the surface of the desk as she takes a note of what the person on the other end of the line is telling her. Boyd hears her say, 'Yes, of course. Quite understand. It must be a very difficult time. I'll certainly ask him to call you. Thank you. Do take care now. Our sincere condolences on your loss.'

And Boyd knows it's another probate job. He hopes it's an elderly person who's died. He finds it hard to cope when tragedy strikes the young.

Houses are such emotive things. He and Vita had done nothing about theirs when he left, but he really should have gifted her his half; it would have been the honourable thing to do. He'd love to be able to do it now, if only his mother would … He can't finish this particular thought.

He waves to Trixie who waves back, and then catches sight of Honey who is watering the plants in the meeting room. She's concentrating on what she's doing and so hasn't spotted he's arrived and he takes a second to watch her.

There is still so much about her he doesn't know. And her dreams don't help. Until this last one, she hadn't had one for a while but, in their early days together he'd often wake to find her struggling against some unseen presence, her arms and legs twitching, her breaths coming in short, sharp bursts. But she never tells him what she's dreaming about. Instead, she fobs him off with, 'Oh, it was just a silly dream. Ignore me.' But he believes it has to be more than that. Just a silly dream wouldn't make her rigid and breathless with fear, would it?

Boyd never used to be a patient man, but with Honey he has had to become one. He has a sixth sense that if he rushes her, he'll scare her away.

'Another probate job?' he asks Trixie as she puts down the phone.

'Yep. I'll email you the details,' she replies.

'Thanks.' He steps past her desk and taps on the meeting room door. 'Hey,' he says to Honey. 'I've got the lock.'

'Oh! You made me jump,' she says, turning and smiling at him. She looks slender and brittle; it's almost as though she could snap were he to touch her. 'I'll make us some coffee, shall I?'

'That would be great, thanks.'

Honey touches him on the arm as she walks by him. It feels like a blessing.

It's nice to say ordinary things to one another. Towards the end with Vita he'd had enough of stinging sentences and weighted silences to last a lifetime.

It hadn't started out like that. At the beginning it had been easy and simple. The two of them had fitted one another, like a hand in a glove.

Take the day they first moved into Albert Terrace. They'd had so little it was laughable. The house had been dark and tobacco-stained. The old man who'd lived there before had gone into a nursing home and his daughter, a plump over-coiffured woman who favoured wearing lime-green leggings and bubble-gum pink tops far too small for her ample frame, had sold the house to pay for her father's care. She'd seemed a nice woman but not one Boyd or Vita would have wanted to spend too much time with.

They didn't need to. They had each other.

In those days Vita would stand, tucking herself up next to him, and he'd drape an arm over her shoulder. They were like a nest of spoons, a Russian doll, so they told one another. All the clichés.

The day they moved in, it rained – thick rods of it – and so they'd had to run from the hired van to the front doorstep. The boxes they carried were soggy by the time they reached the house and they'd laughed because nothing had mattered. Anything that got wet would dry in time. Nothing they had would get spoiled because of the rain. The only thing Vita treasured was her art box. This she carried as though it were a religious relic. They'd covered it with a piece of tarpaulin to protect it and it had sat in the corner of the lounge as they ate fish and chips from newspaper and drank whisky from the bottle in front of the fire.

Vita had undone her plait and fanned her hair over her shoulders to dry it. She'd taken her glasses off and her eyes had glittered and the skin on her cheeks was smooth and creamy. Boyd had never seen her look so beautiful.

And outside the rain continued to fall.

They'd been so young; had believed themselves invincible.

If only someone had been able to warn him of what was to come. Maybe then they could have done something to protect themselves against it; done something to avoid it.

So, on this Saturday afternoon in summer Boyd decides that now is the time to act on his idea for Honey's birthday. He wants to know and he wants Honey to know. For all his patience, he wants some degree of certainty. Any amount, even the smallest fraction of it will do.

At his desk he types what he's looking for into Google and clicks on the first name that comes up. A little while later he says, 'I'm off out for a bit.'

Neither Honey nor Trixie look up from what they're doing, but both raise a hand in farewell. The phone starts ringing again and he hears Trixie say, 'Good afternoon. Harrison's Residential. How can we help you?'

Boyd steps out of the door onto the pavement. The heat hits him like a hand.

He drives to a house on the outer edges of the town. He parks his car and walks up the path. He rings the doorbell. A woman in her fifties with soft, curly hair opens the door. She's wearing jeans and a loose white linen top. She beckons him inside. He follows her. The door closes behind them.

Honey

Boyd's gone out but didn't say where. She's not worried; he often does this. She knows she doesn't, and assumes Trixie doesn't either, want to make him feel accountable; it's his business after all. And so she decides to do her weekly analysis of movements in the market by checking in with the websites of their main competitors. She has a spreadsheet where she collates information on what's sold and when and she's got some software that can translate the numbers into a pie chart showing market share and a graph showing sales over time.

Needless to say, Boyd is very impressed by this but she's not so sure Trixie is. Trixie's always carried this information in her head or so she told Honey when she presented her first pack of information to Boyd. 'All he needs to do is ask me, you know,' she said. 'No need for all this ...' She waved her hand dismissively over the folder. But that night, when Boyd and Honey were in bed, Boyd said, 'Take no notice of Trixie. I love what you're doing.'

As Honey was stroking the skin on the underside of his wrist at the time, she'd wondered whether he meant that, or her work. But he'd turned then and kissed her and, after that, it didn't really matter either way.

Honey scrolls down the houses listed on one of their competitors' sites; the work isn't difficult and she can let her mind wander and so she thinks of Vita in her studio. She thinks of her small, strong body, her long hair, the faint lines around her mouth and, for the first time, she really wonders what Vita thinks of her and Boyd being in her house. Perhaps she should have thought of it before, but she'd been so caught up in the 'them' of her and Boyd and so absorbed by how she feels about their temporary accommodation that, to her shame, she hasn't. Surely it must be awkward for Vita to have her space invaded? She would be used to living alone; it's been six years since Boyd moved out. Honey can't imagine why she agreed to them moving in.

The first time she asked Boyd about his wife, he said, 'Oh, we were married. It didn't work out. We're friends though still. At least we've managed that.'

They were eating breakfast. It was a Sunday very early on. The sex they'd had the night before had been good, not wonderful, but good. After the novelty of the first few times had worn off, they were getting better at being with one another. Or rather Honey was getting better at being with Boyd. She'd never had sex with the same man as many times as she had with Boyd. Being in a relationship was a new experience for her, not that he knew this of course. It wasn't something she ever wanted him to know.

The table in his flat was strewn with sections of the newspaper. Honey was wearing one of his shirts and drinking chilled orange juice. She felt like Julia Roberts in *Pretty Woman* and, seeing where she'd come from and what she'd done before, it was awesome to be sitting opposite this kind bear of a man, with sunlight streaming through clean windows, the only sounds his contented breathing and the rustle of paper.

She decided to risk another question. 'How long were you married?'

'Fifteen years. I think …' He paused, picked up the coffee pot and asked, with that kink in his eyebrow, if she'd like some. She nodded. He continued, 'We got married too young. We thought we knew everything, but we were in our twenties. What does anyone know in their twenties?'

'Um,' Honey said, picking up a spoon and knocking it against the side of the cup. It made a ringing sound. 'Excuse me. I'm in my twenties and I think I know …'

'Oh shit, sorry!' he said, smiling at her.

Already she loved how he smiled at her but of course she really had no idea; she was running on empty, making it up as she went along.

The second time she asked him about Vita they'd just had their first fight. It was about something small and stupid, as most fights are.

Honey had gone for a run. It was an unusual thing to have done, she admits that now. But they'd been cooped up in the flat for the weekend because the weather had been shitty and she was going stir-crazy. There are only so many episodes of *House of Cards* you can watch in one go.

There were times Honey wanted to rip out the dark wood shelves and ornate rugs Boyd favoured and replace them with something simple, light and bright. But it wasn't her flat. She had no rights. She was still renting her bedsit so was strictly just a visitor at Boyd's. They hadn't sorted out any of the grown-up stuff about being in a relationship at that point; she's not sure they have even now.

She knows she veers away from making things official; she's never shared a permanent grown-up address with someone else before.

She is a superstitious soul and fears that were she ever to do so it would be to court disaster. Better to leave things fluid and flexible but, obviously, there are times when she hungers for permanence and for some kind of certainty and not to feel like she is just passing through. She knows it doesn't make sense for her to feel this way, but it's how she does sometimes and how she did on that particular evening.

So she ran. She didn't tell Boyd where she was going. She just wanted to be alone, to give herself what the trendy therapists call some *headspace* and *heartspace*. She needed perspective. She pulled on her trainers and coat. Hardly running gear, but she wasn't going to let the lack of designer Lycra stop her. Boyd was in the bath when she left; she closed the door with the softest of clicks and the air in her lungs felt good as she started jogging through the rain.

Perhaps she stayed out a bit too long, perhaps she should have left a note. She doesn't know. All she knows is that when she got back and let herself in with the key Boyd had had cut for her only the week before, he was standing in the lounge, hands on hips, his mouth set to a grim line.

'Where did you go?' he asked, hardly moving his mouth.

'For a run.' She was panting and drenched in her own sweat and the rain. It was quite obvious where she'd been.

'Why?'

'Just felt like it.' She looked at the odious rug and then back up at him. 'I don't have to tell you everything. You don't own me,' she said.

And there she was being again the surly teenager she'd once been, the one who kicked out rather than being kicked down. Boyd had never seen this side of her before, but she knew this version of herself well. She'd been her many times: with her foster carers, at school. She'd always been on high alert, ready to defend herself.

Boyd took a step towards her and, for the first time, she feared him. It was a knee-jerk reaction; she'd been threatened before. But, she was to learn, Boyd was different. He opened his arms and said, his voice soft and low, like a parent's soothing a child, 'No, I don't own you. But I love you, and with love comes worry. I worry about you and for you. Can't you understand that?'

Honey was hot now and rain was trickling down the back of her neck. She wanted to hit out at him for being so reasonable. She didn't deserve it. She didn't deserve him. And so she hit him. She flailed her fists against his broad chest and he stood and took the blows until she was sobbing and he was kissing her and holding her, his huge hands on her back like folded wings.

Afterwards, when she too had had a bath and changed and he'd made her a milky drink which he put on the floor by her side and she was curled up next to him on the sofa, she said, 'How come you're so good, Boyd? How come it didn't work with Vita when you are such a good man?'

There are some conversations you start that you wish you hadn't, conversations that shift the goalposts. And this was one of them. She thought she wanted to know, but it was as though she was picking at a scab. She didn't want it to come off but still she couldn't stop herself from digging her nails underneath it.

He stretched his long legs out; there was the smallest of holes in one of his socks. Honey could see a slice of his toenail through it.

'You always start off,' he said, 'with the best of intentions. You never believe it's going to fail. Otherwise, why would you start in the first place?' He shifted in the seat a little and continued, 'We met when I was showing a possible purchaser around a set of studios in London. They were crazy times, property was moving so fast, if you blinked you missed it. Vita and her colleagues were sitting tenants and came with the building. She was angry with me for being there because she was passionate about her work and the space she worked in. She was afraid of the coming change. I liked that about her, right from the word go. She believed in what she was doing whereas I,' he paused to wind his fingers through Honey's, 'I wasn't at all sure. I was making good money, but it was meaningless money. No one got emotional about what they were buying; it was business, pure and simple. I wanted more. I wanted to deal with real people, people who wanted forever homes. It was idealistic of me and perhaps I was too young to make the decision I made but, meeting Vita, seeing how much she believed in what she was doing, gave me the courage to jump. And she jumped with me.

'And it was wonderful at the start. I had enough money to buy Albert Terrace. She had a few portrait commissions. We believed in the story of us. We thought we'd be young for ever. We imagined we'd be happy for ever.'

He stopped talking and let his fingers slip from hers. She bent down to pick up her drink and took a sip of it. The warm liquid was soothing.

She'd come this far. She couldn't stop now. 'So what happened?' she asked. 'Why last fifteen years and end it then?'

'People change. Things happen to change people.'

'Were you unfaithful?'

'No.'

'Was she?'

'No. I don't believe so. You always tell yourself you'd know, and I still believe that. No,' he shook his head and stared hard into the middle distance, 'no, she wasn't unfaithful. It wasn't that.'

'What was it then?'

Honey had finished her drink. It had stopped raining outside but it was dark now. She was getting too close to the truth, she thought, and suddenly, she didn't want to know. She feared what he was about to tell her would change things; change how she felt about him, about them.

'I haven't spoken about it for a long time and I'm not sure I can. It's pathetic I know, but some things go so deep …'

'I understand,' she said, reaching up and kissing him. She was relieved. It felt like she'd been given a get out of jail free card. The scab was still in place; whatever it was that was raw and pink underneath was still protected.

'At least we're still friends,' he said, getting up and closing the lounge curtains in a move that told her the conversation was over. 'That's something I suppose,' he added, before taking her empty cup from her and carrying it through to the kitchen.

Honey clicks on the house in Eldon Avenue that one of the London agencies has just sold and adds it to her spreadsheet. She looks up from her screen and watches Trixie for a moment and she's still watching her when Boyd strides back into the office carrying a white envelope. Trixie stands, then sits down abruptly, pats her hair with one hand and picks up the phone with the other.

'Hello there, ladies,' Boyd says, grinning at them both. 'Any messages while I was out?'

Vita

I'm in the park again. I was in the studio and then I left it. I remember walking out of it, through the gate and down the path.

And now I'm here watching the weekend families. Some are at the swings – combinations of parents and children, the occasional grandparent; some are playing football – dads and sons, their dogs bounding in amongst their legs with a wild kind of joy. The grass is dry beneath my feet, the air hot, the sky a cloudless, cornflower blue. My bones feel heavy in my body. It is an effort to lift my feet and take the necessary steps. I know I should go back, back to the studio, the painting, to being the me I have become, the one who doesn't mind, who doesn't want any of this for herself.

I text Colin. 'You around later?'

'Sure,' he replies.

'OK. I'll be in touch.'

Thank God for Colin I think as I turn and slowly make my way home. The children's laughter follows me. In the horse chestnuts at the end of our road, a blackbird is shouting an alarm call. My garden welcomes me almost like it is a pair of arms wrapping themselves around me. I feel a strange sense of expectation at the thought of Boyd and Honey coming home here after work but am not sure whether this is a good thing or a bad thing. I think of the house now that the three of us are living there, how it seems both to have expanded to fit around us and contracted so that we constantly bump up against one another. Having them there is like having them grafted onto my skin and me being grafted onto theirs.

Honey's things are spreading around the house like ink on wet paper: tubs of 'summer glow' face cream nudge up to my creams which claim 'to reduce wrinkles in five days or your money back'; tiny wisps of her underwear hang on the airer in the bathroom and seem to mock my sturdy M&S multi-pack knickers; her books, her bags, her laughter, her grace, her youth, fill the house as they fill Boyd's arms, his mind and his heart.

On the way into the studio, I pluck a dead rose bloom off the bush by the gate; the petals dissolve in my fingers.

Boyd

While Honey's making coffee, Boyd sidles up to Trixie's desk. Saturday shoppers are milling by outside; the sun is hot and high.

'Hey,' he whispers conspiratorially. 'It's Honey's birthday next week …'

'I know.' Trixie smiles a tight smile as she says this.

'… I was wondering if you could hide this for me in your desk?' He holds out the envelope he was carrying when he got back to the office. 'I can't, you see,' he continues, 'Honey looks through my drawers sometimes and I can't hide it at the house, we've hardly got enough space for our everyday things, let alone secret hideaway things, and I can't really ask Vita, can I?'

'No, you can't. I guess,' Trixie's tone is somewhat sharp which makes Boyd look at her in surprise.

Then she says, 'OK.' Her voice is a bit softer this time and she takes the letter from him and slips it into her drawer. Boyd has written 'To Honey' on the front of it.

* * *

Days pass. Sunday comes and goes and then it's Monday again, and Tuesday and then it's Honey's birthday. As they wake he tells her he'll give her the present later. 'OK,' she says. 'That's fine.'

Trixie arrives at work and says, 'Morning.'

Honey is on the phone. Boyd notices her delicate neck bent, the phone held between her shoulder and her chin as she carries on typing.

'Hey there.' Boyd looks up at Trixie and smiles. 'Are those cream cakes I see?'

'Sure are. I'll pop them in the fridge for later.'

'And have you got the you-know-what for you-know-who?' He talks to Trixie from behind his hand like a pantomime villain and she smiles another tight, thin smile back at him.

She nods and, when she returns from the kitchen, gives him the envelope.

He props it in front of Honey's screen and mouths 'Happy Birthday' to her. Honey's smile is totally different from Trixie's; hers is slow, wonderful, conspiratorial. Out of the corner of his eye, he sees Trixie look away and busy herself moving papers around on her desk.

Then Honey says, 'OK, yes. Thanks for calling. I'll get on it straight away,' and she puts the phone down and picks up the envelope.

'What is it?' she asks Boyd who's hovering by her desk, his hands in his pockets jangling the change he keeps in there.

'Open it and see.'

Honey gets her paper knife and slits open the envelope.

'Oh my God,' Honey says when she opens the birthday card. A business card falls out onto the desk, face up.

'Look on the back of the card,' Boyd says. He's taken a hand out of his pocket and is stroking the back of Honey's neck. They have long ago stopped pretending to Trixie, stopped trying to keep their relationship a secret. When this shift happened, Boyd can't remember. One day only he and Honey had known and then suddenly, Trixie did and now Vita does too, obviously.

'It says, "5.00pm, Wednesday 14th".'

'That's your appointment then.' Boyd is still stroking Honey's neck. 'Now turn the card over again.'

Honey reads it out. 'It says, "Elizabeth Holland, Medium". Oh, Boyd. This is fantastic! I've never been able to afford to go to one before. I love it.'

'I knew you would.'

Boyd feels like a child who's just got all his sums right in class.

'I've met her,' he says. 'Elizabeth, that is. I went to her house. Couldn't let her loose on you without checking her out first. She's very lovely. I trust her to treat you gently.'

Honey pushes back her chair and wraps her arms around Boyd's waist. She tucks her head under his chin and squeezes his ample frame saying, 'Thank you. You know how much this will mean to me,' into the folds of his shirt.

Then the phone rings and Trixie snatches at her handset and barks into the mouthpiece, 'Hello. Harrison's Residential. How can we help you?'

Honey

The three of them have settled into a comfortable routine in the house in Albert Terrace and Honey is more and more convinced that, although she's not around much, Vita likes her. Vita is straightforward, outspoken and unafraid and Honey believes she knows where she stands with her; Vita will tell you if you're pissing her off or, if you're doing something that pleases her, she'll tell you that too. Honey hadn't expected to feel at ease here, and the fact that she does surprises her daily.

She also hasn't had the dream again. She believes that, at last, she's pushed it so far back in her mind that it can't find its way out.

Boyd's taken to spending the start of the day with Vita, which is fine as Honey gets to have her coffee and horoscope-check time without him. She can stretch out in bed and watch the early autumn mornings unfold outside the window while he's downstairs sitting side by side with Vita doing the crossword.

From Honey and Boyd's room, Honey can hear the rumble of their voices, the occasional sharp exclamation of joy or frustration and it makes the house seem more alive somehow. She imagines their heads close to one another, the sun inching through the lounge windows at the front of the house and the leather on the sofa creaking as Boyd shifts in his seat. She imagines them as old friends who have lived through difficult times and have come to an accord. She doesn't doubt Boyd's feelings for her nor does she mistrust Vita. From what she's seen of her so far, she has no reason to and again, this surprises her. It is so different from how she felt when she first came here.

Maybe it has something to do with the fact she'd always felt like a visitor at Boyd's flat, but they're more on equal terms here, him and her; they are both guests and it's a kind of respite. She knows he's planning on them going back to the flat once the tax bill is paid and his finances are in order.

He's been visiting his mother in the care home as regularly as he can but always returns from these visits subdued, and Honey doesn't press him for information because she senses that the sadness he feels about his mother, and his father for that matter, go deeper than she first realised. She does sometimes wonder if he talks to Vita about it – she must know more of his history – but for some reason Honey doesn't want to know if this is happening and so she lies in bed and thinks of other things as the two of them are downstairs and the day churns into motion.

Then Boyd comes back upstairs to get showered and dressed and he leans over the bed and kisses Honey long and hard on the mouth and places a giant hand on her head as though he's blessing her and she's strangely content: her head is safe in the sand, her heart is safe in his hands and she's looking forward to the visit to the medium he gave her for her birthday because she has a suspicion that she will learn something which will only add to this contentment. Again, she has never felt this way before and this surprises her too.

And all is made much better because Vita has also agreed to a TV being installed downstairs. Boyd's put it on the wall opposite the alcove in the kitchen and so, some evenings, when Vita gets home Honey is sitting there watching her soaps and Vita tuts and snorts with derision and says, 'My Christ, whatever is this crap?' and Honey laughs and says, 'These soaps are the engine house of the country; they are mirrors reflecting us back at ourselves.' And Vita snorts again and bangs about in the kitchen but Honey knows she's not really cross; she can tell from the set of Vita's shoulders and the way she bends her head as though she's actually half listening to the programme.

And so it's September 14th and Boyd and Honey are getting ready to leave work. Trixie's said she'll lock up and Boyd is giving Honey a lift to the medium's house.

Honey's horoscope this morning said, yet again, that she'd get news from far away but she didn't give it much thought, she's had this particular one many times before. But she was relieved when making the bed to find a penny that Boyd must have dropped. It was facing heads up. This is a sign of good luck and the good luck hasn't yet arrived. Honey is confident it will before the day is out.

'Do you want me to wait for you?' Boyd asks. His shirt is crumpled after a day sitting at his desk. He looks tired. They've just had a sale fall through and it's never nice when that happens: all that work putting the deal together gone in an instant because someone somewhere down the chain has had a change of heart. House buying and selling is such a delicate balancing act: Honey's come to realise it's seventy-five per cent emotion and twenty-five per cent reason.

'It's OK,' she says. 'You're tired and I'd like to walk back if that's all right. It's a nice evening and the exercise will do me good.'

She's not been running again since that fateful night back in the early days. She should do more, she knows, and so it will be nice to walk, and to be alone for a while too. It is all so different to how it was before.

Life is, she's decided, like a pulse, but it beats in a pattern you only recognise when you look back at it. It's all about perspective, is life.

Boyd touches her arm. 'Of course,' he says. 'I'll see you at the house. I'll have some dinner waiting for you if you like. Vita's said she'll be out this evening. She's going to a friend's exhibition in London, said she'll be back late.'

'Oh,' Honey says. 'When did she tell you that?'

'Yesterday morning, I think,' he replies.

Honey only hesitates for a second while she processes this information. She tells herself that it's fine that Vita should tell him these things, that he should know them. And it is fine. It really is. Honey doesn't mind. She has more than enough. She is happy.

But she looks round and sees that Trixie has stopped what she's doing and is watching them. Trixie's still wearing a plaster on her hand. Honey had asked her what she'd done and she'd said, 'Just a silly accident in the kitchen.'

Trixie is obviously listening to them but Honey ignores this, she has more important things to do.

'You ready?' Boyd asks her.

'Sure am,' she says, picking up her bag.

She feels blessed: a good man loves her, she is beginning to like the woman who was his wife, she got this job because Trixie believed in her, she has a bed to sleep in and a roof over her head, she has a bank card and a phone that's not pay-as-you-go, she enjoys her job and she is only twenty-eight. There is still much more before her than behind her. Life is good.

'See you tomorrow,' she says to Trixie who starts as if Honey's made her jump.

'Ah, yes,' Trixie says. 'See you tomorrow. Hope it goes well this evening for you – you know, the medium and all. Hope she doesn't say anything upsetting. Remember what we talked about before?'

Honey laughs, but doesn't reply. She's still sure that the medium won't, still sure that whatever she does say will confirm that Honey is in the right place at the right time doing the right thing, that she is still showing her best side to the world. It's getting easier and easier to do this as each week passes. Sometimes she even wonders if she's forgetting; she's certainly becoming less watchful.

Boyd drives her to the other side of town and pulls up outside a nice house with a yellow front door. There are two bay trees in planters either side of it. The bay trees have been pruned to make almost perfect spheres.

Honey leans across and kisses Boyd. 'See you later,' she says.

'Bye, my love. Hope you enjoy it.'

'Thank you.'

Honey has no idea what is going to happen next. Maybe if she had, she would have stayed in the car and told Boyd to drive her home. Maybe she should have done so. Maybe she should have heeded Trixie's warnings.

When she'd opened her card on her birthday, Trixie had been strangely quiet and then later, when they'd had their cream cakes and Boyd was out on a valuation, Trixie had said, 'Fancy a cup?'

Honey was aware that some days it seemed all they did was make cups of tea or coffee, but they didn't. These were random moments in their otherwise busy days.

'Yes, please,' she'd said.

Trixie had hesitated by the door, leant up against it and said nonchalantly, 'I've heard so many remarkable stories about mediums, you know.'

'Have you?' Honey looked at up her.

'Well,' Trixie said, 'there was this one friend of mine, albeit a number of years ago, who wanted to know if she'd met Mr Right. The woman she went to see said that she could feel the presence of an elderly relative asking to make contact. Apparently this woman had worn a blue housecoat. My friend knew immediately it was her grandmother. Well, anyway, this grandmother warned my friend off the man she was seeing. Told her he wasn't what he seemed and that he would only cause her heartache. And she was right. My friend ended the relationship and two months later read in the paper that the chap in question had been arrested for embezzlement. Oh, and …' Trixie paused.

'Yes?' Honey said.

'… and,' Trixie continued, 'there was this other friend who went to one and was told not to park her car in the lay-by outside her house that Saturday night. Well, she ignored the warning, parked the car and was woken up by some boy-racer crashing into it. Of course, he was uninsured and the car wasn't driveable for weeks. Just goes to show, eh? At least no one was hurt though, which is a mercy isn't it? Does just go to show though.'

'Oh, it does,' Honey replied. She thought briefly of her superstitions; the bread, the salt, the penny, how in summer she searches for three butterflies together, and she believed every word Trixie said.

These are the things Honey notices when the door to Elizabeth's house opens: the woman standing there is shorter than her; she has a round face and soft, curling, fair hair. She must be about fifty. She is dressed in a loose, stone-coloured, knitted tunic which she's wearing over a white camisole and long, white, linen trousers. She has a pair of Birkenstocks on her feet. Her toenails are painted a pale shell-pink.

'Hello,' the woman says, stretching out a hand, 'my name's Elizabeth. People have always tried to shorten it to Beth or Libby or other names, but I like to be called Elizabeth if that's OK.'

Honey shakes her hand. 'Of course,' she says. 'I'm Honey.'

'Yes, your husband said you'd be coming.'

'Ah, we're not married actually.'

'Oh, I see. He's a nice man. I can tell.'

'Yes, he is.'

Honey's still standing on the doorstep. Behind Elizabeth she can see a hallway leading down to what must be the kitchen. Two rooms lead off to the right; the staircase is on the left. Elizabeth's eyes, Honey notices, are a pale hazel; her smile is warm.

'Come on in,' she says, standing back a fraction.

Honey goes in. The house smells of lavender, she can see a scent diffuser on the hall table. In the background is the faint sound of music.

'That's David,' Elizabeth says, laughing lightly. 'Bit of a jazz fiend, I'm afraid.'

Honey doesn't reply.

'Come upstairs. I have a room set by. We can get some peace there. Would you like a hot drink?'

'Just a glass of water, please.'

'Let's get settled and I'll get you one.' Elizabeth starts to climb the stairs. There is a doll in national costume sitting on each step, like a guard of honour almost. They are a kindly presence.

There are four doors leading off the landing. Honey presumes three of them must be bedrooms, one the bathroom. Prints of Beatrix Potter characters hang on the walls. At the end of the landing opposite the window is a full-length mirror. She catches sight of herself. For some reason she looks more afraid than she feels.

91

Elizabeth leads Honey into a small bedroom at the back of the house. In it is a single bed; its duvet cover has daisies on it, and there's a bookcase and a pine dressing table. On the dressing table are about a dozen glass paperweights; their colours are vibrant and energetic. They imbue the room with a sense of movement. Honey had expected a less busy setting than this.

But then they sit, Elizabeth in a chair facing the back wall of the room, Honey in a chair facing her with the window behind her. Outside, the trees are noiseless, the evening hangs in the air. There is birdsong, the faint drone of the town's traffic and from downstairs the faintest beat of David's music.

'So,' Elizabeth says, touching Honey's arm. Her hand is warm. She is wearing no jewellery other than her wedding ring.

Honey notices all these things, maybe to distract herself from the real reason why she's here. Suddenly she's worried about what she might be told.

'So,' Elizabeth says again. 'You relax and I'll go and get your water.'

She's gone for a matter of moments and then she's back. Honey hasn't even had time to study the spines of the books in the bookcase.

Honey drinks the water and puts the glass down on the floor by her chair.

Elizabeth sits back down opposite her. They don't speak for a while, the air in the room stretches and softens. Honey can feel the muscles in her neck lengthen, the breaths she takes are slow and measured and deep. This is a nice place to be, she thinks. Gone is the worry and fear. There is something about this woman that makes both these things disappear.

'My dear,' Elizabeth says, 'we just need to wait. Someone will come, I know it.'

'That's fine,' Honey replies. 'There's no rush.'

Elizabeth continues, 'My sister used to live in Farnham ...'

'Oh,' Honey says, not really sure what this has to do with her.

'... but she moved, about ten years ago. I still miss her. She used Harrison's to sell her house.'

'Ah.' Now Honey knows why she is telling her this.

'She said she got really good service from them.'

Honey's just saying, 'That's good to hear,' when Elizabeth tips her head to one side and screws up her face as if concentrating on something out of sight. She holds up a hand to stop Honey from saying anything more. Elizabeth's mouth twitches and she nods.

'There aren't many here,' she says. 'I would have expected more.'

Honey stays silent; her previous feeling of peacefulness has gone. Her hands are knotted in her lap, they are shaking; her breaths are sharp and shallow.

'OK,' Elizabeth says. 'I'll tell her.'

Honey wants to remain sceptical because she's afraid now of what Elizabeth's going to say. Who is it who's there? What is she going to be told? She can feel her heart getting ready to fall and when it falls she knows she will believe everything she's told.

'There's a woman here,' Elizabeth says. 'She's tall, thin, has the same colour eyes as you. She wants you to know her. She says she is your mother.'

Honey snorts, her heart inches closer to the edge. Elizabeth could say anything about her mother and she wouldn't know if it was true or not because she never knew her. She wants to tell Elizabeth this but the words are stuck in her mouth.

'Did she pass before her time?' Elizabeth asks her.

She shakes her head. 'I never knew her,' Honey says.

Again, Elizabeth tips her head and frowns; Honey can't tell who she's listening to, the presence who is purporting to be her mother, or her.

'Ah,' she says. 'I see.'

Then she says, 'She's telling me she's sorry for what she did.'

'What did she do?' Honey asks.

The air in the room seems heavy now. Whatever is happening outside the window is happening in slow motion.

'She says, she left you. Gave you up and that she shouldn't have. She really believed you'd have a better life without her.'

There is an agonising pause. Again Elizabeth holds up a hand to stop Honey from saying anything. Honey's heart has fallen completely now. It is in her lap with her hands; she can feel it as a wet hammering thing, the consistency of liver.

More silence. There are so many questions Honey wants to ask but she's paralysed with a mixture of fear and wonder.

'But,' Elizabeth says next, 'she knows now that you didn't.'

'Didn't what?' Honey manages to say.

'Didn't have a better life without her.'

This makes Honey angry. 'How dare she say that? How does she know?'

'She says she's been watching you.'

'Holy shit,' she says. 'You mean she knows everything?'

Another pause, then Elizabeth says, 'Yes, but it's OK. She understands.'

'That's good of her.' Honey doesn't mean it. She wants whoever it is who's talking to Elizabeth to have flesh and bones. She wants this woman to hold her, let her rest her head on her shoulder. She wants to be able to smell her; she's never had this. And she wants to be able to punish her, she's never had the chance to do this either.

Honey has imagined what her mother would've been like; she asked foster carer after foster carer until she was eighteen and then, when she had the chance to find out for herself, she chickened out. She convinced herself it wouldn't do her any good and now it's too late anyway because whoever her mother was is now on the other side. There is absolutely no chance of Honey ever knowing her now.

Honey wants to weep and it must be obvious that she does because Elizabeth says, 'It's OK to cry. Let it out, my dear.'

But, no, Honey tells herself; you're not going to. She doesn't want to waste her minutes here. Elizabeth may have more to tell.

'I can see a child,' Elizabeth says now. 'She's holding a child. It can't be you though. The vision is weak. Pardon?' She turns her head and looks out of the window.

Honey follows her gaze, sees nothing but the tops of the garden trees, a slice of sky, the vapour trail of a plane.

'She says she has three things she needs to say.' Again Elizabeth holds up a hand to stop Honey from interrupting. 'There is the child. She wants you to know about him. But I can't quite see ... You will fall, she's saying. Be careful of the step. I can't see the step, but that's what she's saying. I wish I could tell you where it is.'

Another pause. 'Really?' she says. 'She also wants me to warn you: he will find you, you are not safe.'

'Who? Who will find me?' Honey asks the question, although she already knows the answer.

'She isn't saying.'

'But, I have to know.'

She knows, of course she does. Not a day goes past when she doesn't see his face reflected in a shop window, or feel his shadow following her. He is always limping, a slight limp, nothing too noticeable. But she knows he is there and she knows why. The dreams may have stopped for now, but that night on the boat is there; she will never be free of it. Whatever semblance of safety she feels now is an illusion.

'Fuck,' she says under her breath.

'She's sorry,' Elizabeth says. 'Sorry that she can't give you more, better news. But she …'

'How did she die?' Honey asks. This, now, is the most important thing she needs to know. The rest she can think about later.

'A stupid accident,' Elizabeth says. 'She's telling me it should never have happened. She should have come back for you and then it wouldn't have. I can see a road and a lorry and there's a rattling noise, but it's not all that clear I'm afraid.'

Honey doesn't feel like herself. She has no idea who she is. Why is she swearing? The new her doesn't swear, not like this. There is a child. Is it hers? There is a step. Where is this step? He will come back and he will find her. She wishes she'd never come here. She wishes Boyd had never bought her this gift. It is no gift. It is a burden and she doesn't want it. She doesn't fucking want it.

'She's going,' Elizabeth says now.

'Good riddance,' Honey mutters under her breath.

Honey looks down at her lap, at her imagined heart beating inside her closed, shaking hands. She imagines slipping it back into her chest and walking out of this room, and she also imagines throwing it down on the floor and stamping on it. She really has no idea what to do with it. It seems a useless, redundant thing.

And now she cries. Huge wracking sobs. Elizabeth leans back and picks up a box of tissues Honey hadn't spotted when she came in. She offers her the box. They are man size tissues. She's obviously needed them before. Honey takes one and holds it to her face. She shuts her eyes but can still hear Elizabeth's voice, can still feel another presence in the room. It's a faint echo of the woman who had been her mother. It is too much; it is not nearly enough.

'Stay as long as you like,' Elizabeth says. 'You don't have to go until you're ready.'

Honey wants to say, 'I guess you've seen this many times before. There's nothing new in this, is there?' But all she can manage is, 'OK.'

Elizabeth stands and quietly moves towards the door. 'I'll pop back in a bit,' she says. 'See how you're doing.'

When Elizabeth's gone, Honey concentrates very hard but the echoes are getting fainter and fainter until there's absolutely nothing left. She's had so few certainties in her life that believing in her horoscope and living in the gridlines of her superstitions has always given her comfort and a semblance of control. There is, however, part of her now that wishes she didn't. And yet she can't escape them. What's been said can't be unsaid, what she knows now can't be unknown.

Again, she thinks about what Elizabeth told her and tries to make sense of it. She's always really known that she can't escape her past, that this life she's living with Boyd can't last. For the first time she's found somewhere she wants to stay and it is wonderful, and she will try and make it last, make it as wonderful as she can, for as long as she can. But now, here, this afternoon she realises that one day, once again, she will have to leave.

She has the urge to put her hand on something, so leans across and touches the flowers on the duvet cover.

Elizabeth taps on the door and pops her head around it. 'You OK?' she asks.

'Yes, I'll go now if that's all right.'

'Sure. And, come back whenever you wish. I'm always here.'

Somehow Honey doesn't think she will go back.

She gives Elizabeth her empty glass and follows her downstairs, past the dolls. David's jazz is still playing in the back of the house.

'Him and his music,' Elizabeth says lovingly.

They say goodbye on the doorstep. Honey is careful of the step. She has been warned after all.

She's glad now that she agreed with Boyd that she'd walk home. She needs the time to process what's just happened. All around her, other people's evenings are starting: kids are watching TV or playing computer games, dads are mowing lawns, food is being cooked, barmen are wiping down the tables in pubs, dogs are being walked when their owners get in from work. On the surface of this world, all is ordinary, calm.

And yet her heart, now it's back inside her chest, is fluttering. She feels nauseous. She tries to focus on her feet: one step, then another. She walks past houses and shops, past bus stops and parked cars. She glances at garden gates and garages, hears voices and car engines, sees late hydrangeas bow their massive heads, counts from one to twenty and then from twenty back to one again.

Eventually she reaches Albert Terrace. Vita is out, as Boyd said she would be. He's sitting on the battered leather sofa in the alcove watching TV. He mutes it as Honey walks towards him and raises his head. He smiles at her.

'So,' he asks, 'how did it go?'

'Wonderful,' she says. 'All good news. She told me that I was being watched over and cared for and that I'll have a long and happy life.'

He beams. 'I'm so pleased,' he says. 'Dinner's almost ready by the way.'

'Thank you.' Suddenly, Honey is starving.

'Did she say anything else?' he asks. 'About children, or anything like that?'

'Oh yes,' she replies. 'Plenty of kids in the picture too. It was, as I say, all good news.'

Vita

'I shouldn't,' I say, leaning forwards a fraction, offering my champagne glass to the bamboo-thin waiter. I've had enough to drink, but one more won't hurt. He pours me another. He has dreadlocks piled on top of his head in some old lady bun and this makes him look taller and even thinner. But he's got kind eyes and a nice smile.

'Thank you.'

'My pleasure,' he replies before moving on through the crowd.

I hate these sorts of occasions and have no idea why I said I'd come. I hope it wasn't to impress Boyd and Honey. What need have I of their good opinion, or of being thought 'with it' in the art scene? I barely know this artist and he must have copied and pasted his whole address book into the invite email to have included me.

The gallery is suitably impressive: all white walls, chrome fittings and clever lighting. The art is bold and aggressive but I do admire its courage. The room is full of impossibly beautiful people wearing designer clothes, who have probably come here en route to somewhere much grander. They remind me of bees; they flitter and settle and suck the sweetness from the room before lifting, often in pairs, and flying off somewhere else.

The evening outside is one of those soft September ones when

London, and particularly this part of Mayfair, practically gleams. The shops are stocked with elegant things, people laugh as they stand outside bars, the light falls in ribbons.

I had once hoped for something like this for myself, something to prove my parents wrong.

I know I'm a disappointment to them. Always have been, apart from that brief moment when I'd had the picture of Boyd in the RA Summer Exhibition and it looked like my career might be going somewhere. But then it all went quiet and I went back to doing pet portraits for local ladies with blue rinse in their hair and bunions on their feet.

My parents had always wanted me to take risks, live large, live light. I'd been a flower-power baby after all. They'd worn kaftans and looked practically the same with their long flowing hair and androgynous gaits. They'd lived in a commune on a smallholding in Scotland with four other couples and an assortment of children from an assortment of couplings and had commended themselves on their self-sufficiency and how they'd turned their backs on the trappings, both moral and practical, of the modern world. But two things didn't sit quite right with me. Firstly, contrary to the philosophy of the commune they'd always insisted they'd been faithful to one another and that I was the outcome of their exclusive relationship and, secondly, my father was now on Facebook, worked as a storeman for B&Q and ordered his groceries online.

They named me after Vita Sackville-West, had hopes that the commune would have the same Bloomsbury air of free-thinking and risky elegance as she had but, in the photo of my parents in my bedroom, my mother is sitting on a stool, shelling peas into a bowl on her lap, her long hair tied in a plait down her back and she's wearing a pair of large dark glasses which are hiding her eyes. She has always seemed disappointed with her lot.

And Dad? He's sitting in a deck chair next to her, a copy of the *Socialist Worker* on the ground at his feet. He's a tall man, my dad, has something of a crane about him – the bird, not the piece of equipment used on large construction sites. But here he's crumpled, like someone has cut his strings and he's folded in on himself, his long arms and legs encased in hand-knitted woollens and too-short, second-hand trousers.

Neither of them looks particularly happy and, since the picture was taken, the commune has kind of imploded. Two out of the other eight who were not 'officially' together at the start have gone off with one another, bought a bungalow in Worthing and taken up ballroom dancing. Another died a slow and fractious death, always wishing he could do it without medical intervention, relying instead on herbs and positive thoughts, but succumbing in the end and dying, morphine-riddled, but pain free. It had, Mother said, been a mercy in the end. The rest – my parents, the deserted partners of the couple in Worthing, the widow of the dead man – carry on, just about. Very few of the assortment of children who are the result of this failed social experiment ever visit and neither do I.

Since I split from Boyd, I've been keeping myself to myself, making an OK living, enjoying the company of a few, select friends and more recently, enjoying both my evenings out with Colin doing cultural stuff and my evenings in with him doing sex stuff.

I tell myself on a daily basis that none of what's gone before has the power to hurt me, not any more. And nothing that may happen next can hurt me either; I've become adept at believing that the face I show the world is the real me.

I sometimes wonder if everyone does this to a certain extent and that underneath our calm exteriors, the looks we give people on the bus, the 'Thank you' smiles we give shop keepers and the ladies who hand back our clothes in plastic bags at the dry cleaners, we are all a boiling mass of doubt, regret and yearning. What if we actually answered truthfully when someone says, 'So, how *are* you?' Would we, could we, say, 'Well, actually, my heart is broken and it feels as though I'm carrying a ten tonne weight about in my chest. Oh, and by the way, I've always hated the way my right foot turns in a fraction when I walk'?

We spend so many wasted moments convincing ourselves that we don't mind about the things we think we cannot change but, now I'm here, at this preview, I know for sure that I really did want this for myself too. I wanted the white walls, the chrome, the clever lighting, the beautiful people, the bold art.

Of course, I know it's a lot to do with connections and meeting the right people at the right time. I hadn't had a patron and Boyd and I had perhaps been too insular when we were younger; we hadn't played the game.

He'd always had a healthy disregard for the politics of it all. Take this evening for example. He'd have come along, spoken loudly, laughed a lot, shaken critics' small hands in his big hand and steered me out of the door at the end of the evening, his fingers resting on the stem of my neck. It would have been like oil on water to him and we would have talked of insignificant things on the way home.

Not Colin, though. Colin is in the room somewhere now. He's asking intelligent and well-phrased questions and subtly promoting me wherever he goes. I know this, but can't see him in the crowd. Boyd always used to stand out; a head taller than everybody else.

A man is approaching. I don't recognise him but he's definitely coming my way. He's wearing a loud poncho over a pair of white jeans, has a string of beads around his neck and espadrilles on his feet. He is completely bald. Next to him, in my simple shift dress and leggings, my hair tied in its customary plait and wearing my red glasses, I feel like his grandmother.

'My dear,' he says, chinking his glass against mine. 'How lovely to see you. It's been simply ages.'

I'm not in the mood for small talk. 'I'm sorry,' I say. 'Do we know each other?'

He baulks and takes a step back. This is not accepted behaviour. At times like this, one dissembles. There will, after all, be some kind of connection between the two of us. Not least of which will be the artist in question.

'Um,' he says. 'I'm Barney Makepeace. You're Vita, right? We were at college together, shared that space in Fulham until the sodding landlord sold it from under us. Remember?'

Oh, yes, I remember. And now, of course, I remember Barney.

'My God,' I say. 'It *is* you. Sorry for not recognising you. It's been a while.'

And during this time, I say to myself, you've lost your hair, put on weight, changed. You used to wear tight black jeans and black t-shirts, you were never seen without a roll-up or a can of lager in your hand. You used to paint the most spectacular landscapes.

'So,' I continue, 'what are you up to now?'

'Oh, this and that. There were a few barren years, you know, like we all go through.' He laughs and takes a dainty sip of his drink. His fingernails, I notice, are painted with sky-blue nail polish. 'But then I got my shit together. Thanks mostly to Marmaduke,' he waves a hand at the crowd, 'who's here somewhere, and now the pictures are back. Mostly Cornish skies as that's where we're based now. I paint as Rock Johnson now. You may have heard of me?'

His eyes widen, kind of like a dog's might when he's doing something clever like sitting and staying or coming when called. I've heard of Rock Johnson. There was a piece about him in one of the Sunday supplements not so long back. I hadn't recognised the photo of him then either. And his work? Now I come to think of it, his use of perspectives was still good, but his colour palette seemed to have gone awry, although, I think charitably, maybe that was just the print quality in the magazine. I obviously hadn't read the article that closely, otherwise I might have noticed the connection to our college and our inauspicious beginnings in the studio.

'Of course,' I say hurriedly, fearing that his eyes may actually explode. 'There was an article I read about you recently.'

'Oh that old thing,' he says, blushing. 'What a lot of fuss!'

But I can tell he's delighted really.

'And so,' he says, taking yet another sip of his drink, 'what's new with you?'

'Oh, absolutely nothing,' I reply. 'Same old, same old.'

I absolutely don't want to tell him about the pet portraits.

'But surely,' he presses on, 'you must be doing something. An artist never really puts down their brush, do they?'

'I live a quiet life. I get by.'

'And what about that handsome brute you went off with? He still on the scene?'

There's an odd, stabby feeling inside my chest as though I've suddenly developed indigestion.

'No,' I say. 'He's not.'

Three small words: not nearly large enough to describe the pain I'd once felt.

At that moment, Colin appears. Thank God for Colin, I think.

'How are you doing?' Colin asks. He's not holding a glass and looks unruffled and cool in the heat of the room. I am grateful to him for all these things.

I introduce him to Barney and say, 'I'm good, thank you. But we should be getting going I guess.'

I should ask Barney the requisite questions about where he's staying tonight, what his plans are after the preview, when he's going back to Cornwall, but can't be bothered. Right now, I wish to be in my house in Albert Terrace, with its muddle and its memories; I want to be at home. I don't let myself consider whether Colin should be there too or whether I will spend the night listening for small movements and whispered conversations in the room across the stairs.

'Keep in touch,' Barney says as I put my now-empty glass on a passing waiter's tray.

'Will do,' I promise, but I know I won't.

I haven't even really studied the art on the walls. There's always been a press of people near the paintings and I'm not in the mood to battle my way through them. A glimpse here and there has been enough.

It's nice to leave the gallery and step out into the street. Perversely, despite the traffic noise, it seems quieter out here than in the room behind us. My neck under my plait is prickly with sweat. Colin doesn't try to take my hand but still he seems to steer me towards the Tube. He doesn't say much, just the occasional comment. He asks me no questions. Again I am grateful. He is such easy company.

The journey home is uneventful; the train we catch is one of those mid-evening ones after the commuter rush and before the late-night ones where the sleepy or the drunk journey home, swaying between the seats before they find somewhere to sit, the trains where the overriding smell is of burger and chips.

'We'll walk back I presume,' Colin says as we rumble into Farnham station.

It's completely dark now and still warm and as we get off, Colin holds out an arm to steady me.

We walk in companionable silence and then Colin says, 'I liked the art tonight. It was robust.'

Robust is just the right word. Robustness is what my work has been lacking of late. I seem to have lost whatever vigour I once had, the ability to take chances, the time to. I'd once thought there was an infinite amount of time ahead of me, but whatever there was has sped by at an alarming rate and now I look back more than forward and this angers me; I should have more to show for my life than I do.

'It was,' I say, as we turn into Albert Terrace. Some of the houses still have their curtains open and I glance into front room windows, see the buttery yellow lights on inside, the flicker of a TV screen.

We pause outside Colin's house. 'You can come in if you like,' he says.

Again, the lack of a direct question is a comfort.

'I think I'll head home. Got an early start.'

'That's fine. I'll see you soon.' This time he does reach out a hand and takes one of mine in it. He presses his thumb against the soft flesh of my palm and I feel a faint buzz inside my stomach but it's not strong enough to make me change my mind. His face is calm and unlined, his eyes reflect the glow from the streetlights. I like his mouth, his plump lips, his tidy stubble, the way he speaks.

'Thanks for coming with me this evening.' I begin to pull my hand away from his.

'It was a pleasure, as always,' he replies.

I'm starting to turn away from him, my heartbeats steadying, when he says, 'Vita?'

I look back at him. 'Yes?'

'Are you OK?'

'Of course I am. Why?'

'I just hope it's working out all right, you know with Boyd and everything.'

'By everything, do you mean Honey?' I ask, my heartbeats inexplicably quickening again.

'Well, yes and Boyd. I mean it must be odd having them there.'

I think. Is it odd? I'd thought it would be but actually it isn't. There's something right about it, easy almost. It's good to have Boyd there; strangely, his presence provides a kind of comfort. And Honey? It's almost as though she fills a gap, albeit a gap that shouldn't be there and that she shouldn't be filling. Sometimes I hate having them there, but other times? Other times, it seems as natural as breathing.

'I'm fine,' I say. Then realise I've said this snappily so I tilt my head to one side and continue, 'Really I am. There's nothing to worry about. Nothing is changing and it's only temporary. They'll be gone before I know it.'

'As long as you're OK.'

'Yes,' I say. 'I am.'

But as I close the front door behind me and Colin closes his, I stop in the darkness of the lounge. The curtains are drawn to and all is quiet upstairs and suddenly I'm filled with a fury that's as unwelcome as it is unexpected. My heart somersaults in my chest and I stomp into the kitchen to get a glass of water and then I stomp upstairs, not caring if I disturb them, they shouldn't bloody well be here anyway. Everything was perfectly settled the way it was before. It has been six years and never once have I questioned what happened between Boyd and me. It was the natural culmination of what led up to it; there'd been no other choice.

I get into my pyjamas, take off my glasses and unplait my hair and then I use the bathroom. I don't stop midway along the landing to listen out for movement in Boyd and Honey's room but I imagine him turning over in his sleep, his long legs stretching out, his paw of a hand resting on her hip and my heart bangs uncomfortably inside my ribs again as I climb into bed and turn off the light.

I also don't think of Colin in the room on the other side of the wall, or the fact that on the few occasions we've actually fallen asleep together, when he sleeps, he sleeps tidily and noiselessly, doesn't crowd me and keeps to his side of the bed, how he doesn't rest his hand on my hip. No, I don't think about any of this at all.

* * *

The next morning I'm making a cup of tea when I hear the unmistakeable sound of Boyd's footsteps on the stairs.

'Tea?' I ask.

'Please.' He's standing before me running his fingers through his hair.

'How did yesterday go?'

'Yesterday?' He's walking through to the lounge to draw back the curtains.

'Honey's birthday surprise,' I reply as he comes back through to the kitchen and I'm pouring boiling water into the teapot. I'd obviously known about her birthday but hadn't felt it my place to acknowledge it in any way. We weren't on those sorts of terms.

'Oh,' he says, 'it was great, thanks. I booked for her to go and see a medium. You know how she is about her superstitions? Well, I wanted to give her some kind of certainty and thought it would be a good idea.'

He pauses, then continues, 'She got told just what she wanted to hear. Lots of good news, future all rosy that kind of thing. The lady even said …'

He stops mid-sentence and I have a sneaky suspicion I know what he was going to say. I am relieved when he doesn't but instead mutters, '… Never mind. It's not important. How was your evening by the way? Good preview?'

'It was OK,' I say as I stir sugar into his tea. 'Met up with Barney Makepeace. Not sure if you remember him from the old days?'

'Guy who always wore black t-shirts and unfeasibly tight jeans?'

'That's the one.' I hand him his tea. 'He looks a bit different now though.'

'Guess we all do. It's been a while.'

'I suppose it has.' I take a mouthful of my drink, it's so hot it scalds my tongue. 'Shall we see if we can finish off yesterday's crossword then?' I ask.

We settle down on the sofa and he is within touching distance.

'Right,' he says, 'which ones have we still got to do?'

'There's twelve down: "Alarming disclosure of beauty". It's nine letters.'

Boyd shifts in his seat. 'Do we have any of them yet?'

'Sixth letter is H.'

'That's not much to go on.'

I am struck by a powerful sense of déjà vu, that not only have we sat here like this a thousand times before but that we've had this clue before. I look at Boyd. He's frowning and drumming his fingers on his leg and before I know what I'm doing I say, 'You haven't changed. Not like Barney, I mean.'

I think, shit, where am I going with this?

He turns and smiles, 'I'll take that as a compliment.'

There is a heavy pause. I rustle the paper. I am acutely aware of Honey upstairs, of the fact that Boyd has changed; he is older, wiser, his heart belongs to someone else.

'Did you mean it as one?'

'One what?' I snap. I am staring hard at the clues. Thirteen across is 'Two girls on one knee' and it's seven letters. If we get it, it'll help us with twelve down. My mind has suddenly gone blank.

'A compliment,' Boyd says.

'I guess so. At least you still have your hair!'

'And you haven't changed either, Vita. You're still …'

'Still what?' I am losing patience with this conversation, am fearful one of us will say something that will put the delicate balance we've achieved at risk.

'Still stubborn, generous, opinionated, intelligent,' he says. 'And you still have that energy, that sense of beauty that I so loved about you …'

The word 'loved' crashes into me and sounds huge in the quiet of the kitchen. Two things about it are inescapable: firstly, he said the word 'love' and secondly, he used the past tense. I leap up as if stung; the mug of tea I've balanced on the arm of the sofa topples and smashes to the floor. Broken china and tea go everywhere. 'Fuck,' I say. 'Look what you made me do.'

'I made you? What do you mean?'

I can't explain to him what I mean. My head is whirling; I didn't need to hear what he said, I don't need to know it, I don't want to admit what both things about the word may mean. It's a bombshell I can do without.

'Bombshell!' I almost shout it.

'What?'

'"Alarming disclosure of beauty" is Bombshell!'

'You're right, it is. Well done you. That gives us an L for thirteen across. Knee, knee ... The answer's almost within reach.'

Too bloody right, I think, but don't really know where the thought comes from. By now, I'm on *my* knees, cleaning up the broken mug and wiping up the spilt tea. Knee, knee ... and then the word comes to me: 'Patella,' I say, looking up at Boyd. 'Pat and Ella are two girls' names and patella is kneecap.'

'You're on fire this morning, Vita,' he says and thankfully it seems as though he's forgotten what made me leap up and knock over my drink. 'You're way ahead of me.'

But I'm not, I think. I'm actually way behind you. I haven't been able to give my heart to anyone else and still don't really know to whom it rightly belongs. Of course I say nothing though, it wouldn't do either of us any good if I did.

'Well,' I say, 'guess I'd better be getting on.'

'Me too,' he replies. 'And Vita ...?'

'Yes?'

He stands, still holding the newspaper, and he looks at me. 'Oh, it's nothing,' he says. 'It'll keep.'

And then he's gone, back up the stairs, back to Honey, and I'm left with two clues completed and no appetite for my toast and marmalade, just pieces of broken china in my hand and a tea stain on the carpet.

Boyd

From the photographs Boyd's seen, his mother had been beautiful when young: dark hair, full lips, wasp-thin waist. He remembers looking through her albums when he was a boy, the pictures held in by cardboard corners. She hadn't annotated them with dates or places but he'd seen a succession of shots of her as a teenager: her leaning against railings on a pier or standing next to a shining car, her tiny gloved hand resting on the bonnet; or her seated at a table, cocktail glass in hand. She'd been a radiant person back then.

Too young for soldiers, she'd waited until she was nineteen, until the start of the fifties, to spread her wings. It was then, Boyd reckoned by looking at the fashions, that she was photographed leaning on the arms of a succession of handsome boys, her expression guileless and happy.

He must have studied these pictures when they lived in their first home. He remembers his mother stopping on her way to the kitchen, sitting next to him on the mustard-yellow sofa they'd had in those days and saying, 'My goodness, Boyd, how times change, eh?' She'd taken a drag on her cigarette and said, 'But we're fine, aren't we? Just the two of us. You must promise me ...'

'Promise you what?' he'd asked.

She'd paused before she'd said, 'That you'll never try to find your father. Some things are best left. OK?' and she'd let out a mouthful of smoke and through the smoke her face had looked fierce, fierce and like a stranger's.

And, of course he'd promised her. When the smoke had cleared, he'd looked up and seen how her face powder had settled into the creases around her eyes and how there'd been a faint dusting of it on the outrageously wide collar of her patterned dress. He'd promised her because he'd had no other choice. She'd moved away then, the ash hanging perilously from the end of her cigarette.

This was in the mid-seventies when they'd lived in a flat above a chemist's shop in West London and before she'd married for the second time.

Her story had not been a simple one and it had taken him a long time to put the pieces of it together, not helped by the absence of any grandparents to provide corroborating evidence. He often mourned the fact that he'd never been part of a family, part of something bigger than himself and his mother.

She'd been born to an upper middle class family from Bristol. Her father had, he came to learn, been the Company Secretary of a prestigious manufacturing firm – one that made a certain type of valve – and he and his wife lived a life of respectability and calm that came with his close association to the local captains of industry. That was until Boyd's mother discovered men, or one man in particular.

She'd been christened Muriel but had always hated the name so renamed herself 'Belle', and all was going well until – as she was to tell him one afternoon when, again, they were sitting on the mustard-yellow sofa and Boyd was turning the pages in the album and saw a picture of her holding a bouquet of white flowers, standing next to a man on a set of steps – she met Malcolm.

Malcolm had blown into town with the travelling fair. He'd worked the dodgems and Boyd could imagine what had happened; it's a common enough story. Malcolm must have flattered Belle, smiled at her as he hung on to the waltzer's poles, as he hopped panther-like from one to the other in his hip-hugging trousers, a cigarette hanging from his lips, as he made her believe she was the only one.

Belle had got pregnant, had been disowned by her respectable parents, had married Malcolm only to lose the baby and for him to go back to the fair, leaving her a wife with no husband, a mother with no baby, a daughter with no parents.

That afternoon on the sofa, when Boyd had been around eight and they were looking at the photograph of her wedding day, she'd said, 'He was the most beautiful and most dangerous man I've ever known. I loved him with all my heart.'

Boyd had not really understood then of course.

There were other men after Malcolm; plenty of them, as the album testified. There were pictures of Belle with men wearing hats, men smoking pipes, men in thick woollen cardigans, one man with a dog at his heels. But no one stayed. She worked, paid the rent, made her own clothes, smoked too many cigarettes, drank too much, didn't eat properly and still her parents didn't, couldn't, forgive her. Boyd had often wondered if they came to regret their decision, but he'd never know for sure as they'd died long ago. His mother had told him the bare facts in her more tipsy moments over the years but never whether she tried to effect a reconciliation. He doubts she did. Like him, she was, and is, a proud person.

Then, in 1969, she fell pregnant again, with him. His father was, so Boyd came to believe, the husband of one of Belle's friends: a married man with a family of his own who'd never wanted anything to do with either Boyd or Belle. This is what his mother had told him anyway and Boyd had long since been unable to grasp whether it was the men she picked who were flawed or whether it was her; whether there was something inherently unkeepable and unwantable about her.

But in the late seventies she must have changed tack, because then there came three more marriages: the first to Douglas who sold cars at his family's dealership and who was portly and florid and who died of a heart attack five years later; the second was to Patrick, an accountant who slipped and fell on an icy pavement one January evening on his way home from work, knocking his head on an iron foot scraper and dying from his injuries three days later; and the third was to a small, bespectacled vet called Aubrey who had died of peritonitis after a burst appendix a mere six weeks after the wedding.

Whether Belle had loved any of these men, Boyd never knew. But his mother dutifully set up home with each one, only to move on to the next, until Aubrey that was. And, as each left the majority of his estate to Belle, by the time Aubrey died (Boyd had often had Lady Bracknell's voice in his head, extolling the difference between being unfortunate and being careless in his mother's track record with husbands) Belle had amassed some wealth, a vet's practice in a substantial Victorian house in another part of West London, which she quickly closed down, converting the house back to its former glory – and Boyd.

And now Boyd had persuaded her to sell the house and move into a care home in the Surrey hills where she sat jealously guarding what was left to her: her photographs, her money and her disappointments.

And, because he'd broken his promise to her and had tried, once, to find his father, she refused to make things any easier for him. And so they wait, on opposite sides of the fence, glaring at each other over the metaphorical barbed wire of her estate. It is a shame that it should be like this, and is another of Boyd's regrets.

However, it's Sunday and Boyd is driving through the early autumn lanes to see her. Around him the trees are on the cusp, the sun is huge and low, the fields seem to glisten. There is, he notices, a lot of roadkill today: rabbits, a badger, pheasants – a tapestry of guts and fur and feathers. Each time he passes the remains of one, his heart contracts a fraction and he daren't look in the rear-view mirror.

The Lexus is purring, the radio's on and he's thinking of the house in Albert Terrace and of Vita in her studio, her red glasses, her long, thick plait hanging down her back and he's thinking of Honey in the office, gamely manning the phones and dealing with the viewings. It's more difficult for him to get away during the week and although it's hard to leave Honey on a Sunday, he tries to visit his mother once a month at least; it's the least he can do.

He pulls up outside. The house had once belonged to a famous Victorian female novelist and it intrigues Boyd, when he steps through the front door, to think that he's walking on tiles where she once stood.

He rings the bell and gets buzzed in. He says hello to a passing nurse and signs the visitors' book. He is, as every time, stupidly nervous.

'Hello, Mum,' he says as he pulls up a chair next to her.

She's sitting in her chair as if it's a throne. She glances in his direction then looks back at the TV screen where some implausibly bendy gymnast is doing a floor routine.

'How are you?' he asks. It's very hot in the lounge and, despite the best efforts of the staff and the air fresheners attached to the walls, which puff out bursts of fragrance at regular intervals, the room smells of cooked cabbage and wee.

This time she looks at him. 'Not bad, thank you,' she replies.

He notices a nurse signalling to him from the doorway and so when his mother returns her attention to the screen, Boyd unpacks himself from the chair and goes over to the door.

'Yes?' he asks.

The nurse is young and sweetly beautiful; he wonders briefly how old she might be.

'We just wanted to let you know how she is,' she says in somewhat halting English.

Boyd has not seen her before but guesses she's from Poland or somewhere in that direction. One of the other nurses, one who knows him, must have pointed out to her who he is and who he's here to see.

'Oh, thank you.' There is a pause, so Boyd adds, 'And so, how is she?'

'She is very well; blood pressure, everything like that, all good and she is eating well, as always,' the nurse says.

Boyd is disappointed that he's disappointed by this news. Somehow, some part of him had wished for a different, graver update.

He's always wanted to be a good man, to live up to his own idea of himself. He never wanted his mother's disappointments to colour the way he sees the world. He's not always managed it of course, but in the way he loves – or rather loved – Vita, and the way he loves Honey he hopes he is doing his best. If anyone was to give out medals for good intentions, Boyd would certainly be on the podium.

'But,' the nurse is saying, 'she has been complaining of a pain in her back this last week so we are, how you say, keeping our eyes peeled onto it.'

'OK, thank you,' he says, wanting to reach out a hand and rest it on the nurse's arm in a show of solidarity but knowing he shouldn't do this, that it is not allowed or appropriate. 'I should,' he adds, 'get back, you know, to sit with her. I can't stay for long.'

'Ah,' the nurse says, smiling kindly at him, 'yes, she says you are a very busy man with your own house business, yes?'

'An estate agency, yes, but we rarely talk about it, she and I. I've always had the impression she doesn't quite approve of it.'

'I think,' the nurse says, making ready to turn and leave, 'she is very proud of you actually.' She says the word 'actually' as though it's spelt acturarly.

This information unsettles Boyd as he walks back to where his mother is still watching the gymnastics. He wants to say something soothing and kind but when he says, 'Mum, the nurse tells me you've got backache,' it comes out sharper than he'd intended.

'It's nothing,' she murmurs, picking at the hem of her cardigan with a painted fingernail.

For as long as Boyd can remember his mother has always had perfectly manicured hands.

She is, of course, old and frail now, her once glorious hair is grey and wispy and she seems to get smaller and smaller each time he goes to visit her. She does, however, still take pride in her clothes which are always smart and colour co-ordinated and she always wears some jewellery; after all, she has plenty. He has no idea which of the husbands' wedding rings she wears these days, although something tells him it's Malcolm's. He was the only one of them she'd ever said she really loved.

Boyd's childhood hadn't lacked material things, not after she married Douglas anyway. Before that they'd had to be frugal and his mother had worked tirelessly at different jobs in shops and offices to make ends meet and he'd had his odd jobs and washed neighbours' cars. He likes to think she was being heroic, sacrificing her happiness for his, but now feels that he knows her better than this, that her motives weren't always altruistic. He was always well-dressed, mostly well-fed, there was heat and light in whichever flat they were living, but he felt he'd missed out on something significant: that type of connection a son should feel for his mother or that a mother should feel for her son. He'd had the sneaky feeling that she'd resented his presence in her life and would have much preferred it if he hadn't been born at all. He can never remember dancing with her or hearing her sing along to a song on the radio like the mothers in movies sometimes did.

At least, he thinks, as the tea trolley gets wheeled into the room and the gymnastics moves seamlessly to a murder mystery on TV – *Miss Marple* by the look of things – he has Honey now. Her presence in his life is like a fresh start; she helps to keep the ghosts at bay.

He's never been quite sure that his mother understood what happened between him and Vita, how sad and unnecessary it all was, how much it shames him to think of how he behaved but, as she stirs sugar into her cup of tea she says, 'So tell me, Boyd. Are the three of you still living together in that house of yours? You, Vita and *that* girl?'

She says the word 'that' as though she's spitting it out.

'How do you know about that?' he replies. He hasn't told her because he believes she'd judge him for messing up his finances. He hadn't wanted her censure on top of his own.

'Vita visits me now and again.' There is a look of veiled triumph on his mother's face.

'Does she?'

'Well, why wouldn't she? I'm still her mother-in-law after all.'

'And she told you I'd moved back in,' he pauses, 'with Honey?'

'Of course. Something about you needing to save money. You never were very good with money, were you Boyd?'

She takes a sip of tea. A drop of it spills down her chin but she doesn't notice.

He doesn't reply to her question but says instead, 'Well, it's all going really nicely thank you. Vita's being wonderful about it and Honey is so lovely that you can't help but love her. I wish …'

His mother turns her flinty gaze on him. 'You wish what?'

'I wish you'd agree to meet her. She'd love to meet you.'

'I'd like to say, over my dead body,' his mother says, 'but that may turn out to be too prophetic.' She smiles wryly and hands him her cup. 'Put this on the table for me will you?'

The sound is low on the TV but Boyd can still hear the tinny sound of murder mystery music and the rumble of voices both from it and from the other residents and visitors dotted around the room. He dislikes this lack of privacy but thinks he'd be even more uncomfortable if it were just him and his mother in her room.

'Vita's never got over it, you know,' she says now, out of nowhere.

'Over what?' He taps his spoon on his saucer for lack of anything else to do.

'Over you and what happened.'

'And you know this how? Has she said anything?'

'Of course not, Vita has far too much class for anything like that.'

It's odd, Boyd thinks, that his mother should sing Vita's praises

121

now. In the early days his new wife could do nothing right, and so it's even odder to think that she would now willingly come and visit Belle and not tell Boyd about it either. How easy it is, he thinks, to think you know someone when you don't, not really.

'How often does she come?' he asks his mother.

'Now and again,' she says. 'Not often. But she did come recently, or she must have done or I wouldn't have known about your new …' this time it's she who pauses, '… living arrangement.' She says this as though it's something squalid.

'It's only temporary Mum, until I get back on my feet and pay my sodding tax bill.'

The look of triumph hasn't yet left his mother's face; how he wishes for a different parent at times like these. With her, life is so fucking complex, as though everything is some sort of eternal game of one-upmanship.

This time both she and he turn their faces to watch TV and the minutes tick by and eventually he looks down at the tepid half-inch of tea in the bottom of his cup and says, 'Ah well, Mum. I guess I'd better be going.'

And she says, 'That's fine. Thank you for visiting.'

But he knows she doesn't mean it.

On the way back out to the car he feels like he could cry and, driving through the small lanes back out to the A31, it seems to Boyd that he's been in the care home for weeks and yet the sky is the same shade of blue and the leaves on the trees are the same colour as when he got there. He's been with his mother for less than an hour but feels as though he's aged ten years. He thinks, how come our parents do this to us? They reduce us to the dependents we once were, they remind us at all times of how much we owe them and how we can never fully repay them.

He wants to talk to Honey and so dials the office number. She will, he knows, be packing up for the day; he hopes she's had an easy time of it. He pulls over and switches from hands-free because he wants to connect with her via something tangible. The phone rings four times and then she picks up. He can imagine the tilt of her head, the soft skin of her neck.

'Hi, it's me,' he says before she has the chance to say the usual, 'Good afternoon, Harrison's Residential, how may I help you?'

'How did it go?' she asks.

'Pretty awful to tell you the truth.'

'Still, it's done, eh?'

'Yes, it is, for now. There's always next time and the time after that though.' He tries to laugh it off, but is filled with a sudden and inexplicable despair. 'How have you got on today?' he asks in an effort to chase it away.

'Oh, OK. It's been quite quiet actually. I'm just starting to pack up. What do you fancy doing this evening?'

'I'm not sure.'

There is a pause and a muffling of her voice and he can hear the office door open and Honey say to whoever has just walked in, 'Hello. I'll be with you in a minute.' And then she comes back on the line and says, 'I'd better go. Look, if Vita's going out tonight, perhaps we can stay in. Get a takeaway?'

'Sounds like heaven,' he replies. 'Leave it with me. I'll see you back at home, OK?'

He doesn't think it strange that he should refer to Vita's house as home, but maybe on another day, in another place, he may have done.

Next he dials Vita's mobile.

'Mmmm,' she says as she picks up.

123

'You painting?' he asks.

'Yes. How do you know?'

'You always answer the phone like that when you're painting.'

'Like what?'

'You say, "Mmmm" as if whoever it is ringing is a total inconvenience.'

'Well it is. You are.'

She laughs her throaty laugh as she says this, the sound echoes as it always does when she's in the studio and Boyd is momentarily unsure whether he should speak next or whether she's going to say anything more. There is a second's silence and so he says, 'How's it going?'

'What?'

'The painting.'

'Oh, it's crap. I can't get the colour of the pesky dog's coat right. These fucking Cockapoos, no two are ever the bloody same. Now give me a nice traditional Golden Retriever, I know where I am with those.'

In the field next to the lay-by where Boyd is parked are two horses; he watches as one saunters over to the other. The horse is graceful and muscular and rests his huge head on the flank of the other. Then, as if someone's fired a starting pistol, they spring apart and start to run, manes streaming out behind them.

'Why do you do it?' he asks Vita.

'What, paint stupid animals?' she says.

'Yes.'

'For the money. Why do you think?'

The horses have stopped running and in the distance a flock of birds banks in tight formation. Boyd watches them mesmerised.

'You still there?' Vita asks.

'Yes, sorry. Look, I know it's a job,' he says, 'but why don't you go back to doing portraits? Weren't they always your first love?'

'No,' Vita says, 'you were.'

'Pardon?' he says.

'Only joking, Boyd.' She hesitates before adding, 'You're right though, I should think about changing. I fucking hate people's pets. Anyway, you didn't call to talk about my job did you? What did you want?'

Boyd has, over the years, got used to Vita's total lack of charm on the phone and in some ways it's refreshing to talk to her like this. It's normal and natural and comforting. He wants to ask her why she still visits his mother, what they talk about, how often she goes. But he holds back from doing so. The birds have disappeared from view; the horses are quietly eating, their long necks stretching down to the grass. Instead he says, 'I'm just on my way back from seeing Mum and was wondering if you know your plans for this evening yet?'

'Why?'

He can hear her tapping her paintbrush on the side of her glasses. He used to love watching her do this when they first met.

'Honey and I were thinking of staying in, getting a takeaway.' There is silence at the other end of the line, the tapping sound has stopped. 'You could join us if you wish.'

As soon as the words are out of his mouth he regrets them. It isn't what he wants and he guesses it isn't what Honey would want either.

'I'm going out, but thanks for asking,' she replies.

'Anywhere nice?'

'I hope so. Look, I'd better get on. See you later Boyd.'

'Yes, see you.'

She hangs up and he puts his phone back down on the seat next to him, shifts position and starts the engine. Of course he didn't ask her about her visits to his mother and probably never will. One of the horses looks up and stares at him. He pulls out of the lay-by and heads back to Farnham.

Vita

After I hang up, I stare at the screen for a long moment. There is a tightness in my chest I don't recognise.

'Shit,' I say, putting the phone down on the table to the side of the easel. Did I really say, 'No, you were,' when Boyd asked me whether portraits had always been my first love?

I place the phone such that it's dead square with the corner of the table; there's something pleasing in the symmetry of this.

I think of Belle and the care home's unique scent: the warm, slightly sweet odour that seems to hang to my clothes after I leave. I think of Belle and her disappointments, and then, naturally, of my own.

Although I hate the movie and particularly despise René Zellweger's portrayal of the simpering and ditzy Bridget, the line about dying alone and being eaten by Alsatians often ricochets around my head. I don't want to fear ending up alone, but I guess it's natural. I don't want to wonder about my motives for doing what I'm doing with Colin either.

And then my thoughts turn to Boyd and I imagine him driving back through the country lanes and the takeaway he and Honey will have tonight, their used plates stacked in the dishwasher, marks from

Honey's lipstick on the rim of her wine glass, them sitting on the sofa with their legs bumping up against one another as they chat or read. And I think of Belle's small, but perfectly manicured hands. There is no logic to my thoughts and I am cross with myself about this.

I let out a hurrumph which echoes around the studio. 'Enough,' I say, turning my attention back to the picture of the fucking stupid Cockapoo. 'Right,' I tell it, 'it's you and me and I'm going to get your bloody ears right if it kills me.'

Honey

She locks the door as the last customers of the day leave. They'd come in out of curiosity, nothing more. One of the houses Boyd has in the window must belong to friends of theirs, she guesses, and they were fishing for information. However, even under their intense questioning about why 32 Church Road has suddenly come on the market, Honey had remained totally discreet and non-committal; Trixie and Boyd would have been proud of her.

It is when she is turning the 'Open' sign to 'Closed' that she sees him.

She'd always known this couldn't last: her job, her life with Boyd, loving him and being loved by him. Even Vita and Trixie had filled a gap she hadn't realised had been there. She'd never really had any friends before, not proper ones. But, all along, she knew he'd come for her; that this person, the one who'd been showing what she'd thought was her best side to the world, hadn't been the real her. She was, she is, a construct.

What was it the medium had said, that she'd be found? And what had her horoscope this morning said? 'A face from the past will reappear in your life today.'

Holy shit, she thinks, her hand still on the sign.

He's standing in the doorway of the shop opposite. He's looking at his phone, is taller than she remembers, bulkier, but perhaps he's been working out and, after all, she'd only really known him lying down. He's wearing a light brown jacket, jeans and sunglasses and he's leaning against a door post. His skin is swarthy. She'd know him anywhere.

As soon as she could after the explosion, she'd gone to the local library to find out what had happened that night. There was a newspaper report on Google which said:

'Local businessman and entrepreneur Reuben Roberts has sustained life-changing injuries following an explosion on his boat offshore at East Quay Marina last night. The cause of the explosion is not known and no conclusive evidence has come forward from any eye-witnesses to the event. It is believed that Mr Roberts lost a leg in the incident.

'Forensic teams are still at the scene but initial reports point to this being a tragic accident and not the result of negligence or foul play.

'Mr Roberts (52) chairs a number of local enterprises, as well as being the proprietor of a string of successful nightclubs along the coast. His property portfolio is thought to be valued at £20m. His wife, Anastasia (29) is the daughter of Russian billionaire, Sergei Popolov and is herself involved in a number of local charities. Mr Roberts has one child from his first marriage.'

The report went on to say that the boat had been completely destroyed. Over the years Honey has imagined what his injury must have been like, how could she have caused such an awful thing to happen?

It was, however, obvious from this early report that he'd got to the press and the police and convinced them not to look too deeply into the events of that night; Camilla, the woman Honey worked for, had made it clear that Reuben and his wife had friends in high places and that they both had reputations to keep. It seems that money could buy silence after all.

There was a smattering of other reports on the internet and some grainy pictures of Reuben and his wife at gala dinners or on board the boat, but it looked as though the trail had dried up a few months afterwards and the reports petered out, being replaced by articles about both of them opening day centres for disabled kids, holding a charity auction and Anastasia launching *Resurrection*, her own brand of perfume. It had all been glossed over and forgotten, by the public at least.

It may well have been a cover-up, but Honey can still remember the taste of seawater in her mouth, how heavy her arms and legs had been as she'd tried to make it to shore.

Now however and, from what she can see of him from her position behind the door, he looks unscarred: his skin is still dusky and smooth, but maybe his body is a criss-cross of lines; perhaps he had to undergo months of skin grafts and prosthetics' fittings before he could walk again? And it would all be her fault. It was her fault. It is.

She's deliberately not looked for references to him on the internet for years now. In true ostrich form, she's not wanted to know.

It had all started so innocently. She was working behind a bar when her colleague, Sioux, said, 'Hey, fancy earning some extra cash?' And hey, who wouldn't?

She began working the sex lines and was quite good at it. The callers seemed to like her. However, as ever with these things, it didn't stop there. Maybe it's like drugs, she's often thought. You get used to the strength of one and then you want to move on to something that gives you a bigger hit. So she started camming. That was harder – the 'clients' more choosy, and the scoring system and competition harsher – but the rewards were good and, with her bar wages, she was managing to make ends meet, could even afford the odd Starbucks. It sounds crazy, but when you have so little, something like that matters.

And then came Camilla and her escort agency. Honey had once believed that being an escort was accompanying a James Bond look-a-like to the door of a swanky hotel in the West End, holding his arm, only to peel off discreetly and wait to be called upon for erudite conversation when it suited him. She also thought that being an escort meant she'd always get home safely and sleep in her own bed. But it wasn't like that. There were some dreadful gigs, dreadful sex on dirty sheets and then the bookings on the boat and the promise of extra cash.

At the start she'd liked the fact it was glamorous and risky, that she'd been the chosen one. Seemed stupid now. It was, she'd soon realised, like she'd traded her soul, and the money made no material difference to her life at all. She still wasn't able to afford to live anywhere nice or fund a college course. Her life was a vicious circle of her income never quite matching her outgoings. It was as though Camilla's business model was to pay her girls just enough, but not so much that they'd get ideas above their station. In those days Honey's regrets could have filled a football stadium.

Reuben was dangerous and liked it rough but, because he was the pillar of the local community, married to his ridiculously young, beautiful and wealthy wife, what happened on the boat had to be a total secret. Honey was his fantasy, the thing he thought he could get away with, the dark underbelly of his otherwise perfect life.

There were numerous mucky transactions but that one night, that last night on the boat has haunted her ever since.

Honey left the agency soon after, got a cleaning job and, for a while, things were OK until the PTSD set in; she guesses that's what they would have called it if she'd gone anywhere official like the doctor's. All she knew were the panic attacks, the feelings of worthlessness, guilt and shame, the need to hide. So she left her jobs and moved from the coast to here in the hope that she would feel better about herself, and safer too. She'd always believed Reuben would want to punish her for the damage she'd caused, or silence her, or both. Living with the fear of this was exhausting but, as the months went by and he didn't come after her, she started to pull herself together. She got a job in Ali's corner shop, bought fake ID from a guy Ali knew, rented a bedsit with the last of her money and signed on. And then came the interview at Harrison's where, dressed in charity-shop clothes, she told them her name was Honey Mayhew.

She's often thought of the person she was before: her real name – the name her mother gave her – and then she thinks of the foster carers and the dark days and truly believes it's better to have re-invented herself, at least this way she has chosen who she is; she likes being Honey Mayhew. There are still times, however, when she looks at her name on an official document and wonders how long it will be before she's found out. Fake IDs are never bullet proof and though she had done some things to cover her tracks, the worry and the fear of discovery will, she honestly believes, never leave her.

Reuben's still there; he's put his phone away and is scanning the street, studying the shopfronts and the passers-by. In a move she's seen before, he sweeps his sunglasses off his face and fixes his eyes on the door she's standing behind. He shifts his feet and a flash of what appears to be pain crosses his face.

Although she looks totally different, she knows he recognises her too. She'd had long brown hair before, was plumper; the dyed crew cut and diet of anxiety and poverty had, she'd hoped, turned her into someone unrecognisable. But he must be cleverer than that. She is convinced he can see through her disguise.

At the second his gaze meets hers, a woman stops in front of the door and rummages in her handbag for something, blocking her sight of him and, when the woman moves on, Reuben's gone and it's like he's never been there at all. But Honey knows; she knows he knows where she works now.

It takes her another ten minutes to pluck up the courage to pull down the blinds behind the window displays, check the front door is locked and the computers turned off and sneak out the back, watchful, terrified, in case he's found his way round there.

He hasn't.

Her heart is knocking against her ribs. She holds her phone in her hand, ready to dial 999, and starts walking back to the house in Albert Terrace. She's careful not to tread on any cracks in the pavement in the forlorn hope that this will keep the evil undisturbed, but knows deep down that this is a futile gesture and that nothing is ever going to be the same again.

Thankfully Boyd isn't in when she gets back. The house is in semi-darkness now the evenings are beginning to draw in. She guesses Vita must be in her studio and, although she's not ready to face Boyd yet, she craves company and so, leaving the lights off in the house, makes her way through the lounge, into the kitchen and out the back door.

It's all still there, whirling in her head: the sex, the precariousness, the cash, the guilt. She can never let Boyd know the type of person she really is, what she was driven to do, that she is damaged goods. She truly believes he will stop loving her if he ever finds out.

This is awful. She loves being here, she loves Boyd, she likes Vita, she is happy in this house but, just like it was after her session with Elizabeth, she has been reminded that none of this, not one tiny iota of it, can be for keeps.

She's right, Vita's working. Vita's also been busy in the garden, clearing up after summer, getting it ready for winter. Honey doesn't know how she finds the time, but the garden looks abundant, tended. The leaves of Vita's shrubs brush against her legs as she walks down the path and she likes this. At the front of the house the Virginia creeper is starting its autumn blaze.

The sun has slipped below the roofs of the nearby houses, the neighbourhood is Sunday-quiet and suddenly, through the welter of thoughts about what has just happened, the idea comes to her and she feels oddly blessed, blessed that she has the chance to do something to preserve what Boyd and she have together. Whatever may happen next, at least she can give him this.

She knocks on the studio door.

Vita makes an 'Mmmm' noise from within.

'Hi,' she says, 'it's me, Honey. Can I come in?'

Vita doesn't answer so Honey takes that as a yes. Inside, the light from the spot lamps is weird; it's not fluorescent but more like daylight and Honey assumes this is intentional. Vita's sitting in a pool of it, her hair made almost luminous by it. Her woollen dress is the same red as her glasses, it's long and its hem is brushing the floor. Around her shoulders she's wearing a black shawl which she's clipped together with a large silver butterfly brooch. She has a pair of clogs on her feet. Although it's still quite warm outside, she has her heater on. The air smells of linseed oil and turps.

She turns to look at Honey and nods briefly before saying, 'Yes? What is it?'

Honey's getting used to Vita's ways now; her bark is always much worse than her bite. She comes over as perfunctory, but Honey knows she has a good heart. She must have done to have loved, and been loved by, Boyd. However, despite this Honey's suddenly lost for words. As she'd stood outside the door she'd been so sure, but now face-to-face with her, she's not. So, instead, she says, 'Hi. Just wanted to say hello.'

'Hello,' Vita replies, her voice flat and disinterested. She picks up a paintbrush and taps it against her glasses.

'Nice picture,' Honey says lamely, looking at the canvas on the easel. It's of some kind of dog with soulful eyes and who looks like he's wearing some sort of handlebar moustache.

'Fucking Cockapoos. Everyone thinks they're so cute. I can't see the point in them myself.'

'I've never had a pet. Have you?' Honey asks.

'No. Why would I want to do that?'

Vita's washing out the brush now, studying its bristles and not looking at Honey. It's getting darker outside now and Honey feels confused by the colours in the studio: the yellows and browns and blues are shouting at her from the pictures stacked against the walls. She'd thought she would get accustomed to what had happened earlier, but it's obvious she won't, not immediately. She needs to sit down. The silence between them stretches as she tries to think of what to say next.

Eventually Vita looks at her. 'Shit, you OK?' she asks. 'You look awfully pale.'

'I'm fine. Just hungry, probably.'

'Boyd says you're having a takeaway tonight.'

Honey feels a faint frisson when Vita says this. She's not sure what it is, but it's not comfortable. Boyd had said he'd call Vita, but even so, part of Honey still doesn't like the fact that he has. It's stupid of her, she knows.

'We're hoping to,' she says. 'What are your plans?'

Vita pauses, gazes out of the window and then says, 'I'm going to try and get some more of this bloody picture done and then I'm going out.'

She doesn't tell Honey where she's going and Honey doesn't like to ask. Despite how well they seem to be getting along right now, Honey doesn't want to push it. However, she does still need to ask her.

'Look,' she says, shifting her feet. 'I was wondering if you'd do me a favour.'

'Oh,' Vita replies, 'what's that?'

'It may seem a strange thing to ask.'

'I won't know if it is or it isn't until you say it.'

Vita's still not looking at her, but has put down her brush and has picked up a tube of paint and is picking at the label with her fingernail.

'Will you paint me? Paint my portrait, I mean.' Honey carries on in a rush, not pausing, afraid now of how Vita's going to react. 'I'd like you to do it so I can give it to Boyd.'

'You want me to do *what*?' Vita says. 'Why the fuck would I want to do that?'

Honey immediately regrets asking her. What kind of gold-plated fool is she to think Vita would welcome the idea with open arms? And yet, still, it's something that she realises she really, really wants.

'Please,' she says. 'It's the least I can do.'

'What do you mean?'

She closes her eyes. The words are burning her tongue. She's never told anyone before and, although it's obvious why she'd want to now, why should she want to tell Vita?

But she does.

She says, 'There are things about me that Boyd doesn't know and that I don't want him to know, but I think that one day he may find out and I want to do this for him so he'll have something good to remember me by, something that'll remind him of who I am right now.'

The words come out in a rush. Honey realises she must appear like a mad, wild-eyed woman and has no idea if what she's said makes any type of sense.

'That sounds dramatic,' Vita replies. 'We're not in some Hollywood movie, you know.'

'I know we're not. It's just that I'm so worried, Vita. I'm worried that what I've done in my past is going to catch up with me.'

'What do you mean?' Vita is looking at her now, her eyes drilling into Honey's, but her voice is kinder than Honey had expected it to be.

'I've never wanted to deceive him. It's just that there are things I can't tell him, things I did before I met him.'

'Like what?'

So Honey tells Vita about the boat and the explosion. She doesn't say what she was doing there or why, she just tells her about the blast, that it was an accident, that the boat's owner may be after her and that she's sure she saw him earlier today standing on the opposite side of the road to the office. She also tells her about her visit to the medium and what she said about the fall and about being found. She says nothing about her mother though, or the child. It is a kind of half-truth, half-lie, but it has to do. She doubts she'll ever be ready to tell anyone the rest of it.

'My God,' Vita says. 'There's more to you than meets the eye, isn't there?'

Honey bristles at this. Now the words have been spoken, she feels surprisingly light-headed as she says, 'I guess there's more to all of us than meets the eye. Even you, Vita. We all have stories to tell, don't we?'

Vita nods at this and places the tube of paint down carefully on her work table. 'We sure do,' she says, 'we sure do. And Boyd knows nothing of this? About the boat, or the medium?'

'No, I told him the medium had said everything was going to be OK.'

'Yes,' she says, 'he told me what you'd told him.'

'Did he? I hadn't realised he'd done that. You won't say anything though, will you, Vita? You must promise me. He must never know. I've only ever lied to protect him. Well, not lied exactly; it's just I've never told him the truth. I can't, I just can't.'

Vita hesitates, taps her paintbrush on her glasses and says slowly. 'I know I'll probably live to regret this but OK, I promise.'

Then there's another pause and Honey asks, 'Well?' She can feel her phone buzzing in her handbag. Most likely it's Boyd ringing to see where she is. He's probably got back by now and is in the house turning on the rest of the lights, checking what's on TV, getting out the takeaway menu. Her heart stings with love for him and the life they're living together. 'Please,' she says again. 'Please will you do it, paint my picture?'

And, astonishingly, Vita says, 'Yes. OK. I'll do it.' And then she adds, 'You want it to be a surprise, I expect.'

It wasn't a question but still Honey answers it. 'Yes,' she says. 'I do.

So perhaps we could work on it while he's doing evening viewings, or is visiting his mum. What do you think?'

'It will be tricky to find the time.'

Although Vita's said yes, it's obvious she's still not making it easy.

'I know it will and I'm really grateful.'

'I don't want your thanks.'

'I'll pay you.'

'I don't want your money either.'

Vita is a mystery. Right at that moment Honey doesn't think she'll ever understand Boyd's wife, but says, 'Thank you,' again anyway.

'I told you I don't want your thanks.' Vita picks up her brush again and this time she puts it behind her ear and squeezes some paint from the tube she was playing with earlier. 'Look, I'd better get on,' she says. 'And so should you. Boyd will be wondering where you are.'

'OK, shall I let you know when he's next due out in the evening or if I plan to take time off work and if you're free …'

'Yes, yes,' Vita replies, waving a tube of paint in the air.

Honey takes it that she's been dismissed and so she leaves, closing the door quietly behind her. In the distance she can see the lights are on in the house and, as she crosses the small patio where they'd had dinner on their first night here, she can see Boyd moving about the kitchen. He's putting something into the sink and his body fills the window. Although she can see him, he obviously can't see her yet.

'Hello Boyd,' she says as she steps into the kitchen.

'Hello love,' he replies, kissing her on the mouth. 'Where have you been?'

'Chatting to Vita.'

'Oh, that's nice,' he says. 'Now, which continent shall we visit tonight?'

'I fancy Chinese.'

'Perfect.'

And he kisses her again.

Vita

When Colin asks me if I'm sure I've made the right decision in agreeing to paint Honey there's no judgement in his voice. It's not: '*Are* you sure ...?' or even, 'Are you *sure* ...?' He is just curious and I like him very much for this.

We're walking. Around us people in their houses are doing what people do on Sunday evenings: some are eating, others watching TV (I've always hated *Antiques Roadshow* with a passion), some may be hunched in front of their laptops checking off those last few emails from Friday. But Colin and I are walking, of all places, to a church.

He's persuaded me to go with him to a choral thing, something by Mendelssohn apparently and I'm not sure about it, not sure at all. But, in the spirit of trying new things I've agreed to go.

I haven't changed; am still wearing my red wool dress and clogs. I did re-plait my hair, clean my glasses and wash my hands. The cursed dog I'm painting at the moment will have to wait until tomorrow.

As we turn into Upper Church Lane he asks other, more direct kinds of questions. 'Have you,' he says, 'agreed a timeframe for the picture? I know you're busy with the animals. You mustn't let this distract you. I guess she's not paying?'

Against my better judgement, and once again, I have a craving for

142

him to reach out and take hold of my hand. This surprises me because I rarely feel anything like this. I ball my hands into fists and let my arms swing by my side as though I'm marching and say, 'A rough one. Yes. We have to do it when Boyd's not there. It's supposed to be a surprise.'

I realise I haven't answered his first question so say, 'You asked if I'm sure. Well I am. It'll be all right. It's nothing major.'

But I do wonder if I'm being totally honest with myself. What I can't tell Colin is how my sorry heart melted when Honey stood before me, her head to one side, her eyes huge. She looked terrified and childlike and there is, I acknowledge, something about Honey which brings out feelings in me I've been suppressing for years. It's stupid of me, I know. And it's dangerous; I shouldn't allow myself to feel this way. It is all shades of wrong.

I'd been determined not to get involved in either Boyd's or Honey's lives, but the mornings I spend with Boyd and the odd balance Honey displays between worldliness and victim unsettles me, even more so now Honey's told me about her past. It's shifted the emphasis between us and I feel as though I should actually be the strongest of the three of us; I never expected to be in this position, not in a million years.

Every time I think of what happened to her and what is happening to her now, my heart flutters and parts of me feel like they're melting; my knees go soft, the edges of my ears burn as if calamity is just about to strike. They say this is how parents feel when they think of the dangers their kids face, when they understand how precarious their safety is, how something awful can happen in the split second you're not looking and, after all, I know all about that, don't I?

They say we're hard-wired to protect those we love and that with love comes a fierce burning in our bones that means we will grab on to a toddler who's standing too close to the edge of a pond, that however much at fault our loved one might be we will puff out our chests and stand up to anyone who threatens them, who seeks to diminish them in their own eyes; we will stare down an attacker or retaliate with strength we didn't know we had if it will save someone we love from harm. And it's only afterwards, when we realise the full import of what we've done and what we've risked, we are blinded by the flashing lights behind our eyes and our breath comes in short, sharp bursts as we say, 'What if? What if I hadn't done that, been there, intervened? What if it had all gone horribly wrong?'

But right now I'm walking with Colin and I've agreed to paint Honey's portrait. This, I tell myself, has to be enough for now.

Colin's wearing a moss green corduroy jacket with leather patches on the elbows. You'd think it would look naff, but it doesn't. Colin always looks stylish and unruffled: long legs under designer jeans, a black polo shirt, his tawny skin. He looks every inch the architect he is.

Before I got to know him I'd obviously a) thought he was gay and b) assumed he worked in finance. But in both these things I'd been wrong and now, knowing him as I do, it makes sense that he's firmly, but undemandingly, heterosexual, and an architect; it is the only profession that would suit him. He runs a small practice, which is just him, and Beryl who answers the phones and does the books. He does house extensions mostly, sometimes office conversions and the odd barn, but what he really hankers for, or so he's told me, is the chance to work on a ground-breaking design, the type that'll get him noticed by RIBA and, more importantly, Kevin McCloud, or as Colin refers to him with a rare kind of bite, 'Kevin Fucking McCloud'.

Colin had briefly been married to Suzanne, they'd had no children and the marriage ended in an amicable divorce. He's never told me why and doesn't seem to keep in touch with his ex-wife. We never talk about this either and this suits me fine.

'As long as you're OK with it,' Colin says now. It's been so long since either of us last said anything that I've almost forgotten what we were talking about.

'I am,' I say.

We've reached the church and are joining a line of people walking up the path to it. Suddenly I falter. I hadn't realised it would affect me this way.

'Colin …'

'Yes,' he turns to face me.

'I'm …' but I can't say it.

I haven't been in a church for nearly seven years and never quite understood why I chose to have the service in a church then anyway. After all, I wasn't – I'm not – religious and wasn't brought up to believe in anything other than the practical scientific theories of evolution and human greed. There has never been an atom of faith in my life and, I'd long thought, this was just as well. Just imagine if I had believed? Just think how much more the betrayal would have hurt.

'I do hope you're going to like it,' Colin says, guiding me, his hand under my elbow. We sit on the spectacularly uncomfortable pews and wait for the concert to start. And, as we wait, I browse the programme and then lift my eyes to the ceiling – its vaulted wonder, the huge stretches of wood, the massive blocks of stone, the carvings and the gilt and the colours and the majesty of it. I can't breathe. It's all too much. Boyd would never have brought me to a place like this.

And then the music starts. It's Mendelssohn's 'Hora Est; Te Deum;

Ave Maria' and, by the look of things it lasts a whole fucking hour. How I'm going to get through it, I don't know. But, as the voices lift singly and in harmony and, as they tell some sort of story I can't fathom, my heart quickens, there is that tightness in the middle of my breastbone again and I give myself up to it. I'm barely aware of Colin by my side, sitting steadfastly, listening carefully. Instead I'm lost in something that's fearful and wonderful, something full of a nameless grief and an irrepressible joy.

It's as though whatever it is I've been avoiding admitting to is taking shape in front of me, is becoming something tangible that I could, if I wanted to, reach out and touch.

Dusk is settling outside, the colours in the stained glass windows deepen and, if I could cry, I would do this too. I haven't cried in years and, although every fibre of my body is urging me to, I can't.

When it's over, we leave, say polite things to one another, remark on the church, the music, the others in the audience. We walk slowly back to Colin's house where we make some supper and open a bottle of wine. To all intents and purposes the evening is continuing calmly, but inside I'm still reeling.

Later, we have sex. I can't call it making love. It's efficient and tidy and I relish having Colin's firm, sleek body between my legs, like the way he tastes of cheese and wine. I like the way his fingers play me as though I'm some kind of musical instrument.

But afterwards, as we lie in the quiet of the house, I imagine I can hear Boyd's and Honey's soft breathing next door. It's almost as though their heartbeats are matching mine and I don't like this, not at all.

'You OK?' Colin asks at last. 'You've been very quiet this evening.'

'I'm fine.'

'Have I done anything wrong?'

'Of course not.'

'So you're happy?'

Am I? Can I honestly say to him that I am? I thought I was and that everything was in its place, that I was immune and resolute, but then there's Honey's request, and the voices and the church and the memories and there's Boyd next door, his arms around a woman who is not me.

'Yes,' I say. 'I'm happy.'

And in my head Colin is asking me to stay the night, he's saying, 'I want to wake up with you. I've never woken up in the morning with you.' And he's asking me to tell Boyd about us, for it all to be in the open so we don't have to sneak around any more, so I don't have to close his front door quietly so that no one can hear me, so I don't have to creep into my own house in the middle of the night afraid that this, whatever it is I am doing with him, will be discovered.

Yes, I want all this, but he doesn't say these things. Instead he places his warm lips on my neck and says, 'That's OK then. As long as you're happy, I'm happy.'

* * *

It's ten days later. September has slipped into October; the horse chestnut leaves are turning and it's the day of Honey's first sitting.

Honey's taken the afternoon off work, ostensibly to meet a friend for a cup of tea and a piece of cake. It was, she told me, the best lie she could come up with.

'Pretty crap lie,' I said to her under my breath as Boyd stacked the dishwasher the previous evening. 'Do you even have any friends that Boyd doesn't know about?'

'You'd be surprised,' Honey had said winking and smiling at me.

Damn her, I'd thought. How can she look so innocent while saying something so false and knowing?

Damn her, I think, as Honey settles herself on the stool in my studio. It's sunny out but the sun is low and mellow, not the hot high heat of summer – a good light for painting. It casts a gentle kind of shadow across Honey's face.

I start to sketch.

'Try not to move too much.'

'Sorry.'

'That's OK.'

It's quiet in the studio, just the faint murmur of music from the radio and a silence between us that's just the wrong side of comfortable and then Honey says, 'Tell me about how you and Boyd met.'

'Why?'

'I'm curious. He's told me some things.'

'What things?'

'About the collective where you worked, how he sold it out from under you, how he liked what you believed in.'

'He said that?'

'Yes. He liked your passion.'

'They were interesting times,' I say, tipping my head to one side to look at Honey from a slightly different angle. 'Can you move a fraction to your right?'

'OK.'

I tap my pencil against my glasses and say, 'We were very young.'

Honey stays silent and, for want of anything better to do and to avoid the uncomfortable silence of a moment ago, although it goes against my better judgement, I carry on. Each word seems an effort, but it's a relief to say them. 'We were so sure we were going to change the world. There was me, a guy called Barney and one called Hugo. We were the main three I guess. Others drifted through, but we rented the space, did the odd commission to help pay our way. It was always so fucking cold in there: huge high ceilings, badly fitting windows. Can't remember what we ate but we drank a lot of red wine, smoked a lot too. I felt marvellous to tell you the truth. As far away from my parents as I could be.'

'Your parents?'

'They live in Scotland.'

'Boyd's never mentioned them.'

I pause and look at the floor. I've often wondered what he's told her about him and me. Not much by the sounds of it. But has he shared the awful part, the part with all the pain and confusion in it? Maybe he has and Honey doesn't know what to say. But, surely he's said something to her about why what happened to us happened? I daren't chance it just in case he hasn't. It's not my place to, and anyway I don't want to. Instead I say, 'I think you'll find there's quite a bit Boyd hasn't talked about.'

I regret saying this as soon as the words are out of my mouth but Honey's still sitting peacefully, the light falling in waves over her.

'He told me,' Honey says after a short pause, 'that he came to value the place. Your landlord was throwing you out?'

It's good to be back on safer ground and so I say, 'Yes, the bastard. I remember the first time I saw Boyd though. I thought him a bit of a knob to tell you truth. He was so ungainly, so eager to please. Like a St Bernard puppy.'

'So how did you get together?'

Do I really want to tell her this? I don't like to think why he hasn't. 'He trod on my picture,' I say.

'He did what?'

'I was drying a canvas against the wall and he stumbled and put his whole fucking foot through it. You can imagine his embarrassment.'

'I can.' Honey is smiling now, her head bent in that birdlike way again. 'I bet he wouldn't stop apologising!'

'No, not until I agreed to go out for a drink with him.'

Neither of us speaks for a while and I say, 'I took him to the most shocking place I could think of. It was a bikers' pub. The local Hells Angels used to go there. I asked him for a snakebite and bless him, he had no idea what it was.'

The light is starting to change very slightly and, in the garden, a blackbird has set up an alarm call. I study what I've done so far. A few lines, a suggestion of the girl's head, those cheekbones, eyes. Already I know this picture will be a good one because I'm good at this. Even painting my husband's lover is something I will do well. Perhaps, I think, as I outline the side of Honey's neck that's bathed in the remaining light, it's because I can see her through Boyd's eyes.

And I remember the smell of the pub and the beat of the music where he and I had had our first drink, him balancing his large body on a barstool and saying good things, things that were intelligent and that mattered about art and property and ambition and about relishing the quiet moments and how I'd wondered briefly as I sipped my pint of snakebite why I was beginning to like this unlikely man so very much.

'Is it odd?' Honey asks.

'Is what odd?'

'Talking about him to me.'

'You'd think it would be, but it isn't. Not really.'

But it is and I hate it because of where it might lead.

There is another pause. The only sound is that of graphite on paper.

'I've not had many friends,' Honey says.

And, although I have no real idea where this comment came from, I find myself replying, 'I haven't either. Not really. I was quite close to Trixie for a while, but we've kind of drifted apart lately.'

'Life can do that to you.'

If I was to analyse this conversation and break it down into its component parts, I would realise the things that were missing, the things we didn't tell one another: anything about Honey's parents for instance, or mine; my wedding to Boyd and how Belle had boycotted it; the sharp wind that blew around my ankles as I stood on the registry steps; the day we moved into Albert Terrace and the rain and sitting in front of the fire drinking whisky from the bottle and making love on the floor with Boyd's body warm and damp and covering mine.

I didn't tell her how Boyd had built this studio for me, laying brick upon brick, cementing himself to me, how he positioned it so the windows would face north, how he measured them to be just so for the light, how he dug the path that links the studio to the back gate and how he cleared the path down the side of the park so I could wheel my bike down it. I didn't tell her about when I painted his portrait and how he'd sat for me, his face that blend of animation and peace, that almost-smile, his eyebrow, the one that lifts and falls as if it's got a mind of its own. I didn't tell her how he'd promised we'd have at least five children, take holidays by the sea, or that we had had sex here, right here, on the floor, near where she is sitting and that he'd come in me and it had trickled out of me and been warm against my thighs.

I also didn't tell her about Colin and the comfortable sex and easy conversations I have with him. And I didn't tell her what happened in the room where she now sleeps with Boyd, or ask whether Boyd has told her any of it. Nor did I tell her how sometimes I listen to them in the night and imagine Boyd's body on hers or how I wait for her to have that dream again so that once more I can hear the sound that sounds like a child crying in my house.

However, for all these things that separate us, I think, as I lean up to erase a sketch mark from the paper, there is the one immutable thing we have in common: Boyd.

'I think,' I say, 'we ought to leave it there. He may be back soon.'

The sitting has lasted an hour and a half but it seems like only a few seconds have gone by.

'OK,' Honey says easily, slipping off the stool. 'Can I see it?'

'I'd rather you didn't.'

'Oh, OK.'

'Not yet, anyway.'

I put down my pencil and fold the cover of the pad over the drawing. 'It's only a preliminary sketch,' I say.

'Can I bring you down a cup of tea, or something?' Honey asks.

'That would be nice, thank you.'

And then Honey's gone, with her inexplicable past, leaving me with mine, wrong-footed again. I'd thought this would be a business transaction: I would paint Honey's picture, Honey would sit quietly while I did so. I hadn't expected to feel like someone had come and taken the box where I keep my most secret self and started prising the lid open and that all the unspoken things that are lying inside it would be at risk of flying out.

The mask I wear when I'm smiling at people on the bus, or saying

'Thank you' to the ladies in the dry cleaners, or when I'm with Colin, or Honey, or Boyd, is slipping. I can feel it starting to peel and, for all the mess and the canvases and the pictures of bloody animals and my bicycle and the radio still playing quietly in the background, the studio suddenly seems emptier than it's ever been. I never expected to feel this type of loneliness again.

Honey

The weather's unseasonably warm for October; a kind of Indian summer. The sky is cloudless, high, a washed-out blue and, in the sunshine, it feels like it could still be July.

It's been a good day at the office: Warwick Road completed, Boyd received a new instruction in Silver Street, but Honey is uneasy, she feels that any moment Trixie or Boyd will notice that she's constantly looking out of the window, stopping by the doorway and gazing out into the street.

She is watching for Reuben to come back, waiting for him to do so.

She's lost count of the number of times she's imagined him there: a flash of a jacket, him walking by, his slight limp, the colour of his skin. Then her breaths come in short, sharp bursts and she has to do something to distract herself. Surely Boyd and Trixie must have noticed. It's getting harder and harder to keep on pretending that everything is OK. The medium's warnings sit heavily on her shoulders, her heart flips giddily; she has no idea how much longer she can go on.

And then Trixie surprises her by saying, 'Hey Honey. Do you fancy grabbing a drink after work today? We haven't been out together for

ages – if at all, come to think of it. We should, shouldn't we? If you're not doing anything this evening that is?'

'Oh, that sounds lovely,' Honey says. 'I'll tell Boyd when he comes back from the viewing. You're right, we should go out. I know I could use a drink!'

* * *

The lighting in the wine bar is odd, pools of intense white light beaming down onto the wooden floor and, outside the perimeters of these pools, the rest of the space is in shadow. They're sitting in a booth towards the back of the bar, a scrubbed pine table between them. On the table there's a single lighted candle, a salt and pepper pot, a rack of serviettes and a menu leaning up against the wall.

'What would you like?' Trixie asks.

Trixie's left her car parked at the back of the office. Boyd has said he'll give her a lift home when he comes to pick Honey up and Trixie has said she'll get a taxi into work tomorrow morning.

Giving a rare insight into her private life she'd also said, 'Can't really afford it, going out or paying for the cab, but I deserve a treat don't I? And it's a relief not having to …'

Here she'd stalled and hadn't said any more.

Honey is studying the menu, is glad she's wearing her short-sleeved cream mohair sweater, black leggings and knee-length low-heeled boots: it's a look that fits in here. She's not wearing any jewellery but has outlined her eyes in kohl, in what Boyd calls her Claudia Winkleman kind of way, and has dabbed frosted pink lipstick on her lips.

'Mmmm,' she says, resting her chin on her palm, 'a glass of white wine I think. What about you? I'll get them if you like.'

'No, it's OK,' Trixie says hurriedly. 'Think I'll have the same. Anything to eat?'

'No, thanks and you must at least let me pay for my drink,' Honey says. 'I'd happily pay for yours, too.'

'I said it's all right,' Trixie snaps and then says, more softly, 'if we go Dutch that'll be fine. I'll go and order for us, shall I?'

Trixie looks tired and the skirt she's wearing is worn, a bit of the hem has come loose. She looks like a slightly faded version of the woman who interviewed Honey all those months ago.

Honey closes the menu and smiles at Trixie as she stands up and starts to make her way across the room, travelling through the spot-lit areas until she reaches the bar.

As Trixie's waiting for the drinks to be poured, Honey notices her look back to where she's sitting but then she gets distracted by her phone and is checking emails when Trixie says, 'Here you go,' and puts the glasses down on the table.

'Ooh, thank you!' Honey lifts hers and taps it against Trixie's. 'Cheers!'

'Cheers!' Trixie replies.

They drink.

'This is nice,' Honey says. 'I was saying to Vita recently that I don't actually have many friends. Perils of being a bit of a nomad I guess.'

'Guess so.' Trixie takes another sip. She doesn't speak and bizarrely Honey feels a nip of unease, a need to fill the space and silence between them with words.

The wine bar is filling up around them; knots of men are standing at the bar drinking lager from long glasses, and the tables towards the front are filling up with couples and a group of friends on a girls' night out. There is the babble of voices and the soft bass of the bar's background music.

The wine is slipping down nicely; Honey is relaxing and her edges are beginning to soften.

'Um,' Trixie says. 'You said the word 'nomad' just now. What did you mean by that?'

'Did I?' Honey's taken one of the paper napkins from the rack and is folding it into squares, half then half again; she presses it between her palms and looks up at Trixie. 'Did I really?' she says again.

Trixie takes another drink, leaving another gap in the conversation. Again, that strange need to fill it comes over Honey. Her vision is getting blurry and she's feeling raggedy at the edges. It's a nice feeling though, as if her muscles are melting.

Camilla's warnings about club drugs had been frequent and loud, but where Honey is now is a separate world to Camilla's. This sense of peace and wellbeing is because Honey is, for once, relaxed, happy. Alcohol can have a greater effect when you're contented than when you're miserable. At least this is what Honey has learned over the years.

'Well, you know when I came for my interview,' Honey says, 'I mentioned that my past hadn't been orthodox, I guess that's what I meant. I remember you were so kind. You said that we're all made up of fault lines and scars, or something like that. You were the first person who'd not pressed me for details and I really appreciated that. It was hard enough being at the interview and,' she pauses, 'that was before I'd even met Boyd!'

'Ah, Boyd,' Trixie says. She runs her fingers down the outside of her glass, chasing the beads of condensation. She's almost finished her drink; Honey, on the other hand, still has half of hers left. 'So,' Trixie continues, 'you were saying about your past …'

Honey takes a large mouthful of wine. It's like when she was talking to Vita; she imagines she will feel lighter if she confesses. So she does.

'You,' she says, 'you and Vita are the only people I've ever told and this is because I trust you both. I've never had the luxury of being able to trust anyone before and you must promise not to tell Boyd. Ever. Promise me?'

'Of course.' Trixie says. 'You can trust me.'

And so she tells Trixie about the man on the boat and the explosion and how she had to jump to safety and swim to shore and how she believes he is coming to get her.

'I've seen him,' she says, 'outside the office. On the other side of the street. It's just like the medium said it would be.'

'Ah, the medium,' Trixie reaches out and takes hold of both of Honey's hands.

The napkin Honey's been folding is a discarded, crumpled mess on the table by now but Trixie's hand are warm. She holds Honey's for a few seconds and then says, 'I'll get us some more drinks, shall I? Then you must tell me everything the medium said. I've been anxious to know but didn't dare ask.'

'No, I'll get the drinks.' And Honey stands quickly and strides across to the bar. She feels a bit dizzy as she approaches the bar, blinks once, then twice.

The crowds are thickening, the sound of voices and music is getting louder, the wine isn't as chilled this time and it doesn't taste the same as the first drink, but still Honey drinks it as she tells Trixie about the medium's predictions about the step and how she's been told she'll fall and how the man from the boat will find her. The words trip off her tongue as if they have a life of their own; she couldn't stop them even if she wanted to.

'You poor thing,' Trixie says as Honey finally finishes. 'How have you borne this? Did you tell Boyd what the medium said?'

'Of course not. I told him she said everything will be fine. I wouldn't want to worry him, he's too good for that.'

'Yes,' Trixie says. 'He is. But Vita knows, you say?'

'I told her what I've told you and actually,' Honey pauses, tips her head on one side and says, 'it's a relief to have done so. I thought I was strong enough to keep my own counsel on this, but obviously I'm not. I …' she pauses again, '… once hoped I would be other than I am.'

Boyd comes to collect them about half an hour later. She and Trixie spend the intervening time talking about work and Boyd's mother. And then they're in the car and Boyd is driving, his large hands on the wheel, his head turning every now and again to talk quietly to Honey sitting next to him in the front. She can feel Trixie's presence in the back but everything is getting hazy, it feels like she's floating. It's relief she thinks, relief at having told Trixie some of the truth. She realises Trixie hasn't said anything about herself, and nor had Honey asked. She feels a little guilty about this.

Honey doesn't actually remember much about the journey home; obviously Boyd was in the car and she seems to recall him talking to her, his voice low and soft. She does remember, however, Trixie leaning forward and touching Boyd on the shoulder as they pulled up outside her house. 'Thank you for the lift,' she said and Honey remembers them waiting in the car until Trixie had unlocked her front door, stepped inside, turned – a silhouette against the orangey light from her hallway – and waved.

But not much more than this. She thinks Vita poured her a glass of water when they got in and that she said something sharp and disapproving to her. She also thinks music was playing, something that sounded like Bob Dylan. She didn't know Vita liked Bob Dylan.

She also thinks Boyd made love to her; recalls feeling wanton and snaking her arms around his neck in bed and thinks she cried out, but can't be sure. She also seems to remember Boyd sitting on the edge of the bed sometime during the night and that his shoulders were moving as though he was weeping. But this may have been a dream. What she does know is that she didn't dream about the explosion and that she woke feeling like shit with Boyd standing over her with a cup of coffee in his hand.

'Good Lord woman, you were in a fine state last night,' he says tenderly, putting the mug down on her bedside cabinet.

All she can say is, 'I'm sorry,' but it seems a feeble attempt at an apology. All she'd had were two glasses of wine and yet she'd felt this soaring, this huge feeling of liberation, this loosening of all the ties that had seemed to bind her. As she was unburdening herself to Trixie, it was as though the puppet master who'd been in the shadows for so long had been banished, the strings he'd been holding had been cut and she'd morphed from marionette to real person, someone new and unblemished, someone who had nothing to fear.

Through the foggy bits in her mind come these recollections and she wonders whether, were she to tell Boyd about her past, she'd feel this same sense of being reborn. Would she, could she ever dare to?

She'd once read somewhere that it's harder to share your secret with someone than it is for that someone to hear it. And whoever it was, was right. There's that moment when the words are out in the air and can't be unspoken and are preparing to fall and then when they do, there is that moment when the person listening decides what to do with the information and nine times out of ten, it doesn't change anything. Trixie and she will go on as usual, just like she and Vita are. By unburdening herself the way she did, she hasn't burdened either of them, of this she is sure, but Boyd is another matter altogether. No, she will never be able to risk him knowing. He is looking at her with such love, such trust. She will do anything to keep both of these things.

'I think you'd better take the day off today,' Boyd says, as he takes a shirt from the wardrobe and starts unbuttoning it and slipping it from its hanger.

'No, I'll be fine,' Honey murmurs, having to close her eyes again. The room is not so much spinning now, but is rocking not-so-gently from side to side. She is aware of the cup of coffee he's brought her, but the thought of drinking it makes her feel yet more nauseous.

'As your boss, I insist.' Boyd is putting on the shirt as he says this and she watches the way the material covers the flesh of him and finds that tears have sprung unbidden to her eyes. 'Whatever is the matter?' he asks, picking out a tie.

'Nothing. But maybe you're right. I'll stay home for now. Maybe I'll come in later.'

'No, take the whole day. Sleep it off, take a bath. We'll do something nice this evening, OK?'

She can't quite fathom how he's really feeling. His voice is still gentle and kind and he could be thinking this amusing rather than sinister and yet …

… yet she notices a tension and wariness in his shoulders as he moves around the room that she's not sure she's seen before.

But she's too sleepy and hungover to think about this too deeply and so she gives in to it and eases herself back down the bed. He comes over and arranges the duvet around her.

161

'I'll see you later, love,' he says and then he kisses her on the forehead and leaves the room, quietly clicking the door behind him.

Honey dozes. The room fills with the musty scent of sleep, dust and hangover and, when eventually she wakes, the light behind the curtains tells her it's around midday. She yawns and stretches and tries to move her head. It's feeling better and, in the distance, she hears the sound of Vita climbing the stairs. She holds her breath. She hadn't expected Vita to be home today.

Then there's a knock on the bedroom door.

'Come in.'

Vita doesn't, but just pops her head around it instead.

'Came to ask if you needed anything,' she said, her tone brusque and business-like.

'Oh, that's really kind of you. I'd love a cup of coffee. I couldn't face the one Boyd brought me earlier.'

'Oh, OK. I'm only asking because Boyd rang me and told me to.'

And she's gone, her footsteps retreating down the stairs: clump, clump, clump. There is nothing ambiguous or subtle about Vita sometimes and it often puzzles Honey as to how the brushstrokes on her paintings can be so beautiful and delicate.

Honey burrows back under the duvet and listens to the sounds of Vita moving about downstairs. There's a knock on the front door and Honey hears voices. Vita's talking to another woman, their words rise and fall but Honey can't make out what's being said. For a moment she thinks whoever it is must have gone because there's been a period of silence, but then the voices start up again – some murmurings, followed by a sharp laugh and then the front door closes again and it's quiet.

It's odd but she hasn't been lazy like this for ages. In the old days she wouldn't think twice about staying in bed all morning, but recently, the new her – the her who is with Boyd – has been driven and focussed and organised. She's liked this new version.

However, lying there waiting for her coffee she lets her mind drift back to those old days and her heart starts knocking in panic. Suddenly she feels unwashed and sticky, she feels dirty. She grabs hold of the duvet cover and clenches it in her fists as though it's a lifeline. As the saying goes, you never truly know what you've got until it's gone, or if not gone, then at risk of going.

Her thoughts are interrupted by Vita delivering her drink.

'Here you go,' she says, coming into the room this time and putting the mug down next to the other cup by the bed. Honey notices Vita doesn't look at her, or the bed.

In Vita's other hand is a bouquet of flowers: large white lilies and tiny coronets of gypsophila.

'Trixie brought these round for you,' Vita says. 'There's a card.' She puts the flowers at the bottom of the bed.

'Oh,' Honey replies, rearranging the pillows around her head like a consumptive Victorian heroine; this isn't her at all, she thinks. She's better, much better, than this and yet she says, 'Thank you. Gosh, that's kind of her too.'

'Boyd must have told her you'd had a bad reaction to the wine, or something.'

'It is odd,' I say. 'I only had two glasses.'

'Mmmm.'

Honey can tell Vita doesn't necessarily believe her but then Vita's gone. She doesn't say goodbye, or see you later, she just goes, leaving the coffee on the bedside table, and the flowers at Honey's feet.

The card says, 'Hope you feel better soon. Thanks for a lovely evening, Trixie.'

Honey will put them in some water later but for now she looks at them, at the waxy petals of the lilies and the blooms of baby's breath and feels a strange kind of unease.

By the time she gets up and has had her bath, Vita has gone out. She makes some soup and sips it watching some inane programme on TV. She checks her horoscope. It says, 'You will receive an unexpected gift today.' She checks the time, it's almost four. Boyd should be home soon.

Vita

I didn't expect this. When Boyd and Honey moved in, I expected my life to remain unchanged. I would work, go out to exhibitions and galleries, have sex with Colin now and again; I would eat the same food, drink sparingly, do my garden as always and then they would leave. But now it seems my life is concentrating itself once again on this house and the people in it. Boyd's presence is comforting and comfortable. Honey is quirky and full of a contradictory kind of poise; some days she's relaxed and happy, others she's wired and watchful. I find I am interested in and confused by both these people and the vigour and uncertainty they've brought with them.

I feel responsible for them in some strange way, that I am the adult and they the children. Like I had when Honey had been in my studio, I feel the loneliness of being the one in the middle not able to tell Boyd what I know, not able to help protect Honey. And, I keep telling myself, I shouldn't want to do either. It is not my place to. I am a free agent; nothing should be able to touch me, not now.

I feel cramped by their presence in the house, the scattering of their belongings, and I feel liberated by it. I have no fucking idea what I'm doing and, when Honey is in bed with her inexplicable hangover and Boyd is out at work, I am unsettled, as if something is out of alignment.

I've just taken the flowers Trixie brought round up to Honey and texted Colin, 'You around later?'

He replies straight away, 'Yes. Do you fancy doing something this evening?'

'Maybe.'

'OK, I'll text you in a bit.'

My exchanges with Colin are not loaded with ambiguity or open to misinterpretation and this pleases me. I hope we will go out tonight. I've seen an advert in the window of the local bookshop saying that the author of a book about Ancient Rome I've recently read is giving a talk. Maybe we can go to that, or maybe not.

However, there is a gap, an absence I can't put my finger on. The weather's still good and so I decide to go for a walk. I can't face the studio today; not the portrait of Honey nor the picture of the stupid little Pekingese I'm doing for a friend of the woman who owns the Cockapoo.

And so I leave the house and make my way to the end of Albert Terrace; I'll do a circular route, ending up back in the park, like I've done before. I remember why I used to walk it too. After the time I'd spent with my face to the wall, there'd been the walking. I'd walked and walked, in the mornings, afternoons, at night. I'd left without telling Boyd where I was going or when I'd be back, I'd left him behind in so many ways. And yet he'd always be there waiting for me when I got in and he'd help me take off my coat and then touch me briefly on the shoulder as I turned and moved away from him. I hadn't let myself be consoled and I hadn't consoled him either.

By the time I reach the park, school is out and there are knots of kids around the swings, their mothers sitting at a distance in the unexpected autumn sun. I can hear the children's shouts but see them only as blurs of school uniform against green grass. I refuse to watch them, I can't bear to. It's like this every time I come here; I know I shouldn't, but somehow I can't keep away.

And then one hurtles into me, coming at me from an angle. He's obviously not looking where he's going.

'Oof,' I say, as he crashes into my legs and topples over onto the ground, his body still plump with childhood, his skin pale, one sock down, the other up.

He starts to cry.

'Hey,' I say, bending down to pick him up. 'It's OK. No damage done. Look, there's no blood.'

The boy gazes up at me and then down, firstly at his knees, then at the soft palms of his hands. I'm right, there's no blood and I wonder if secretly he's disappointed by this. The tears are hovering on his eyelashes. He looks bewilderingly beautiful.

'Off you go,' I say. 'Best go and find your mum, eh?'

He nods, his lips trembling. He wants to be brave, I want to hug him to me. He's around six years old, I'm in my forties and yet neither of us really knows how to behave. He runs off and I wait until I see him safely reconciled with his mother.

When I get home, Boyd is back. He's left his briefcase and jacket on the sofa at the back of the kitchen. I fill the kettle noisily, crashing it against the sink and slamming it down on the counter, expecting him to appear and ask after my day like he used to do.

'Stop it,' I tell myself as I wait for the kettle to boil. 'Why the fuck would he?'

I check my phone, there's no message from Colin as yet and this surprises me. I'd thought he may have been in touch by now.

I hesitate, uncharacteristically uncertain. The incident in the park has unsettled me further.

'Fuck,' I say out loud. 'Fuck, fuck, fuck,' and, leaving the kettle to switch itself off, I stomp upstairs to my room.

Boyd and Honey are talking but, as I reach the top of the stairs, there's something about Boyd's voice which makes me pause. I don't want to listen but can't help it.

'Were you?' Honey is asking.

I hear the creak of the bed as Boyd sits on it, can imagine his face, the lift of his eyebrow, his full lips.

'Well?' Honey asks again. 'I can't remember exactly, but I think you were crying. You were sitting in the same kind of place as you are now, your head in your hands. And you were crying. Weren't you?'

'Do you ...' Boyd says quietly, 'think you may have been dreaming. You were a bit tipsy!'

'I was more than tipsy and I have no idea how it happened. I've even wondered whether there was something wrong with my drink!' She laughs as she says this, an easy, light laugh and then, serious again, she says, 'But if you were upset, you can tell me. You know that, don't you? Did I do or say anything to upset you?'

I rest a hand against the wall and wait. I should move on, go into my room, change my clothes ready for when Colin gets in touch. Yes, I think. These are the practical, sensible things I should do and yet I wait, convinced in some strange way that what will happen next will have something to do with me.

'No,' Boyd replies. 'It's nothing you've done.'

'What is it, then? Is there a problem at work, something you haven't told me? Oh, shit, you're not ill, are you?'

My mind's-eye moves from the figure of my husband, as he sits on the bed, to Honey. I imagine Honey is standing by the window, the evening sun starting to fall in stripes across the carpet. Honey's head is tipped to one side in that bird-like way of hers. The flowers Trixie brought will be somewhere in the room, too.

'No. But there is something you should know. Something I should have told you ages ago.' Boyd's voice is low and quiet.

'You're scaring me now.'

'Don't be scared.'

I hold my breath. I know what's coming. So he hasn't told her then. I think back to the morning when he said what he said and I knocked my tea off the arm of the sofa. Had he been trying to say something about this then, that he hadn't told Honey and that I mustn't either. Shit, I think, how can this house survive seeing it's full to bursting with the three of us, our belongings, and so many unsaid things? Sometimes, in the middle of the night, I can feel it all pressing in on me; it's as though the house is going to explode.

But now Boyd is saying, 'It's just that sometimes being in this room gets to me.'

'This room? Why?'

'You once asked why Vita and I split up. Do you remember?'

'Yes,' Honey says in an almost-whisper that I have to strain to hear.

There is an agonising silence and then Boyd says, 'We had a child. A son. This was his room.'

As he says this, I expect the roof to collapse and the wall against which I am leaning to crumble. I expect a huge wind to rise and raindrops the size of fists to fall on my head. But this doesn't happen. Instead there is yet more silence, heavy and portentous. Whatever Honey says next will, I believe, shape the rest of our lives.

'My God, Boyd. You should have told me. Why didn't you tell me this?'

'I tried once, early on. That night you went running. Do you remember?

She pauses, then says, 'I remember.'

Stop it! The words are screaming inside my head. Stop talking about yourselves. Remember my boy, how it felt to hold him, the shade of blue his eyes were, a shade for which there is no word.

And then he tells her, or as much of it as he can. He can't know of my pain, the vacuum, the sheer magnitude of my loss, my rage, my never-ending search for someone to blame, for someone to fill the void. Loss: such a small word, such a massive, massive thing.

'His name was – is – William. We thought we'd end up calling him Will, but somehow he stayed as William. He looked like a Will, though. He had the most amazing blue eyes, Vita's eyes.'

'What happened?' Honey's voice is soft and loving and I hate her for it. How dare she feel pity, feel anything at all? What right has she?

'Sudden infant death. He died in his sleep when he was three months old.'

And again it's as though someone has come along and torn my heart from my chest. I can see the scatterings of broken ribs, the trails of blood, can hear the howls of my pain and of Boyd's as he holds our son's body: all that promise gone, a whole life gone, my life gone in one short moment.

I'd always believed that Boyd had not really understood the savagery of hoping every month that this would be the one when the dot, or the line or the words would tell me I was pregnant. I mean, how could he? It wasn't his body.

We'd left it late and I blamed myself for this. I can't remember now why it seemed so important that we did but eventually, everywhere around us, people were having kids. Trixie had had hers, the artists with whom I'd studied sent photos of round-faced, chubby-armed babies in their Christmas cards and I would pummel the flat of my stomach with my fists and ask myself why I hadn't.

Boyd had promised me a horde of children, five at least. We'd buy them bunk beds, extend into the loft, we might even move house. We'd talked about caravan holidays, burying them in sand up to their necks at the beach, us reading stories to them, the smell of cheese on toast for supper, doing homework by the fire. All this.

By the time we started trying I would have settled for just one. One precious child I could be a good parent to, a better parent than mine had been to me. And Boyd? I'd wanted Boyd to have a son. I'd wanted to peg their jeans (his vast, our son's tiny) on the line, to watch them kick a ball to one another in the park. I'd wanted Boyd to teach our son to drive. All this.

Then, eventually, I fell pregnant. I liked to imagine I knew when it had happened, that there'd been something special about the way we'd made love that particular night.

Boyd was flummoxed, as I'd imagined he'd be.

'I know it's what we wanted,' he said, 'but now it's here, is it OK to be scared?'

'Of course,' I'd replied. 'I'm terrified too.'

And I was. As I watched the stretching of my skin I was at times ecstatic, at others crippled by fear. And when the baby began to kick, it was hard to explain to Boyd what it was like; it was music and movement and flawless. I'd felt that my baby and I were dancing together, that I was already holding him in my arms, swaying, tracing figures of eight on the carpet and drawing in the sweet smell of his head, his tiny fist wrapped around my finger.

My spine slackened, my hips spread, my tummy button protruded, my breasts became full and round and hard. I was fuelled by a primal instinct and a huge ball of unnameable, unmanageable love. I'd waited so long for this.

We decorated the nursery pale yellow, bought a cot, a mobile of farmyard animals to hang over it, tiny white sleepsuits, packs of minute socks, a crib to put by our bed so I could reach over and gaze at him in the night. We got a baby monitor, muslin cloths, nappies. The house took on the appearance of a Mothercare store.

And then came the birth. I remember telling Trixie every last detail of the drive to the hospital, the waiting, the cannula in my wrist, Boyd pacing the room, the nurse with the cool, small hands, the rush of the last moments and then how William had arrived: bloody, marvellous, triumphant.

And I nursed him.

That raw pull of his mouth on my nipple, the delicious pain searing across my shoulder blades as he fed.

The solid mass of him, sturdy yet fragile against my bare skin.

And Trixie was there, with casseroles and clean laundry and she let me weep when I wanted to and shuffled Boyd out of the room, sending him on errands when he was being helpless and in the way.

And I watched Boyd with our son, his head cradled in Boyd's huge hands. I watched the tricky process of Boyd placing William on the changing mat, the intricate application of creams, the way Boyd would lower his lips and place a kiss on his son's belly.

And I imagined a future for me and my son. From the moment my eyes met his, I saw it stretching out in front of us: football, driving, girls, doors slamming, limbs lengthening, his first shave, his first job, how he'd call me 'Mum', his voice deep, a man's voice. I saw him become a father and hand me his child and I would see my son's face reflected back at me. All this.

And then there was the morning when I woke suddenly, breathless, afraid of the inexplicable silence from the baby monitor by the bed. Normally, I would hear a faint whistle or snuffle as William slept, the rustle of bedding, even a bird singing outside the window of his room. But that morning: nothing.

'Boyd?' I hissed. 'Boyd, there's something wrong.'

I threw back the bedcovers, my breasts full and leaking. William hadn't woken for his early morning feed as he normally did and I'd slept through; I hadn't been watchful. My heart was hammering.

'What?' Boyd answered, still sleepy.

'It's William. There's something wrong with William.'

And he was out of bed and at the door in one bound. His hair, I noticed, still tufted by sleep.

I remember how we knocked against one another as we turned into William's room and how, without being able to say how, I knew that my baby was dead.

And Boyd was holding William, placing him on the floor and massaging his heart, was lowering his lips to my son's mouth in a different sort of kiss. Then he lifted his face to look at me, grief already etched on it in what looked like black marker pen. 'Call an ambulance,' he said in the sliver of silence between my howls. 'Go. Do it now.'

And everyone was gentle with us: the paramedics, the hospital staff, our GP, the midwives, the counsellors, Trixie, the couple who lived in Colin's house before Colin. Everyone.

But however kind these people were, what no one could do was bring my baby back.

And now Boyd is saying, 'And nothing was the same again. How do you recover from something like that? That's why I've always said it's amazing we're still friends. There was so much damage, untold damage after he died. It's just that occasionally I can still feel him, here in this room. I'm sorry. I shouldn't I know. This is about you and me. I've done my mourning, or anyway I think I have. Last night was an aberration, nothing more.'

I can't bear to listen. After all, there is nothing Boyd can say that I don't already know, haven't already felt a million times. And I feel his betrayal again and again. Can he really have finished grieving? How dare he even consider it? How can his tears last night have been an aberration? Either he is lying or he's a cold and unfeeling bastard. I can't believe he is. The mornings we'd done the crossword together recently had been special and I'd thought I still knew him, but maybe we're both still acting; maybe we haven't actually forgiven one another yet.

And, as I creep into my room and silently close the door, I can imagine Honey walking over to where Boyd is sitting and wrapping her slender arms around his shoulders and breathing in his familiar, musky smell. I imagine Honey kissing Boyd, pulling on his lips with her teeth and Boyd's cock, his wonderful, vast cock, which I've held in my hands and in my mouth, stirring, and him reaching up and pulling Honey down to him and in that moment I hate Honey, I hate Boyd and I hate the grief that never seems to let me go.

The last day

On the last day Graham Silverton has finished loading the poles onto the lorry, has climbed up into his cab and is staring at the docket in his hand. He punches the postcode into the satnav.

It's blustery, there's still a chill in the air and, as he starts the engine, the radio comes on. Some idiotic DJ is playing *California Girls* by the Beach Boys.

'What the fuck?' Graham mutters, putting the truck in reverse and harrumphing to himself.

Summer seems a lifetime away still; they've yet to book their holiday. His wife has said she'd like to go to Cuba this year. 'Cuba?' he'd said, 'why on earth would you want to go there?'

Behind him the poles rattle a bit like distant applause.

Honey

She'd thought she knew Boyd, but this man sitting on the bed in front of her is an almost-stranger. But, she reasons, there are things about her he doesn't know so maybe all relationships are based not on what's real, but on what's perceived to be real. However, she needs to say something, so says, 'We don't have to stay here, not if you don't want to. We can move out, find somewhere else. I didn't realise. You should have said.'

'I thought I could cope, that we'd both moved on, but – and this might sound strange – in some ways it's been good, being here.' He pauses, then says, 'I think we should stay, it would disrupt things too much if we left now.'

'Disrupt Vita, do you mean?' She has no idea where the words come from, she doesn't mean them, not in a nasty way, but worries that Boyd may not understand so she clambers on the bed behind him, wraps her arms around his chest and rests her head on the broad sweep of his shoulders.

He sighs, but doesn't answer.

'You should have told me before now,' she whispers into the wool of his jumper.

'I know, but I didn't know how to.'

At least she can understand this. It's the same for her. She is, however, surprised that Trixie's never said anything, never even hinted at it.

'Should I say anything to Vita?' she asks.

'I wouldn't. She's very proud, very private. Her grief isn't something she can talk about. That was part of the problem I think. We fought a lot during those last months before I left. Mostly in this room actually, it seemed to be the place where both of us felt him most keenly.

'We'd tried for ages, you see. To have a child, I mean. Our friends, and Trixie, of course, had their families already but we started late and then it didn't work. We had tests and there was no obvious reason why, so the doctor said just to keep trying and we did, but the joy went out of it all so quickly and then, amazingly, Vita got pregnant. They often say it's at the point when you give up that you relax enough for it to happen. Maybe that was the case, I don't know. We'd always wanted a big family.' He pauses, then adds, 'My mother was ...'

'Yes,' Honey says softly, drawing in the Boyd-ness of his scent and the washing powder they use and wanting more than anything for him to turn and lay his body over hers.

'My mother was uncharacteristically excited. I hadn't expected her to react the way she did. She was besotted with William. In some ways I think when we lost him, it became another thing for her to blame me for. But it wasn't anyone's fault. What happened is so rare. He presented no symptoms; it came out of the blue, so there was the shock too. We had no time to prepare. We never got to say goodbye to him.'

'Tell me what I can do.'

Now he turns and gathers her to him. She nestles in the circle of his arms and he says, 'Never leave.' His lips are soft against the skin of her neck. Then, he pulls back a bit and looks her in the eyes. 'Just stay with me. When you were out of it last night, there were moments I watched you and it scared me to think I might ever lose you too. I couldn't bear that.'

'I'm not going anywhere,' she tells him but her stomach clenches as she says this. How can she ever reconcile who she really is with who Boyd believes her to be?

He moves away from her then and goes over to the window, his body a black mass against the light.

'The flowers are nice,' he says.

'Trixie brought them round.'

'She said she was going to. Guess she feels a bit responsible.'

'What for?'

'For you getting so ...'

'I reckon there must have been something wrong with the wine; it doesn't usually affect me that way.'

'Thank goodness,' he says, smiling at last. 'Or maybe not!'

She can remember more about the sex now and, of course, now knows that Boyd had been weeping, but they have survived this moment, she thinks, and is grateful that they have.

* * *

In the days that follow, they are quiet and kind to one another and, on one occasion, she touches Vita briefly on the arm as she's standing at the kitchen sink.

'Hey,' Honey says, 'you'll let me know if there's ever anything I can do, won't you?'

Vita turns to look at her, her eyes glittery and hard. 'I have no idea what you're talking about,' she says, but Honey thinks she does.

Now she can sense William's presence in the house and realises that he must be the child in the medium's vision, the one her mother was holding. Holy shit, she says to herself now and again when she thinks of this and, one evening when Vita is out and Boyd and Honey are eating, she asks him where William is buried.

'I'll take you there one day,' he says. 'It's not far.'

'Did it …' she taps her fork against her plate and clears her throat.

'Did it what?' he asks.

'Did it rain after the funeral?'

He puts his knife and fork down and looks over at her. 'Why do you ask that?'

'Just curious.'

He's silent for a moment and then says, 'Yes, it rained.'

'That's good.'

'Good?'

'It means he found rest and is content.'

'That's bollocks, surely.'

'It's nice to believe that it might not be bollocks,' she says 'Isn't it?'

He doesn't answer. She knows he humours her superstitions, but she does wonder whether she's gone too far this time. After all, this matters, it really does.

Little does he know the full version of her visit to Elizabeth's. Elizabeth had seen a baby. That baby must have been William. Honey knew that now and if Elizabeth had been right about the child, then she was most likely right about Honey being found. OK, Honey hasn't seen Reuben again and she hasn't fallen, but she firmly believes both of these things will happen somehow and put an end to this life she's living. They will mean the end of Honey Mayhew.

Vita

'I heard you,' I say to Boyd as he stands next to me at the sink.

It's Thursday. It's six-thirty in the morning and the lamps are on in the lounge and the house is warm. Boyd is up earlier than normal and is wearing joggers and a sweatshirt; his face still has that just-slept-in look. We're waiting for the kettle to boil.

'Pardon?' he asks over the sound the kettle is making.

I've been waiting for days to say this, but now that the moment's here, I hesitate, unsure and wary. What good will it do? I'm not even sure of my motives but I plough on regardless. Sometimes I wonder what I've got between my ears; it's certainly not brains.

'I heard you when you told Honey about William. I was passing.'

'Passing? How could you be passing?'

I can't read his tone. He isn't looking at me, but he's staring down at the washing-up bowl. He reaches out a hand and touches a teaspoon on the draining board and moves it a fraction.

'I was on my way to the bathroom.' I'm not looking at him either, I can't.

'Mmm.'

I know he's not convinced.

'Why hadn't you already told her?'

Now he turns and gazes down at me, I glance at him out of the corner of my eye.

'I don't know, Vita,' he says. 'I really don't. I tried, believe me. Many times, but it was almost as though, if I told her, it would change me in her eyes. I wanted to be the man she believed I was when she fell in love with me, not the man burdened by ...' He doesn't finish the sentence.

I know it's a cliché but it really feels like my blood is boiling. Burden? Hadn't William been a gift too?

'Oh, Boyd.' But I don't say what I'm really thinking which is, You are wrong, you are so wrong. How can you not have let her know this? And what about the grief? Don't you still carry a picture of your child in your wallet like you used to do?

The kettle boils, the kitchen fills momentarily with steam and then it dissipates. The silence is overwhelming. I think of Honey asleep upstairs and that she has no idea of this thing between me and Boyd, this iron bond.

And then I think about her secret and the words are in my mouth. I would be a hypocrite if I expected him to have told her about William and didn't expect him to need to know about her past. Surely it's my duty to clear the pathway between them? Secrets do such damage.

But I stop. What about Colin? If I'm such a great exponent of the truth above all things, I should come clean with Boyd about Colin and I should tell Colin about William. I should say to Boyd, 'Oh, by the way, I'm having a relationship with the guy next door. We go places together, eat food together, have sex. I don't love him, or at least I don't think I do, but he knows every inch of my body – just like you used to.'

No, some secrets should remain secret. I don't analyse why I think this, but I am convinced that a) it's not my place to interfere, b) I should not go back on my word and c) I don't want Boyd to know about Colin, or that sometimes I think Colin is my last line of defence against an unknown enemy – those old-lady-eating Alsatians and the muddle of feelings I am not brave enough to face up to.

'But it's done now,' Boyd is saying. 'She knows now.'

'Yes,' I reply. 'It seems that she does.' And I am furious; a wave of anger hits me, it's cold and hard and relentless. 'Oh, sod it,' I say, 'forget the fucking tea, forget the fucking crossword today, I'm going to have my shower.'

Walking away from him is a wrench; it's like there's a sundering in the air as, once again, what lies unspoken between us raises its head and stares at me with its pale eyes.

I don't look back at Boyd as I make my way across the room but, as I climb the stairs, I hear him sigh.

Honey

Boyd's diary is full of calls to vendors, purchasers and solicitors and he has a valuation to do at one. Honey notices that there's something different about him but for a moment can't pinpoint what. Then it comes to her, he's not wearing a tie.

'You forgot your tie,' she says, looking over at him as she signs off an email and presses 'Send'.

'I know,' he replies. 'Left in too much of a rush this morning I guess.' He winks as he says this.

He'd been downstairs as usual, talking to Vita as they'd made their tea and Honey's coffee. She'd presumed they were doing the crossword and then she heard Vita stomp up the stairs and go into the bathroom. She checked the clock. Vita was having her shower earlier than normal.

And then Boyd had come upstairs. He'd locked the bedroom door and had made love to Honey quickly and fiercely. He doesn't usually, not in the mornings and especially not on a weekday, but he'd been insistent and the sex had been wonderful; they'd both come silently and had lain there afterwards tracing their hands over each other's skin for a while, and so had, unsurprisingly, been a bit late leaving for work. Honey hadn't even had time to read her horoscope but had seen his tie on the arm of the sofa and had assumed he'd pick it up and put it in his pocket to wear later.

But here he is in the office, without it.

'Do you want me to go and buy you one?' she asks.

'Or, I could pop back to the house and pick one up for you,' Trixie says, standing up and smoothing down her skirt. She's wearing the turquoise top Honey's always liked. It goes with her colouring. 'I've still got a key.'

'No, don't worry, you two,' Boyd says. 'I've been in touch with Vita and she's bringing it in. She said she was passing anyway.'

Honey purposefully doesn't look at Trixie when Boyd says this. Why would his first instinct be to call Vita? This puzzles her briefly but then the phone rings and it's business as usual for a while.

Of course, she'd thanked Trixie for the flowers and Trixie had said something non-committal, like 'We must go out again.' but Honey had the feeling she didn't really mean it.

She'd moved the flowers downstairs as soon as she could because their scent had become too overbearing in the bedroom and anyway, since Boyd had told her about William, there'd been something too funereal about the lilies. They hadn't lasted long and one day she'd come home from work to find Vita had thrown them away and washed up the vase.

A few moments later Trixie asks if either of them wants anything from the storeroom.

'No thanks,' Honey says. 'I'm good.'

'Me too,' Boyd replies.

'Just need to check on something,' Trixie says and opens the door and goes down the step, but then the main door opens and Vita wheels her bicycle in.

'Hi,' she says.

'Hey there,' Boyd replies, leaping up from his seat and going over to her.

'Your tie.' She plucks it from the bag she's got hooked over her shoulder. Honey notices their hands don't touch as she passes it to him.

The weather's turned a little now and Vita's brought an eddy of damp, cold air in with her.

'Thanks,' Boyd says and, in a gesture that Honey guesses both she and Vita have seen countless times, he hitches up his collar and starts to tie the tie.

He smiles first at Vita, then at Honey, his left eyebrow doing that thing it does.

'Trixie in?' Vita asks.

'In the storeroom, checking something,' Boyd replies.

'I'll pop my head in and say hi, then.'

Vita leans her bike up against the wall and Honey hears her call out hello and Trixie's muffled reply. She's only in there for half a minute or so and then she comes back up the step, wheels her bike back out of the office and is gone. Honey goes over to where the wheels have left wet marks on the carpet and picks up a stray leaf the colour of thick-set honey. She throws it in the bin.

The day presses on. Trixie and Honey do their work, Boyd takes and makes his calls and then he goes out to do the valuation.

He's been gone for about half an hour when Trixie says, 'Bugger, I left my office keys in the storeroom. You wouldn't be an angel and get them for me would you?'

Honey doesn't think it's strange she should ask her this. She knows Trixie's in the middle of something complicated and it pleases her to do something for Trixie now and again, kind of gives her the moral high ground.

Honey's saying something to Trixie about printer cartridges and is looking over her shoulder as she steps down into the storeroom.

Of course she falls. The wooden step underneath her foot, the one Boyd warned her about when she started working at Harrison's, seems to give way and she slams down onto the concrete floor, her right leg twisted painfully under her. She calls out.

Trixie comes running. 'Shit,' she says, 'you OK?'

'I think I may have broken something,' Honey says and then everything goes black.

Boyd

His phone is on silent but he can feel it vibrating in his jacket pocket. However, he can't answer it because Mr Edwards is in full flow about his house. 'Been here fifty years,' he's saying. 'Man and boy. Carried my Gladys over the threshold so I did. Lordy, we've had some times here I can tell you.'

Boyd wishes he could say something meaningful in reply but his phone is still vibrating and he has no real idea what to say to Mr Edwards.

Gladys died six months ago and Mr Edwards is selling up to move into a retirement flat. Apparently his son and daughter-in-law are going to help him with the move but, looking around the house, it's going to be some task. Every room is crammed with furniture and paintings. Mirrors dot the walls and Boyd can tell that the wiring and plumbing will need replacing, as will the kitchen and bathroom.

It's a house that's stood still while the world around it has kept on spinning. But, Boyd thinks – as Mr Edwards finally bustles out of the box room saying, 'Best let you get on, there's not room for two of us in here. I'll get the kettle on, shall I?' – what's also stayed still is an idea of love and loyalty and togetherness.

Everywhere Boyd looks are signs of a life lived with rectitude and care: in the sitting room the antimacassars on the armchairs have been hemmed by hand with tiny, even stitches; the books in the bookcase are arranged alphabetically and on every available surface is a photograph in a frame of a boy who turns into a youth, then into a man, then a man holding a baby – and so the photos multiply, depicting people Boyd knows are loved unconditionally. He doesn't have time to explore this feeling though because as soon as he hears Mr Edwards carefully making his way down the stairs, he plucks his phone from his pocket.

He wouldn't ordinarily, not during a valuation, but there's something about the insistence of the calls that has unsettled him.

He's missed five calls from the office and one from Trixie's mobile. This doesn't look good. Trixie knows where he is and that he doesn't like to be disturbed, it's not polite when he should be concentrating on the vendor. After all, each person's story is different. Trixie's left a message so he taps into voicemail. Her voice is breathless and panicked and he can't catch all that she says but he gathers there's been an accident and that Honey is hurt. It's enough for him to take the stairs two at a time and burst unceremoniously into Mr Edwards' kitchen and say, 'Oh, I'm so sorry, but I have to go. There's been an accident at work. My colleague ...' Boyd baulks at the word 'colleague' but stammers on, '... has been hurt. Can we finish the valuation another time, please? I'm so sorry to do this. You must think I'm very rude.'

'Not at all,' Mr Edwards says, switching the kettle off and putting the spoon he's holding back in a drawer, 'you must go. We can do this another time. I'm not going anywhere for a while!' He smiles at Boyd as he says this, his eyes a sparkly blue in the creased skin of his face.

'Thank you. I'll show myself out.'

Boyd reaches out a hand. Mr Edwards takes it in both of his. 'I do hope everything is all right, Mr Harrison,' he says. 'Take care of yourself, won't you?'

If Boyd hadn't been itching to leave, these few words may have led him to wonder what it may have been like to have had a father figure in his life, someone who would regularly hold his hand in theirs and say, 'Take care of yourself, won't you?' but he's walking quickly from the house. He fumbles in his pocket for the car key and, unlocking the door, hurls himself behind the wheel. As soon as the phone connects, he dials the office. 'It's me,' he says. 'I'm on my way. What's happened?'

And Trixie tells him that Honey has fallen down the step into the cellar, that she blacked out for a moment but came to soon after and that she's sitting down with her right foot up on a chair in front of her, drinking a cup of tea. 'We think it might be broken,' Trixie says. 'Her ankle that is. I think you may need to take her to A&E.'

'Guildford or Frimley?' he asks her.

'I don't know which is best. I'll check the traffic and let you know when you get here. OK?'

'OK, and ...' Boyd is finding it difficult to swallow, it seems like his heart has lodged itself in his throat, '... thank you, Trixie. Thank you for everything.'

'Oh, don't be silly,' she says. 'It's the least I can do.'

* * *

Honey looks unfeasibly young when Boyd eventually crashes through the door to the office. He has abandoned his car at an angle in the service yard out back; anyone watching might think he is some sort of criminal leaving it for a quick getaway.

'What have you done?' He thinks he's most probably shouting but he's scared, and his fear is making him shout.

'I'm OK,' she says, smiling wanly up at him.

She doesn't look OK at all; her ankle is swollen and must be very painful.

'Come on, let's get you to hospital. That needs an x-ray. Trixie?' He turns to Trixie who's sitting on the edge of her seat, gazing intently at the screen of her computer.

She looks up at him. 'Yes?' she says.

'What news on the traffic?'

'It'll be quicker to go to Guildford by the looks of it. There are roadworks the other way.'

'Thank you.'

'Would you ...' she asks.

'What?' He's shouting again.

'... have time to answer a few work questions?'

'No, of course not,' he snaps. Then adds, 'Sorry, didn't mean to snap. I'll ring you from the hospital when I've got Honey sorted.'

Trixie makes a strange snorting noise but Boyd's too preoccupied to pay much attention to her, or the noise.

'Come on,' he says more gently now, helping Honey up on to her good foot. 'Is it very sore? Did you bump your head? Can you put any weight on it?' The questions come thick and fast and he doesn't give her any time to answer them. Instead she rests her weight up against him and together they shuffle from the office and back out to the car.

Trixie follows them to the door and, as she makes to close it after them, Honey turns to her and says something about the prediction coming true but Boyd doesn't hear her properly as a lorry is reversing into the yard, beeping as it does so.

But he does hear Trixie say, 'Don't be silly. Of course it's not that. It was just an accident.'

And then the door to the office closes and he helps Honey into the car.

'Try not to go to sleep,' he says. 'Don't they say that after a bump to the head?'

'I don't know whether I bumped my head or not,' Honey replies, leaning back against the headrest and closing her eyes.

'Don't!' He is shouting again. 'I'll put the radio on. Listen to that, it'll help you stay awake.'

'God, it hurts,' Honey says, gingerly lifting her right knee.

'Put the chair back as far as it'll go so you can stretch out a bit. OK?'

'OK.'

He tries to keep the conversation going on the journey, but it's hard because he has to concentrate on the traffic and his mind is whirring ahead to what might happen when they get there. He'll have to drop her off and then leave her as he parks the car. How long will they have to wait? Will it need to be put in plaster? What does all this mean? When should he tell Vita? Should he tell Vita?

The DJ is wittering on about the number of shopping days left before Christmas when Boyd looks over at Honey as they are held at some traffic lights. She has her eyes closed.

He hates to disturb her. She looks pale and drawn. And frightened too. She looks how she looks when she wakes from her dream, the one where she cries out and struggles against him as if he's trying to smother her. She has, he's noticed, been more jumpy of late, always looking out of the office window, checking over her shoulder if they're walking anywhere. He'd thought by now that she would have started to be more relaxed with him but, if anything, she's getting more and more anxious.

Eventually they get to the hospital and he helps her in and leaves her leaning up against the reception desk as he goes to park. It takes ages to find a space and, as every moment passes, he becomes more and more frantic.

When he does finally return to A&E, she's nowhere to be seen. He asks at reception but they're not sure if she's been called or not. Best to wait and see, he's told.

He checks his phone. Thank God, she's texted. 'Gone for X-ray. Will keep you posted.'

So, he decides to go to the X-ray department to find her. He follows the maze of corridors, passing doors to wards and volunteers driving the infirm around on mobility buggies. There is an air of preoccupation and incipient drama everywhere. He should call Trixie, and Vita, but right now all he can think about is finding Honey.

He asks at another desk and is told that yes, she's being seen and should be out soon and so finally he lets himself breathe properly and sits on a hard red plastic chair to wait for her.

And that's where he is when he hears his name.

'Boyd? What on earth are you doing here?'

'Mum?'

Sitting in a wheelchair in front of him is his mother. She's dressed in a jade two-piece, has her make-up on and her nails are painted. She reminds Boyd of the Queen.

Suddenly he's exhausted. He doesn't want to have to explain why he's here. He certainly doesn't want this to be the first time Honey and his mother meet.

So instead of answering her, he asks, 'Why are you here? Is everything OK?'

'Just routine,' she answers and, looking over her shoulder, sends what he thinks is a warning look to the nurse who's pushing her along. 'Isn't it?' she says, addressing the nurse.

The nurse smiles at Boyd and nods. 'Yes,' she replies. 'Just routine. Is this your son then?' she asks, placing a hand on Belle's shoulder.

'Yes,' Belle says. 'This is Boyd.'

There is an awkward silence and then Belle says, 'Well, best be getting on I guess. Time and tests wait for no man. I'll see you soon, no doubt, Boyd.'

She doesn't bother to wait to hear the reasons why he's there but instead she raises a hand and waves imperiously as she gets wheeled away. How, Boyd wonders, has it come to this? We used to be close. Well, we had a kind of closeness anyway; we were mother and son, but now can only be like this with one another. It's a crying shame, a fucking crying shame.

But he knows why it is so. After all, hadn't he done the one thing she'd expressly asked him not to?

* * *

It was September, a warm day. He was eighteen, impatient and angry. He'd done his A-levels and was waiting to go to university but knew that before he did, he had to try and find his father. He'd always known his father's name; after all it was on his birth certificate: Percy Harrison.

The name Percy had always conjured up the image of a man who was slightly fat, with thinning hair and a meticulous way of moving.

Boyd had absolutely no idea how his mother could have fallen pregnant by this kind of a man.

He'd had many theories about their affair over the years. Maybe it had been one between two like-minded people separated by circumstances, you know the wrong place/wrong time kind of thing, and that the years of silence that had followed had been heart-breaking for both of them. Or maybe Percy's wife had once been Belle's friend but she'd become ill in some awful way and so Percy and Belle had decided that the only honourable thing to do was for Belle and her baby to disappear to reduce the amount of harm done. Or, perhaps Percy had taken advantage of a lonely and desperate Belle at a neighbourhood party: a fumble in the coat cupboard that went too far, that could, in different circumstances and at a different time, have been considered rape.

Whatever happened, Belle remained tight-lipped about it throughout Boyd's childhood. She'd said, 'I made a promise that I'd never let you contact him; we're not supposed to have anything to do with him. It was part of the bargain.' She didn't tell him what the rest of the bargain had been.

But Boyd had lost patience with this. He wanted to confront the man, seek some kind of connection. He'd spent too many years fatherless and was, to all intents and purposes, to remain so despite his mother's spate of marriages. Not one of these marriages had given him a father.

And so he looked Percy up. It wasn't difficult to find him. He went to the library and sourced local newspaper coverage from where his mother had been living at the time and found articles about Percy: he'd won a marrow-growing competition in 1972, had championed a pedestrian crossing outside the Post Office in 1979. In one article they gave his address as Sussex Gardens and so Boyd had started his search there.

And, it seemed, Percy hadn't moved house, not in all the years that had followed. Instead he'd stayed in the bay-fronted semi he'd been living in when Belle and he had done whatever it was they had done to produce Boyd. And so it was that on a warm September evening Boyd stood on the pavement opposite, watching as his father mowed his front lawn.

The man didn't bear any resemblance to the picture Boyd had carried around for so long in his head. Instead, in front of him was a tall, well-built man. He had a mop of dark hair which he kept brushing out of his eyes with one hand as the other kept the mower steady on its journey up and down the lawn. This man wore a loose, white shirt and faded jeans, his skin a kind of burnished gold in the setting sun.

Boyd watched his father as the occasional car trundled up and down the suburban street. Boyd didn't think about his mother, and his childhood faded to no more than a sepia tinge of days punctuated by school, meat paste sandwiches and reading in bed. This moment was all that mattered. This was going to be the day that defined him. He would be a man with a father, a man who knew where he came from and where he was going to.

He stepped off the pavement and crossed the road. As he approached the end of his father's drive, he paused, but then Percy looked up and caught sight of him. Instinctively Boyd raised a hand in greeting. Percy frowned and, bending down, switched the mower off. The silence in the street was deafening. Behind him stood the house, impenetrable, a sun setting in each of its windows. The two men walked towards one another.

'Can I help you?' his father said.

'I …' The words died in Boyd's throat.

'I know who you are,' Percy said, running a hand through his hair and keeping it there as if to shield his eyes from the sun.

'You do?'

'Of course I do. Your mother insists on sending me pictures.'

'She does?

'Yes.'

Boyd couldn't fathom what his father might be thinking. His face was half-hidden by his hand but his body language was wary, as if he was poised for flight.

'Although,' Percy continued, 'it's against the terms of our agreement.'

Boyd was starting to feel foolish. He shouldn't have come. Maybe his mother had been right and it was best to let things lie. And he'd promised her. Countless times he'd promised her not to go in search of his father, and yet here he was standing at the end of his father's drive wishing he was anywhere else on the earth but there.

'She hasn't told you then?'

'No.'

Percy had dropped his hand by now and had put both in the pockets of his jeans. Boyd could hear the rattle of a few coins, maybe a set of keys, as Percy turned and looked briefly and somewhat furtively over his shoulder at the house behind him.

When he turned back to face Boyd he said, 'The deal was that if I gave you my name and allowed her to change hers to Harrison by deed poll, she'd not make any other claim on me. The most important things for her, apparently, were for the three of us to have the same name and for you to have the box on your birth certificate filled in. I gave her some money too, at the time. Money I could scarcely afford, I'll have you know.'

Two things struck Boyd about what his father had just said. Firstly, the way he'd said the word 'apparently' had been snide and somewhat cruel and, secondly, Boyd had come to the realisation that Percy's other family still had no idea that he existed.

'They still don't know, do they?' he said.

'Who?'

'The people in there.' Boyd pointed at the house.

'No, and they must *never* find out.'

'You must be so ashamed of me.'

Percy took a step towards Boyd at this point and took one hand out of his pocket and stretched it out as if to touch Boyd on the arm. 'It's not that,' he said. 'It's just I've never dared get close to you. I have too much to lose.'

If Boyd expected an apology to follow, he was disappointed. In his heart he'd heard his father say, 'I'm sorry, son. I'm sorry I can't be the father you deserve. It's a fucking tragedy but that's the way life is. I'd do anything for it to be other than the way it is.'

No, Percy didn't say this. Instead the front door of the house behind him opened and a girl of around twenty stood on the doorstep and called out, 'Dad? Mum says tea'll be in five minutes.'

The girl was tall, slender and dark-haired. She was, Boyd later realised, his half-sister and he didn't even know her name.

Percy had dropped his hand and turned to face his daughter. 'Tell her I'll be in soon,' he said. 'Just finishing up out here.'

'Go,' he said, looking back at Boyd. 'Just go. It's for the best, believe me. Your mother and I have an agreement and this isn't part of it.'

As he finished this sentence Percy's mouth moved silently as if the words, 'I'm sorry,' were making their way involuntarily out of it. But still he didn't say them and, as Boyd began to walk away, he heard the girl say, 'Who was that Dad?' and his father reply, 'Just someone asking for directions, that's all.'

The consequences of this meeting on the driveway on that evening in September were cataclysmic. Percy must have told Belle of Boyd's visit because after saying, 'You broke your promise,' to Boyd, Belle didn't speak to him for three months and has never really forgiven him for it since.

And so Boyd started university effectively motherless and fatherless and he drank too much and slept with any girl who would sleep with him and he did barely any work and he ate bad food and did no exercise. Before losing William, it was the lowest point of his life and, even now, sitting on a hard plastic chair in a hospital corridor waiting for Honey to reappear with the whoosh of the wheels of his mother's wheelchair still ringing in his ears, the weight of this rejection sits in his chest as though someone has buried a cannonball there.

But even so, Boyd has always tried to be the better man. He knows that honour and love lie in the small acts of kindness between people and so he's tried, both with Vita and with Honey to be a good man, to put them first and him second. He built Vita's studio for her, he waited for as long as he could for her to recover from William's death and, although it shames him, he'd truly believed that leaving was the kinder thing to do. And he loves Honey; for all her frailties and for all she hasn't told him, he loves her the best way he can. And, he's also, over the years, tried to be a good son to his mother. Yes, he may not love her, not in the way he should, but yet he tries; he is loyal and steadfast and forgiving. These are the qualities Boyd believes in and which, he hopes, he demonstrates in the small moments, in the day to day. Even so, there is something, some unresolved question hovering around his heart. He doesn't know what it is, but it's there, like smoke or cloud cover.

'Mr Harrison?' A nurse is standing in front of him.

'That's me. How is she? How's Honey?' he asks.

'She's fine. Follow me and we'll get her discharged. It's going to take a while for her to get used to the crutches.'

The nurse smiles at Boyd as she says this and Boyd stands and makes his way down the corridor after her.

Vita

'Oh, what are you doing here?' I'm surprised to find Trixie in the house when I get home.

'Waiting for Boyd,' she replies.

'I didn't know you still had a key.'

'I keep it in the office, just in case.'

'Oh, I see.'

Having her here is a painful reminder of when she used to come round after William died; her presence now though is different, less comforting. She had been sitting down, reading, a mug of tea on the table in front of her, but now she's standing, as though poised for a fight.

It's bad enough, I think, coming back home when it's just the three of us and there's Boyd and Honey's stuff around and I can never predict what state the kitchen will be in, what there'll be to eat in the fridge. But this? Having Trixie let herself in like this is a diabolical liberty. Oh, to have those days again when it was just me living here! Suddenly I want this fiercely and then, just as suddenly, I don't.

'Honey's had an accident,' Trixie says, somewhat defensively I think.

My heart judders to a stop. This, I realise, is what fear is; that fear of something happening to someone you care about and the twin pillars of powerlessness and powerfulness that sit at the centre of all of us which tell us, 'Yes, you can save them,' and 'No you can't.'

I think of the child in the park, of the tumble of limbs as he fell in front of me, his face as he looked up at me. I feel a shooting sensation down my arms and my palms tingle.

'An accident?' I ask.

'Yes, she fell down the step into the storeroom. Boyd's at the hospital with her now. She's probably broken something, but is otherwise OK, I think.'

Then there's a knock at the front door. I open it. It's Colin.

'Oh, hi,' I say.

'Hi. You ready?'

'Just about.'

But I'm not. I don't want to go out. I want to say here and wait for Boyd, but I mustn't. I can't.

'Oh,' Colin says, catching sight of Trixie, 'I didn't know you had company.'

'This is Trixie,' I say. 'She works with Boyd. And, Trixie, this is Colin – he lives next door.'

They nod at one another and smile but I can't seem to say the word 'accident'. I don't want Colin to know, not yet, not until I know more about what's happened. Instead I ask Trixie to tell Boyd that I won't be back until late, but would like it if he could ring me to let me know how Honey is.

'Will do,' she says.

And then Colin puts his hand on my shoulder and says, 'Let's go, eh? We don't want to be late.'

I don't look at Trixie as we go out the door and as I close it behind me.

Honey

'Come on then hop-a-long,' Boyd says, opening the car door when they get back to the house.

Getting into the car had been a struggle even though the chair was still pushed back so she could stretch out her leg. The plaster cast reaches to just under her knee and is very heavy, it's going to take her a while to get her balance and learn how to operate the crutches.

'Cheeky sod,' she replies, as he bends down and helps lift her leg, turning her in the seat and then putting a hand under each of her armpits and hauling her to a standing position. Next, he leans her up against the car and grabs the crutches from the back.

Slowly and clumsily Honey makes her way down the path. It's about six and dusk is well-established, the street lamps are on and the lamps in nearby windows are a pale yellow glow.

Boyd is following her; she glances back at him, at the concern etched on his face. He's carrying her handbag and for some reason this makes her want to laugh.

'Suits you,' she says.

'Eh?'

'My bag. Looks good on you!'

'Now who's the cheeky sod?'

The front door opens and Trixie's standing in an oblong of light.

'Oh,' Honey says, surprised to see her there. 'It's you.'

'Yes,' Trixie says, stepping back and letting her edge past her, the muscles in Honey's arms are already starting to feel sore from the effort. She's going to have to get much better at this. 'I have a key,' she says. 'Boyd gave it to me ages ago.'

There's something about the way Trixie says this which makes Honey uncomfortable but she can't pinpoint why and shrugs it off. 'Vita in?' she asks.

'She was, but she's gone out.'

Boyd's put Honey's bag down and is resting one of his huge hands on the small of her back as if to guide her.

'Out?' he asks Trixie. 'Do you know where?'

'No, but the guy from next door ... Colin is his name? Anyway, he called round and they went out together. She said she'd be back late but wants you to call her, to let her know about Honey.'

Honey is standing in between Trixie and Boyd, looking from one to the other and wishing that Trixie would move so that she could manoeuvre herself to the sofa, when she catches a look that passes between them. It's an odd look, not one she's seen before. It's half-surprise and half-complicit, as if they are reading each other's minds and are wary about what they can see.

'Colin?' Boyd asks. 'You sure?'

'Yes.' Trixie has, at last, moved and Honey sits down and Boyd, of course, rushes over to put a cushion under her foot. 'It looked like they were quite familiar with one another,' Trixie says. 'At ease, you know. As if they know each other well.'

At this point Boyd turns and strides into the kitchen, making a low growling kind of noise that Honey's not heard before either and

Trixie leans in slightly and says in a sugary voice, 'Can I get you anything, Honey? Cup of tea perhaps?'

Honey nods and says, 'Thank you, that would be nice. And ...'

'Yes?' Trixie says, again in that sweet voice but looking over now at Boyd, a slight frown creasing her brow.

'... can you pass me my bag?'

Trixie hands Honey her bag and joins Boyd in the kitchen where Honey can hear them talking about work. They don't mention Vita again but she can sense that something's shifted, that Boyd minds that Vita's gone out somewhere with Colin. Boyd asks Trixie about the sale of the house in Cumberland Avenue but the noise of the kettle boiling drowns out her answer.

Honey plucks her phone out of her bag to check her emails. She hates not being on top of her work but, before she reads them, she notices there's a text from a number she doesn't recognise. She's not really concentrating when she clicks on it but then it feels as though someone has punched her in the stomach as she reads, 'Sorry about your fall. Was watching from the other side of the street. Kind regards, The Boatman.'

'Shit,' she says under her breath and quickly closes the message down and slips the phone back in her bag. How the fuck did he get her number? She thinks back to the people she's given it to recently: a delivery guy, the man in the shoe repair shop, the mechanic at the garage who had MOT'd Boyd's car. She's been getting sloppy. She should be more careful, more watchful. And now Reuben has texted her and who knows what he may do next? Don't they say that revenge is a dish best eaten cold?

She feels dizzy and puts her head in her hands. She wants to cry but knows she can't. She mustn't give Boyd any further cause for concern. Today has been difficult enough as it is.

'Here you go,' Trixie says, putting a mug of tea on the table next to the arm of the sofa.

Honey manages to mutter a thank you and then says, 'I …'

'Mmmm?'

Trixie's tidying, plumping up cushions, straightening Vita's magazines. Boyd's on the phone; Honey can hear the rumble of his voice.

'I wonder if you'd ask Boyd if he could help me upstairs when he's finished on the phone? I think I'd like to lie down. Today's kind of taken it out of me.'

'Of course, I will,' Trixie says, smiling.

At least I'm safe here, Honey thinks. While Boyd and Trixie are around, I am safe. And so she decides to tell her. 'Trixie?' she says.

'Mmmm?' Trixie says again, putting on her coat.

'Oh, it's nothing. I guess you want to get back to Richard.'

Trixie makes a strange sound as Honey says this; like she has a pain lodged somewhere deep inside of her. Then she says, 'No, it's OK. He can wait. What is it? Do you need me to get you anything?'

Honey thinks then about the times Trixie must have spent here; maybe she and Richard had come round for dinner with Vita and Boyd back when life was simple, before William. Trixie would have left her boys in the care of a babysitter and they would have got a taxi and Richard would be wearing a loud, striped shirt, the type someone who works in the City would wear. Honey can imagine them sitting around the table with wine in glasses in front of them, the smell of lamb and rosemary in the air. Their laughter would be easy, intimate and candles would flicker and not one of them would know how dramatically things were to change. Not one of them would have imagined that one day she'd be here, with her foot in plaster and her belongings upstairs in the room that she now shares with Boyd.

And she can see Trixie here after William: Trixie ironing Boyd's shirts and dusting the mantelpiece; Trixie in the kitchen stirring soup on the stove, creeping upstairs every now and then to check on Vita who is lying in her bed, curled up like an ammonite.

Boyd is still on the phone so Honey murmurs, 'I got a text. From the man in the boat.'

Trixie looks surprised. 'How do you know it's from him?' she asks.

'He signed it "The Boatman".'

'What did it say?' Trixie carries on putting on her coat; she's adjusting the collar, picking up her handbag.

'That he knows about my fall.'

'You mean he was watching?'

'Yes.' Honey glances towards the kitchen. Boyd is standing with his back to them and Honey is filled by a powerful kind of love for the goodness in him. He can't know. He must never know the type of person she used to be: the things she did, the damage and pain she caused. She is sure his love for her isn't strong enough to bear these truths, she doesn't want to give him any more pain than he's already suffered.

'You still got the message?' Trixie asks.

She nods. She's conscious that they're whispering and that, if he were aware of it, this may make Boyd suspicious.

'Block the number and then delete the text. Don't respond to it whatever you do.'

'I wasn't going to …'

At that moment Boyd turns and starts walking back towards them. 'Right then, ladies,' he says, beaming. 'What are you two conspiring about?'

'Nothing,' Honey says but imagines the guilt written large over her face in capital letters. 'I did ask Trixie to ask you to help me upstairs, but now you're off the phone, I can ask you myself!' She is tipping her head to one side as though she's flirting with him and hates herself for doing so but needs to distract him, make sure he has nothing to be suspicious of.

'Sure thing,' he says, bending down to pick up her crutches.

'You certain you'll be OK,' Trixie asks. 'You spoken to Vita yet?'

'No,' Boyd replies and, again, a look passes between them that unsettles her. 'I'll call her later,' Boyd says, touching Honey briefly on the knee and smiling down at her.

Suddenly and stupidly, Honey feels like she's a child in a grown-up drama and that she's not being told the full story. She's on the verge of tears but reckons this must be shock and tells herself not to be so silly.

'Come on, hop-a-long,' Boyd adds, helping her to stand and slotting the crutches under her armpits.

Honey has the feeling that hop-a-long is going to be her name for a while yet.

'I'll be off then,' Trixie says.

'Thank you so much for everything.'

Boyd lets Honey lean up against him as he reaches out and puts a hand on Trixie's arm; she moves the keys she's holding from one hand to another and shifts her feet.

'Oh, it's nothing,' she replies. 'What are friends for? I'll see you tomorrow, Boyd.'

'And me?' Honey asks, letting the warmth of Boyd's body seep into hers.

'You're not coming into work, surely?' Trixie's voice isn't so sugary now but Honey guesses it's because she's tired.

'I'd like to. I'll go stir-crazy here on my own all day.'

'Vita may be home,' Trixie says. 'Perhaps she can keep you company for a bit.'

'Maybe,' Honey says and then adds, 'and thank you …'

'What for?'

'Everything.'

'That's OK,' she answers. 'As I said, it's my pleasure.'

And Honey believes her. And then with a nod to Boyd, who has withdrawn his hand from Trixie's arm and is now resting it on the back of Honey's neck instead, she leaves. The door clicks quietly after her and yet again Honey feels like weeping and yet again she tells herself this is because of the shock of the fall.

As they make their way slowly upstairs, Boyd tells Honey he'll have to inspect the step down to the storeroom at work, fill in health and safety forms, inform the insurers. She says there's no need, it was her fault – she wasn't looking where she was going – and he says it can all wait until tomorrow. The important thing is for her to rest.

She hobbles to the bathroom and then, back in their room, overwhelmed by tiredness, slips out of her clothes and hops into bed.

'Can I get you anything to eat?' Boyd asks.

'No, thanks. I'm fine. Just need some sleep. I'll be dandy in the morning.'

He kisses her on the lips, puts her phone next to the bed, opens a window to give her some fresh air and says, 'I'll leave you for a bit then. Call me if you need anything and I'll check on you in a while anyway, OK?'

'OK,' she nods, and then he's gone from the room and she hears him going downstairs.

She reaches out for her phone and blocks the number as Trixie had told her to do and then deletes the message. It feels good to do this; a lucky escape, like she's been given a second chance.

She dozes and a bit later is woken by the sound of Boyd's voice. He's talking on the phone on the patio below their bedroom window.

If it's difficult enough overhearing a conversation you're not meant to overhear, what's more difficult is only being able to hear one side of it. It means that you have to imagine what the other person's saying and the chances of getting this wrong are massive. She lies very still and quiet; her foot feels heavy, her head is full of cotton wool and yet she can still make out Boyd saying, 'No, there's nothing you can do. She's sleeping. You don't have to come back, but … you should have told me, Vita.'

There's a beat of silence before he says, 'Why? Because it matters. I thought we were friends.'

Another beat of silence.

'How long has it been going on?'

There's a pause while Vita says something and then Boyd says, 'He doesn't seem your type.'

There's something in the tone of Boyd's voice that Honey doesn't recognise. It's sharp, like a parent's when they're talking to a child who's let them down in some subtle, yet catastrophic way.

He's talking again. 'Were you ever going to tell me? I mean, you going to move in with him, or him with you? Am I in the way?'

Honey notices the word 'I' in this last question; it's like a pin scratching her skin. He should have said 'we'.

She realises he's talking to Vita about Colin and this is what the look that passed between him and Trixie was all about and it hits Honey suddenly and irrevocably that Vita being with Colin is making Boyd unhappy for some inexplicable reason. Why should he mind? Shouldn't he be happy for her? It certainly makes Honey happier.

Boyd must have moved back inside or further down the garden as she can no longer hear him. It's completely dark outside now and she imagines the sky dotted with stars. She sleeps again but doesn't dream about the man in the boat. She'd expected she would, but she doesn't.

Boyd

The next morning Boyd is filling the kettle, half listening out for Vita's footsteps on the stairs. He was here yesterday morning doing the same thing and it seems a lifetime ago but it isn't, it was only yesterday and they still have five across to do: the clue is 'tart quality' and the answer's eleven letters long. They already have an N and a Y but are stumped and, without it, they can't answer seven across.

As he switches the kettle on, he thinks of Honey upstairs, her face pale against the pillowcase, the sooty smudges of tiredness under her eyes, those cheekbones. She'd slept heavily, he'd thought she would have her dream again but she didn't.

He'll have to go and inspect the step today; see what it was that caused her to fall. He checks the clock, it's six-forty. Vita's late coming down this morning, he thinks.

And then the front door opens and she's standing in the lounge, the sky behind her is still navy, she's carrying her coat over her arm. She looks guilty and, for a second, a pain seizes Boyd's heart as if she's been caught out deceiving him in some unspeakable way. Just for that second he's forgotten they're no longer together, that Honey's upstairs. Vita's obviously just come in from spending the night with another man and, apparently, this is all as it should be.

211

'Good morning.' Vita is speaking as though she's just arriving at a business meeting. The guilt's gone and in its place is her usual defiance, her brittleness.

'Morning. Kettle's on,' Boyd replies, tightening the belt on his bathrobe and looking down at his feet. He's wearing slippers and has the sudden urge to laugh, as though he's trapped in some awful sitcom.

'How's Honey?' Vita asks, thankfully pulling Boyd back to the tea, this morning, the crossword.

'OK, I think. She slept well.'

'That's good.'

'Nice evening?' he asks as he puts tea bags in the pot. He tries to say this lightly, but has the feeling it's come out as somewhat barbed.

'Yes, thank you.' She's put her coat down and has picked up yesterday's paper. 'You still haven't got five across then?' she says.

'It's been a bit busy round here.' Again, his voice is sharper than he intended it to be.

'I bet it has.'

And then he's imagining her with Colin: her in bed with Colin, Colin's hands on her skin.

The words seem to come out of nowhere. He wasn't expecting or planning to say them.

'Tell me you're happy at least. With him, I mean. That he makes you happy,' he says.

There is a long silence and then, looking steadily at him, she clears her throat. 'It's not a hearts and flowers thing, Boyd,' she says. 'We're good friends, that's all. It's ...' she pauses.

'Yes?' He's fingering the knob on the lid of the teapot in an effort to distract himself.

'… convenient.'

'Is that all you want?' This question also comes unbidden and he knows as soon as he's asked it that he has no right to do so, no right at all. 'I'm sorry,' he adds quickly. 'I shouldn't have asked that.'

'No,' she replies, 'you shouldn't. You,' she looks up in the direction of the bedroom where Honey is still asleep, 'are the last person who should be asking me that. And that's why I tried to keep it quiet, why I don't want a fuss. It's nice as it is.'

'Does Trixie know?'

'What is this, Boyd? Why should it matter if she does or doesn't. It's nobody's business but my own really, isn't it?'

Boyd can't answer this and so, in an effort to change the subject, he says, 'Trixie stayed on for a bit last night. Saw us get settled in after we got back from the hospital.'

'Did she? That was nice.'

'I really don't know what I'd do without her, you know.'

'She's still part of the furniture, isn't she?'

Vita looks tired, Boyd thinks. He wants to be able to take a step towards her, hold out a hand and place it on the back of her head, feel her hair under his fingers like he used to, but he knows he shouldn't be thinking this at all.

And then she's saying, 'Is that tea going to pour itself or what?' and automatically he picks up the pot.

She's still holding the paper and says out of nowhere, 'Astringency.'

'Pardon?' He's adding milk, just the amount he knows she likes.

'That's the answer to "tart quality". It's "astringency".'

He hands her a mug and says, 'Oh, of course it is. How did we not get that?'

'Must be getting rusty, I guess.' And, he thinks, it's not the only thing they're rusty at. They should be better at doing this than they are and he shouldn't mind about her and Colin. They've been through too much to get to where they are now, after all, haven't they? 'I'll take Honey hers,' he says, 'and then shall we crack on with twelve down?'

'Actually Boyd, I think I'll head on up if that's OK and have my shower now. I need to change my clothes.'

As he watches her go, he feels an ineffable sadness settle on his heart at the thought of her 'convenient' relationship, at the thought of her wearing the same clothes as yesterday, of her getting out of bed next door and putting them back on to make the short journey home, at the thought that she will peel these clothes off again upstairs and get dressed into something else and go into her studio and carry on painting the pictures of the bloody dogs she hates painting. This isn't the life he would wish for Vita. He wants something better for her than this. He wishes it was still in his gift to give it to her, and this surprises him.

He doesn't know Colin all that well but guesses he's a nice bloke, that he'll have Vita's best interests at heart but there is, in the back of Boyd's throat, a taste of something bitter and the thought that actually Colin may not be good enough for Vita, not good enough at all.

These thoughts are buzzing in his head as he carries Honey's coffee upstairs. He can hear the shower running in the bathroom and deliberately doesn't think of Vita's small, firm, familiar body, her sturdy legs, her hair, the water channelling between her breasts. No, he doesn't think of these things but instead he tiptoes into his and Honey's bedroom and stands for a long moment looking down at the girl he loves now as she sleeps, at the small frown puckering her brow.

'Hello there, sleepyhead,' he says at last, putting the mug down.

Honey stretches and winces as she tries to move her foot. 'Shit,' she says, 'I'd forgotten that for a moment.'

'That's a fine way to greet me,' Boyd chuckles as he says this.

'Sorry,' she mumbles. 'I meant of course, good morning, Boyd.'

'That's better.'

'Is Vita home?' she asks. 'Is that the shower I can hear?'

'Yes, she's just got in.'

'Ah, OK.'

Boyd realises that neither of them, it seems, is brave enough to ask the other how they feel about this latest development. And so it looks like it's going to be one of those things that just gets accepted, isn't questioned, isn't analysed. And, he thinks, this is probably for the best.

'I'd better check my phone,' he says as Honey hoists herself up in bed and takes a sip. 'And you'll be wanting to check your horoscope, I guess.'

'Guess so. Didn't have time to check it yesterday; it may have told me I'd take a tumble if I had!' She laughs, picking up her own phone and staring intently at the screen.

Boyd's phone has been on silent and he's missed three calls from Jean, the manager of Queen Anne's, his mother's nursing home.

'Fuck,' he says under his breath, 'what now?' and hurries out of the room to listen to the messages.

'Hello Boyd,' Jean's voice is husky on the voicemail, huskier than it is normally. 'It's Jean. From Queen Anne's. Just wondering if you could give me a call back? It's quite urgent. Thank you. Hear from you soon, I hope.'

She's left a breathy gap between each of these sentences as if struggling to work out what to say. The first two calls are just missed calls, she's left this message on the third. He dials her number and is standing at the top of the stairs when she answers.

'Boyd,' she says. 'I know it's early but thanks for calling back.'

He can picture her at her desk with its jumble of papers and the painting of Stonehenge on the wall behind her.

'Sorry I missed your calls. What's up?'

'Um,' she replies. 'This is tricky. I don't quite know what to say.'

'Just say it. Whatever it is, we'll cope I'm sure.' He still has no idea what she wants, what she's got to tell him.

At that moment, Vita opens the bathroom door and, with a towel wrapped around her body and another around her head, starts walking towards him. In their room Honey is chuckling at something she must be looking at on her phone as Vita steps by him.

'It's Jean,' he mouths at her.

Vita nods briefly and goes into her bedroom, closing the door behind her.

Boyd doesn't think about the damp towel, the drops of shower water that may still be on Vita's eyelashes, about Colin and Colin's hands on her. No, he doesn't think of any of these things, or so he tells himself in the split second before Jean speaks again.

'Your mother's in hospital,' she says quickly. 'She was admitted yesterday.'

It takes Boyd a moment to compute this. He'd seen his mother at the hospital yesterday, she'd said she was just in for a routine check-up and he'd believed her.

'Which hospital?' he asks, although of course he already knows the answer to this.

'Royal Surrey. We've only just received her permission to tell you.

I have to admit, it's been difficult these past few weeks, not being able to pick up the phone to you to tell you about the tests, the diagnosis.'

'But she's fine, isn't she?' Boyd's brain is playing catch up with his heart, his heart is beating a million times a minute it seems, while his brain is moving in slow motion. 'I mean, she had a backache when I visited her last, but otherwise, she seemed fine. They said her blood pressure was OK and that she was eating well. She said she was just in hospital for tests. It was just routine.'

There is an agonising pause and it's as though Boyd already knows what Jean is going to say next.

'It's cancer, I'm afraid, Boyd. It's in her bones and now her liver. It's a matter of palliative care from now on. I'm so terribly sorry.'

'Why didn't she say? How come I'm the last to know?'

'I can't answer that, I'm sorry. You know what she's like.'

He'd thought he did, but now he's not so sure. He's known this woman who is his mother all his life and yet he can't tell whether she's kept her illness a secret up to now in order to protect him or to punish him.

'I should go and see her,' he says. 'Today. I should go now, shouldn't I?'

'It may be an idea, Boyd,' Jean replies. 'I am so terribly sorry.'

'I'll be in touch later when and if I've been able to speak to her doctor, OK?'

'OK. And do take care, Boyd. Everyone here is thinking of you.'

They say goodbye, or Boyd assumes they do; he can't quite remember as he puts his phone in the pocket of his bathrobe and stares at the closed door to Vita's room. He should tell Honey, he should phone Trixie to say he won't be in the office again today, he should do both of these things and yet, the most logical and important thing he actually wants to do is to tell Vita this news; it's as though only she will understand the full enormity of it.

He's just raising his hand to knock on Vita's door when Honey staggers out of their room and, leaning up against the wall, says, 'What is it Boyd? What's happened?'

And so he tells her instead and she says, 'I'll come with you. To the hospital. I should come, shouldn't I?'

'You don't have to. You should stay here and rest.'

'I want to come. I want to be there with you.'

And he loves her for saying this, for wanting to do this thing for him. And, if he's honest with himself, he's relieved; it will be a comfort having her there. Even though she and his mother have not met before, this might be the easiest and best way for them to do so. It may be one of the last chances they have.

'I should tell Vita though,' he adds, as he steers Honey back into the room and helps her sit down on the bed.

'You do that while I try and get dressed,' she says. 'And then I guess you should put some clothes on too, eh?'

'You're right, I should!'

But before he does, he walks slowly until he's outside Vita's door and this time he knocks and she says, 'What?' and he says, 'It's Mum,' and she flings open the door and is standing there, her hair in waves around her shoulders, her eyes vulnerable and exposed without her glasses, and she is saying, 'Christ, Boyd. What's she gone and done now?'

It's awful telling Vita, especially as he's so short on actual facts. All he can say is that his mother is suddenly dying. This morning when he got up, she'd been 3D and alive and difficult and feisty and angry and part of the backdrop to his life. Now, a mere hour later, she's slipping out of the picture frame, already fading. And, surprisingly, Boyd finds he's furious about this.

He feels beleaguered: first there was telling Honey about William, then Honey's accident, then finding out about Vita and Colin, and now this? What's life going to throw at me next, he wonders?

Later, when all three of them are downstairs, Honey having fashioned a way of getting down them on her bottom with Boyd behind carrying her crutches, Boyd finds the house too small and crowded. Part of him thinks he should face this alone but another part wants the company of one or either of these women, but actually not both.

'I'll come,' Vita had said. 'To the hospital. I'll come with you.'

'It's OK, Honey's coming.'

'But Belle doesn't know Honey. Not like I do.' She's standing in the kitchen now, her arms folded across her chest. She's wearing black leggings, red boots, a smock-type thing Boyd hasn't seen before. Her hair is back in its plait, her eyes behind her glasses and she's radiating some fearful kind of energy he doesn't quite understand.

In the lounge, Honey's sitting on the sofa, her leg up. She's wearing a long flowery skirt, her denim jacket. She looks impossibly young and vulnerable and he's standing in between the two of them, a surprising mess of emotions. He'd sometimes wondered what life would be like without his mother and her disappointments but now, faced with the news Jean's just given him, he finds he's not at all ready to find out.

'Vita,' he says, 'will you help Honey into the car while I ring Trixie. She'll be wondering where I am.'

'I can manage,' Honey says, struggling to her feet and hopping over to pick up her crutches.

'Don't be so silly.' Vita takes the crutches from Honey and helps slot them under her armpits and then, steering her gently with one hand, she takes the keys to Boyd's car out of his hand with her other and they make their way gingerly to the door.

Boyd dials the office number. 'Trixie?' he says, as he watches them go. 'It's me.'

The shock is starting to wear off but even so, telling Trixie about his mum is harder than he thought it'd be. Of course, she says, 'Don't you worry about anything here, Boyd. I'll look after everything. You just go and see her. I'll hear from you later no doubt.'

'I was,' he says, 'going to come in and inspect the step down into the storeroom, take photos, and the like. Promise me you won't touch anything or go down them yourself today. Promise me.'

'I promise,' she replies.

'I'll call you later, OK?'

'OK, Boyd. Take care now.'

There's a strange gap in the conversation. They've spoken on the phone countless times and yet this time Boyd can sense an undercurrent, something Trixie's not saying but that she wants to.

'Who?' she says into this gap. 'Who's going with you, to the hospital, I mean? You're not going on your own, are you?'

'Vita and Honey are coming. Vita's helping Honey get in the car at the moment.'

'Oh, I see,' Trixie says. 'Well, in that case I'd better let you get on.'

There's another gap into which Boyd says, 'Thank you, you're a godsend. Don't know what we'd do without you.'

'Well, yes, that's as may be,' she replies, before saying, 'Go on, you'd better get going then. And Boyd …?'

'Yes.'

'I hope it goes OK, at the hospital. You know.'

'I know. Bye for now Trixie.'

'Bye.'

Vita's closing the car door as Boyd steps out of the house and turns to lock up behind him. It's only just gone nine and yet he feels he's already lived half a lifetime today.

Honey

It's strangely OK to be shepherded down the path by Vita; she's strong and capable and her hair smells comfortingly of lemon shampoo. Boyd's car is where he left it yesterday, facing the bottom of the road.

'We should arrange another sitting, I guess,' Honey says to Vita as they reach the gate. 'For the portrait, I mean.'

'Mmmm,' Vita replies. 'Suppose we should.'

'I mean, while I can use this,' Honey adds, pointing to her foot, 'as a reason to stay home.'

'Mmmm,' Vita says again, manoeuvring Honey around the car to the passenger door, snatching at the handle and yanking it open. 'Here,' she says, 'I'll help you in.'

And that's when it happens. Honey's lowering herself into the seat and preparing to swing her legs around when she looks off into the distance and catches sight of him standing under the horse chestnut trees at the end of the road. The leaves are full of blight at this time of year, have begun to turn and there are drifts of them crowding up against the fence bordering the park.

He is leaning against the tree, hunched inside a leather jacket, smoking a cigarette.

'You OK?' Vita asks, as Boyd slams the front door shut; scaring a bird from the tree and causing Reuben to look directly at them.

'Of course,' Honey says. 'I'm fine.'

But he's still there as Boyd turns the car round at the end of the road. He's still there as they drive away. Honey closes her eyes and imagines opening them to see that he's gone, that he was never there in the first place but instead, when she opens them, his reflection is getting smaller and smaller in the wing mirror.

Neither Boyd nor Vita say anything at the junction or as Boyd pulls out into the flow of traffic.

Vita

It's been years since I've been in a car with Boyd.

We had a car seat for William which we put in the front and I'd sit in the back and crane my neck around the headrest, constantly checking on him on the few journeys we did together before he died. I'd watch his tiny lips move, him punch the air with his fists, open his eyes wide when we went under a bridge. I can't remember what we did with the car seat afterwards.

Other than that, I always travelled in the front seat, next to Boyd as he drove, and so it's odd now being in the back, staring at his left ear, the jut of his jaw, and seeing the top of Honey's head in the seat in front of me, a few dark roots showing in her cropped, peroxide hair. At a set of traffic lights, Boyd reaches across and squeezes Honey's knee.

Isn't it strange how you never know you've lived the last day of one kind of life until you realise that kind of life is over, and you're looking back at it and can pinpoint the exact day that everything changed?

And so there must have been the last day on which I rode in the front of Boyd's car as we drove to a place we'd planned to go to together, as a couple, with me comfortable and relaxed and knowing that when we left, we'd leave together and drive home again; there must have been the last day I ironed a shirt of his as his official wife, not his estranged or separated wife, or angry or grieving wife; there must have been the last day we made love – his tender hands, his full lips, the way we came together, practised and easy with one another; there must have been the last day when we smiled at one another – the simple, open smile of two people who love each other, who share a life and home and photo albums and the word 'us'; there must have been the last day we went to the supermarket, bought bread and milk and eggs and carried them through the front door in plastic bags. There must have been a last day before William died.

I've never thought of this before or wasted time remembering all these last days; what would have been the point? It wouldn't have changed anything.

He'd said he'd leave and I hadn't asked him to stay, it had been the easiest of the options available to us at the time. Without him in the house, there weren't the daily reminders of what we'd lost and I could pretend everything was as it should be without him there. I'd not wanted him to be able to see my pain or to see his, which he'd worn like a cloak he hadn't seemed able to take off.

It'd been as though we'd never shake off the grief; how was I to know that even though it's obviously still there, it's been – and can be – overlaid with the day-to-day, the small joys of seeing a magnolia in full bloom, hearing the pouring out of birdsong, mixing just the right shade of paint? These tiny blessings can't erase the enormity of my grief, but they can – and do – soften it a little. But even so, how can Boyd now say he's done his grieving, that it's over completely? I don't think I will ever be able to forgive him for that.

Maybe if we'd been more patient, with ourselves as well as each other, we wouldn't have ended up like this, with me in the back of the car, Boyd and Honey in the front, all of us going to visit his dying mother on a morning when I woke up in another man's bed. Maybe we would have come to an accord, understood each other's grief better. After all, grief is ever-changing, but he and I would have had to be living together to know this, wouldn't we? Doing it all from a distance: him in his flat, me in the house, each of us pretending nothing mattered any more – had this all been one huge mistake?

Maybe if Boyd hadn't come back to live in the house, hadn't brought Honey with him, I wouldn't be in this situation now either. Maybe him doing so had been one huge mistake too.

'You OK in the back there?' Boyd asks as we reach the A31. He looks back at me briefly, raising his left eyebrow in that way of his.

'Of course I'm all right,' I snap.

Boyd stares ahead once more and I rest my chin on my fist and gaze out of the window.

I really have no idea why I decided to stay over at Colin's last night. I'd got home from another bloody visit to another bloody woman with a stupid yappy dog to find Trixie in the lounge having made herself a hot drink, and she'd told me about Honey's accident. The walls of the house had moved in a foot or two, like they were squeezing me out, or so it seemed.

But then Colin had called round. We were going to the cinema in Aldershot to see a live screening from the Royal Opera House. Maybe it had been then I'd decided that it was time to come clean in the only way I knew how, by staying out overnight.

'Nearly there,' Boyd says now, as we merge on to the A3. I can tell he's nervous, he's never really been comfortable around his mother. And then he looks across at Honey and says, 'You doing OK? Not in too much pain?'

I want to throw something at him.

I don't hear Honey's reply because I'm gazing out of the window again, thinking about last night and Colin.

'Enjoy that?' he asked as we left the cinema.

'Mmmm, yes, thank you.'

'Back to mine? I've got some of that Epoisse cheese you like. Thought we could have some with a glass of port before you go back next door.'

Or perhaps it had been then that I'd decided.

Or perhaps it had been after we'd eaten the cheese and drunk the port and had sex and bizarrely I'd felt like weeping.

In any case, there'd come a point in the evening when it was obvious Colin was expecting me to slip out of bed, get dressed and leave as I always did.

'OK if I stay?' I'd said.

'Are you sure?' He raised himself up in the bed and looked me squarely in the eye. His skin was caramel coloured in the diffused light from the landing; it was smooth and silky.

I was lying with my hands behind my head, revelling in being naked, of having just come and, for that moment had felt defiant, the opposite of victim, and I remember wondering why it was I'd never told Colin about William. He'd traced the faint stretch marks on my belly but had never commented on them and this was yet one more thing I was grateful to him for. He'd also never asked why Boyd and I had split but had taken it as a given. As I've said, Colin is the most undemanding man I've ever known; I don't like to think this is because he doesn't care enough to be demanding, but that he respects my space, much as I respect his. And also, I didn't want him to know the broken, tragic me. I want to be this Vita, this strong, sure island of a woman who makes no demands and expects nothing in return.

'I'm sure,' I said.

So maybe it had been then I'd decided to stay.

Whenever the decision had been made, what I hadn't bargained for was walking into my house this morning and finding Boyd standing there looking at me the way he was, the air between us stitched tight.

* * *

When we get to the hospital, it's like we're in some kind of farce.

We park and Boyd strides off to find a wheelchair for Honey.

'I'm not having you hop all the way there on your crutches, you'll be exhausted,' he says as he gets out of the car. 'You'll wait here with her, won't you, Vita?'

'Sure.' But I don't really want to, I want to get going, get it over with.

With Boyd gone I don't know what to say to Honey. Should I make polite conversation? Could I? I've never really been alone with Honey anywhere other than the house or the studio and it's odd being here, in public, away from the security of what's normal. It's like I don't know how to behave or what role I'm supposed to be playing.

But then Honey says, 'I feel such a fool, you know.'

'Why?' I snap again. Honey's comment has taken me by surprise.

'Falling over the way I did. I mean, I'm a grown-up, I shouldn't be falling down steps.'

'How did it happen?' I try a more conciliatory tone. 'Trixie told me some of what happened, but can you remember anything?'

'Not really; I was going down into the storeroom and then I was falling and it went black for a while. I knew I'd broken something as soon as I came to. After all, it's what Elizabeth had predicted.'

'Elizabeth?' Who the fuck is Elizabeth, I think?

'Yes, you know. The medium I went to see. She said I'd have an accident so I'm presuming this is it.'

Honey's voice quavers as she says this, which I find odd. After all, Honey had seemed to be coping so well with everything. She's been so bloody pleasant and amenable and hasn't made a fuss that I'm surprised by how she says this and how she's nervously tapping her fingertips on her knee as if to try and steady herself.

There's a gap in the conversation which I feel honour-bound to fill, so say, 'Ah, yes, Elizabeth.' And then I gaze out of the window and at last see Boyd making his way across the car park with a hospital wheelchair.

Thank God. Now at least we can get on. I am, I realise, stupidly nervous about seeing Belle. My visits to Queen Anne's have mostly been an act of bluff and bluster.

Boyd opens Honey's door and leans in and I say, 'You took your time.'

'Charming,' he replies. 'Next time you can go and find the sodding chair then.'

'Boyd?' Honey says, looking up at him. 'It's OK. We're OK, aren't we, Vita?'

I harrumph and get out of the car. 'Come on,' I say, 'let's get Honey into it then.'

Together we help Honey into the chair and Boyd pushes her along the path to the hospital entrance. His shoulders, I notice, are tensed and hunched up almost to his ears. I wonder what he's thinking. After all, this is where I gave birth, where we'd come to try and find out why William had died, where we'd endured a litany of doctor-speak and the words 'rare' and 'tragic' said far too many times into the space that was beginning to grow between us.

I stride ahead, leaving Boyd and Honey to follow in my wake. It is starting to rain: cold, penetrating rain. 'Bloody brilliant,' I mutter under my breath as I take shelter in the doorway. God, I hate it here.

We manoeuvre Honey into the lift and then out of it again; we tramp along long, winding corridors until we reach the ward his mother's in.

'No,' says a short, squat nurse who is as round as she is tall. 'Absolutely not. You can't visit until Visiting Time. That's why it's called Visiting Time and, in any case, there are only two visitors per patient and…' she stares at Honey's wheelchair with her beady eyes, 'it's best not to bring *that* on to the ward.'

'Fine,' Boyd says, his mouth set in a firm line. 'We'll wait until Visiting Time. Honey'll hobble on her crutches and only two of us will see my mother who, by the way, I only learned this morning is actually dying, at any one time. Does that work for you?'

I have rarely seen Boyd so angry and my heart tips a little in my chest. Of course, he'd been angry with me when he'd said he was leaving and I'd heard an echo of that anger when he rang last night to talk about Colin and in what he'd said to me this morning when I came home, but this kind of frustrated rage is something new and has, I think, everything to do with his mother.

'Of course,' the nurse replies, all sweetness and light now she knows what Boyd's dealing with. 'That's fine. And I'm so sorry about your mother. You can wait in the family room down there,' she points to a doorway just past the entrance to the staircase, 'or go to the restaurant. They do a mean panini.'

When the nurse has bustled off, Boyd looks firstly at Honey and then at me. 'I …' he says.

'You need to go and get some answers, don't you?' I say.

He nods. 'I need to try. There must be a doctor here somewhere who knows what's going on.'

'We'll be fine. Just go.'

I don't mean this. I want to go with him; the urge to do so is like a stabbing pain in between my ribs but I know I can't. It's not my place to, not any more.

He bends and kisses Honey on the lips. I turn and get ready to march off before remembering that I'll have to wheel the bloody chair when Boyd has gone.

Honey says, 'Take care. Try not to worry too much. OK?'

'OK,' Boyd replies. 'Thank you, for being here.'

I really can't bear it much longer. How can Honey have the fucking right to be here? However lovely and bird-like and kind and quirky she may be, however much she may love him, and he think he loves her, she's only been around for five minutes, hasn't gone through what Boyd and I have gone through. She hasn't even met Belle yet for fuck's sake!

But, I reason, there's nothing I can do, nothing I should do. Not now, not here. Here and now is about supporting Boyd through this ordeal, so I march back over to the wheelchair and say, 'We'll be in the restaurant having one of their world-fucking-famous paninis then. Come and find us when you can?'

And I kick the footbrake and begin to wheel Honey away. I don't look back at Boyd but concentrate instead on the way Honey's hair tapers at the back of her neck and tell myself to remember this when we have our next sitting. There is something unbearably fragile about Honey's neck; her skin is creamy-white.

Hours pass, or what seems like hours. Honey and I eat our paninis, drink coffee, say the occasional thing to one another but otherwise we stare out of the window or check our phones. I'd texted Colin to tell him what was happening and he'd replied, 'Oh, I'm so sorry to hear that. Take care. Speak soon.' Another clear, clean answer from him: no ambiguities there.

'I'd better see how Trixie's getting on,' Honey says, getting ready to dial the office.

'I'll get us some more coffee then.'

As I'm waiting to pay, I stare at the display of chocolate bars and, for some strange reason I'm young again and back in Belle's monster of a house with its dark furniture and huge windows. Belle's sitting in an armchair, holding the ridiculously small handle of a ridiculously small cup between her perfectly manicured fingers. I feel like Gulliver in Lilliput next to her. It's the first time we've met.

'So,' Belle is saying, squinting a little in the afternoon sun flooding through the French doors at the back of the room, 'you're Vita.'

The room's cluttered and filled with a pervading sense of disappointment. Without being told it, I know I somehow don't come up to scratch. Maybe I should be broad-hipped and domesticated, a cake-baker and expert flower-arranger. But then maybe even if I had been, I wouldn't have met with her approval.

'Yes,' I say. 'I'm Vita.'

Boyd is in the kitchen refilling the pot. I wish he'd come back; the room is an unfriendly place without him in it.

But when he does come back, he and his mother continue the dance they'd played on the doorstep and in the hall and as she carried in a plate of biscuits. It is a kind of dance I've never experienced before. It is evident that there's something between them that's massive and unspoken and unforgiven.

After that first visit, relations had thawed a little. Not much, but a little, and Belle didn't come to our wedding.

'I haven't done everything I've done to see you get married in a Registry Office,' she'd said.

However, when at last I fell pregnant, it was as though a cloud had lifted.

We're back in the sitting room of the huge house but this time Belle is fussing over me. 'Come now,' she's saying, 'you must rest. Put your feet up on this stool. Have a Garibaldi.'

I hate Garibaldi biscuits, but take one as Boyd comes back into the room from the garden where he's been propping up a bit of broken fence.

'Thank you, Boyd,' Belle says. 'Now have some tea and look after this wife of yours.'

Boyd winks at me and I nearly choke on a bit of the bloody Garibaldi.

On the way home in the car, I'd turned to Boyd and asked, 'What is it between the two of you? You and your mum? You ever going to tell me?'

'It's complicated,' he said. 'Sometimes I think it's too complicated even for me to understand. I really don't know if I could explain it to you.'

But he tries and so I learn about his father and the visit Belle has never forgiven him for.

And then William is born and Belle is in her element.

She fusses and knits and interferes and says, 'He looks just like you did, Boyd, when you were born. You were such a handsome chap then.'

And then William dies and Belle's grief has become mixed up in the thing that lies unforgiven between her and Boyd and in the fact that I let him leave me and that he went.

I've only been to visit her at Queen Anne's a few times but enough for it to seem like a habit.

Belle had been hostile at first. 'What do you want?' she'd asked in a beaky sort of voice. I'd been quite surprised by the change in her since William's funeral. She'd shrunk and her voice had become more tremulous, less certain.

'Just thought I'd pop by and see how you were,' I said.

'Well, I'm fine, as you can see.' She obviously wasn't. 'Have you heard from Boyd?' she added.

'We're in touch, now and again.'

She made a kind of snorting noise, a mixture of disapproval and disgust and I remember looking out into the garden, at the lawn sloping away into the distance. There were a few white plastic tables and chairs on the patio but it was November and so no one was sitting out there. Rain spattered against the window.

I felt compelled to say it, even though I didn't really want to. 'I'm sorry,' I said.

'What for?' She turned her laser-beam eyes on me.

'That it didn't work out, between Boyd and me.'

'Mmmm,' she replied. And then in a rare move she reached out a hand and said, 'It was an awful time. I can't imagine how you must have felt.'

I didn't know whether to believe her or not but most of all I thought it's not how I *felt* but how I *feel*. The loss is still fucking there. All of it: losing William, losing Boyd, losing the chance to be a parent, the future my child should have had, the person I could have become.

But all I actually said was, 'It's good we're friends, at least we have that.'

When I told her about Boyd's request to come back and live at the house, she'd been incredulous, even more so when I told her about Honey.

'How can you countenance it?' she asked.

And so the bluff and bluster kicked in and I said, 'Oh, it'll be fine. It'll be cool.'

I pick up the tray and carry the coffees back to where Honey is sitting, telling myself that, after all, whatever happens, the woman in the nursing home, the woman in the bed in a ward in this hospital, is still – and always will be – the grandmother my son would have had, had he lived.

'Thank you,' Honey says. 'Trixie was on the other line so I'll call her back in a bit.'

'Mmmm,' I reply, stirring my coffee vigorously. I'm not really interested in what Honey's just said. Trixie and I were close once, but obviously weren't so nowadays, we didn't need to be. All that water, all those bridges, again

But then I notice that Honey hasn't touched her coffee, her hands are in her lap and she's shaking.

'Did you see him?' Honey asks.

'Who?'

'The man, standing under the trees at the end of the road earlier as we drove away. He was watching us.'

I tap the stirrer against the side of the mug and then put it down on the table top. An uncomfortable feeling of dread fills my chest. You know, that knee-melting, ear-burning thing again. But I say, 'Nah, I didn't see anyone.'

'Oh, OK. Perhaps I was imagining it. I always get a bit freaked out about hospitals and while I was here yesterday I saw a broom leaning up against a bed and that always means death and so maybe I was distracted by that and imagined it.'

I have no idea what to say to this. After all, wasn't there going to be a death now anyway? I choose not to reply but take a sip of my drink and notice that when Honey eventually picks hers up, her hands are still shaking. I put my drink down and sit on my hands to stop myself from reaching out to touch her.

We sit for the most part in silence until Boyd comes back and he too buys something to eat and the three of us wait for the much-advertised Visiting Time to start.

'How did you get on?' I ask as he sits down, his as-yet uneaten panini on a plate in front of him.

'OK. One step forward, two back.'

'What do you mean?' Honey leans over and touches his arm.

He looks at her and back at me. It's like he's watching a tennis match, I think.

'I saw a doctor, but he's not *her* doctor. All he could say was that her doctor should be on the ward sometime this afternoon and to try and catch him then. You'd think I'd have a right to know what's happening to my own mother, wouldn't you?'

'But you know what she's like,' I say.

'Yes, I guess I do. I had thought though, that just for once, especially now, she'd thaw a little, take me into her confidence.'

Honey and I exchange a glance as Boyd says this. He takes a bite of his panini. Swallows. Wipes his mouth on a napkin.

It's as though both Honey and I are waiting for the other to react, to get up and put our arms around this bear of a man whose heart, it seems, is breaking. I believe it should be Honey who does this, but I want it to be me.

The last day

Graham Silverton has been doing this job for ten years. He'd once hoped to spend his time doing something more extraordinary, like digging wells in Africa or discovering a ground-breaking cure for some unspeakable disease, but he hadn't worked hard when he'd been at school, preferring to play the fool and impress the girls than get to grips with algebra and the subtexts in Shakespeare's plays. And then came marriage and a mortgage, children and Henry the cat and so now he's a driver for a builders' merchants, plays darts down the pub on a Friday night with his mates and spends Saturdays on the touchlines of football pitches watching his son not quite being the brilliant player he'd dreamed he might.

As Graham drives he glances at people's houses and gardens. He studies the faces of the people in the vehicles next to him at traffic lights and junctions and he listens to the radio, wondering whether there's another life out there he could be living. Sometimes he sees a beautiful woman on the pavement and thinks thoughts he shouldn't think about hot skin and risky sex but then he remembers his wife, his kids, his house, mortgage and cat and becomes the perfectly ordinary man he mostly believes himself to be.

On the last day, as he's driving along the ring road, an Aston Martin sweeps by him, all sleek and shiny. He watches it disappear round the bend and then checks the time. He's running a little late with this delivery so decides to take a short cut through town. He knows the way so doesn't need the satnav. He indicates and switches lanes ready to take the next exit.

Boyd

When at last he's allowed on to the ward, Boyd's first thought is how tiny his mother looks in the hospital bed. He pulls up a chair and sits, placing his hands on his knees. Her bed is next to the window and, outside, the clouds are steely and bulbous. It's an ugly autumn day.

'You needn't have come,' she says.

'We wanted to.'

'We?'

'Yes, Vita and Honey came too.'

'Why would they come? Especially *that* woman.'

Boyd hesitates for a second, not totally sure which woman his mother is referring to, but then says, 'If you mean Honey, well, she wanted to come. She wants to have the chance to meet you, you know before …'

He tails off and his mother jumps in with, '… before I snuff it, you mean.'

'Well, I wouldn't have put it quite like that.'

'Mmmm,' she closes her eyes and turns her head away. 'I'm tired,' she says. 'Not sure if I'm up to visitors today.'

'Oh come on, Mum,' he says. 'We've come specially and Honey's got a broken ankle. That's why I was here yesterday.'

240

Without her make-up and clothes, his mother is a different person: gone is the aura of pretence she's always worn, the pretence that says everything is fine, when really it isn't. Of course Boyd has always known this, but like the rest of the world he's been beguiled by the image his mother has put across. She's always had the ability to make him feel like he doesn't deserve to breathe the same air as her, as if she's in some way superior to him. The only time he'd seen her unmasked was at William's funeral. Then she'd been pale, subdued, overwhelmed, as had he and Vita, of course, but it was odd seeing his mother like that; it had made him wonder whether the fact he's not seen her clearly all these years was actually not her fault, but his.

Perhaps he had just been looking at her from the wrong angle.

And now she's here, pale and overwhelmed again, dressed in a white cotton nightie, the skin around her neck mottled and wrinkled, her hair flattened on one side from when she'd been sleeping. The perfectly dressed and coiffured woman of yesterday has, it seems, been replaced by a stranger, much like she'd appeared to him all those years ago when she'd made him promise not to find his father …

She hasn't replied to Boyd's comment about Honey's ankle and so he continues, 'I was hoping to speak to a doctor while I was here.'

'Why?'

'To find out what's going on. How I can help.'

'You could ask me. I'm not dead yet.'

She's picking at the bedclothes with her fingernails and then winces.

'You in pain?'

'Of course I am.'

'Why didn't you tell me sooner? About the cancer I mean. You should have told me.' He hadn't wanted to say this, not this afternoon, not on this first visit, but he knows he has to sometime and so he does, he has.

'What would have been the point? You couldn't have done anything.'

'Not medically perhaps, but we could have talked about it.'

'There wouldn't have been any point in that either. There's nothing to say. I'll stay here while they get my medication sorted and then they'll find somewhere for me to go for the palliative bit. It's quite simple.'

Boyd really can't fathom his mother. It's as though she's talking about a neighbour, not herself, and so he blurts out, 'Aren't you cross?'

And then Belle looks straight at him. There is, he can see, some of her famed beauty left. It's in the directness of her gaze, the way her mouth moves. Somewhere deeply hidden are remnants of the woman in the photographs he'd pored over as a boy.

'Of course I'm cross,' she says. 'I'm bloody furious. But it's happening and I can't stop it. I just wish ...'

'Yes?' He leans in; he feels huge next to her. His mother had always been a large presence in his life. She might have been small in stature but her presence had made her loud, difficult and permanent. And now? Now there is something temporary about her; as if her colours are fading, like how book covers bleach if they're left too long in the sun.

'Oh, it doesn't matter.' She puffs out a breath and grips on to the blanket again.

'I'll get a nurse,' he says.

'Don't fuss. For heaven's sake, Boyd. Just leave it.'

They fall silent for a moment or two and Boyd's aware of the other patients on the ward, the purposeful stepping of the nurses, the bleep and drip and shuffle of medical paraphernalia, the distant sound of sirens, and he thinks about all the dramas being played out across the country; the tiny ones and the vast. He thinks of the births and of other deaths and of hearts being broken and of people making love in hotel rooms, people who have left their real lives behind them for an hour or so.

Then his mother says, 'Vita! How lovely to see you.'

'Hope you don't mind,' Vita says as she approaches the bed. 'I was anxious to know what was happening. We drew straws, Honey and I, and so I'm here to find out.'

Boyd watches Vita; she is terribly recognisable and yet unfamiliar in this strange setting. He has the overpowering urge to feel her body against his, tucked in by his side like it used to be.

For a moment, this triangle – him, her, his mother – is making sense again and he's back in his mother's house: it's the afternoon, he's coming in from mending a fence and finds his mother and Vita talking about biscuits and babies.

But he mustn't think this and so he says, 'How is she? Honey, I mean?'

'She's fine. She was on the phone to Trixie when I left her in the restaurant.'

'I'll go and get her in a bit, bring her up here.'

'You can go now if you like,' Vita says. She's taken her glasses off and is cleaning them with the hem of her top.

'You're still doing that then?' Belle asks.

'What?' Vita replies.

'Cleaning your glasses like that.'

'Guess I am.'

Boyd's wife and mother smile at one another and Vita moves a blanket from the armchair next to Belle's bed and sits down. 'Right,' she says, 'tell me what bollocks the doctors have been telling you then, Belle. Moan as much as you like. I can stay all afternoon if you'd like me to.'

Yes, thinks Boyd, this is how to treat my mother. He's always pussy-footed around her far too much, been too needy. Perhaps if Vita had been around more during these last few years, he and his mother wouldn't have got into this impasse and, shit, he thinks, I still have Honey to consider. How on earth is all that going to play out?

He leaves them chatting, or being as chatty as Vita and Belle can be. Vita had told him that her relationship with Colin was no hearts and flowers thing and, come to think of it, Vita's never had a hearts and flowers relationship with anyone, not even him. She's always been muscular, unforgiving, principled, fearless: the absolute opposite of Honey.

Honey

It's a relief to be alone for a bit. The past twenty-four hours have, if she's honest, been a bit of a challenge.

When she had eventually got through to Trixie, she'd sounded a bit odd – flustered and out of breath – but had said she'd been tidying up a bit, so maybe that was why.

Honey slips her phone into her bag and leans back in the chair. The last coffee Vita bought her has gone cold but that's OK, she's happy sitting here watching the world pass by. She sees children and pensioners and harried medical staff in white coats with stethoscopes around their necks, she sees busy receptionists and volunteers driving mobility buggies. It's its own world in here: it has its own ecosystem, its own sets of rules. She is just a visitor, a passer-through.

Her leg is hurting and so she props it up on a chair and, for want of anything better to do, plucks her phone back out of her bag and unlocks it. There's a text she must have missed the last time she checked. It's from a number she doesn't recognise and yet, instinctively, she opens it.

It says, 'How are you today? Regards, The Boatman'.

She drops the phone on to the table top, the plastic cover makes a slapping sound. Such is the force of its fall that the phone spins for a few seconds until it settles and stills. However much she stares at it though, however quietly it is sitting on the table, the message on it will still be there.

Why did she think that just by blocking the first number he would stop? After all, wasn't he there watching her as they drove away this morning? Didn't Elizabeth say he'd find her in the end? It's easy to buy another pay-as-you-go phone and it's easy to keep on buying them and sending texts. And she can't change her number without Boyd getting suspicious. A heavy weight settles in her stomach, she lowers her head and is aware that she's twisting her hands again. It's not going to be long before Vita realises that there's more to this than Honey's told her. She is, she realises, starting to let the cracks show. She knows she's never going to be free of her past, not until Reuben Roberts holds her to account or makes sure she stays quiet for good. After all, he's lost something precious. He needs someone to blame and it was her fault, all of it was her fault. She wants to run, but obviously she can't. 'Fuck,' she says out loud. 'Fuck.'

'Honey?' Boyd is walking towards her. She looks up, startled. 'You OK?' he asks.

She swallows hard, reaches out for her phone and puts it back in her bag. She imagines the text has burnt a hole in the screen.

'Of course,' she says. 'As OK as I can be. My bum's gone numb from sitting here for so long and I'm desperate for a wee.'

She's acting and she knows it and it's taking up every ounce of her energy and concentration. She really wishes it didn't have to be like this.

'Come on then hop-a-long,' he says, helping her up. 'There's bound to be a loo on the way to the ward.'

'I'm going to meet her now?'

'Yes. Vita's sitting with her at the moment, but said she'd make way for you when you arrive.'

'That's kind.'

Honey's nervous, stupidly nervous. She feels dishevelled and far too young to be going through all this. She wants to run away from this, too, and obviously, she can't.

Boyd is helping her into the wheelchair; he's putting her bag on her lap and is resting a huge hand on her arm. His touch is warm and reassuring and it reminds her how much she loves him. She thinks back to that time in the car wash, the first time they made love, she thinks of the nights falling asleep next to him and the mornings waking up with him there.

She thinks about the grief she's helping to shelter him from and the decision he made to leave Vita, she is helping him here too; it is her job to make sure he is as happy as he can be with what he's got now. Boyd is no hero, not in the Hollywood sense of the word, but he is a good man: a good, loyal, steadfast, honest man who wears his heart on his sleeve. She owes it to him, she tells herself, to see this through.

They're making slow progress and stop off on the way. She struggles into the cubicle in the Ladies' and then touches up her make-up and runs her fingers through her hair.

'How is she?' she asks when she's back in the chair and once again Boyd's pushing her along. Her crutches are tucked down by her side and the handles are pressing into her thigh.

'Who? My mother?'

'Yes.'

'Angry, and afraid.'

'This must be so hard for you. I can't imagine what you're going through.'

But she can, just a little. She's imagined meeting her mother over and over again and, since her session with Elizabeth, now knows that it'll never happen, that whatever chance she had to know her own mother has gone. At least Boyd's had a history with his. He'll have some memories to hold on to.

As they journey through the hospital's corridors she's aware of her phone and the text on her phone and the thought strikes her that maybe she's been doing this all wrong. The thought shocks her. She'd been so sure she was doing the right thing in keeping her past a secret from Boyd. But what would happen if she told him everything? If he loves her, surely he'll understand? She shifts in the seat, fusses with the strap of her bag and can hear Boyd breathing as he pushes her along.

'Here we are,' he says as they arrive at the doors to the ward. 'You ready for this?'

'Not in a million years,' she says, trying to laugh but it comes out more like a strangled sob.

He leans down and kisses her full on the mouth. She loves the way he kisses her, he tastes of coffee and cheese and Boyd.

They leave the chair in the corridor and she hobbles in to the ward. His mother's in a bed by the window and has her eyes closed.

Vita stands as they approach and says, 'Right, I'll wait in Main Reception. You can pick me up on your way out, OK?'

'Thank you, Vita,' Boyd says, touching her briefly on the arm.

She shrugs him off and says, 'Pah! No need to thank me.' And then she bends over the bed and says, 'I'll be off now, Belle. I'll see you again soon.'

Belle nods, but doesn't open her eyes.

Vita looks at Honey and gives her a small, tight smile and then she leaves. Honey misses her immediately. She'd provided a buffer between her and Boyd's mother. Without her, Honey is in uncharted waters.

'Here,' Boyd says, taking her crutches off her. 'You sit down, between Mum and the window.'

She sits.

Belle still hasn't opened her eyes.

'Mum?' he says. 'Honey's here.'

Belle must once have been beautiful. There is a soft majesty to her features, a kind of *Vogue* glamour thing. Even without make-up, and with her hair squashed on one side and the neckline of her nightie having slipped to show a thin, freckled shoulder, Honey can understand how Boyd's mother would once have commanded the room, that whenever she walked in, men would stop what they were doing, fix their eyes on her and watch as she walked by.

When Belle says, 'I know she's here,' it takes Honey by surprise. She hadn't realised Belle had heard Boyd.

Tentatively Honey places her hand on Belle's, fully expecting her to pull it away, but she doesn't. They sit there for a long minute and then finally, Belle lifts her head and looks straight at Honey.

It's like she can see right through to her thoughts and is busy reading them. Honey feels vulnerable and exposed and very, very known.

'So,' Belle says, 'you're the other woman.'

'She's the only woman, Mum,' Boyd replies. He's sat down in the chair Vita had been sitting in and so his mother would have to turn her head to look at him. She doesn't. 'I've done nothing wrong. You know that. Vita and I …'

'Vita and you are still married in the eyes of the law,' she says.

'But in name only. She's totally cool with the situation and she and Honey get on well, don't you?'

He looks at Honey as he says this and she nods. What else could she do? They do get on well. Honey likes Vita and thinks Vita likes her too, she is painting Honey's portrait as a surprise for Boyd, Vita has Colin and a life of her own and has, Honey believes, moved on.

'Yes,' she says. 'We do.'

Belle grimaces and Honey feels her hand tense under hers.

'You OK, Mum?' Boyd asks. 'Do you want me to get a nurse?'

'Of course I'm not all right,' she snaps, turning to look at him. 'I'm dying for heaven's sake. And,' she turns back to look at Honey, 'because I am, I am entitled to ask you this.'

'What? What do you need to ask me?'

'I need to know where you're from, what your background is. Boyd's told me so little. If I'm going to have to leave him in *your* care, then I need to know.'

A nurse comes over, soft-soled, plump under her uniform. 'How are you doing Mrs Harrison?' she asks. 'Can I get you anything? A cup of tea maybe? We'll have to do your blood pressure in a bit if that's OK?'

Belle waves the nurse away with the hand Honey's not holding. 'Don't fuss me,' she says. 'Just do what you have to do when you have to do it and leave me alone the rest of the time.'

'There's no need to be rude, Mum,' Boyd says.

She doesn't acknowledge him but looks at Honey again and says, 'Well? Who *are* you, Honey Mayhew?'

So, is this it? Should she tell them both everything, right here, right now? Is this the place and time? Boyd can tell Vita later and then, when it's quiet and he and Honey are alone, Honey can ask Boyd if he wants her to leave.

The text is still sitting like a malevolent toad in her phone. There is no escape and she can't go on pretending. Whatever half-truths she's told Boyd in the past about her foster homes, the itinerant jobs, the grotty places she's lived in, now is the time to set the record straight and tell him that she sold her body for money, took innumerable risks and consorted with crooks, that she was there when a boat exploded and a man lost a limb and people could have died, that there's someone out there who's after her, who she believes either wants to hurt her because she hurt him, or silence her because she knows too much, or both.

She looks across at Boyd, at the way his hair tufts over the top of his ears. He's watching her, his left eyebrow raised, he's resting his hands on his knees. She can see the fair hairs at his wrists and again thinks of the car wash and how she'd noticed them then; she remembers how he touches her, the warmth of his breath on her skin, what it feels like to have him in her, how his mouth twitches when he comes. She remembers the small kindnesses he performs: coffee in bed while she checks her horoscope, going out at midnight to the petrol station to buy a can of Diet Coke when she's had too much wine. She remembers the mumble of his and Vita's voices while they're doing the crossword first thing each morning, how he is sitting here next to the mother he's never really known how to love, how he is both fatherless and childless and will soon be motherless and she can't. She can't do it to him. She can't let him know who she really is. She has to give him the version of her he thinks he already knows.

She squares her shoulders and moves her foot a little, her toes are cold and she has pins and needles. 'I'm a product of the State,' she says. 'What you see is what you get. I never knew my mother, nor my father. I was in care from an early age but had good foster parents, went to school, did my exams, worked in temporary jobs, tried to make ends meet and then I got the job at Harrisons. The rest is history, as they say.' And she repeats for good measure, 'So, what you see is what you get. Isn't that right, Boyd?'

'And I like what I see,' he says, smiling broadly at her.

She is lying, of course. She seems to spend her life lying and can tell Belle doesn't believe her. Belle's too shrewd to do so, but she doesn't contradict her or press her for more details.

She just says, 'I think I'll have that cup of tea now, Boyd, if that's OK?'

'Sure, Mum,' he says and stands up. 'You want anything, Honey?' he asks.

'No thanks, I'm fine.'

He wanders off and, as soon as his back disappears around the corner, Belle flips the hand Honey's still holding over and grips hers fiercely.

'Don't you hurt him,' she says. 'Don't you dare. He's had enough hurt to last a lifetime.'

'I know,' Honey says. 'I know he has. Hurting him is the last thing I want to do.'

'It should never have happened.'

'What?'

'He and Vita should never have split up. They should have worked it out. Once you have a family, you have to fight to keep it. It was the one thing I could never give my son. It is the biggest regret of my life. He and Vita could have, should have tried again, had another child. It wasn't too late, not for them, not then.'

'Belle?' Honey says. 'Don't. Don't say that. What's the point in saying that? What's done is done.'

'It's all right for you to say. You're young, you have choices. Will *you* give Boyd a child?'

This last question takes Honey by surprise. 'We've not talked about it,' she says. 'It's still early days. We'd need to get sorted financially first and move out of Vita's house.'

Her head is reeling. How could she ever have a child?

'Promise me you'll try,' Belle says, still holding on fast to her hand. 'Let me die knowing that Boyd'll have that at least.'

Honey recognises emotional blackmail when she sees it and Belle is heaping it on in spades. She can't answer her so instead says, 'Oh look, here's Boyd with your tea.'

They leave her shortly after, the question lying unanswered between them. Honey didn't promise and Belle didn't mention it again. Honey knows it's hard for Boyd to leave, but he needs to get to work; the distraction will help and there's stuff that needs doing. Trixie's been emailing both of them all day with updates and questions and it's not fair to have left her to hold the fort for so long. Life goes on, or the life Honey's living now has to go on anyway. She has to keep going until she runs out of options.

Boyd hasn't seen his mother's doctor but at least he knows that she's being cared for, as much as she'll allow, that is.

'I'll come back tomorrow,' he says to her as he helps Honey back onto her feet and passes her her bag.

'There's no need,' Belle says.

'Of course there is.'

'Suit yourself.'

'I will.'

He doesn't kiss his mother when he leaves.

They meet Vita at the entrance to the hospital; she's sitting on a bench, muffled in her coat and staring into space. Strangely, it's good to be back with her. Her company is a comfort.

When they get home, Honey manages to delete the text and block the number yet again, Boyd leaves for work, Vita goes into her studio and Honey's left alone in the house. She hobbles to the sofa, picks up the remote and switches on the TV but is, she realises, exhausted and is soon asleep. And, this time, she does dream.

She's dreaming she's in the water; it's cold and salty and the waves are bumping up against her like hands, the moon is a white coin in the sky and behind her the boat is burning and she can hear shouts. This time she doesn't make it to the shore but there's a small dinghy alongside her and someone is stretching down into the water and saying, 'Here, hold my hand. We'll pull you up.'

And inside the boat are Vita, Trixie and Belle, their faces are silvery in this light and Belle says, 'It's her. It's that woman.'

And she's gripping on to the side of the boat and each time she gets a finger-hold, one of them bends down and prises her fingers off as the others are batting her away with their oars and still she can hear shouting and smell burning and the waves are covering her and she can't breathe. She can't breathe.

Vita

Sitting in the hospital's reception had been torture. Seeing Belle had been torture too. It was so fucking sad to see her the way she was – so diminished, still so angry. I'd really tried when I'd been with her to put on a brave face, say what she'd expect me to say and what Boyd would expect me to say, but inside my chest, the best and bravest parts of me were tumbling around in tiny, sharp-edged pieces.

I hated the thought of Belle meeting Honey and what they might say to one another. What if Belle liked Honey more than she'd liked me? I knew this wouldn't be hard, even given the recent thawing of relations between us.

As I watched the comings and goings of visitors and nurses and people driving buggies and young kids and the teenagers who have that amazing ability to walk in a straight line whilst looking at the screens of their phones, I wondered what on earth I should do with all the past that's stuffed inside of me like loft insulation or the innards of soft toys? How do I make sense of any of it now there's this new order: Belle dying, Boyd in love with Honey, Honey's massive secret, my spectacular ability to walk around with the wool firmly pulled over my own eyes?

And I hated sitting there because I was back in the place where

William had been born, where Boyd and I had come the first day after he died; back where the cracks in our marriage had begun to appear.

This is what I'm thinking when Colin says, 'I'd like it if you came,' and picks out an onion from the vegetable rack in the cupboard next to the sink and starts to peel it.

He's making dinner: something exotic, spicy and carefully crafted.

It's not often he says things like this, in fact I can't recall him ever doing so before, but ever since Boyd and Honey have known about me and Colin, there's been a subtle shift in the balance of things. It had been fine when it'd all been a secret, it was almost as though I hadn't admitted it to myself. But what had seemed convenient and pleasant before now seems portentous and uncomfortable.

'Boyd knows about us,' I'd said to him the day after Honey's accident.

'Ah,' he'd replied. 'I guess that's a good thing.'

'Mmmm, I'm sure it is.'

When I think back to this conversation, I realise I hadn't looked him in the eye during it and surely that must have spoken volumes?

He chops the onion and I feel my eyes smarting. 'Shit,' I say, grabbing a piece of kitchen paper.

'You OK?'

'Of course.'

I'm sitting on a stool at the breakfast bar in Colin's immaculate kitchen, a glass of wine on the countertop by my elbow. Outside it's November, the air crackling with the first frost of the winter. It should be nice to be inside on a night like this; I should be enjoying the warmth and safety, the pungent smell of frying onions, the vibrant greens of the herbs Colin's washed and left to drain by the sink. But all I can think about is the comfortable muddle of my own house the other side of the party wall. There, I can put my feet on the sofa without fear of leaving a mark, I have Boyd's company and Honey's, and the company of their scattered belongings. I am part of something crowded and bigger than myself at home. I had got used to being on my own but now I have a role, a part to play. Here, everything is minimalist and clean lines. Here isn't where I belong.

Colin's taken out as many of the non-load-bearing walls as he can and made the ground floor of his house into something that to me looks like a marble run; it reminds me of one of the few games I'd had as a child on the commune – a maze through which I had to run a ball bearing until I got it into the centre when a bulb would light up and a buzzer sound. The walls of his house are white; his furniture is mostly either pale wood or light grey with a few statement pieces: a copper sculpture of interlocking circles, a Mondrian print, a faux tiger skin rug.

'Well?' he asks, as he tips the jasmine rice into the rice steamer.

I still like the way he moves, his tidy gestures, his compact frame, the contours of his muscles underneath his shirt, but am beginning to ask myself if this is enough.

I'm wearing jeans, a pair of socks Boyd left behind when he moved out the first time, a loosely knitted black cowl-necked jumper. My hair, as ever, is in its plait and I'm wearing my glasses. I cross my legs, take a mouthful of wine and say, 'Remind me when it is again?'

He stops what he's doing and turns to face me. I have the feeling he's going to walk towards me and touch some part of me. I both want this and I don't, and so I put my wine back down on the counter and slip off the stool, saying, 'Shall I lay the table?'

'Thank you,' he replies. And, moving back towards the hob, says,

'The party's next Saturday. We don't have to stay for long, but I should show my face. I'd like to. After all, I designed the house! And it would be great if you could come; I'd love for you to see it.'

But part of me doesn't want to go, doesn't want to get involved in this part of Colin's life. It'd been OK when we'd gone to the art gallery, to the recital in the church, to the cinema and to other innocuous, generic places; those had been events in which I'd had nothing invested, they didn't matter, not really. But this would be different. This would be him and me being like a couple and, for some bizarre reason it's almost as though by going there with Colin I'd be putting a distance between myself and Boyd, and Honey, and Belle too.

Belle had been moved to a hospice and was waiting, ever more impatiently, for the end to come. Boyd and Honey and I, and sometimes Trixie too, had settled into a routine of visiting her, although it was still tricky for Honey to get around and would continue to be while her leg was still in plaster.

It had been a combination of Honey's broken ankle and a particularly busy time at work for all of us that had meant Honey and I had not yet got around to arranging another sitting for the portrait. However, we'd fixed one for this coming Sunday, the day after Colin's clients' housewarming party.

'Sorry?' I say to Colin, aware that he's speaking but, because I'm not listening, I haven't heard him.

'I was saying, shall we use chopsticks with the meal? If so, they're in the sideboard, second drawer down.'

'Wilko Cap'n,' I say, doing a mock salute and trying my very best to smile at him. He really doesn't deserve to be treated the way I'm treating him. For reasons I can't explain, we haven't had sex and I haven't stayed the night since Honey's accident.

I march over to the sideboard, a ball of fury lodged in my chest. I'm impatient with the sideboard's Scandi glamour, impatient with the faux tiger-skin rug, with the Mondrian print, with the walls, with the front door and the path down to the road and the way I imagine the frost is even now settling on the bare branches and the railings and the tops of the streetlamps.

We eat in relative silence. A few weeks ago it would have been companionable, but now the silence has a kind of edge to it.

'I guess you're not stopping over this evening,' Colin says as he pours the last of the wine from the bottle into my glass.

It isn't a question but even so, I look up at him, over the top of my glasses and say, 'I don't think so, thanks anyway. Got a busy day tomorrow and need to get an early start. But dinner was lovely. Thank you.'

When we've finished eating, he quietly and efficiently clears the plates and stacks the dishwasher. I help, and soon the kitchen's back to its normal pristine state, its white high gloss cupboards gleaming.

We don't kiss one another goodnight but I touch him lightly on the arm as he hands me my coat. 'Hope you sleep well,' I say.

'Thank you,' he replies.

As the front door closes behind me, I tell myself it doesn't matter. He and I are fine; we understand one another and yet, sitting at the base of my heart is a knot of regret that I don't quite know what to do with.

The night is clear and cold, the sky almost black, the few stars I can see through the light pollution glitter like small pieces of tinsel and I'm right, the frost is starting to settle. The breaths come out of my mouth in small, dense puffs as I walk the short distance to my house.

Inside Boyd's watching something dreadful on TV. From the nasal, smug tones coming out of the speakers it's a re-run of a *Top Gear* episode, I imagine. It's times like this I really regret letting him persuade me to have a TV installed. We'd never needed one before.

'Nice evening?' he asks.

'Yes, thank you.'

'Honey's turned in. She fancied an early night.'

'OK.' I convince myself I don't care where Honey is, or that Boyd's sitting on the sofa in the extension to the kitchen dressed in his jogging bottoms and an old sweater he had when we were together. I remember him wearing it when he was lying on the sofa with William on his chest. William had been fast asleep, his body rising and falling along with Boyd's breathing. 'I think I'll turn in too. It's been a long day and I've got an early start.' I haven't, not really, not an unusually early one. But saying this maintains the lie I've just told Colin. I wonder whether if I say it enough times I'll actually begin to believe it.

'Well, goodnight then,' Boyd says. 'See you tomorrow. If you're up too early though, you'll miss our crossword session.'

He chuckles at something on TV and I stay silent because I don't know what to say and so I turn and make my way upstairs, the babble of TV voices and roar of car engines following me.

Maybe I should knock on the door of Honey and Boyd's room and say goodnight to Honey too, but I resist. It gives me a buzz that I'm able to do so. When I'd been at Colin's, I'd wanted to be here with them, but now I'm here, I want to be on my own.

I don't need these people. I bloody well don't need anybody.

* * *

But, naturally, I go to the housewarming party with Colin on Saturday. He drives and Classic FM's playing on the radio. The weather's stayed cold all week and even at six, it's frosty; the air the kind that burns the back of your throat if you breathe it in too deeply.

'Here we are,' he says as we turn into a concealed entrance in some village in the Surrey Hills. 'The drive's a bit of a statement too.'

He hasn't told me anything about the house other than that he likes the clients and is pleased with the end result, and so I'm not prepared for the mansion that appears in a clearing in the trees at the end of the driveway. I should have known it'd be magnificent. After all, the gates were grand enough, and then there were the lights throwing up beams of intense white at even intervals into the shrubbery along the drive. The drive had been laid to gravel, making even the tyres of Colin's ordinary Toyota sound like they belong to a high-performance car.

'Christ, Colin,' I say, as the house comes into sight. 'It's fucking huge. Why would anyone want to live in something so huge?'

'It's just a home,' he replies. 'Some walls, floors, windows, a roof. All houses are basically the same, it's the small details that make them special: the way sunlight stripes a wooden floor, the curve of wood in a banister, a grey marble fireplace against cream walls, the furniture, the things people do and say while they're living there.'

'Mmmm,' I am unconvinced. 'It still baffles me why some people feel the need to live in houses like this.'

He pulls into a space in front of the triple garage next to an Aston Martin.

'That's not his car,' he says. 'My client's, that is. That must belong to a guest. Steve's got a Ferrari.'

'How did they make their money?' I ask as he switches off the engine and I open the door.

'Care homes, I think,' he says. 'Steve set up a business, then sold it to a US consortium. Made a fortune. This is their dream home, or so his wife told me at the start. There'd been an Edwardian house on the site but they had it knocked down, built this in its place.'

Wouldn't it be odd, I think, if this Steve had once owned Queen Anne's where Belle had lived until recently? If he had, then in some way, Belle's money would have helped to pay for some of this usurper house sitting smugly before me in its landscaped grounds.

The house is what I can only describe as a fusion of styles: part flamboyant Art Deco, part restrained Edwardian good taste but, when we go through the front door, I realise that here is where Colin's talent shines through. On the outside there may be some degree of vulgarity and ostentation in the brickwork, light fittings, exquisitely clipped topiary plants in garish silver pots, but inside the house is all clean lines, balanced spaces and understated elegance.

There's a double-height lobby just inside the front door which is lit by a massive chandelier hanging from the vaulted ceiling all the way down to the space above our heads. Four reception rooms lead off the hallway and, so Colin tells me as we make our way through to the kitchen, there's a games room and gym on the other side of the house, mirroring the wing on this side which houses the kitchen, breakfast and utility rooms. The stairs are at the end of the hallway, dividing when they get to the first floor and, on each side of the house bedrooms lead off both landings. Each bedroom has its own en suite and, he says, there's a party house and indoor swimming pool in the grounds behind the garages.

'Fuck me,' I say under my breath as we walk into the vast kitchen. 'You could fit my whole house into the utility room of this thing!'

A man is approaching. 'Colin!' he says, 'I'm so pleased you could come.'

'This is Vita,' Colin says and I shake the proffered hand. It is warm and large and reminds me of Boyd's.

'Hi,' he says, 'I'm Steve. This man here is a genius.'

'So he tells me,' I say, laughing lightly, wishing I was the sort of person who could get away with saying things like this, but even as the words come out of my mouth I regret them. This isn't me. Steve's let go of my hand and so I whip off my glasses and start cleaning them with the hem of my sleeve.

Steve is tall and well-built and obviously looks after himself. He has grey hair, intelligent, piercing blue eyes and looks as though he wouldn't be afraid of making tough decisions at work.

'Ah, Vita,' he says, 'you're the artist, aren't you? Colin's told me all about you.'

'Has he?' I ask. I'm surprised and annoyed by this. How dare Colin talk about me in my absence? What gives him the right? I put my glasses back on.

There's an awkward pause and then Steve says brightly, 'You must come and meet the Mrs,' and he leads us over to the woman who must be his wife. She's directing a waitress towards a group of guests standing by a set of huge bi-fold doors and saying, 'Just keep the food and drink flowing, OK?'

He introduces her to us, saying, 'This is Rachel. The power behind the throne.'

God, how I hate it when men talk about their wives like this. Boyd never did, and he never would, and I'm surprised when Colin laughs politely in agreement.

Like Steve, Rachel is well-groomed and wearing something that's obviously not off the peg. Her hair, face and nails are expertly done, but she exudes warmth and genuineness and, standing next to her in my denim tunic and cheesecloth shirt, black leggings and DMs, I feel OK, like she and I could be friends. Not that I could be friends with her guests though. The huddle over by the patio doors are all Botox, fake tan and sycophantic laughter. Whereas Steve and Rachel have some undefinable kind of class, their guests certainly don't.

The only way to cope with this evening is to drink and so, as Colin is taken away by Steve to be introduced to the rest of the guests as the architect of this wonderful house, I hang back, take the glass of champagne the waitress is now offering me and down it in one.

I swap my empty glass for a full one as another waitress skims by, and take another mouthful. I haven't eaten much today and already the alcohol is making my blood buzz. On the other side of the room Colin is doing what he does best: fitting in, being undemanding, giving me space. He knows I hate small talk and that I don't actually want to be here at all and have only come as a favour to him. But, as Rachel puts a proprietorial hand on his arm and guides him through the crowds of house-admirers, I feel a stab of something. I assume it's impatience and annoyance. No way is it jealousy.

When Boyd and I had been together, I'd never had cause to be jealous and, whatever it is I feel now he's back living under the same roof and has brought Honey with him, that's not jealousy either. It is, I acknowledge, a huge mix of emotions: it is regret, grief, affection, care, but not jealousy. I help myself to yet another glass of champagne.

A florid, rotund man is approaching with a look of expectancy on his face as if I will immediately know who he is and be dying to speak to him. 'Ah,' the man says, 'are you Mrs Colin?'

'No,' I reply, looking down at my feet, 'I'm not.'

The man, however, must have the hide of a rhino because he doesn't take the hint. 'But,' he continues, 'you came with Colin the Architect, didn't you?' He says it as though the word 'Architect' should have a capital A.

'We're just friends,' I say through gritted teeth. 'Now, if you'll excuse me, I need the loo.'

I leave the man standing there looking foolish but I don't care. I wander away from the hubbub of noise and activity in the kitchen into the quieter corridors and spaces on the other side of the house. Here, I stare out of the huge windows on to the cleverly lit gardens, the frost is deepening as the evening wears on and the lawns are sparkling with a million pinpricks of silver.

Are we just friends, I wonder? Me and Colin? I can see my reflection in the glass and for the first time I really question what I'm doing and why I'm doing it. Having sex with Colin had seemed an uncomplicated thing before Boyd came back, but now Boyd knows about us it's starting to mean something different.

'There you are.' Colin appears behind me. 'I wondered where you'd got to. You hate it here, don't you?'

'They're not my kind of people.'

'Much like they weren't my kind of people at the art show we went to in London.'

'Touché,' I say, smiling at him. 'But to be honest, they weren't mine either. I only went because it was expected of me.'

'I know,' he says.

I'm not in love with Colin, not in the breathtaking, heart-stopping way I should be, but I admire his intelligence, clear-sightedness and patience. I also know, however, that this definitely isn't enough. I want more. I'd had it once and thought I could live without it when it went away but, as I stand in this magnificent house in its magnificent grounds, I realise that actually

I can't. And, given all that I've convinced myself of lately, this is an awful admission to make.

'Come on,' I say, 'let's get back to it.'

'We can leave if you like.'

'I'll give it another half an hour!'

'That's good of you.'

We're teasing one another and it feels good to do so. I need to make an effort to ensure the pall that settled on me when we arrived starts to lift. It's not fair on Colin otherwise. He doesn't deserve it. 'Anyway,' I add, 'I could use another drink.'

By the time we leave I've had too much champagne, said things I shouldn't have said to some of Steve and Rachel's guests, dropped a glass onto the slate floor of the kitchen and said, 'Fuck it,' too loudly when I did so.

Colin steers me out of the house and the cold air hits me like a fist and I retch into one of the exquisitely cut topiary plants, saying, 'I think I'm a little bit drunk.'

'You don't say,' Colin replies, opening the car door. 'You get in. I'll de-ice the windows.'

And, as I sit there waiting for him to get in too and drive me home, I know I won't stay the night with him tonight, and that perhaps I won't stay the night with him ever again.

* * *

The next morning I'm late down and Boyd's already got the kettle on and is leaning up against the counter, newspaper in hand.

'You look awful,' he says.

'Why thank you. What a nice thing to say!'

'I'm sorry,' he smiles at me. 'It's just you look tired. Late night last night?'

'Bit too much to drink if I'm honest.'

'Ah, that'll be it. We never learn, do we?'

I'm not sure who he's referring to with the word 'we'. It used to mean him and me, but obviously doesn't any more.

'Where did you go?' he adds, reaching round me to grab the mugs out of the cupboard.

'One of Colin's clients had a housewarming party,' I say.

Boyd will know that I didn't stay the night at Colin's; would he wonder why?

'Shall we get cracking on the crossword?' he asks.

'Do you mind if I pass? Think I'll take my tea back upstairs if that's OK.'

'Of course. I should get going anyway. I told Trixie I'd be in a bit earlier today. Honey's staying here, having a day off.'

'Is she? That's nice.'

I never was much good at lying and so, hastily grabbing the tea Boyd's made for me, I drag myself back to my room. As I get into bed, I try very hard not to think of Colin in his room on the other side of the wall, try not think of his firm body, his caramel-coloured skin. I pick up my phone and send him a text. 'Sorry for last night,' it reads. 'I didn't acquit myself very well.'

He replies immediately. 'That's OK. No damage done.'

But I wonder whether actually more damage has been done than either of us appreciates. And, I notice, he doesn't suggest we see one another today, or later, or even sometime next week.

I can hear the unmistakable sounds of Boyd getting ready for work: his footsteps on the stairs, the way he clears his throat, the mumble of his voice as he says something to Honey. And then, very soon, he's gone. The front door closes behind him, he's scraping ice off the windscreen of his car and then his engine starts and he pulls away. I've watched him do this so many times that, even though I'm in bed and the curtains are still closed, I can see him as if I am looking out of the window. Doing so is almost like a magic trick.

I've finished my tea and lie back and shut my eyes. My head is pounding and the room's a bit jittery.

There's a knock at my door.

'Yes?' Reluctantly, I open my eyes and haul myself into a sitting position.

The door opens and Honey pops her head round it.

'Hi,' she says, 'just wondered what time you want me? In the studio?'

I hadn't forgotten but had hoped Honey had.

'What have you told Boyd you're doing today?' I ask in lieu of an answer.

'He's suggested I read *The Magus* by John Fowles so I've promised him I'll make a start on that and then stagger around the kitchen and get dinner ready for when he comes home. I feel awful not going into work today, but it's also nice to have a day off. Can't remember the last time I did, one that wasn't caused by this,' she points to her foot, 'or Belle.'

'It was probably the time we started the portrait,' I say. 'Your last proper day off, I mean.'

Even in her pyjamas, without make-up, and with bed hair, Honey is still unbearably beautiful. I feel a hundred years old in comparison. Obviously, the hangover isn't helping.

And Honey seems relaxed today, at ease. It's been a while since she has been. Honey has become much more twitchy of late, but today she is a like a teenager for whom the sun is shining. You know how teenagers can be: all doom and gloom one minute, all light and laughter the next …

She laughs, 'You're right, it probably was.' And then asks again, 'So, what time do you want me? It is …' she hesitates, shifts her foot, clunking the plaster cast up against the door and saying, 'argh!' before continuing, '… very kind of you to do this for me, for us.'

'Well, it's not for "us" is it? After all, Boyd doesn't know about it.'

'Not yet, no.' If Honey's upset by my tone, she doesn't show it. 'But he will. One day, he will.'

'Shall we say eleven?' I say, trying to be a bit more conciliatory.

'Perfect. I'll see you in the studio then,' Honey replies, stepping back through the door.

'Let's hope the light stays on our side,' I add as the door closes. 'The light on these cold, clear days can be great for painting …'

But Honey's gone, and I can hear her uneven tread along the landing and then the bathroom door closes.

I snuggle back under the covers and let my mind wander.

When William died, I'd really believed that Boyd and I were strong enough to cope. After all we'd had so many years of it just being the two of us that we hadn't got used to it being any different, not really. William was, of course, all-consuming and the centre of everything, but it hadn't yet started to feel ordinary, we were still feeling our way. It should have been easy to revert to how it had been before.

And we always believe we will survive, don't we? When something awful happens, the first thought isn't, 'This will finish us.' It is, 'I will do what I can to protect those I love from the pain of this.' Isn't it?

But in the days and weeks immediately afterwards, I turned away from Boyd, believing it to be a wholly justifiable thing to do because my pain was greater than his. Trixie practically moved in, bringing round casseroles and ironing Boyd's shirts. She'd leave the office and pop by at lunchtime to make me a bowl of soup or scrambled eggs and I'd stay in bed, where I am now, with the windows closed and the curtains drawn.

Then the weeks turned into months and still Boyd got up every day and went to work; he did the shopping, tidied the garden, replaced broken lightbulbs, didn't try to touch or comfort me. He'd suggested grief counselling but I'd told him to fuck off and had rebuffed him so many times at night by then that he'd given up trying. And I'd gone walking. I'd walked for miles and miles in the park and around the neighbouring roads and had come home foot-sore and drenched and hadn't let him comfort me then either. And then one day, the day that, in retrospect, marked the official beginning of the end of us, he came home from work to find me in William's bedroom, putting baby clothes into bin bags.

'What are you doing?' he asked.

He stood in the doorway, his huge frame sagging with exhaustion.

'What does it look like?'

'Isn't this something we should have discussed? I mean ...' he hesitated, taking one step nearer to me.

I remember feeling a pulse of impatience, as if his presence was sucking all the oxygen from the room.

'What? What do you *mean*, Boyd?'

It was as though there was a splinter under my skin and I had to keep digging until I got it out. I was wearing an old t-shirt, a pair of leggings, my hair was loose and unwashed and I hadn't cleaned my glasses for ages and it was like I was seeing everything through a filter.

Outside it was raining and I also remember thinking how fucking appropriate it was that it should be. The rain fell in rods from low, dark clouds like it had on the day we'd moved in and like it had at William's funeral.

'I mean,' he tried again. 'I mean, what gives you the right to do this today? What if I'd wanted to do it months ago but didn't dare because you weren't talking to me and I couldn't check if it was the right thing to do or not? Or, what if I never want to do it but want to keep his things, this room as it is now, for always?'

Of course, I didn't hear the other arguments, the totally reasonable things he said which were, in retrospect, nothing but a cry for help. No. All I heard was 'what gives you the right?'

'The *right*?' The words exploded out of my mouth. 'Because he was *my* son. I was his *mother*.'

'He was my son, too, Vita.'

If I think of all the ways Boyd could have said this, they are countless. He could have been angry, resentful, violent, and would have been totally within his right to be any of these. But he actually said it like he was admitting defeat. His sadness filled the room and I didn't want it, couldn't handle it, not on top of my own.

We'd painted the walls of William's room duckling yellow before he was born, it seemed an absurd colour now he'd gone. I hated it. I carried on stuffing his things into the bags and turned my back on Boyd.

It was a shameful and cruel thing to have done.

For Boyd it was the last straw. I never really blamed him. After all, he'd been the one keeping going; he'd carried on earning the money to pay the bills while I hadn't been to my studio since the day William died.

'I,' Boyd said, coming over to me and placing one giant hand on my back as I was bending over to pick up a dropped sock. The sock was the size of a business card. It was pale blue with white spots. 'I don't think I can do this any longer,' he said.

'OK,' I said.

OK? Is that how you finish a marriage? Can it be that two tiny letters could actually dismantle the years we'd been together: the meeting, the moving in, the sex, the laughter, the arguments, the eating and sleeping and dealing with his mother? Is it a fitting way to bookmark the absolute and total grief we found that, in the end, we couldn't share?

'I'll be gone by the end of the week. It'll be good for us both to have some space, won't it?'

'I guess so,' I replied, putting the sock into the bag and tying its handles.

The rain was still falling when Boyd lifted his hand from my back and left the room.

I put the bag into the cot and held on to the wooden bars of it, my knuckles showing white in the gloom.

He moved out a week later and his absence was a solid thing.

At first I was relieved that he'd gone, relieved that I no longer had to be responsible for his sadness or feel guilty about mine. If he'd asked to come back at any point during those first weeks and months, I would have turned him away. But then I started to take the first small steps through the grief: began to paint again, launched my website, ventured outside, talked to my neighbours and shopkeepers and yearned for Boyd to come back so that I could forgive him and be forgiven by him. But he didn't, and no way was I going to ask him to.

We talked often though, about everyday things: his work, my work, his mother, the house, the garden but, as time passed, I didn't tell him about Colin and he obviously didn't tell me about his early days with Honey. I've often wondered why Trixie didn't do so and feel her betrayal over this keenly. And so, over the years, my heart became the barren, hard muscle I showed to him when he at last did ask if he could come back; it became the sad, weary and confused thing it is now he's here and has brought Honey to live in the room that had once been our son's.

* * *

The studio always takes ages to warm up so, pulling on a pair of jeans, my Ugg boots and an old sweater I make my way down the garden, unlock the door and switch on the heaters.

On my way back up to the house I look over at Colin's windows; they stare inscrutably back at me. I pull the cuffs of the jumper down over my hands to stop the cold air from getting to them and let out a kind of strangled snort. I remember this jumper; Boyd had bought it for me one Valentine's Day and had presented it to me in a Harrods' bag.

'What the fuck?' I'd said. 'You surely haven't gone and spent a fortune on me?'

He'd grinned and his left eyebrow had raised just a fraction in that part-sardonic, part-little-boy-lost way and said, 'No! I got the sweater from a charity shop, just put it in the bag to amuse you.'

I'd lifted myself onto my tiptoes and kissed him lightly on the mouth. 'How well you know me,' I'd said and I meant it.

Now, I notice that a thread's coming loose on the hem. I'll have to refasten it at some stage, or maybe I won't. It'll be some kind of poetic justice should the whole bloody thing unravel.

I'm still feeling crap after last night's excesses and so, when I get back to the kitchen, I take a couple of painkillers, make myself a cup of tea and a slice of toast and settle down on the sofa. I pick up the crossword but don't even take the cap off my pen.

At just before eleven, I've finished the tea and toast but have mostly been sitting with my eyes shut. I open them when I hear Honey bumping her way down the stairs.

'Let's get going then shall we?' I say, more officiously than I'd intended. My head's still thumping and I wish I hadn't agreed to paint her bloody portrait in the first place.

'OK,' Honey replies, smiling widely.

Honey's also wearing a pair of jeans but has rolled one of the legs up to make room for her plaster. She's also wearing one of Boyd's jumpers. I want to laugh at this, but find myself unable to. As always, Honey looks infinitely more glamorous than I feel.

We make our through the kitchen with its smattering of used crockery that no one's been bothered to stack in the dishwasher yet, an almost-empty bottle of wine that Boyd and Honey must have shared last night, yesterday's newspaper on the counter where Boyd must have left it. I both celebrate and mourn this mess, these signs of occupancy, signs of life.

'I can hobble back and get a coffee, or something for you later, if you like,' Honey says, taking my arm and adding, 'You don't mind, do you? But I'm feeling a bit unsteady right now.'

'Of course I don't mind,' I say, again more sharply than I mean to.

Once in the studio, I put on the radio and turn the volume down low and we settle into our seats. Then I put the canvas on the easel and pick up my palette and brushes.

It's warm in here now and the windows are huffing up so that it feels a bit like we're in a cocoon. There's some comfort in us being here again, like it's become a habit because it's the second time we've done this.

'How was Belle last time you saw her?' Honey asks as I start mixing the paints.

'Oh, as you'd expect: scared, bad-tempered, worried. How long ago did you see her?'

'We went on Wednesday after work. She slept through most of the visit though. The nurses said it would be because of the medication.'

'Ah,' I say.

'When did you go?'

'I was there on Monday; said I'd go again tomorrow.'

'Did you get on with her? I mean, before, well you know before …' Honey's voice trails off.

'She's never been the easiest of people. At the beginning she was downright hostile, which surprised me because Boyd said they'd never really been close and so it wasn't as though I was taking her precious son away from her. You know how some mothers can be with their sons …'

I'm appalled by what I've said so add hastily, 'But then, later on, she seemed to soften a bit.'

'Was that when you had William?'

I hate it when Honey says William's name and put down my brush so I can do something else with my hands for a moment. I tuck a stray lock of hair behind an ear and say, 'Yes. I guess so.'

'Sorry,' Honey says. 'It must be hard to talk about it. I shouldn't have brought it up.'

I'm painting again, putting some shade under Honey's chin. 'It's OK,' I say. 'It was all such a long time ago.'

And I'm back, back when I painted Boyd's portrait, back when things were simple and good between us. When love was the only option, life was straightforward and it showed in his portrait; his honest face, his goodness shining through. It would, I reckon, be a very different kettle of fish if I decided to paint him now.

'Boyd seldom mentions his dad,' Honey says next. I know she's trying to change the subject and I should be grateful, but here's yet another subject that it's hard to talk about.

'He never spoke about him much to me either.'

'Hasn't Belle ever said anything to you?'

'No. Not really.' I change brushes, put a touch of white in Honey's hair, where the light from the window is falling onto it. 'Although she did say once that she found it hard to forgive Boyd for breaking his promise.'

'What do you mean?' Honey shifts in the chair.

'You OK?' I ask. 'Do you need to prop your leg up a bit?'

'That would be good actually, thank you.'

I move a stool from underneath one of the benches and plop a cushion on top of it. 'There you go,' I say. 'That better?'

'Much, thank you.'

We fall silent again for a moment and then Honey tips her head on one side and says, 'What *did* you mean, you know when you said about Belle not forgiving Boyd?'

'I'm not sure I should say.'

I remember our first conversation, here in the studio when I'd said there was a lot Boyd didn't talk about. How things have changed, I think now.

'I won't tell him. It's just I'd love to know more. He's like a closed book as far as his dad's concerned.'

I switch one of the bars off on the heater, then I clean my brush again and this time pick up some Permanent Mauve to do Honey's eyes. I tap the brush against my glasses and say, 'Apparently she'd made him promise not to try and find his father. It was part of a deal she'd struck when Boyd was born that neither of them would. I think, from what Belle said at the time, the man was married and didn't want his family to find out. But then …'

'Yes?' Honey asks, leaning forward and resting her chin on her hands for a second. 'God, it's hard to sit still, isn't it?' she says, laughing a little.

'Yes, it is but please try to do so,' I say, a little crossly. I hadn't wanted to be interrupted, not just at that point. I continue, 'Well, then apparently Boyd did go. Just before he went off to university, he tracked his father down, went to see him, got turned away.'

'That must have been awful.'

'It was and then Belle got all silly about her will and power of attorney and said she'd never forgive Boyd.'

'Do you think she has, or if she hasn't, do you think she will, you know, before she …'

'Before she dies, you mean? I'm not sure in either case. I bloody well hope so. He doesn't deserve it, he really doesn't. I mean, I admire Belle for what she did, bringing him up on her own and all that, but I've never liked the fact that she's always held him hostage over this thing. After all, anyone would like to know who their parents are, if they didn't know, wouldn't they?'

Honey makes a strange, small sound, halfway between a 'Mmmm' and a sob and then her phone starts ringing.

'It's Trixie,' she says, 'I'd better get it.'

I nod and take off my glasses; again, everything is nicely blurry without them on. I take a tissue from the box on my work table and start to clean them.

I'm only half listening to what Honey's saying and am aware of the tinny sound of Trixie's voice on the other end of the line but I can hear her saying something about vendors and Boyd and a house in Montague Gardens. I'm just putting the tissue into the pocket of my trousers when I sneeze.

'Bless you,' Honey says, holding the phone away from her face for a second and then, when she starts talking again, she says, 'Oh, it's only Vita.'

What Trixie says next must be a question because Honey says, 'Oh, we're just hanging out. Nothing special.' There's a brief moment when no one moves or speaks: not me, or Honey, or Trixie on the other end of the phone, until Honey asks, 'Has Boyd said what time he might be home? I promised to cook for him tonight. Can you ask him to let me know?' She giggles and smiles at me.

I give her some sort of smile in return, or I hope I do.

When Honey's finished the call, she says, 'How are we doing? Do you want to stop? I'm happy to fit in with you.'

It's already one o'clock; the last two hours have raced by. My headache's eased, but I have that empty feeling that comes with a hangover; something only a bowl of soup will fill.

'Let's give it a few moments longer, shall we?' I say.

'I'm in your hands.'

Again, we are silent. I would like to say it is an easy, companionable silence but Honey has changed. Gone is the relaxed and happy Honey from earlier, now there's a different Honey sitting before me, her shoulders tense, her hands twisting on her lap again. It's like someone's flicked a switch.

'Actually,' Honey says, 'there's something else I'd like to talk to you about.'

'Is there?' my heart quickens inexplicably.

'I've been getting mysterious texts,' Honey blurts it out almost too quickly for me to understand what she's saying. 'You know,' Honey continues, 'I told you about what the medium said about the fact I would be found, well I think the texts are from the person who's looking for me.'

'Why do you think that?' As she talks the world shrinks to just this: Honey, the man who is out to get her and my powerlessness to do anything to stop it.

'They started after I saw him, or thought I did. You remember? Outside the office? And then again, under the trees the day we went to visit Belle? You said you hadn't seen him, but I'm sure he was there. Anyway, whoever it is uses different numbers. When I first got a message, I deleted it and blocked the sender's number but then another one arrived from another phone and so I deleted it and blocked that, but I'm afraid that another message will come and that they'll keep on coming.'

'Why do you think that?'

'He signs the texts, "The Boatman".'

'So you think it's got something to do with what that medium told you?' I've given up all pretence of trying to continue with the painting now and am watching Honey carefully.

'Well she did say I'd fall as you know ...' Honey points to her leg and tries to smile, but it's unconvincing.

'Oh, I'm sure it's all a load of tosh,' I say with more confidence than I feel. 'But I think you're right. Just ignore them. It's probably just a hoax. Don't give whoever it is the oxygen.'

'You won't tell Boyd, will you?' Honey asks.

'Of course not. I've already promised I won't. What sort of person do you take me for?'

'Thank you, and thank you for listening. I don't know what I'd do without you.' Honey slips off the chair and shuffles over to me and places a hand on my shoulder. I want to be able shrug it off, but I can't, Honey's too fragile; if I did brush her away, I'm worried she might break. Then I wonder whether this is what it's like to be a parent, absorbing what you're told and by so doing taking away its sting? The young can be intolerably selfish, they never stop to question what effect they are having, what legacy they leave behind.

Honey takes a deep breath and then asks me whether she can see the picture and whether it'll be ready for Christmas.

'No, you can't see it,' I say, 'not until it's finished and no, it won't be ready in time for Christmas. We need at least one more sitting, now scoot and let me clear up. I'm in dire need of hot soup and a nap.'

'And I'd better start reading that bloody book and get my thinking cap on as to what I'm going to cook Boyd for dinner.'

And with that, Honey's gone. There's a blast of cold air as she opens the door to the studio. The chill hangs around me for a moment until the warmth surges back again. Again, the studio seems unreasonably empty.

'Fuck,' I mutter, more out of habit than anything else, as I carefully turn the portrait around so it's leaning against the back of the easel and start to tidy up. I wish more than anything that I'd never made that stupid promise not to say anything in the first place. I should tell Boyd everything Honey's told me, I know I should.

Honey

She's looking in the fridge when the thought strikes her. Perhaps she should have asked Vita if she'd like to eat with them tonight. She decides to mention it when Vita comes in to make the soup she said she's going to have.

Honey's phone bleeps with a text and she presumes it's Boyd letting her know what time he'll be home. She's found some chicken and an avocado and, rootling around in the cupboards, has also discovered some spice mix and tortilla wraps and so has decided to make fajitas for dinner. They'll have a nice bottle of red to go with it and put their feet up. Ah, she laughs silently, put our feet up. As if she can do anything else with hers!

She looks at her phone before checking the wine rack and clicks on the text. It's from a number she doesn't recognise.

'Not long now,' it says. 'You'll be out of plaster soon.' And, of course, it's signed 'The Boatman'.

And suddenly she's furious. How dare he? How *fucking* dare he? All she has achieved here is under threat because of him and this time she's not going to stand for it. And so she does what both Trixie and now Vita have told her not to, she replies. But she doesn't reply as who she is now, oh no. She replies as the person she used to be, before she became Honey, before she started living this life with her best side facing the world and the other, the darker side, turned away from the light.

'Just fuck off,' she types. 'Fuck off and die.'

* * *

Honey remembers the moment she decided to change the trajectory of her old life, the life when she'd been called the name her mother gave her, when she'd been the girl who'd negotiated her way through foster home after foster home: the first one with the man with the hands, the others where she'd tried to be a daughter and failed, where each time she felt she'd come up short, been a disappointment, to them and to herself in some intangible way.

She'd woken that particular morning to find the bruises from the last time with 'The Boatman' hadn't quite faded. She'd gone with him because of the money. She'd had to; she was literally living hand-to-mouth. Everything was precarious and insubstantial. Her life was crap and, waking that morning to that particular sun at the window, that particular configuration of dust motes in the air of her room, that particular person who called out something in the street below, that riff of birdsong, she'd decided that the life she was living was no answer and it was much, much less than she deserved. The only person she'd ever been able to rely on had been herself and so that was the moment she'd decided to do what she did.

* * *

Honey's often wondered which the strongest emotion is. Is it love, or hate, or remorse? What is it that compels us do extraordinary things? And by extraordinary, she means not just things that are out of the ordinary, but things that are extreme.

As she stares at the text she's just sent she realises that right here, right now, the strongest emotion in her life is guilt: guilt over what she did before she met Boyd, guilt that's she's never been brave enough to tell him, guilt that the woman he thinks he loves isn't the real her, guilt that it seems as if her whole life, her whole fucking life, has been some kind of act and finally, guilt over sending the text telling Reuben to 'fuck off and die.' She really shouldn't have done that.

How could she have got herself in this situation? She'd always promised she'd travel light, not put down roots, leave before she got found out. It had always been the only way. She'd done it before. And yet here she was, trapped again. Would she never learn? She knows the only solution to this is to leave; only now it's not an option, it's an imperative. If she stays, she will end up hurting the people she loves more than if she leaves them before it's too late.

The thought of going is heartbreaking and she will have to choose this moment carefully too. She will have to armour herself against the fallout. Already, her arms and legs (even the one in the plaster cast) feel like liquid and a white heat burns behind her eyes. It takes all her energy to swallow.

The ingredients for the meal she's going to cook Boyd are laid out on the counter in front of her. She's leaning up against the counter. It feels like there's a hand grenade in her chest.

Boyd

December's been wet and warm. After the gin-like clarity and chill of November, the run up to Christmas has been soggy, lacklustre and unseasonal.

And Belle is still dying, slowly and irrevocably.

It's Christmas Eve and Boyd is downstairs putting his gifts for Honey and Vita under the tree. It's odd, he thinks, how we measure life by significant events like Christmas and birthdays. This Christmas will be his second with Honey. He's lost count of the number he's had with Vita. They didn't even have one with William.

The lights on the tree are blinking at him; Honey's idea. He would have preferred static lights, as would Vita, he's sure. But Honey wanted 'bling' as she called it, though now the lights are kind of fuzzy. He rubs his eyes. He has, he realises, been crying.

'Stupid bloody sod,' he mutters, arranging the presents so that they look more plentiful than they really are. His gift for Vita was an easy choice now they've got the TV: the box set of *Breaking Bad*. He knows she'll like it; it'll appeal to her sense of the macabre. But Honey had been more difficult to buy for. He'd thought about a diamond, a designer handbag, a holiday. They'd never actually been away anywhere together, mainly due to money and, with things as they still were, none of the above were really possible. So he'd gone for an iPad. He has no idea whether she'll like it, but it was easy to buy and easy to wrap.

If he had unlimited funds and unlimited choice what he'd like most of all would be a place of their own again, for it to be just the two of them once more. He likes living with Vita, of course he does, but it's not ideal, it can be confusing at times and it shouldn't be a permanent solution. He feels he is hampering Vita, stopping her from living the kind of life she wants to live. He wonders sometimes if he's stopping her moving in with Colin, or Colin moving in here. In truth, he wishes he knew more about Vita's relationship with Colin. She never talks about him. They don't see one another very much these days either and she's not stayed out overnight again, not to his knowledge anyway.

All of them deserve a better solution than this. And he's worried; at times he feels that he's carrying an alarm clock around in his pocket and that one day, when he least expects it, it will go off.

He's got a long way in saving up for the tax bill, but there's still a chunk of money to be found from somewhere and because he still doesn't know in what sort of state his mother's affairs will be at the end, he can't – and shouldn't – depend on anything coming from that direction.

The wrapping paper on the presents shimmers; there are gifts to him from Honey and Vita and from Vita and Honey to each other. There are also the ones Trixie gave him at work yesterday: one for each of them. He's given her some perfume, her boys money in an envelope and handed her a bottle of wine for Richard. There's also a parcel from Colin to Vita and this makes Boyd feel uneasy.

He switches off the lights and starts to make his way upstairs. Vita's in her room and Honey's reading. Her plaster's due to come off on the 29th and she can't wait. Neither can he, these last couple of months seem to have gone on for ever.

'All OK downstairs?' Honey asks as he closes the door behind him. Neither of them bother locking it any more.

'Yes, all set.'

Vita's going out for Christmas lunch with Colin and some friends of his. 'We're all single, unattached, childless,' she'd said. 'Should be a right barrel of laughs!'

And so he and Honey will be having Christmas Day here. He's planning on visiting the hospice first thing; he's bought his mother a set of handkerchiefs with 'Belle' embroidered into their corners. He knows she won't use them and that it's a waste of money and effort, but some part of him hopes he'll keep them after she's gone, as a memento.

Honey looks tired. She's been having the dream quite often recently and although he says, 'You can talk to me about it if you like,' she always says, 'It's OK. It's nothing.' And yet it's not nothing. It's obviously very much something.

She is different, more on edge. He's noticed her stopping in front of the windows at work and scanning the street as if she's looking for someone. She's constantly checking her phone and seems to be losing weight. He feels she is slipping through his fingers and it seems there's nothing he can do to stop her from doing so.

And then his phone rings.

'Who can that be?' he says, picking it up and staring at the screen.

Of course it's the hospice.

'Boyd?' the voice at the other end of the line says.

'Yes.'

'It's Sophie here. I'm afraid she's taken a turn for the worse. We think it won't be long now. Can you come?'

And so they go. They leave the presents by the tree and he, Honey and Vita drive in silence through the Christmas streets. It's a bit like it was after Honey's accident with the three of them in the car, but it's also very different this time.

He thinks of the households they pass, of the kids tucked up in their beds and the stockings and mince pies left out for Santa. He thinks of the mothers and grandmothers whose job it'll be to make the lunch, of the fathers making sure they've bought batteries to put in the kids' toys, of the flocks of turkeys sitting ready in fridges and baking trays and of the legions of crackers laid out on tables and the small schooners of sherry and too much pudding and arguments and tears and people saying 'I love you' and 'I hate you' and 'I can't do this' and 'You just don't understand' and how, at Christmas, everything concertinas into something bright and hard and significant.

It's a strange day. We hurtle headlong towards it; we tell ourselves it'll be all right if only we are together and yet, there will be those for whom the balance isn't quite right. Like him, for instance: his mother is dying, he never got to know his child and the woman who was his wife is no longer really his wife and is sitting in the back seat of the car plaiting her hair and cleaning her glasses with the hem of her scarf while the woman he loves is sitting in the front, her foot in plaster, her heart full of secrets she won't trust him with.

And he thinks of those who love each other but who are separated by people, or places, or principles. And he thinks of those who don't love each other but who decide to stay together also because of these things.

As he turns the car into the hospice entrance Boyd realises he's scared. He's scared of what he is about to face and what it could mean. He's never known any other life than this one with his mother in it and there's some part of him, a small voice tucked deep within his ribs that's saying, 'From here on in you need to be honest with yourself. Are you really who you want to be? Are you where you want to be, doing what you want to do?'

Sophie greets them at the door. 'Thank you for coming,' she says in an almost whisper. 'I hope you don't mind, it is Christmas Eve after all.'

'We're glad you called,' Boyd says.

He's always felt oversized here but now he feels like a giant walking through the night-quiet corridors. And, whereas he'd felt earlier that the balance between him, Vita and Honey wasn't exactly right and wasn't the right solution, now it's just as it should be. When he'd been with his mother and Vita at the hospital, he'd felt part of a triangle but now, flanked by these two women, he feels more part of a circle. He's very glad both of them are here.

And, when they get to his mother's room, he realises that what Sophie said was obviously true; it won't be long now. He'd thought his mother had looked bad before, but now her skin had shrunk on to the bones in her face a bit like cling film. It is almost translucent. She's the size of a sparrow and he can barely make out the rise and fall of her chest.

The cancers have spread so that there is, according to the nurses, hardly any part of her now that isn't affected.

It was when it got to her brain that the decline had started in earnest and it was then that Boyd had started to mourn in earnest too. Not that he really knew how to, it was more a heaviness in the pit of his stomach and as if his legs were weighed down with lead. Filled with part-dread, part-remorse, he'd started to grieve in advance of her death in case he found he was unable to do it properly when the time came.

Not that he need have worried because, seeing her like this, the grief comes over him like a wave and it is different from how he'd felt after losing William; each grief, he's come to realise, is a different shape and colour. And, he'd thought he had managed to pack William's grief away, but here it is sitting alongside the grief he's feeling for his mother, still pulsing, still vibrant.

'I have to sit down,' he says to Honey and Vita.

Vita organises chairs for him and Honey and says, 'You can prop your foot up on here, Honey,' as she manoeuvres a footstool in front of Honey's chair.

'Thank you,' Honey says in a whisper.

'I'm sure she can't hear us,' Boyd says, fidgeting in his seat. 'What about you?' he asks Vita. 'Where will you sit?'

'I'll wait outside if that's OK,' she says. 'It feels a bit crowded in here.'

'No, you stay, I'll go.' Honey tries to stand, but Vita's already half-way through the door. She closes it quietly behind her.

'I don't know how to do this.' Boyd looks over at Honey who's sitting in a pool of yellow light from the lamp above the bed. It's like we're on some strange desert island, he thinks. The rest of the world has faded until it's no more than a speck in the distance.

'You don't have to do anything,' she replies. 'Just being here is enough, I'm sure.'

'Some part of me thinks she'd rather die alone. She's always been such a proud person, maybe she doesn't want me to see her like this.'

Honey reaches over the bed and touches his hand. 'They say that, when it actually happens, most people don't want to be on their own. I've heard many stories about people holding on until their loved ones arrive.'

'And I've heard as many stories about people waiting until their loved ones leave before they die.'

She squeezes his hand. 'Look,' she says, 'you can't know for sure. Not now. The important thing is to do what's right for *you*. If you want to be here, then stay.'

'You're right.' He disentangles his hand and runs his fingers through his hair. Suddenly he is inordinately tired. 'I'd never forgive myself if I wasn't with her at the end.'

There's a soft knock at the door. 'Everything OK?' Sophie asks.

'We're fine, thank you.'

Sophie comes in and studies Belle's face. 'She looks peaceful,' she says. 'She won't be in any pain now.'

Boyd wonders how Sophie can know this, but decides not to question it; it's better to think that this is so.

And so they wait and the minutes tick by to Christmas morning.

If Boyd had expected some kind of revelation or reconciliation at the final moments, he was to be disappointed.

He and Honey sit mostly in silence. Occasionally Honey limps out of the room to check on Vita. 'She's OK,' she says as she comes back in. 'She's reading and chatting to the nurses on the night station.'

And as they wait, he remembers random things: his mother on a beach building sandcastles, the smell of her cigarette smoke and the shush-shush sound her dress made when she walked. He remembers the string bag she took shopping, how she could never open a tin of corned beef with the little key thing but always said, 'Here, you do it Boyd. It's a man's job.' And he remembers standing outside her bedroom at night listening to the sound of her gentle weeping when she thought he was asleep. He remembers her disappointments, her lavender perfume, her brittleness, her smile.

It's just gone four in the morning when Belle makes a strange kind of noise, one long exhale almost like a laugh. He and Honey look at her and then at one another and they know without saying anything that she's gone.

And suddenly nothing matters any more, everything stops. There is only emptiness and silence.

Then, as if she's got some kind of sixth sense, Sophie knocks on the door again. 'You OK?' she asks, coming into the room.

'I think she's gone,' Boyd says.

'Yes, she has.' Sophie holds one of Belle's hands as she says this. 'I'll get Vita, shall I?'

'Yes please.'

'I'm sorry,' Boyd says as Vita enters. 'I'm so sorry.'

'You have nothing to be sorry for,' she says.

'I shouldn't have brought you here.'

'It's OK. It's not the same.'

He stands and moves towards Vita. Something urgent inside of him is telling him to hold her, that maybe sharing this grief will allow them to better share their grief over William. She steps into his arms and rests her head on his chest. It feels good to have her there.

He knows Honey will understand. He hopes she will.

* * *

They leave the hospice around six. What happens next is left in the hands of the staff.

'You go home,' Sophie tells Boyd. 'Come back on the 27th. We can sort the paperwork out then. And you can collect her things then too. Don't worry about it now. Just get some rest, all of you.' She looks at him, then at Vita and then at Honey, who's still sitting next to the bed with her foot on the stool.

Boyd guesses Sophie must have seen it all over the years she's worked there and so him being there with Vita and Honey isn't strange, or wrong, or anything in between; it is just how it is.

When they get back to the house in Albert Terrace, Boyd feels as though something seismic has shifted in his life and in its place is a huge slab of loss and relief and remorse.

'I'd better pop round next door,' Vita says, picking up her gift to Colin from under the tree as Honey limps into the kitchen to fill the kettle. 'I can't face going out for lunch, not now.'

'Don't blame you.' Honey is leaning against the counter top.

Boyd looks at Vita who's hovering by the front door and then at Honey. 'I think I'll go up and try and get some sleep,' he says.

And, to his surprise, he does sleep. He doesn't dream. Instead, his head is full of a dark mass he will later know to be sorrow.

Vita

'I'm sorry,' Boyd says. 'I'm so sorry.'

'You have nothing to be sorry for.'

'I shouldn't have brought you here.'

'It's OK. It's not the same.'

Boyd stands and moves towards me. I'm aware of Honey on the other side of the room but the thought of her bewilders me. I step forward and rest my head on Boyd's chest. He wraps his arms around me and for a second I let myself believe that nothing's changed, that Honey isn't here, that it is years ago and that his mother's death is about me and him and that no one else matters.

I imagine that this is a last day before a next day when I will wake and find him beside me.

I close my eyes and draw in the scent of him; his body is warm and vast and I am, I realise, still exhausted, my bones are heavy, my heart has slowed. If I were allowed to, I could fall asleep here, now. If I were allowed to I could, despite everything – all that lies unspoken and unforgiven between us – let myself love him again, let myself love him still.

Boyd

He goes back to the hospice on the 27th but says to Vita and Honey that he wants to go alone.

The three of them had spent Christmas Day and Boxing Day skirting around one another, watching old films on TV, eating when they felt like it. They'd opened their presents late on Christmas Day evening and had drunk too much whisky and Vita had gone next door for a while and Boyd and Honey had slept without touching, Belle's death a solid and impenetrable thing between them.

At the hospice he is given a case of his mother's things which he takes into the family room and opens. Inside he finds a half-used pot of face cream, a book she never got to finish, her nightdresses, a pair of slippers and the handkerchiefs he'd given her for Christmas, still wrapped in gift paper. He also finds an envelope and inside the envelope is the jewellery she'd been wearing when she was admitted. There are all sorts of other things that had belonged to her, too, all slightly faded and worn and terribly, terribly sad.

And there's also a copy of her will in a brown envelope. Someone has written, 'For Boyd, in the event of Belle's death' on the front of it. And there's a letter in a white envelope with Boyd's name c/o Belle, and the address of the hospice. He doesn't recognise the handwriting.

'Shit,' he says as he lifts both of these documents out of the mêlée of his mother's things.

He's aware of the noise of the traffic on the main road and of birds singing and the hum of electricity and of people talking in the room next door and he wants to open the documents and yet he can't.

They sit on the table in front of him: one white envelope, one brown.

Eventually, he leans forward and picks up the brown envelope.

So, it appears that Belle had made a will and in this will she's left everything to him: the residue from the sale of the house that had been the vet's practice, all the savings she'd accumulated from her other husbands and a significant amount in premium bonds. There is a note with the will from an accountancy practice in Godalming giving the total figures as of a month ago. Even after the costs of Queen Anne's, it is a huge amount of money. She's also left a small legacy and all her jewellery to Vita and there are instructions to get rid of everything else, including the furniture she'd taken to the care home, to cremate her at Guildford Crematorium and to inter her ashes near to her parents in Bristol. How odd, Boyd thinks, that after everything they did to drive her away and keep her away, she would want to return to them in the end. Maybe all children want that, maybe this particular bond never breaks.

He is surprised. Never in his wildest dreams had he expected her to leave everything to him. He'd assumed she would bypass him in some way, give it all to a cats' home or something which would punish him yet further for breaking his promise to her. But, maybe all parents forgive their children in the end too; maybe this particular bond never breaks either. He wonders whether her parents might have forgiven her had she let them.

It will take time to calibrate this. It will also take time to sort out probate and realise the assets, but this, he knows, is the answer to his financial worries. Now he can pay the tax bill, Anthony will be happy at last, he and Honey can move out of Vita's house back into their own flat and he and Vita can come to an agreement about the house in Albert Terrace. At last, he can give both Vita and Honey the futures they deserve.

He puts the will back in the suitcase and lifts out the white envelope. It is a letter from his father and it says:

'Dear Boyd,

Your mother has told me her news. I am, of course, deeply saddened to hear it and, with all my heart, wish her a pain-free end. She has always been such a force of nature and someone I have admired very much and, if things had been different for me, I would have honoured my obligation to her. I want you to know this.

She has also told me of the arrangements she has requested for her funeral, but I have decided that it would be best if I did not attend. It would only rake up the past and I would not want to burden you with my presence. But please know you will be in my thoughts, as you always have been.

With my kindest regards and deepest sympathies,

Percy Harrison.'

It is something, Boyd thinks. It is not nearly enough, but at least it's something. After all this time, after the abortive attempt to get to know him all those years ago, this is a meagre offering, but at least it's not silence and, Boyd realises, the fact that he has been in his father's thoughts matters a great deal. It's as though a link in the chain that had been broken was now fixed. Here is some kind of resolution. It's not what he'd hoped for, but this and the proof of his mother's unusual and changeable love for him also written down in black and white are, in the end, more than he ever thought he'd be given.

His mother's body has been moved to the undertakers. He's registered her death and is in touch with the Crematorium about the funeral. They have an opening on 3rd January at eleven which he's booked.

And so, he bundles all this together: his mother's things, her will, the letter from his father, the arrangements he's made so far and leaves the hospice. He'll tell Vita and Honey about it all later. But, for now, he needs to get back to work, to focus his mind on something other than these huge things.

* * *

At the office, Trixie gives him an update on the current purchases and sales and clucks around him, fusses and hangs up his jacket and asks him every five minutes if he's OK.

'I'm fine, thank you,' he tells her. But he's not; he's not fine at all.

Towards the end of the day, however, he remembers something he's forgotten to do. He never, he realises, checked on the step in the storeroom. It's been weeks since the accident and he's been negligent in not checking on it, but he had told Trixie not to do anything with it, to leave it as it was.

He opens the door and switches on the light. The step is in perfect order. There is not a crack or flaw in it. How, he wonders, could Honey have fallen down it? She said she'd felt something give, as if a bit of the wood had broken away. It's lucky, he thinks, that they don't need to report the incident to their insurers. If it had been any other employee they would have done, but Honey had insisted it didn't matter, that it had been her fault. But, he acknowledges, he'd always thought that the step had been damaged in some way and that this is what had caused her to fall. Odd, he thinks, as he puts on his jacket, says goodnight to Trixie and heads for home.

Vita

I'm taking some washing out of the machine, Honey's upstairs reading, the heating is on and is clicking away the way it does. It's dark outside.

I'd expected Boyd to come home hours ago but he hadn't. It had been awful waiting for him but at last I hear his key in the lock and here he is in the kitchen. He looks shattered.

'How did it go at the hospice?' I ask.

'Oh, OK. I went into work for a bit afterwards, you know, to take my mind off things.'

'I don't blame you.' I shake out a towel and start to fold it.

'They gave me her things,' he says, 'even the present I got her for Christmas. She never opened it, you know.'

I have no idea what to say. I pick up another towel. Thank God for towels, I think. At least I can keep my hands busy.

'Where's Honey?' he asks.

'Upstairs. She said she was going to have a lie down and read for a bit.'

'I'm glad. She deserves the rest.'

She deserves the rest, I think. For fuck's sake, what about me? Don't I deserve a rest too? But I say nothing. I still don't know what to say.

'Um …' Boyd jangles his keys, staring down at them. I imagine the metal of them must be getting hot in his hands by now. 'Um …'

'Yes,' I say, trying not to sound impatient.

'She left a will you know,' he says.

'Did she?'

'And there was a letter from my father with her stuff, addressed to me. Here,' he holds out a white envelope, 'you can read it if you like.'

I put down the towel I'm holding and take it from him.

'Thank you,' I say.

'She left me everything, you know: all the money, everything. And there's a lot of it too.'

'Oh,' I say. I'm surprised and I'm not surprised. I'd always wondered if she would, in the end.

'And she left you her jewellery.'

'Me? Why on earth would she do that?'

'Why do you think, Vita?' he says.

I really don't know, I can't think. I look at him. His face, his dear, dear face is crumpled with grief and loss.

'I'd better go and tell Honey,' he adds.

'Yes,' I say, 'I suppose you should.' I stare at the envelope, anything to avoid looking at him again but there's a tiny beat of triumph in my heart at the thought that Belle left her jewellery to me and not to Honey. Hah, I think. Hah!

'At least this means we can move out, get out from under your feet,' he says. 'Honey'll be pleased. This way I can pay the tax bill, sign this house over to you and we can go back to the flat, leave you in peace; it'll be just like it was before.'

No, I think. No it won't, you stupid, stupid man. Nothing will ever be the way it was before, not ever. I wasn't at peace then and I certainly won't be at peace when you're gone. I open my mouth to tell him this but I'm terrified of saying it. It is the sort of thing that once said can't be unsaid. Neither he nor I are ready for it and I wonder if we ever will be.

I couldn't protect him from the pain of William's death, but maybe I can protect him from the pain of knowing that I've been wrong and misguided and foolish, that I now know for sure that if I were allowed to, I could love him again, love him still.

He puts his keys down on the kitchen counter and starts to climb the stairs. I open the letter. I can't watch him go.

Honey

She'd tried not to mind when Boyd held Vita just after Belle died. She really had. But, to tell the truth she did mind; not because she doesn't trust him around her – she's convinced they're nothing more than just good friends these days – but because it was a reminder of what they'd once been to one another, what they'd shared and lost, all the heartache as well as the joy. It's something she can never compete with. Vita had fitted in against him so comfortably. Suddenly Honey had felt too tall and bony, too young and soiled for him.

Her horoscope today says she should align herself with winners as some of their competitive spirit will rub off on her. She has no idea what this means and frankly, it makes her a bit cross. She'd wanted something a little more tangible and her-specific; something to do with the fact that today her plaster comes off, something that will reassure her that she'll get no more texts from The Boatman. It's been a while now and there's been nothing; in some ways she hopes the reply she sent did the trick and he has fucked off and hopefully died too.

Boyd said he'd drive her to the hospital but she would have been OK getting a taxi as she really wishes he wouldn't take the time off work. They're so busy right now, which is odd seeing that it's the 29th

December and you'd think everyone out there would be too full of mince pies and sitting paralysed amongst the piles of wrapping paper, but there was a rush to get some sales completed by Christmas which has left a backlog of all the other stuff that Trixie and she have to do. Not that she minds; it's good to be busy. It means the business is doing well.

Since Belle's death, things have been different though. Boyd's told her about the will and the money and the letter from his father and has said that they'll be able to move back to the flat in March when the current tenants move out. It'll be odd not to be here. Despite everything she has the feeling she's going to miss this house, and Vita too.

She does wish, however, that Boyd would cry because he hasn't, not really. She has to remind herself that it took him years to be able to cry about William's death, so maybe it'll take years for this other death to work its way through too. All she knows is that during these last few days both he and Vita have been quiet and very sad. They move around the house as if in slow motion and seem always to talk in whispers to one another as if any loud noise will puncture something precious.

Even though they knew it was going to happen, there's a world of difference, it seems, between the idea of death and it actually taking place. Honey has never known it before, not so close up, and what shocked her most was its absolute irrevocability. Once Belle had gone, she'd gone totally. They say that the spirit can rise out of the body and that those who mourn can witness it going, but it was nothing like that with Belle. She did that funny kind of breath and then there was nothing, absolutely nothing; it was as though the room had emptied and that she and Boyd, and then when Vita came in, none of them were really there but were looking down at the empty room as if from a great distance.

'What's Vita doing today?' she asks Boyd as they pull away from the house on the way to the hospital.

She checks in the wing mirror, there is no one standing under the horse chestnut trees this time.

'I don't know. I think she might spend some time in the studio. She said she's got a commission to work on.'

Honey shifts in her seat, trying to get comfortable. She can't wait to get this damned thing off. 'Anything else we need to do for the funeral?' she asks.

'I don't think so. Everything's sorted.' He hesitates; some fuck-awful song is playing on the radio. She wishes he'd turn it off. 'What saddens me,' he says, 'is that it's going to be such a small affair: just us, Trixie and maybe some people from Queen Anne's and the hospice. After the life she's led, how vibrant and angry she was for most of it, it's tragic to think there'll only be a handful of people seeing her off. If only ...'

He pauses again, lifts a hand off the steering wheel and runs it through his hair.

'If only what?' she asks, although she thinks she knows what he's going to say. She's right.

'If only there was a grandchild,' he says, 'one who, in years to come, might be interested in the woman who'd been their grandmother. My father's other family will never know her either and that's tragic too.'

'I know,' Honey says. But she doesn't. For someone like her who's got no relatives at all – that she knows of anyway – it's hard for her to imagine a future filled with descendants and family stories. And, although what Belle said to her about her having a child is still lodged somewhere between her heart and her brain, she hasn't been able, or willing, to process it yet. Despite all the promises she'd made herself the last time she got a text from 'The Boatman', it seems she is still very good at not making any decisions and keeping her head resolutely in the sand.

They get to the hospital on time and park and walk in, Honey holding on to Boyd's arm and, when the plaster eventually comes off, she feels giddy with relief. Her ankle's pale and tender and they say she'll have to do some physio and wear a kind of support stocking for a while, but it's not just the freedom of movement and the lightness of her leg but having use of her hands again that's bloody wonderful.

'I'll have to take you dancing,' Boyd says, brushing his lips over hers when they're back in the car.

'You'll have to learn how to dance first,' she replies, kissing him back.

'Cheeky sod,' he says, smiling at her.

* * *

It's not exactly dancing, well not the kind of dancing she'd expected, but on New Year's Eve Boyd takes her to a party at a pub in town. There's dinner and a disco and they eat and shuffle gingerly to the music and chat to people he knows vaguely through work. Vita's out with Colin, or so she says, and at just before midnight Honey texts her to say 'Happy New Year' and Vita texts straight back, although Honey knows they're doing this more for form's sake than anything else because of Belle's funeral, which is mere days away.

They have, however, scheduled another sitting, their last, for the day after tomorrow when Boyd will be in the office catching up on paperwork and Honey will be at home nursing the hangover she's still expecting to have. With the news that they're going to be moving out in the spring, suddenly the need to get the picture finished is becoming more important. It feels like both Vita and she are working towards a deadline now.

Honey kisses Boyd at midnight and peels herself out of his arms to go and open the front door of the pub; it's not quite as it should be because she should actually be opening all the doors but the logistics of this defeats her.

'What on earth are you doing?' he asks, coming up and standing behind her as she waits on the threshold breathing in the damp night air.

'I've got to let the old year out,' she says, 'before the New Year can come in.'

'You're one crazy lady, you know that, don't you?'

'It's nice to have something to believe in.' She nods and leans back, resting her head against his chest.

'I love you,' he whispers into her hair.

'I love you too.'

Boyd's ordered a cab and, when they get home around one-thirty, Vita's not home.

'I guess she must be staying next door,' Boyd says as he closes the front door behind them. His voice is expressionless.

Honey takes him by the hand and starts to lead him upstairs saying, 'Come on then, stud. Let's do it.'

She feels desperate, as though she really is on the cusp of some momentous change. She hadn't realised, until she'd opened the door of the pub and they'd stood there and it all seemed so calm and beautiful, that actually what she was doing was acknowledging that at the passing of the old year, and with the heralding of the new, the moment she'd been dreading was now within sight.

They make love and it's fantastic. She wraps her legs around him and when he comes she is full of him and somehow it feels different this time. Maybe it's the fact they're both a little drunk, maybe it's the grief and this tiny moment when they can escape it, and the fact that Vita's not in the room across the landing. All she knows is that afterwards she realises that in her desperation she has never known this total abandonment, this total connection before.

'We're getting good at this,' Boyd says, raising himself on one elbow and looking at her, his left eyebrow kinked.

'I should think so too. We've had plenty of practice.'

She tucks herself into the crook of his arm and they doze as the night ticks on. She tries not to think of tomorrow, or the next day, or the day after that, or of anything other than being here, now, with this man and whatever shade of love it is that they've coloured themselves in. And she doesn't have the dream.

The next morning, Boyd brings her a cup of coffee and she checks her horoscope as he gets ready for work. It might be New Year's Day but he says he wants to go in and catch up on a few things. Honey's taken today, tomorrow and the day of the funeral off work, or rather Boyd has told her to. 'You need a rest,' he'd said. 'Get that ankle of yours well and truly mended.'

Vita's still not back and so, when he's gone, Honey goes downstairs and opens the front door to check whether the curtains are open or not at Colin's. It would be nice to know if Vita's OK. She's been strangely quiet since Boyd told her they'd be moving out.

As Honey steps out onto the path, she glances down the road and Reuben is there again under the horse chestnut trees. It's spitting with rain and he's leaning up against the trunk again, staring at her. He's wearing a jacket with the hood up, his hands are in the pockets, he isn't moving. Her blood chills.

'Shit,' she says.

And it all comes rushing to the surface again: her guilt, the need to leave, the fact that she's the only one who can protect Boyd from the real her.

She doesn't look at Colin's house but hurries up the path, or goes as fast as she can with her sore ankle and slams the door behind her. She hauls herself up the stairs to check her phone. There's no message. She goes into Vita's room and peers around her curtains. The man has gone.

'Fuck. Fuck you,' she mutters as she climbs back into bed and draws the covers around her.

Boyd

It's the 2nd of January; the day before his mother's funeral.

'Did you have a good New Year?' Boyd asks Trixie as she puts the phone down and turns back to her computer.

'It was OK. Quite quiet.'

'Were the boys at home?'

'No, they were off doing their own thing. I don't blame them; if I was them I wouldn't want to spend an evening in the company of us old fuddy duddies!'

'Oh, surely not,' Boyd says, laughing. 'There's nothing remotely fuddy duddy about you.'

'Don't you believe it,' Trixie replies, a slight sharpness to her tone.

If Boyd is surprised he doesn't show it, but a tiny alarm bell rings in his head at the unwelcome thought that all might not be as it seems with Trixie. She's been, a bit like Honey has, a little on edge of late; it's nothing he can put his finger on, just a slight raggedness around the edges.

She's continued to be kind and patient with Honey and friendly towards Vita and for this he's grateful and so, maybe, it's because of this that he says what he says next.

'Do you fancy going for a drink after work tonight? To celebrate the New Year? I could do with a change of scene before tomorrow.'

'That would be nice,' Trixie says. 'If you're sure you don't need to get back to Honey ...' there's a pause before she adds, '... or Vita.'

'I'll let Honey know. It'll be fine.'

'And you're sure it's OK to shut the office tomorrow? For the funeral, I mean?'

'Of course. We'll put a notice on the website and the door and if you could change the answerphone message, that'll cover it. I'm sure people will understand.'

'They bloody well should,' Trixie says and, again, Boyd feels a frisson of unease at the vehemence in her voice.

He calls Honey and explains that he's taking Trixie out for a drink.

'That's a nice idea,' Honey says. 'Just text when you're on your way back and we can decide what to do for dinner?'

'Will do.' He pauses and then asks, 'Is Vita home yet?'

'Yes, she's here.'

He's saying goodbye as an email from the solicitor doing the conveyancing for the house in Silchester Avenue pops up on his screen.

* * *

'Bet you're going to find tomorrow difficult,' Trixie says as they settle into a booth at the pub.

'Yes, I will. We all will, I mean,' he adds hastily.

She's drinking red wine and he a beer. He'll let himself have one and then if Trixie wants another drink, he'll switch to something soft so that he can drive her home. Like when she went for the drink with Honey, she's said she'll get a cab in the morning and collect her car then. 'I'll drive straight to the funeral from the office,' she said.

'Is Richard able to come?' Boyd asks, picking up his pint.

'No, I don't think so.'

'That's a shame.'

'Yes, it is.'

They are silent for a moment. Around them the bar is bustling with people, a fire is crackling in the grate and a David Bowie song is coming out of the speakers. Boyd stretches his legs and cracks his knuckles. He feels strangely relaxed, almost as if time's on hold and all that matters is here, now. He's always felt easy in Trixie's company.

'Are you going to be OK, though?' she asks. 'I mean, there'll be painful reminders, won't there?'

Her question prompts Boyd to analyse his feelings, something he's shied away from since his mother's death. 'Yes and no,' he says, after a while. 'It'll be different because it's not a church service like we had with William. I presume you mean it'll be painful because of him?'

Trixie nods and takes a sip of her wine. She is looking directly at him. Her eyes are bright and clear. She has, he notices, a faint blush on her cheeks and has done her hair a little differently; it's more puffed up than it was earlier in the day. He watches her lips as she runs her tongue over them, the wine has stained them slightly, making them redder than they usually are.

'And,' he continues, 'it's different because ...'

'Yes?' She leans forward, resting her chin on her hands.

'Well, because there's a certain rightness to burying one's parents, that's the natural order of things. What's not right is burying your child. No parent should have to do that.'

It's been ages since he's spoken of this, and he wonders whether he's actually ever articulated it in quite this way before.

'It was an awful time, wasn't it?' she says.

'We wouldn't have got through it without you. You know that, don't you.'

She nods again and picks up her drink.

And he remembers how good she was in the days after William had been born and then during those awful months after he died. How she'd try and coax Vita out of bed and how she'd kept him on track at work, carefully and quietly doing the things he'd let slip. And she'd never once complained or taken either him or Vita to task. There were no, 'Isn't it time to pull yourself together?' kind of speeches and no platitudes either. She'd seemed to know exactly how much it hurt without him having to tell her. He wonders now if he's ever thanked her enough for this.

But whatever she'd done, it hadn't been enough to stop him and Vita from falling apart. She'd not been able to forewarn him that day he'd got home to find Vita packing up William's clothes, stuffing them into a black sack, her hair all wild, her face fierce and strange.

It had, he remembers now, been pouring with rain. Work had been awful, with a sale falling through at the last minute and the despair he'd been feeling since William died was, if anything, growing heavier rather than lighter.

He and Vita had said some dreadful things to one another that afternoon in the gloom of William's bedroom, the duckling yellow paint on the walls seeming to mock him. He'd felt so buoyant when he'd decorated the room in the weeks before the birth. How stupid he'd been to have believed it would all be all right. Such presumption, he'd thought at the time. How could he not have predicted what would happen? Why wasn't he prepared for it?

And he'd slept on the sofa for the few days it took him to move out and when he had, he'd expected the pain to lessen. Without the daily reminders – his wife's slow footsteps on the stairs, the way the light fell through the window in the room that had been his son's, her talking to him about the weather or what was on the news, her voice always holding a rebuke – he'd thought his grief would ease. But the pain hadn't diminished like he'd expected it to.

So many people have told him over the years that time is a great healer, but Boyd knows this is rubbish. Time doesn't heal a broken heart, it only hardens it. It covers it with a layer of something that's as thin as silk and as strong as steel. And it's always there – the soft, damaged heart – underneath, ready to be exposed should this layer ever slip. He'd told Honey he thought he'd done his mourning, but he hasn't.

'Penny for them,' Trixie says, interrupting Boyd's thoughts.

'Oh, sorry. I was miles away then.' He smiles apologetically at her.

'That's OK. You have a lot on your mind.'

'You could say!' he replies. 'But enough about me. Tell me, how are things with Richard? Has he got any promising leads, job-wise?'

Trixie sighs and runs a fingertip around the rim of her glass. A man standing at the bar laughs loudly and music's still coming out the speakers; it's Michael Jackson this time.

'No,' she says. 'No strong leads. He tells me he's got some enquiries out, but that for a man his age in the current economic climate we shouldn't expect anything anytime soon. I try to understand, of course I do. But he doesn't make it easy.'

'What do you mean?'

'Oh, it doesn't matter. Not right now. You have enough on your plate.'

Boyd reaches out a hand and touches Trixie's arm. 'You know you can talk to me anytime, don't you? About anything? I owe you so much, it's the least I can do.'

'Thank you,' Trixie says, her voice a little strained. She swallows hard and looks down at her glass. 'Time for another?' she asks.

* * *

When Boyd gets home, Honey and Vita are sitting companionably in the lounge. Vita is reading but doesn't look up as he comes in. Honey is looking at something on her phone.

'What have you two been up to?' he says, placing a kiss on Honey's head and touching Vita's shoulder as he walks by her to go to the kitchen. 'I'm famished. What's for dinner?'

'You didn't text,' Honey says. 'So I'm not sure.'

She doesn't sound cross; but perhaps she should. Boyd has stayed out later than he said, but when Trixie asked if he wanted another drink, he couldn't refuse. She'd seemed to need the company.

'Right,' he says, 'fish and chips it is, then. You joining us, Vita?'

'OK,' she says, putting down the book she's reading and then adds, grudgingly it seems, 'thank you.'

He pops back out to pick up their supper and they eat it on trays watching TV. It's a way of passing the time, Boyd thinks. Tomorrow is edging ever nearer.

And when tomorrow comes, the weather is bright and cold for a change. The sun is low and large in the sky and his mother's funeral passes without a hitch: the cortège arrives, there is a service, there are no hymns because Belle didn't want any, and the curtains close on the coffin; he can hear the sound of the rollers rolling it away.

Sophie's come, and Jean from Queen Anne's, and Trixie, of course. And Colin has come too. Boyd's not sure how he feels about Colin being there. Colin and Vita stand without touching; they barely speak to one another and Boyd finds he minds this more than if Colin had spent the whole service with his arm around Vita, whispering words of comfort into her ear.

There's a brief moment when he catches Colin on his own. Vita has gone to the Ladies', Honey is talking to Trixie and he and Colin are waiting by the door. The organ is playing its last notes and the few people who came are trickling away. He studies Colin, briefly taking in the colour of his skin and his poise, and thinks back to that first evening when he'd come out to water his tomatoes and how Boyd hadn't known then about him and Vita.

'Thank you for coming today,' he says now.

'That's OK. I wanted to be here,' Colin pauses, 'for Vita,' he adds.

'Mmmmm.' Boyd finds he doesn't know what to say next. He sees the undertaker wave at him and knows he has mere seconds to say whatever it is he wants to say. 'Don't hurt her,' he says, his mouth tight, his heart a silent, thudding thing.

'Hurt Vita?' Colin asks.

'Yes.'

'If anything, I think it's going to be the other way around,' Colin says, smiling a little sadly, Boyd thinks.

And Boyd doesn't have time to ask him what he means because the undertaker is still waving at him and he has to go.

And when it's all over, he and Trixie go back to the office and take down the sign from the door and update the website and Trixie re-records the answerphone message and Colin and Vita and Honey go back to Albert Terrace where, Vita says, she needs to carry on working on a picture she's got on the go. There is no wake. Sophie has slipped away, back to the hospice and Jean has gone back to Queen Anne's.

He emails the Crematorium to ask about the interment of his mother's ashes in Bristol. There is, he realises now, no rush for this.

He sends the email as Trixie says, 'I'm just nipping out to get some milk. We're running low.'

'OK,' he says. 'Thank you. And thank you for being there today.'

'Oh, that's OK. It's what friends are for,' Trixie says, putting on her coat and opening the door.

Honey

She's on the boat. She can hear the smack of the waves against the hull. She doesn't want to be here.

'You will go,' Camilla said, lifting her drawn-on eyebrows and tapping the desk with a talon-like fingernail. 'You will do what you have to do and he will pay us. This is how it works. You're in too deep to get out now. You know he'll always ask for you. That's the deal. He can't risk anyone else knowing. It's a matter of damage limitation and so it has to be you. If you hadn't gone that first time, then maybe someone else would be in the position you're in now. But you can't change it. So just suck it up, lady, and go and do what you're paid to do.'

And so Honey goes because he asks for her. Again and again she goes to the boat and he fucks her and hurts her and she's shamed in her own eyes because she takes the money and because she's too weak to say no.

Until that particular night.

Earlier she'd awoken to all the particular alignments: the sun, the dust motes, the shout, the birdsong, and she'd made her decision and now she's here and he smells of cinnamon, one of his arms is pinned across her chest and he's holding on to her free arm and her other arm is wedged under her. He's pulling at her clothes and she's saying 'No,' and his mouth is opening and closing but no words are coming out of it.

'No,' she says, louder this time. 'You're hurting me. Stop. You have to stop.'

But he doesn't, he never does. He likes this. To him it's a game. To Honey it's not.

And so she says it. 'Gas! I smell gas.'

She has to; it's too late to stop it now. This is the only way she can break the cycle of this.

His mouth moves again, his eyes are black buttons, like a toy's eyes. They don't seem to move or reflect the light. They go on for ever into the back of his head.

She feels his weight shift a fraction and slips out from under him. It's like she has scales, like a fish does and that she will die if she doesn't get into the water. Her lungs are gills. She has openings in her chest that flap with her breaths.

'Shit,' he says. He says it loudly and definitely. 'Did you knock something, you silly bitch?'

She shakes her head and her vision blurs but she can make out a pile of red cushions, a black marble counter top, a silver ice bucket. She is inching away from him, he has his back turned to her and has lifted his head as if he is an animal scenting danger in the air.

'I can smell it too,' he says. 'Go. Just go.'

He doesn't have to tell her twice. She runs up a set of white steps, the railing she's holding on to already feels hot.

But what he doesn't know is that when she arrived and said, 'I need the loo,' and he'd said, 'Go on then, be quick,' she'd fractured the seal on a pipe to one of the gas cylinders he has on board and which she knows he never stores safely. She'd used a wrench she'd brought with her and had hidden in her handbag and which she'd then dropped overboard as he got undressed and lay down on the bed in the cabin, his skin dusky against the pale sheets. And, as he pinned her down and she was saying, 'No,' she'd known the gas was leaking and what she had to do next.

And so, when he says, 'Go. Just go,' she goes and, as she runs, she picks up the box of matches she'd hidden behind one of the steps up onto the deck. Her hands are shaking and it's hard to light the match but she lights it and drops it and prays it reaches its target. It is a mad plan and she's sure it's not going to work.

But it does, and there's an explosion and that sound of tin foil crackling and she is jumping off the side of the boat and swimming through the heavy water.

And this time it's definitely not a dream.

* * *

January and February slip by almost unremarked. Every day she tells herself that today will be the day she will leave and yet still she hasn't. There have been no more texts and she hasn't seen Reuben under the trees at the end of the road.

Countless times she tries to tell Boyd, but she always stops herself, fearful of the damage it will do. She tells herself that if he really loves her, he'll forgive her anything, but she doesn't want to put this to the test. She is afraid to find out that he doesn't. That's the trouble with ultimatums, you always run the risk of not getting the answer you are hoping for.

* * *

But then it's early March, Honey's in bed with Boyd and he's snoring gently next to her. Dawn is beginning to break and Honey is pregnant with Boyd's child and knows for sure that her time here has finally run out.

She has to go because what she did she did on purpose and Reuben knows this and now he's done what's he done, she realises the game he's been playing is coming to an end. He's getting ready to make his final move.

They say what you don't know can't hurt you. She can't risk Boyd finding out about the baby. She must take herself away from here and start again because she can't bear to see the look in his eyes when he finds out what she's done and how she could be putting his unborn child at risk by staying.

The decision is out of her hands and, after all the times she's made up her mind and then changed it again, it's a relief to know that, at last, the end is in sight.

She lies totally still, fearful of waking him. Boyd snuffles and turns his massive body a little so that he's facing away from her. This makes it easier for her to bear; she doesn't know how she is going to manage without him and his goodness in her life.

The portrait is finished. She and Vita had their last sitting on the 2nd January while Boyd was at work and then out for a drink with Trixie, and Vita's been working on it in the weeks that have followed: the strange, quiet weeks after Belle's funeral when Boyd was preoccupied with sorting out her will, paying his tax bill, signing the house over to Vita and making the plans for him and Honey to move back into the flat. The portrait is wrapped in brown paper under the bed and she's supposed to be hanging it in the flat as a surprise for Boyd.

This is what she's told Vita and, with her head deep in the sand, there've been times recently when she believed it actually might happen. But then the letter arrived. It was hand-delivered. She'd told Boyd it had been a voucher from the dry cleaners. It came in a plain white envelope with her name on it, and inside was a type-written note in block capitals. It said: 'I AM COMING FOR YOU. IT WON'T BE LONG NOW. WHEN YOU LEAST EXPECT IT, THAT'S WHEN I'LL COME.'

If she wasn't pregnant, she'd tell herself to stick it out. She likes to think it was when they'd made love after the New Year's Eve party that this child had started and she already loves it with a fierce, piercing passion and so that's why she has to go. She is being punished because she didn't open all the doors on New Year's Eve. She's being punished because she's never really been good enough.

This child is, she believes, the child in Elizabeth's prediction. For so long she's thought the baby was William, but now she knows it wasn't.

Boyd wakes and kisses her. She lets him hold her and breathes in the scent of him, the colossal, magical scent of him. She stamps it onto her heart, telling herself that this will be the last day he will ever hold her like this. She must be strong. She cannot falter or change her mind. There can be no coming back. Not this time. Not ever.

She'd once thought guilt was the most powerful emotion, but now she believes it's love: she will do this extraordinary thing because she loves him with all her heart.

* * *

It's late afternoon and there's no one here, but still she moves slowly and silently as though afraid she'll be discovered. Vita has gone out for the day and Honey has told Boyd she isn't feeling well and will stay home today. She must be gone by the time they both get back.

She glances around the lounge. Everything is as it should be. The air in here is familiar. If she were to place the flat of her hand on the wall next to the fireplace she'd feel the echoes of all they've said and done pulse through her fingers like the bass notes of a song.

She creeps upstairs and gathers her stuff from the bathroom and from the dressing table in their bedroom, she slips clothes off their hangers, picks up the book she's reading from beside the bed. A business card falls out of it. It has Elizabeth's name on it. She bends down to pick it up, puts it in the bag too.

There, under the bed, is the portrait, wrapped in brown paper, ready to be hung in the flat. They're due to move out of here next week but she can't go, not with him, not now. This, she tells herself for the millionth time, as she plucks her toothbrush from its glass in the bathroom, is the best way. It is the only way.

Her phone rings. She takes it out of the pocket of her jeans and looks at the screen. Of course it's Boyd. Boyd is calling. There's a flicker of something in her belly; it could be the fear of being found out, or most probably it's the baby telling her to hurry up.

Boyd's call could be about anything: to ask what she'd like to have for dinner tonight, to remind her to get the carpets in the flat cleaned before they move back in, to tell her he loves her. She lets the call go to voicemail and lays the phone down on the bed, up near her pillow, where he's sure to see it. She touches it with one finger as if to bless it, as if her fingerprint can hold a record of everything she wants to say.

She has deleted all the messages, there must be no trail.

The iPad Boyd gave her for Christmas is downstairs, her browsing history cleared and she's de-registered her email accounts and destroyed the letter.

She zips up the holdall. The noise is exceptionally loud in the silence of the house. For once, even the town's streets seem empty of traffic; the birds in the garden are mute. There's still a hint of winter chill in the air.

This isn't the first time she's done this. She's left before. She always leaves. For a short while she'd believed that this time it could be different, that this time she could stay, but now she knows this is the only way. Doing this will put the wrong things right. It will keep the people she loves safe. Honey Mayhew is on her way out. Soon she will cease to be.

She's standing on the doorstep, the house is behind her. The salt she scattered on the doorstep has long since been hoovered away. She hopes Vita and Boyd will forget about her soon too.

Best foot forward, she says to herself and then smiles ruefully. She's better, obviously she is – after all the accident was months ago – but her ankle still gives her gyp on occasions; she imagines it always will, when the weather changes maybe. It'll be something she can complain about when she's old and cranky.

She starts walking. She gets to the end of the path, wheeling the bag behind her. She turns left, walks along the pavement past next door's gate, doesn't look back, counts the houses down, 21, 20, 19 … until she gets to the end. Opposite the Terrace, there's a border of scrubland and then the main road

At the corner, she gets ready to cross.

It's hard leaving Albert Terrace; hard to leave the house with its navy-blue door, its riot of a garden and the people who live there.

If arriving was difficult, leaving is the hardest thing she's ever had to do.

She looks to her left and then to her right; a blackbird sends up a torrent of song, like an alarm and, of course, he's there.

Reuben is standing on the opposite side of the road as she knew he would be. She'd always known somehow that the day she left would be the day he'd come and now he is crossing the road and walking towards her, limping slightly.

She can already feel his arm gripping hers, see the glint in his dark eyes. She remembers his hands hurting her, his dark, beady eyes.

She lets go of the handle of the case and stands completely still apart from a slight tremor in her hands. She bunches them into fists and waits. There is nowhere to run.

'So,' he says when he reaches her. He's wearing a brown leather jacket, his skin is dark, he has a day's worth of stubble on his chin. She's got one foot on the pavement, one on the road. He is positioned in front of her, blocking her way. He is broad and strong.

She takes hold of the handle again, what feels like a hundred butterflies are ricocheting in her chest. 'So, it's just you and me,' he pauses, draws his lips back over his teeth and says slowly, 'again.' A bead of spit has gathered in the corner of his mouth.

Honey swallows; she mustn't let him see her fear.

'How did you find me?' she says.

'It wasn't difficult. I have people who do this kind of thing for me, quite regularly actually. I usually leave the dirty business to them, but this time it's different. This time it's personal.'

He takes a step closer to her so they are face to face. She notices the lines around his mouth are deeper and darker than before. He shifts his feet, placing them about a foot apart in order to give himself more balance.

'Have you any idea,' he says, 'what it's like to lose a leg?'

Another step closer. She can smell his breath; it is sour, with a faint trace of alcohol on it.

'Have you?' he asks. He reaches out and grips her arm like she thought he would, the pressure of his thumb on her skin is familiar. It is almost as if the bruises are still there and are rising to meet him. She can feel the weight of him on her, the rock of the boat in the water; see the red cushions, the black marble counter top, the silver ice bucket. She can feel his arm pressed down on her chest so her ribs are hurting. She can taste the fear.

She shakes her head.

'I didn't think so, you bitch.' He spits out the last word.

She takes a step back and bumps into her bag. Around her now are cars and people walking. Boyd may be driving home and may see them. He may stop and wind down his window and lean his massive body towards them and say, 'Everything OK, Honey?' And she'd nod and say, 'Yes, it's fine. He's just asking the time.'

Or maybe Vita will cycle past, or Colin will walk by and they will dispel the threat of this by saying something innocuous like, 'Where are you off to, Honey? Can I help you with your bag? It looks heavy.'

Or maybe Boyd won't come, nor Vita, nor Colin, and this man, this Reuben Roberts, will put a hand in his pocket and bring out a knife. She can already feel the slice of metal against her skin, see the blossoming of blood, feel the child she's carrying freeze in her womb. This is what revenge looks like. This is it happening.

He's saying, 'This is just a warning. I've been watching you. I've been waiting for my moment.' He's loosened his grip on her arm and raises a hand to her face, letting his fingers hover over her mouth. 'I can destroy the pretty little life you've built for yourself here in an instant.' He clicks his fingers, moves his mouth right up to hers, and says, 'Just like this,' and he blows on her, his breath is fierce, warm and sticky. 'I presume they don't know, these *good* people you live with?' He stresses the word 'good' and makes it sound ridiculous, makes it clear he thinks they are ridiculous for believing in her. 'What would they think if they knew what their precious girl is capable of? Would they ever sleep safely in their beds again?'

'What do you want?' she asks.

'To scare you,' he says, 'and this is just the start. I have many things planned for you, Sweetums.' His voice is snide; his eyes hard and dark. His teeth, she notices, are incredibly white, luminous almost.

And suddenly Honey's had enough. Suddenly the pieces fall into place. She's spent what seems a lifetime trying to prevent the very thing that's happening right now from happening. She's hidden and lied and been afraid and has left the people she loves rather than staying and fighting. What ever happened to the girl who used to stand and fight, she thinks?

And, what is the worst that can happen? She gets found out, the truth is told, she goes to jail, loses everything? No. There are things she will not lose: her child is one and Boyd is the other. The girl who she'd been before is still there after all, the girl who will kick out rather than be kicked down. She takes a step forward. Her neck is aching, she's been holding her breath and her chest is hurting. It feels as though she's being starved of oxygen.

'No,' she says. It comes out as a whisper.

He laughs, 'Ah, try talking a little louder, my love.' He leans in again, 'I remember you used to cry out loud enough before. I always thought that you actually liked it rough and were just pretending you didn't, but you didn't fool me, you whore.'

'No,' she says again and this time it comes out strong and clear. 'No, I hated it and I hate you and don't even think of blackmailing me. I know far worse things about you than you know about me.' She doesn't pause. The words come out in a flood. 'You think I'm worried about being found out? Surely you have much more to lose than me? Your precious wife? Your precious reputation? Your hands are dirtier than mine, Mr Roberts, much, much dirtier.' And when she's finished speaking, she raises her hand to his mouth, pushes her face against his and blows. 'Your life can go up in a puff of smoke, just like this.' She clicks her fingers and turns on her heels and starts to walk back along Albert Terrace.

'This isn't over,' he calls from behind her.

If anyone were watching they might think they were two friends joking with one another, or two lovers having a tiff, raising their voices over the hum of distant traffic, birdsong, airplane engines. To a passer-by there is nothing suspicious about this exchange.

She looks over her shoulder and says, 'Bring it on.' Her voice is still strong, still clear. 'And,' she halts, turns around again and says, 'you can stop the texts and the letters; they mean nothing, they don't scare me. You are nothing to me, nothing. Do you hear?'

In the distance a siren bleats, she's aware of a car door being slammed shut, her skin is hot, the air on it is cool. The butterflies are somersaulting, she can feel her muscles clenching around her baby. She is an animal poised to strike. She is a mother fighting for her child and to keep the man she loves.

'What texts?' he calls out. 'I haven't sent you any texts, or letters. That's not my style, you should know that by now. I'd do nothing that can be traced back to me.'

'Pardon?' She starts to walk back towards him. 'What did you say?'

'I said, I haven't sent you any texts, you stupid little girl, but believe me, this isn't over.'

327

And then he's going; he's crossing back over the road, limping still. He's walking away from her and she's following him, trundling her case after her. 'What do you mean?' she says again. 'If you didn't send the texts, then who did?'

As he reaches the other side of the road, he stops and looks at her and says, 'I don't give a fuck, Miss Honey Mayhew, not one flying fuck. But that's not my style, not my style at all.'

Honey is in the middle of the road; her feet are frozen to the tarmac, her heart is racing.

A flatbed lorry is approaching; she can hear the rattle of metal poles.

If it isn't Reuben Roberts, then who's been sending the texts? Who sent the letter? What has every fucking horoscope she's read actually meant? Was what Elizabeth said all baloney? Who was actually in control of this? What is real and what is made up?

Instinctively she puts her hand on her stomach and then suddenly she knows. The realisation hits her like a gust of wind, or a freak wave, or something else that's unexpected and unpredictable. She has to get back to the house and she has to go now.

She turns around. For the first time in a long time, she's back in control. The thought makes her heart sing. She can beat this. Honey Mayhew is here to stay.

The flatbed lorry is closer now, the poles making a sound like a hundred hands clapping.

The last day

On the last day Graham Silverton's short cut has taken him on a route which passes the end of Albert Terrace.

He stopped for lunch on the M3, some god-awful egg sandwich which has been repeating on him ever since. He should have chosen the beef one. The radio is still playing, the DJ now reading out requests from people in love with one another. He's saying, 'This goes out to Rob from Abigail. Abigail says she knows she's not been easy to live with lately, but you are her rock and her soul mate; she can't imagine life without you.' The record Abigail's requested is *Hello* by Adele.

Graham snorts. What a fucking cliché, he thinks.

He sees the slender woman with short, blonde hair in the road. She's facing Albert Terrace. She is standing stock still. He sees the case at her heels. He sees a man in a brown jacket walking away from her, limping slightly.

Graham swerves a little to avoid her as Adele's is saying something about saying hi from the other side, or something like that.

Graham Silverton doesn't see what happens next.

Vita

I'm cutting the stems of some tightly-budded daffodils one of my clients has given me as a thank you. I wish people wouldn't do this. I like flowers, always have them in the house if I can, but I hate thank yous and would much rather that people just pay me the money they owe me and say goodbye. All this fussing about doesn't sit comfortably with me.

I've just finished the portrait of a cat. A cat! Whatever next! The cat was, I have to admit, a pretty thing with a sweet round face, green eyes and a stripy coat but, for heaven's sake, wouldn't a photo have done the job?

The house is very quiet. I'd half-expected Honey to be home when I got in but no doubt she and Boyd have gone off somewhere, to the flat maybe.

'Sodding fucking things,' I say as I sweep the stem ends off the worktop and into the bin. I look around for a place to put the vase. 'Suppose it'll have to go on the mantelpiece,' I say to no one in particular.

I'm just carrying the vase out of the kitchen when there's a knock at the door.

I plonk the vase down and go to answer it.

'Mrs Harrison?'

Two police officers are standing on the step.

I nod. No one has called me that for years.

'Can we come in?'

* * *

How on earth am I going to tell Boyd?

I ring the office and ask Trixie where he is.

'He's out doing a valuation,' Trixie says. 'He should be back in about twenty minutes.'

'Oh, OK. Thanks,' I daren't look down at my feet because it feels like the floor is moving.

'Why? Is there anything wrong? Can I pass a message to him?'

'No, that's all right.'

And I hang up before Trixie can say anything else. Our conversation sounded normal, but there was nothing normal about it at all.

The evening is drawing in, people are making their way home from work, the cafés in Farnham are closing, the staff are wiping down the tables and stacking the chairs just as the restaurants are preparing for the evening trade. Everything is so fucking ordinary, but nothing will actually ever be the same again.

I couldn't let the police tell him. There was no way I'd allow a police car to pull up outside the office and for Boyd to watch the officers' slow, measured walk to the door. They're not happy about it but I insist I have to do this myself. 'Just try and stop me,' I say to the well-meaning policewoman with the slightly large hips, and so I get on my bike and I cycle. I cycle past Colin's house and I don't think of him. I pass the end of the road. All that's left there now is the skid mark from tyres. It's obscene how quickly it's all got tidied away.

An accident, they'd said. No one to blame. Honey had been in the road, the driver had tried to avoid her, but she'd stepped out in front of him. He'd braked so hard that his load of metal poles had slipped their constraints and rattled onto the tarmac; he was still at the police station making a statement. 'He's in bits,' the officer had said.

I wanted to say, 'I should fucking hope so,' but in the end I hadn't.

How could it have happened? Where was Honey going? Why had she packed a bag? She had, they'd said, fallen as if she'd been walking towards Albert Terrace when she was hit. Was she leaving or coming back? So many questions and I didn't have the answers to any of them.

'Oh, hi,' Trixie says as I push my bike in through the door, much like I'd done when I'd brought Boyd's tie in for him all those months ago. 'What are you doing here?'

'Is Boyd back yet?'

'Yes. He's just getting something from the car.'

I notice that Trixie is looking paler than normal, and thinner. It's as if one good push could snap her in two.

And then Boyd walks in. He's tall and square and slightly rumpled after his day's work; his shirt has come untucked a bit at the front and is creased and he's undone the top button. I know he'll have planned to straighten himself out shortly and will run his fingers through his hair just in case a customer should call into the office, even at this hour.

'Vita?' he says when he sees me.

I lean my bike up against the wall and go over to him. I'm holding both my hands out as if making ready to catch him when he falls.

I tell myself that it's always impossible to tell someone you love bad news about someone they love, especially when you love that someone too. And this is when it hits me; I loved them, both of them. I love Boyd. Christ, I think. I do still love you! I am allowed to love you! How could I not have known it? And Honey? Well, yes I loved her too. Why I should have done is a mystery: was it partly because I saw her as the child I should have had, or was it partly because she was a beautiful person who the man I love was in love with? Or was it a combination of both, or was it neither? What I do remember is how she touched my arm that first day, how it had felt right, possessive, careless, full of nameless love. The kind of touch I'd once believed would be mine for always.

I should have kept her close to us, protected her. I believe I have let them both down in an unspeakable way.

'Oh shit, Boyd. There's something I have to tell you. It's about Honey.'

And when I've told him that Honey is dead and that her body has been taken away and that there'll have to be a postmortem and that the police are involved and that the driver is being questioned, he has sunk to his knees. This mountain of a man has collapsed as though someone has taken all the air from him; he is kneeling on the floor with his head in his hands and I am crouching over him shielding him with my arms. We are in almost exactly the same position as the day William died.

Trixie is crying quietly and unobtrusively, the tears are dripping off her chin. She looks a hundred years old. 'I'll make tea,' she says.

'Where was she going?'

This is the question Boyd needs the answer to but neither Trixie nor I can answer it.

'It's not possible. There must be a mistake. She can't be.'

He keeps saying this over and over as if it's a prayer. What have we done to deserve this?

The rest happens in a daze. Boyd drives me to the hospital where he has to identify Honey's body. I am by his side and there are no words I know to describe how dreadful it is: Honey's face pale, totally flawless, the gentle curve of her skull, the jut of her shoulders over the top of the sheet. She looks so much like she is sleeping, as if one touch would wake her and she'd open those violet eyes and a long, slow smile would creep over her mouth and she'd whisper, 'Hi there, Boyd.'

I have no idea how Boyd will bear this loss when he has had so many losses in his life already.

And there are questions. So many fucking questions.

And in the long, excruciating hours that follow, the nightmare worsens. We are told that Honey was pregnant, that her real name wasn't Honey Mayhew, but Tracy Jones; we are told that Tracy Jones had been implicated in a boat fire four years before, but had never been charged because there wasn't enough evidence and the boat owner, even though he'd sustained life-changing injuries, had decided not to press charges.

I know some of this, of course, but not all of it and the world I thought I knew has tipped off its axis and here is a new world order where nothing is how it seemed. It will take years to get my head around this. And that's just me. What about Boyd? I have no way of knowing how to help him.

'What can I do?' I ask as, at last, around midnight, we emerge from the brightly-lit entrance of the hospital and get back into Boyd's car.

'There's nothing you can do,' Boyd says to me now, staring straight ahead, his eyes glazed, his skin grey with tiredness and grief. 'I always thought it was too good to be true. I had the feeling she'd leave me one day.'

'You don't know she was leaving.'

'Then where was her phone, why had she packed a bag? The police say she didn't have a phone on her.'

'Oh Boyd, I'm so sorry.'

He turns his ravaged face to me and says, 'I know you are. It's good to have you here. I couldn't do this without you.'

And we drive home slowly through the lit streets, the blossom on the magnolia trees we pass en route are cupped and white and waxy.

We drive to the house where, when I step out of the car, I will think back to the day Honey arrived and how it would have been easier if I'd hated her, if I had really been immune, if my barren-hard heart had stayed barren.

We drive to the house where we will find Honey's phone on the pillow of her and Boyd's bed. We will find her iPad with her browsing history and email accounts deleted. We will find the empty hangers and clear dressing table. Her toothbrush will be gone from the glass on the shelf. Boyd's toothbrush will stand alone in it and mine will be in its separate glass on the window sill. There will be no music anywhere, no heartbeats, no Honey. We will find the portrait I've done of her wrapped in brown paper under the bed.

Trixie

Until recently, the best time of Trixie's day had been the moment she'd shut the door of her four-bed detached executive home on its estate of four-bed detached executive homes, got in her car and driven to work.

She liked this moment because it was a liminal one. In it she belonged neither in one place nor another, she was free to be whoever she wanted to be.

Behind her Richard would be sleeping, his face covered with untidy stubble, his lashes, long and sweeping as they'd always been, resting on his cheeks and reminding her of watching him sleep in their early days together when she had been in love with him.

And before her would be Boyd: his left eyebrow's strange kink, his wide smile, his ponderous walk, his goodness, his unattainability.

Boyd's goodness had been the one thing that had helped her forget Richard, forget the silence now Joel and Jonty weren't living at home any more.

His unattainability had broken her heart.

Sometimes she would pause on the doorstep of her house and listen. She'd imagine she could hear the tumble of her sons' footsteps down the stairs and her own voice shouting, 'For the last time, boys, we HAVE to go or we'll be late.' More laughter from the kitchen, more tumbling of footsteps along the hallway and she'd rattle her keys and say, 'I'll leave without you,' and Joel would stand before her, his head on one side, his freckles, his grin, and say, 'Well, that'll kind of defeat the object, Mum, as you're only going 'cos you have to take us to school!'

That was in the days when she worked for Boyd part-time as something nice to do while Richard was at work and the boys were at school. But, since Richard had lost his job and the boys had gone to university and not come back again afterwards – for which she doesn't blame them in the least – she has worked full-time to fill the empty hours and keep a roof over their heads.

It has been an awful responsibility, and now her favourite moment of the day isn't the one when she leaves for work because Honey's there. And Boyd loves Honey, Honey loves Boyd and everything is spoilt and wrong. Her heart may still be broken but this time it's all just so fucking wrong.

She'd mistakenly thought Honey wouldn't pose a threat: she was too young, too awkward, had no advantages, was Trixie's inferior in every way and it pleased Trixie to play lady bountiful; it had been a while since she'd been able to. But what she hadn't bargained for was the girl blossoming the way she had after she came to work at Harrison's. Also, she'd stupidly said to the girl at her interview, 'Come back tomorrow and meet Boyd, just in a belt and braces exercise. I know he's going to love you too.' It was a comment that was to prove uncomfortably prophetic.

Trixie had picked up the shift in atmosphere as soon as Boyd and Honey walked in the door after the valuation at 'Chimneys'. She tried not to notice, but their obvious discomfort was writ large on their faces. She'd gone from intrinsic member of the team to spare part in a matter of moments and it had made her blood boil. Thinking about it now still does.

Then she'd heard Boyd book a table for two and, on the Monday morning when they'd arrived together she knew, she just bloody well knew that he'd had sex with the girl. She'd sworn then that Honey would have to go.

Boyd owed her after all she'd done for him. And, after all, wasn't it her life's goal to protect him from harm? Honey was never going to be anything but bad news.

So, on that morning at the height of summer, she left her four bedroom detached executive home where Richard was still sleeping. Around her were small signs of neglect: hanging baskets left unwatered, the paint on the eaves blistering in the summer sun, the Euonymus, which hadn't been pruned back, swamping the other shrubs in the bed to the right of the driveway.

She has worked hard to keep everything going: somehow she keeps the car running, praying each day it doesn't break down on her, and their insurance premiums and bills are just about covered. It was a godsend that Richard's severance money was enough to pay off the mortgage, but they still had to live, eat and sub the boys' meagre incomes. Who'd have thought that a university education would prepare you for nothing better than working nights at a BP garage (Joel) or stacking shelves in ASDA (Jonty)? They have inherited none of her drive it would seem, just their father's lack of it.

And Richard? God. Some days she wishes he'd just not wake up at all. At least then she'd have his life policy payout and she could get rid of this god-awful house, her pretentious neighbours, and establish herself in a small townhouse, have a social life of sorts and a cat. Richard has always hated cats.

It's almost as though the same thoughts loop in her head every morning and it is no different on this day. By the time she'd parked up out back at the office, she had yet again reached the point of wanting to get a cat and was still ruminating on this when Boyd got back from the valuation at Morris Road, turned his chair to face her and said, 'You going to say hello or what?'

'Hello, Boyd,' she replied and forced herself to smile at him.

But then he did that strange kink thing with his eyebrow and her frosty heart melted. She could never stay angry with him for long. It wasn't his fault. It was that girl. She'd bewitched him.

She thought of Vita and Boyd as they had been, safely married to one another with her, Trixie, at the centre: needed, valued, admired. The next in line.

She thought of Vita and Boyd torn apart as they had been, him lonely and grieving and her, Trixie, the only one who'd really understood. The next in line.

She thought of herself and Boyd together: his body next to hers in bed, him smiling at her and saying 'we' and meaning him and her. Her, in her rightful place.

Anything was preferable to the three of them – Vita, Boyd and Honey – living together in some strange hippy commune the way they were. Anything was better than Boyd actually being in love with Honey.

Trixie had thought long and hard about whether to tell Vita about Boyd and Honey before Boyd did, but decided against it in the end. She wasn't sure even now why this was – maybe it was to protect Boyd, maybe it was because it would be showing her hand too early, maybe it was because by doing so it would make their relationship official.

Whatever the case, Honey's ownership of Boyd, Boyd's vulnerability, Vita's obvious pain and Trixie's powerlessness were the things that hurt most.

'Honey out?' he asked now.

'Yes.'

'Did she say what time she'd be back?'

'No.'

He jangled some change in the pocket of his trousers. 'Any news from the Carrington's solicitor?'

'They emailed about an hour ago. Exchange should happen around two o'clock. I'll wait and go for my lunch then if that's OK?'

'You're a star, you know that, don't you?'

Boyd stood and moved over to her desk. He smelled of washing powder and soap and emitted a kind of heat she revelled in. He was the best thing in her life at that moment. For that tiny minute she ignored the goblin on her shoulder stamping his feet and saying, 'But he's with Honey now. He loves Honey.'

Boyd took his hand from his pocket and pressed it down on her desk and leant his weight against it.

'Everything OK?' he said. 'You seem a bit quiet. What's news with Richard and the boys? Any luck on the job front? For Richard I mean? I feel I haven't asked in a while.'

She looked up at him, there was a ping as an email arrived but she ignored it. She sensed the phone would ring any moment. She only had a few seconds when it would just be him and her, even if they were talking about her husband. 'He's got a few applications out, or so he says,' she replied. 'But it's slim pickings right now. Especially for a man of his age.' She didn't tell Boyd the other reason why it was so hard for Richard to get another job. The lack of a satisfactory reference didn't help.

It had all gone so well for a while. Richard had worked for a bank in the City; the hours were long, the company he kept was intense, the politics were bruising, but he'd seemed to relish it for a while until a new man took the helm and the atmosphere changed. Yesterday's men were just that and Richard was one of them. Slowly but inexorably his job changed. His responsibilities reduced, his credibility was undercut and he'd come home each day fuming and sour. But he didn't do anything to change it and that was his downfall. He just didn't play the game.

Then he called his new boss a fucker and that was that. No disciplinary hearing, no right of reply, just dismissal. They paid to make him go quietly, which he did but he hadn't stopped complaining since, and Trixie had had to bear the brunt of it: Richard's view on bankers, Richard's view on the government, Richard's view on Brexit. But what Richard didn't do was get up and *do* anything. He stayed in bed until ten, watched daytime TV, gambled a bit, looked at porn on his computer and expected Trixie to make his dinner when she got home. He was barely recognisable as the man she'd married.

It was no life. Not even half a life.

'I'm sure something'll turn up,' Boyd said, moving his hand a fraction so that it touched hers. Her heart jolted in her chest as though someone had applied paddles to it.

'Better get on,' she said and snatched her hand away. She turned and stared resolutely at her screen.

At that moment Honey walked back into the office.

'Oh, hi,' she said, totally and utterly unaware of even a fraction of the thoughts in Trixie's head.

Boyd's smile was like sunshine and Trixie watched as his eyes followed Honey moving around the kitchen and putting a small carrier bag of what must have been food into the fridge.

Honey called out, 'Shall I put the kettle on? Tea anyone? Boyd? Trixie?'

'You bet,' Boyd said.

All Trixie could do was nod, but Honey had obviously seen her because a few minutes later she put a mug down on her desk. 'There you go,' she said. 'I'll get on with the invoices this afternoon if that's OK?'

Again, all Trixie could do was nod and soon the three of them were settled to their work. The afternoon sun was beating against the windows. Now and again Trixie looked up and studied the shape of Honey's head, marvelled at the perfect shape of her skull, her slender neck, her creamy skin. God, how she hated the girl. How she wished she'd never come in the first place. How she wished she would just go away and never come back.

She hated Honey for being so loved; she knew in her heart she didn't deserve to be.

Sometimes Trixie tried to imagine what it was like in the house in Albert Terrace. How, she asked herself, could Vita stand knowing that just a wall away Boyd was sleeping next to someone else? Trixie imagined the small puffs of Honey's breathing, the curve of her cheek on the pillow, Boyd's hands on her.

Trixie could have been making Richard's dinner while she was thinking these thoughts, or changing the sheets on their bed, or standing in front of the TV doing the ironing. It was hard to make sense of it. It had been so long since Richard had touched her; she thought if he were to have done so now, her bones would have broken. The silence in her house was all-consuming.

Occasionally she texted her sons. They'd send one word replies back or, sometimes, a smiley face and she'd close her eyes and try to remember how it had felt to hold them when they were babies: the total abandonment of their limbs in her arms, the faint beat of their butterfly hearts under their tender ribs.

If only, Trixie thought, if only I had the power to change things. Surely there was something she could do to alter the trajectory of her life, of Vita's, and of Boyd's.

It was painful to do so, but she did think back to when it had been the four of them: her and Richard, Vita and Boyd, and of the comfortable dinner parties they'd had, the shared jokes, looking across the table and watching Boyd's dark eyes glimmer in the candlelight. Everything had been its in rightful place then. She had been in her rightful place. She had been the next in line.

* * *

And now it's March. She's sitting in her car in the service yard at the back of the office. The Grundon bin is next to her.

It's late. It's the day of the accident and she has watched the horrendous scene of Vita telling Boyd unravel before her eyes like they were all in some god-awful movie.

Vita and Boyd are still at the hospital. She hasn't told Richard the news yet and he hasn't been in touch to see where she is. She has no idea how she is going to atone.

It was not supposed to end this way.

343

Boyd

It's the day after. Sleep is impossible, the space next to him in the bed stretches for miles and the quiet is devastating. And, every time he closes his eyes he sees her: the lorry hitting her, the obscene spiralling of her limbs. He hears the soft crunch of her body as it hits the tarmac, the squeal of brakes, her scream, that last puff of breath on her lips.

He turns away from where she should be next to him but the dawn is already pushing against the curtains and so he gets out of bed and, pulling on his joggers and a sweatshirt, he goes downstairs.

Vita's already there. She's sitting on the sofa, wrapped in a tartan blanket and nursing a mug of tea, yesterday's crossword is on her lap. She hasn't started it.

'I didn't hear you get up,' he says.

'I didn't want to wake you.'

'I wasn't asleep.'

'No, I didn't sleep either.'

He leans against the kitchen counter and stares out into the garden. His mind is like a kaleidoscope and Honey's face is in every fragment, and her voice and the feel of her skin, that soft cry she'd cry when he made love to her, her terrifying dreams.

'What are you going to do today?' Vita asks him.

'Go to work.'

'Really? Are you *sure*?'

'I have to do something, otherwise I'll go mad.'

'I don't think you should.'

'I need to. I need to keep busy. You know how I am.'

Of course she does, he thinks. It was like this last time.

Every inch of him feels numb. If someone was to come along and pinch him, he wouldn't feel it, but still he gets dressed, stepping carefully around the spaces that Honey's things used to fill.

He tries not to think of Vita and how she will spend the day. Will she see Colin? Will she go to her studio and paint yet more of the stupid bloody dogs she hates to paint? Will she sit on the sofa with her cold tea and undone crossword and grieve? Yet again, he thinks, I've brought chaos down on Vita's head and she really doesn't deserve it, any of it.

* * *

Trixie's already in the office when he gets there. She looks exhausted, her face is pale and blotchy as if she's been weeping and although she looks busy, moving things around on her desk, her movements are hesitant and wary.

'You're in early,' he says as he sits down and switches on his computer.

'I couldn't sleep,' she replies.

'No, neither could I.'

'I'm not surprised.'

She moves over to stand next to him and puts a hand on his shoulder. 'I'm so very sorry,' she says.

'It's beyond words. I can't make sense of any of it. Did she say anything to you, about leaving, about her past? Did you know she was pregnant?'

'Pregnant? No!' Trixie says, her voice small and barely audible. 'I didn't. Oh God. That just makes everything so much worse.'

'Did you know she wasn't really Honey Mayhew? Her real name was Tracy Jones apparently.'

'I knew she'd had a chequered past. She told me she was convinced someone was out to get her. Maybe that's why she changed her name? She told me … She told me what the medium really said.'

'She *what*? Do you think this is what it's all about?'

'It could be, part of it anyway.'

'What did the medium really say?'

'That she'd fall, that whoever it was who was coming after her would find her.'

'Was she leaving me?'

'Maybe.'

'Who else knew?'

'Vita did.'

'Vita?'

Trixie doesn't answer him but her hand is still on his shoulder. He can feel that she is trembling.

Boyd's screen flickers into life. His screen-saver is a picture of Honey. 'Shit,' he says. 'She's everywhere.'

It is quiet in the office, just the faint hum of their computers and the buzz of the fridge in the small kitchen. And then into this quiet, Trixie says, 'I did it to protect you. But I didn't mean for it to end this way. You have to believe me, Boyd.'

There is an awful pause. Boyd turns his head to look at her. Her eyes are bright and glittering. She looks an almost-stranger to him.

'What did you do?' he asks.

Trixie

'What did you do?' he asks.

How can she tell him? Her reasons are buried so deep that they've taken root in every muscle and sinew. She has no idea how she is going to get the words out.

'There's so much you don't know,' she says.

'Then tell me.' He is staring straight at her. His left eyebrow is not raised this time, his lips are set in a firm line. He terrifies her.

'Can ...' she says.

'Yes?'

And then the words come. All of them, everything she's ever wanted to say to him.

'Can you imagine,' she says, 'what it's been like for me? First you and Vita – I tried to convince myself that I could cope with that, after all there was a sense of rightness to that: you and Vita, me and Richard. But then when William died and you and Vita split, I had to stand by and watch that, too. I waited. I waited for you to see me. See *me*, Boyd. But you never did. I've been here from the very start, remember? When it was just you and me and Harrison's Residential. When Vita was painting portraits, before William was born, I was here. I did everything because of you. I was the next in line.'

She pauses, swallows, then continues. 'Why didn't you choose me, Boyd? And you never asked what it was *really* like for me living with Richard, how much I've had to put up with. You never guessed, did you? And then there was Honey. And I knew, I just knew that she'd end up hurting you.'

'What didn't I guess?'

His face, his wonderful, kind face looks like someone has come with a scouring pad and rubbed off the first layer of skin. Outside, the day is starting: shoppers are walking by, there are cars, other people's lives are churning into action. But here, in this office, at this moment, there is only waiting: no emails, no calls, no customers or solicitors' letters or wide-angle shots of dining rooms to file.

Trixie knows she mustn't cry. If she cries, she will be lost. She has to tell him. She's waited long enough. She owes it to him and to herself.

'I remember,' she says, 'one particular day last August. I'd just got home from work. A song was playing on the radio. Sinatra. I've always loved Frank.'

'Yes?' Boyd says, he's shifted a bit and her hand has fallen from his shoulder. She is standing next to him, looking down at his broad back, the precise place where his hair meets the collar of his shirt. She is aching to reach out again and touch him.

'That evening the neighbourhood was busy with its end-of-day stuff: kids cycling home from wherever they'd been, parents driving back from work or, if they'd already got in, husbands dragging out their lawnmowers to give the lawn what they would be the last mow of the season whilst their wives fixed dinner.

'When I got home I called out but was greeted by silence. However, as soon as I stepped into the kitchen I knew something was wrong:

the counters were full of dirty dishes, empty cans of beer everywhere. I remember one was on its side and was gently weeping small tears of Boddingtons. But what was worse was our gravy boat, the one Richard and I got for a wedding present, in pieces on the floor by the fridge.

'I looked in the dining room then the lounge but no one was there, only an overflowing ashtray, playing cards in piles on the coffee table, an open newspaper, one lone sock on the carpet.'

'Go on,' Boyd says. 'I'm listening.'

'I looked for Richard,' Trixie continues, 'but he wasn't in our room, nor in either of the boys' rooms thankfully, but I found him curled up on the sofa in the box room, his hand under his cheek as though he was a child, one bare foot sticking out, the other tucked under his body. He was snoring.

'I called his name a couple of times and he stirred eventually, accusing me of being home early. But I wasn't early, it was gone six. I asked him in heaven's name what had been going on.

'He told me he'd had a few mates round and that things had got a bit rowdy.

'It was then, I guess, that the love went for good. If he loved me, how could he treat me this way? And it was then I knew for a fact that I loved you. Even though you hardly ever asked how I was, *really* was, I'd always loved you, Boyd.'

'You loved me?'

'Yes, of course. I still do,' she says, the words she'd been carrying around for years in her messed-up heart coming out of her mouth at last.

And she loves him because he's good and kind and huge and honourable and because he's not Richard, and because it's her turn.

The gravy boat had been a wedding present, a gift from her mother's sister, long since dead, as is her mother – and her father for that matter. She remembers how it felt to unwrap it, when everything was so full of promise. Richard's betrayal of all she'd held dear is, she's long since acknowledged, a monstrous thing. She's hated not being important, or central or valued or admired by anyone any more.

Boyd had been the only good thing in her life. And it was then, when she was standing over the shattered remains of the gravy boat that she'd decided she would do anything, and she meant anything, to protect him from getting hurt again, to make him notice her, make him love her.

'I cut my hand on the gravy boat,' she says, 'and the next day as I was putting more paper in the printer, Honey asked me what had happened. I told her it was just a silly accident in the kitchen.' And she remembers flexing her palm where the skin under the plaster was still stinging.

She'd gone to bed at some point the night before because when she woke up that morning, Richard had still been there, smelling of stale beer and body odour.

He'd muttered, 'Trix?' as she pushed back the covers to get out of bed.

Now is the time, she'd thought. Now he's used the name he used to call me back when things were good, now's the time for him to reach out and hold me and tell me everything is going to be OK. If he does then I won't do anything, I won't do it. But Richard didn't do any of these things. All he said was, 'Trix?' before he turned over to face the window and pulled his side of the duvet over his head.

'And so?' Boyd says now. 'What *did* you do? Why are you so sorry?'

* * *

Honey was easy meat. She was too gullible and trusting. This had surprised Trixie, she'd assumed it would be harder than it was.

First there was her visit to the stupid medium.

It was Honey's birthday. Boyd was out on a valuation but had just given Honey his gift and they'd had their cream cakes.

Trixie had said, 'Fancy a cup?' to Honey and stood and made her way to the kitchen. 'Yes, please,' Honey replied.

Trixie hesitated by the door, leant up against it and said nonchalantly, 'I've heard so many remarkable stories about mediums you know.'

'Have you?' Honey looked up at her.

And so she told her the story she'd made up about Mr Right and the premonition about the car and the girl had believed every word of it. Trixie could tell that Honey was lapping it up. It helped when you were talking to someone as superstitious and susceptible as Honey. After all, the girl religiously checked her horoscope every day, did all that not going out a different door to the one she came in business and, in summer, constantly searched for three butterflies together as she believed this would bring her good luck.

If Honey hadn't been with Boyd, Trixie may have thought these habits endearing, but Honey was with Boyd, she'd taken Vita's place, was living in Vita's house, was stamping all over Vita and Boyd's grief, had taken Trixie's place in the queue and was a threat to Boyd's happiness. So Trixie didn't consider Honey's superstitions endearing, she thought they were stupid and wrong-headed and, more than anything, she wanted Honey to …

It is hard for Trixie to finish this thought.

She'd wanted Honey to go, but she'd wanted it to be Honey's decision. That way she, Trixie, wouldn't be to blame.

Honey was tapping the card on the desk and staring into the middle distance. Trixie had had no idea what she was thinking as she filled the kettle and switched it on and, as it came to the boil, she felt a small shiver of satisfaction. Maybe, she thought, things were entering the next phase at last.

* * *

Then there'd been the night she and Honey went out for that drink.

She'd rung Richard and told him she was going out and all he'd said was, 'Oh, OK. See you later then.'

It'd been on the tip of her tongue to ask him what he was going to do for his supper and how his day had been but, she reasoned, why should she bother? He hadn't asked after her day, or even who she was going out with. As she'd put the phone down, there'd been a dull kind of ache around her breastbone, some kind of longing – for a better, purer life and a connection to the wife and mother she used to be – but she'd shaken these thoughts off. Tonight was going to be about something different, tonight she was going to be someone different.

'What would you like?' Trixie had asked.

Honey had asked for a white wine.

'Anything to eat?' Trixie said, gazing down at her black skirt and wishing she'd worn something a little less frumpy to work. She hoped Honey would say no. The wine was expensive by the glass.

As she waited for the drinks to be poured, she looked back over at Honey. She was looking down at her phone, her head bent, her neck smooth and golden in the candlelight.

Then, when the barman wasn't looking, Trixie took the twist of paper from her pocket and tipped a tiny amount of its contents into Honey's drink.

Back at the table Trixie sipped at her drink. Richard had once told her, long ago when he had to interview fresh-faced new recruits for the bank, that if you are quiet the other person will fill the space left by the words you don't say, and it was often revealing when they did so.

The wine bar had filled up around them, knots of men were standing at the bar drinking lager from long glasses and the tables towards the front were peopled with couples and a group of friends on a girls' night out. There was the babble of voices and the soft bass of the bar's background music. The wine was slipping down nicely, her hard edges were beginning to soften.

'Um,' she'd said. 'You said the word 'nomad' just now. What did you mean by that?' Trixie took another sip of her drink, left a gap in the conversation, hoped Honey would fill it. She did.

As Honey talked, Trixie ran her fingers down the outside of her glass, chasing the beads of condensation. She'd almost finished her drink but Honey, she noticed, had still got half of hers left. 'So,' she continued, 'you were saying about your past ...' She hoped Honey hadn't spotted that she was pressing her for details now.

Honey took a large mouthful of wine and grinned sheepishly at her. 'You,' she said, 'you and Vita are the only people I've ever told and this is because I trust you both. I've never had the luxury of being able to trust anyone before and you must promise not to tell Boyd. Promise me?'

'Of course.' The words tripped off Trixie's tongue. She wanted to order some more wine to make sure Honey kept talking but didn't dare break the moment. As soon as she could she'd suggest a refill. This was going so much better than she'd dared hope.

And then Honey told her a remarkable story about her being with a man on a boat and how there'd been an explosion and that she'd jumped, swum to shore and how the man had been injured and that she still believed he was coming to get his revenge. Trixie took hold of Honey's hands. She held them for a few seconds and then said, 'I'll get us some more drinks shall I? Then you must tell me everything the medium said. I've been anxious to know but didn't dare ask.'

'No,' Honey said, 'I'll get the drinks.' And she stood quickly and then was gone, striding away through the oases of light. Trixie prayed, she actually prayed to God that when Honey came back the moment wouldn't be lost.

The crowds were thickening, the sound of voices and music getting louder. The wine wasn't as chilled this time and Trixie didn't enjoy it as much but still she drank as Honey talked, as Honey told her about the medium's predictions about the step and how Honey was going to fall and how the man from whom she'd escaped would eventually find her.

'You poor thing,' Trixie said when Honey stopped talking. 'How have you borne this? Did you tell Boyd what the medium said?'

'Of course not. I told him that she'd said that everything will be fine. I wouldn't want to worry him, he's too good for that.'

'Yes,' Trixie said. 'He is. But Vita knows, you say?'

'I told her what I've told you and actually,' Honey paused, tipped her head on one side, her eyes were huge and terribly sad in the low light of their booth, 'It's a relief to have done so. I thought I was strong enough to keep my own counsel on this, but obviously I'm not. I …' she paused again, '… once hoped I would be other than I am.'

Trixie let this last comment go because she didn't quite understand it. Her head was reeling from all Honey had told her. This time she thanked God for her forward planning, the tongue-loosening properties of the drink and what she'd added to it, and for loneliness. There would, she now knew, be a way to finish this.

Boyd came to collect them about half an hour later. They spent the intervening time talking about work and Boyd's mother, who Honey was yet to meet. Trixie managed to hide her surprise on discovering this, she'd assumed otherwise. And then they were in the car and Boyd was driving her home, his large hands on the wheel, his head turning every now and again to talk quietly to Honey who was sitting in the front seat next to him. If only, Trixie thought, from her vantage point in the back, if only he knew the whole story …

At home Richard was already in bed: a whole day of her marriage had passed with her only seeing him briefly, speaking to him briefly, loving him not at all. But, at least the house was clean and tidy this time and, before she went to bed, she made herself a sandwich and a cup of tea and fired up her laptop and did a Google search for 'explosion', 'boat', 'marina'.

* * *

'What did I do?' she asks Boyd now. 'I saved you from her, that's what I did. She was damaged goods. She would have left you anyway. She would have ended up hurting you one way or another. I just helped her on her way.'

The world has contracted so that it's just her and Boyd. They are the only two survivors from some sort of holocaust.

'It was easy,' she says. 'I told Honey how mediums' predictions can come true, I put stuff in her drink that night we went out so that she would talk, and when I found out about her past, I sent her texts from "The Boatman" from pay-as-you-go phones, I damaged the step in the office so that she'd fall and then fixed it again the next day. And,' she hesitates, 'then, when at last Honey replied to one of the texts, telling me to "Fuck off and die", I knew I'd hit home and, after a suitable gap, I posted a letter through the door of your house saying that "The Boatman" was on his way. I did all this so that she'd leave. I waited for her to buckle. I knew in my bones that she would.'

It feels amazing to say this. Amazing and dreadful. She knows her life will never be the same again but still, she'd been right to do it, hadn't she? She'd been fearful for Boyd; after all she loved him, didn't she? She'd also been jealous all the times she'd been side-lined: after Honey's accident; when Boyd went to the hospital with Vita and Honey the day they got the news about his mother; Honey's friendship with Vita – all this had hurt. It had *offended* her that Honey should be taking centre stage the way she was, that *she* should be taking Trixie's place. She'd been justified in doing what she did, if only Honey hadn't left the day she did, if only she hadn't been crossing that particular road at the particular moment when the lorry came around the corner, if only …

'But,' she says, 'I never intended it to be like this. You have to believe me. Can you forgive me?'

Boyd

He thought he'd known what grief was: he'd lost a son, he'd left his wife, he was motherless, had always been fatherless and now the woman he loved was dead. But this? This 'confession' he'd just heard coming from the mouth of the one person he thought he'd always known and who he'd always trusted, this was somehow worse. It was worse because it was intentional. Trixie had meant to do these things. She said it was because she loved him, but what sort of love leads someone to cause such awful damage?

And now she was asking him to forgive her.

'I never intended it to be like this,' she was saying. 'You have to believe me. Can you forgive me?'

He studied her face. How much of this was his own fault, he wondered? How many signs had he missed?

'You seriously expect me to forgive you?' he asked. 'I should have you fucking arrested, that's what I should do.'

She nodded a tiny nod. Her fists, he noticed, were clenched, her back was ramrod straight.

'No,' he said. 'No, I will *never* forgive you and I want you to leave. Now. Go. And never, ever come back.'

He watched as she picked up her bag, put on her coat and walked out of the door. There was nothing left, absolutely nothing. He had lost everything.

Vita

And so there's another funeral, another coffin. And this time, like we had with William, it's a church service.

'Whoever she really was,' Boyd had said, 'she may have believed in God. We should at least give her the chance.'

And then he'd said, 'I never did get to take her to William's grave. I should have done. I really should have done.'

Boyd has told me about Trixie's confession but it's almost too much to compute. And when Boyd asked me what I knew, I told him what Honey had said.

'I should have made her tell you the truth, or I should have told you,' I'd said. 'That way, none of this would have happened. But she made me promise not to.'

It sounded such a feeble excuse in the light of this massive thing that has happened.

There have been, I think, so many huge betrayals and it is only now I understand the full import of what Honey told me, how scared she had always been.

Trixie doesn't come to the funeral.

Everything Trixie has ever done is tainted now.

So much lies unforgiven.

But this time, unlike at Belle's funeral, the church is almost full. Boyd's customers come, and the boy at the shoe repair place, and the people who run the dry cleaners, and Elizabeth, the medium Honey had been to see, and so many other people I don't know but whose lives Honey had touched.

The lorry driver sent flowers. There were no charges to answer. He hadn't been speeding and there was nothing wrong with his lorry. She had stepped out in front of him. That was all there was to it. How he will ever live with what happened though, I have no idea.

In the days that followed the accident I often thought about him. His name is Graham Silverton. He's married, has kids. I wonder whether he dreams it, over and over again like I do.

Amongst the congregation I spot a man in a brown jacket who limps when he walks. He wears dark glasses throughout the ceremony. I don't know who he is.

The rest of the congregation sings the hymns Boyd has chosen and Boyd reads 'Do not stand at my grave and weep' and cries huge, wracking tears and all I can do is stay close to him and hold his arm as if my small body could shore him up and stop him from falling.

And still I haven't wept. Not for William, nor Boyd, nor Belle nor Honey, nor even for Trixie. One day I know I will have to.

And Colin is there, too, but I know that whatever it was I had with him is over.

I'd thought I wouldn't spend another night with him, but I did. New Year's Eve had been our last night together. There'd been no massive row, no cruel words spoken, just a gradual fading; like ropes loosening. We'd got up the next day and moved away from each other inch by inch ever since. Perhaps this process had started the night of the party at his clients' house, perhaps it had started earlier; perhaps it had reached its conclusion when the pallbearers had carried Honey's coffin into the church.

What is for certain is that there's no room for Colin in my life now and there probably hasn't ever been because, and this might sound a strange thing to admit to now, even before Honey came into our lives, I'd never stopped loving Boyd and, even if I didn't know it, Colin did. I have no idea how he did, but maybe he knows me better than I thought, better than I know myself. 'It's OK,' Colin said when I went to see him the day after Honey died, 'I understand.'

And I replied, 'I'm sorry. I didn't know, when we started I mean, that in the end I'd still be needed like this. My place is with Boyd. You do understand, don't you?'

'Yes,' he said. 'I do.'

* * *

It's afterwards and we're standing outside the church. Boyd is talking to the vicar and around us the trees are freckled with blossom. Colin is wearing a dark suit and tan shoes. He is tidy and contained, his skin is smooth, his beard tidy.

It's like my head and heart have become disconnected.

Colin puts a hand on my arm. I look at it and recall how it used to be when he made love to me.

'Love never ends with a clean break,' he says. 'That's to say, no one comes with a ruler and pencil and draws a line under how you feel and says, "There now, that's sorted. You won't yearn or hope or wish or remember or regret any more." The phone might ring and you have no idea what to say, not like before when it was easy and comfortable and normal and right and this doesn't change anything. What you felt for whoever it is, like what I've felt for you and what you've felt for Boyd and him for you and for Honey, and all the interconnections that exist, don't go away. They stay out there in the air like invisible cobwebs binding us to one another. Like ours will bind us, in some way. Always. I don't need to tell you this though; you know it already, don't you?'

'Yes,' I say. 'I do.'

And in that moment, it's over. It is simple and sad and he's right, I will still love him in a way, but not in the way I love Boyd, the way I've always loved Boyd.

* * *

Boyd and I are standing in front of the fireplace in the lounge of the house in Albert Terrace. I've shown Boyd the painting I've done of Honey but neither of us is ready to hang it on the wall yet and I wonder whether we will ever be.

The daffodils I'd been arranging when the police came are in a vase on the mantelpiece. They are fully open now.

'The painting's wonderful,' he says. 'I love it.'

'I'm glad. It was her idea. She said she wanted to leave something good behind.'

'I don't think she ever planned to stay. She was always going to leave, wasn't she?'

'I don't know. Honestly I don't.'

'Do you think we'll ever know whether she was going or coming back?'

I lean up against him and he puts his arm around me. I tuck myself into him like I did before.

'I don't know,' I say again.

'I'm glad you're here,' he says.

'I'm glad I'm here too.'

There is a pause and then I say, 'I'm sorry.'

'What for?'

'I should have told you about the danger she was in. She was both of our responsibility. It seems odd to say it, but it's true. She was ...' I falter.

'Go on,' he says.

'So much like a child to me. Is that an odd thing to say, seeing how you and her were ...' I can't finish the sentence.

'No, it's not odd,' he says. 'Love comes in many shapes and colours. You can never predict it. I guess ...' he hesitates. 'We both wanted to protect her, in our own way.' Then he asks, 'Do you think grief ever ends?'

'Has yours for William?'

He looks down at me, his eyes are dark, his face achingly familiar. 'No,' he says, 'it hasn't. I thought once that I'd finished mourning him and that I could escape it, but it's lodged too deep inside. I should have told you all this years ago, shouldn't I? I shouldn't have let you believe I'd finished grieving for him because I never will. I shouldn't have let you believe I'd stopped loving you either, because I hadn't, not really.'

And it's then that it happens; all that was out of alignment falls back into place. The disconnect, the raw, pulsing loss, the memory of Boyd's head bent low over our son's body blurs as though I'm looking at it without my glasses on. Gone is the anger and the confusion and all that's left is the sharp sting of a remarkable kind of grief, both for the son we lost and the girl whose life blessed ours for a while.

There have been so many last days in my life with Boyd. William's death and Honey's are utter tragedies and I miss them both more than words can say. For them there will be no next day but I realise that, for those of us who are left behind and who have to cope with these aching absences, after every last day, there comes a first.

I realise that, although we may not have known that it was the last day – the day when what we believed to be true was true, when what we loved was there to be loved, when what certainty we depended on was certain, and we may mourn all these things when they're gone – what is sure is that we will sleep and rise, and a new day, the first day of a new kind of living, a new way of looking at the world, will come.

I look up at this man and think of all the days he's been in my life both as a presence and an absence; the space he filled and the space he left behind have always been the parameters that have helped to define me.

And I think how love, like life, never follows an ordered path from A to Z; it meanders and stalls, it constantly bewilders and surprises us and how seldom it is that we are actually at peace in amongst the dark dawns and the last days, how rarely we can stand still and say 'I love and am loved'.

* * *

It's late August, another last day.

On the mantelpiece is a vase of phlox from the garden.

Boyd and I are looking at the portrait of Honey on the wall above the fireplace, the memories of her and of William are inked onto our skin like tattoos and we are together, waiting for what might come next.

I can feel the heat of his body next to mine and know that after this last day, this other life, later will come yet more grief and a kind of forgiveness and, when he's ready, a different type of love.

But I don't say anything, because sometimes just being there when it matters most is the only thing that matters.

This Time Last Week

An ordinary morning;
conversation and see-you-later,

routine goodbyes and plans
for an ordinary day.

How special that was,
seen now from the lack of it,

how fragile the charms
protecting us from this.

Alan Hester

ACKNOWLEDGEMENTS

It is safe to say that this book would not exist if it wasn't for the dedication, insight and support of my agent, Broo Doherty. My gratitude and twirling are infinite, Broo.

Also, the whole team at The Dome Press have been just wonderful. Massive thanks are due to both my editor, Rebecca Lloyd, and to David Headley for championing this book, and really special thanks are due to all-round guru, Emily Glenister: you are simply a star. I am also grateful to Sophie Goodfellow at FMcM Associates for her PR magic, to Penny Hunter for her careful copy edit, and to Mark Swan for the beautiful cover design.

Other thanks are due to Jill Pickett for Honey's scene with Elizabeth and to Andrew Hooper of Hoopers Residential for letting me quiz him about the working life of an estate agent. All mistakes, omissions or errors of judgement in these matters are entirely my own.

Thanks are also due to Robert Seatter for allowing me to use some words from *The Book of Snow*, to Alan Hester for his poem 'This Time Last Week', and to Chez and Dave for good times in Kalkan and for introducing me to Chez's brother, Boyd, thus giving me the idea for the name.

Many lovely people have helped me stay on my writing feet over the past few years and so to Adrienne Dines, Alison Sherlock, Amanda Jennings, Annabelle Thorpe, Colette Dartford, Hilary Boyd, Hilary Hares, Iona Grey, Isabel Costello, Jane Cable, Jane Adams, Jenny Ashcroft, Josh Williams, Julie Cohen, Kendra Smith, Kerry Fisher, Liz Fenwick, Louise Ordish, Lynn Smith, Rosanna Ley, Shelley Harris, Stephanie Butland, Susan Martineau, Sue Squires, Tracy Rees, all at Reading Writers and in Kathryn Maris's classes at The Poetry School, my Creative Writing students at Bracknell & Wokingham College, my lovely poetry publishers, Two Rivers Press, and my cup-half-full guru (you know who you are) I say a HUGE and soppy thank you.

This book is also in memory of AH and to acknowledge the work of the Genesis Research Trust (www.genesisresearchtrust.com).

Finally, thank you to my parents (to whom this book is dedicated), my family and cats for putting up with me, but especially to J, J, L & T.